Lazarus Kaine

A Novel

Joel Eden

Lasaria Creative Publishing

LAZARUS KAINE

Copyright © 2008 by Joel Eden

All rights reserved. No part of this book may be reproduced or transmitted in any form or by any means, graphic, electronic, or mechanical, including photocopying, recording, taping, or by any information storage retrieval system, without the formal written permission of Lasaria Creative Publishing except in the case of brief quotations embodied in critical articles and reviews.

For more information, go to: www.lasariacreative.com.

Because of the dynamic nature of the Internet, any web addresses or links contained in this book may have changed since publication and may no longer be valid.

This is a work of fiction. All of the characters, names, incidents, organizations, and dialogue in this novel are either products of the author's imagination or are used fictitiously.

ISBN-13: 978-0-9818367-1-3
ISBN-10: 0-9818367-1-2

Printed in the United States of America.

What we fear, we create.

—Unknown

Chapter 1

"So, you're telling me that this woman simply got out of bed in the middle of the night, walked into her closet, closed the door, and died." Brooks squeezed the bridge of his nose.

Fairfax County police detectives Brooks Barrington and Tessa McBride pushed aside a collection of crisply tailored power suits and slim-fitting designer dresses to look at the body. The dead woman lay in the fetal position, surrounded by sneakers, sandals, and expensive pumps. Wearing only a gray American University T-shirt and a pair of white cotton panties, her hazel eyes were locked in a cold stare.

"What's her story, Tessa?" Brooks peered into the closet.

"Her name is Jill Forcythe. Thirty-one years old. Single. Commercial real estate agent. Her sister, Karen, arrived this morning at about seven o'clock to give her a ride to work. When Karen knocked on the door, Jill didn't answer. Karen had a key to the condo, so she let herself inside. She looked around, didn't see her sister, and assumed that Jill had run out to get coffee. Karen decided to look in the closet to see her sister's latest shoe purchase. She opened the closet door and found Jill on the floor."

"Cause of death?" Brooks couldn't take his determined gray eyes off the woman's motionless face.

"We don't know yet. The ME and two crime scene investigators have been here for a couple of hours, but they haven't reached any conclusions. Stan said he would do the autopsy this afternoon."

"Why is she in the closet?"

Tessa ran her right hand through her short black hair. "I have no idea."

"Do we at least have a time of death?" Brooks bit his lower lip.

"Between midnight and two o'clock this morning."

"Any sign of forced entry?" Brooks probed.

Tessa took in a deep breath and blew out a gust of frustration. "No. The doors and windows were all locked and intact." She stared a hole in her small notepad, which was filled with insignificant details.

"Any indication of a struggle?"

"She doesn't have any defensive wounds on her body, and we haven't found any battle bruises. There are no scratches on the back of the door, so I don't think she tried to force her way out of the closet. She looks normal in every way, except for her hands. She clenched her fists so tightly that her nails dug into her palms." The dead woman's mauve manicured nails had pierced her skin, causing small trails of blood to trickle over her wrists.

"Why do you think she clenched her hands so tightly?"

Annoyed by the lack of evidence and pissed at her perpetually delinquent partner, Tessa rolled her jade-green eyes. "I don't know. I don't have any answers." She clapped the notepad shut and shoved it into the inside pocket of her black sports coat.

"This is ridiculous," Brooks snapped. "I can't believe you've been here for two hours, and you haven't learned anything useful about this case."

"Dammit, Brooks, don't give me shit about my lack of progress when you can't even drag your butt out of bed and get to a crime scene on time."

Brooks turned away from his partner's icy glare. She had every right to blast him for his behavior. Rubbing his bloodshot eyes, he sat down on the bed. His head felt like it had been trampled by a herd of wildebeests. Remnants of a large sausage pizza, five beers, half a chocolate cake, three shots of tequila, and two candy bars churned in his stomach. His weathered face hadn't been near a razor in three days. A crusty patch of ketchup clung to the left lapel of his navy pin-striped suit, serving as a lasting memory of a juicy double cheeseburger he had demolished three days ago. His thick salt-and-pepper hair looked as if it had been styled with a leaf blower. He smelled like old sweat.

"I hate to see you embarrass yourself like this," Tessa said with a mixture of anger and concern.

"I'm not embarrassing myself."

"Your fly is open."

A rush of humility flew through Brooks as he scrambled to adjust his pants. "Sorry about that." Trying to salvage what was left of his self respect, he focused on the case. "I'm gonna take a look around in the bathroom," Brooks announced in his heavy Southern accent. He limped into Jill's master bath and checked her cabinets for prescription drugs and illegal substances, but found only some over-the-counter pain killers, a box of allergy medication, and a full bottle of cold medicine. Struggling with his prosthetic leg, Brooks hobbled out of the bathroom. "Hey, Tessa, take me on a quick tour of this place."

Located on the seventh floor of Tysons Tower, Jill's two-bedroom condominium overlooked Tysons Corner, a thriving community of high-tech companies and upscale restaurants. Just thirty minutes from Washington DC, the Northern Virginia suburb had grown exponentially during the Internet boom and had served as a mecca for affluent young professionals.

"OK, Detective McBride, tell me what you see."

Tessa examined the woman's home for a couple of minutes and then delivered her assessment. "Jill had a flair for decorating. This condo looks like it came straight out of a magazine. My mother would love for me to live in a home like this."

"You mean your apartment isn't decked out with fancy curtains and classy artwork?" Brooks studied a large painting of two geese on a beach in front of a lighthouse.

"My apartment looks like it was decorated by Stevie Wonder," Tessa grumbled. "Look how perfectly the four cranberry red pillows are positioned on this beige sofa. And the white carpet looks brand new. This chick was a neat freak."

Jill's spare bedroom contained a full-size bed, covered with a navy blue quilt. "It appears that this room hasn't been occupied for quite some time. It's too clean. Too perfect." Tessa opened the bedroom's closet door. "Nothing but Christmas decorations and empty shoeboxes in here. Guess she hasn't had any guests for some time."

As the detectives moved into the kitchen, a pleasant aroma welcomed them from a small vase of potpourri that sat next to the sink. Tessa filled her lungs with the scent. "Mmmm, I love the smell of lavender. Very feminine."

Brooks opened the refrigerator and saw a carton of skim milk, orange juice, a head of broccoli, two bags of baby carrots, six red apples, and twelve containers of low-fat blueberry yogurt. "Good Lord, what kind of person eats this stuff?"

"A person who cared about her health, unlike someone I know." Tessa exaggerated a disgusted glance at Brooks's chunky love handles.

"Keep your healthy opinions to yourself, you carbohydrate-hating fanatic," Brooks said. "Let's see what we can find in the master bedroom." He sucked in his gut as he meandered down the short hallway, but after just a few grueling steps, he gave up and let his belly flop back over his belt.

In the bedroom, Tessa and Brooks scanned the pictures covering the walls surrounding the queen-size bed. "She loved Paris, teddy bears, and folk art," Tessa said. "Probably a sweet girl. Shame she had to die so young."

Finding a handheld organizer on her nightstand, Brooks accessed Jill's appointment calendar. For this day, Wednesday, June 15, she had scheduled three business meetings and a yoga class.

Snapshots on her dresser revealed that Jill remained close to her Chi Omega sorority sisters from American University. The auburn-haired woman flashed her white smile in every photo. "Tessa, look at this. Out of the nine pictures on Jill's dresser, not one of them includes a male. Don't you think that's odd for a good-looking woman like Jill?"

"Not necessarily. I don't have any pictures of men on my dresser."

"My point exactly. You're not normal. Geez, you haven't had a date since when? The Reagan administration?" Brooks put up his hands to protect his face from a swift left hook that could have launched at any time.

"I am not discussing my love life with you. And for your information, it was the Clinton administration. The first term." Tessa let a smile spread across her flawless light brown face.

Brooks chuckled under his breath and ambled back to Jill's bedroom closet. A heavy dose of seriousness kicked in when he took another look at the deceased woman on the floor. As he leaned in to inspect her body, a bizarre chill raced across the back of his neck. He looked at Jill's clenched fists and imagined how she must have felt just before she died. His heart began to beat faster, and he broke into a cold sweat. Then his hands clinched. He could hear his pulse pounding in his temples, and his eyes lost focus. He felt as though an elephant were jumping on his lungs. His body trembled. A sharp pain ripped through his chest and down his left arm. His left hand went numb. Waves of nausea crashed into his stomach. The closet whirled around him as a dizzy spell encircled his head. He cringed when he felt a hand touch his right shoulder.

"Brooks, are you all right?" Tessa struggled to heave him out of the closet. She helped him back to Jill's bed.

"I'm fine," he gasped. "I just need to get some air." Brooks took a couple of shallow breaths and told himself to relax. After a few minutes, his eyesight cleared, and he could breathe deeper. "Where is Jill's sister?"

"Waiting downstairs in the lobby."

"Good. I need to talk to her." His head began to throb as he stood up.

"Are you sure you're all right? You look pale." Tessa scrunched her eyebrows.

"Yes, I'm fine. And I always look this pale." Brooks forced a pathetic grin, hiding the fact that he was afraid he had just had a heart attack.

"Do you think Jill committed suicide?" Tessa supported his left arm as she walked beside him down the hall toward a set of elevators.

"Why would she kill herself?"

"Maybe she was lonely. People do strange things when they're alone."

"An attractive, intelligent woman with money—I don't see it. If she was lonely, it was by her choice."

"You know, it's quite possible that she died of natural causes."

Brooks remembered the icy chill that ran across the back of his neck and the intense agony that tortured his body while he was in the closet. His instincts told him that whatever happened to Jill sure as hell wasn't natural.

Chapter 2

Matt Curtis psyched himself up for a fierce confrontation as he navigated through a maze of cubicles on his way to a Wednesday morning status meeting with his project team. A senior manager with LightCurve Consulting, Matt was in charge of a large project dealing with a financial system implementation. The project had turned into a death march. Since the engagement had started in January, his seventy-five-member team of consultants had fallen six weeks behind. Their June 30 delivery date had been pushed into mid-September, and it was probably going to get worse.

After he poured himself a cup of lukewarm black coffee, he walked into a conference room and waited for the inquisition to begin. Four managers who reported directly to Matt dragged themselves into the conference room looking like weak calves waiting to be turned into veal chops. No one said a word.

The managers wore their finest standard-issue management consultant uniforms: dark gray pin-striped suits with starched white shirts and conservative red ties. Armed with powerful laptops, pricey PDAs, and Blackberries, the managers lived in a world filled with bits, bytes, and blocks of complex computer code. Clean-shaven, with unimaginative haircuts, the four men were cast from the LightCurve mold. Hypersmart Type A personalities, they would run through a brick wall for their company.

Matt's athletic build did not fit into the high-tech geek pigeonhole. His black double-breasted suit and amethyst tie screamed individuality. With a head full of dark brown hair, sharp blue eyes, and a pair of deep dimples, his face belonged on a baseball card or inside a football helmet.

The men sat in soft, black leather chairs at a mahogany conference table, anticipating the arrival of their client, Arman Guerrero, vice president of finance for Carponi Communications. They stared out the wide windows that overlooked the streets of Reston, Virginia.

"Our timeline has slipped. The Carponi people changed their requirements again," Ben Knight reported. "Now we're at least ten weeks behind schedule—probably more. Guerrero's gonna blow a gasket."

"Look, whatever happens in this meeting, we need to stay calm and professional," Matt said. "Don't get defensive or emotional. Focus on the facts. And let's hope that we get out of here with a minimal loss of blood."

At 11:00 AM, Matt's executive assistant, Kim Taggert, escorted Guerrero into the conference room, followed by Dan Calvert, a LightCurve senior partner.

Matt shook his client's hand. "Good morning, Mr. Guerrero."

"Morning," the man grunted. He took a seat at the head of the table and unbuttoned his dark suit jacket. A bright yellow tie draped over his protruding stomach.

Taking his seat, Matt looked over at his boss. "Dan, I wasn't aware that you were going to join us this morning."

"Arman asked me to sit in on this status meeting." Calvert positioned himself in the chair next to Guerrero. A forty-five-year-old executive with thin wisps of chestnut hair strategically combed over his extra-long forehead, Calvert wore a charcoal suit with a custom-tailored gray dress shirt and matching tie. His $900,000 annual salary gave him the luxury of wearing ridiculously expensive suits with diamond-studded cufflinks.

Matt's stomach churned. He cleared his throat and handed his client a stack of paper. "Thank you for meeting with us today, Mr. Guerrero. I developed an agenda for our discussion and a brief presentation that describes the current status of the project."

Guerrero crushed the papers into a tight ball and threw them into a trash can. His lumpy bald head wrinkled. "You're more than six weeks behind on this project, Matt. Explain to me how you plan to make up the ground you've lost and deliver my financial system on time." He folded his short, chubby arms as he waited for an answer.

Beads of sweat formed on Matt's upper lip. "Well, Arman, we've encountered quite a few challenges over the past few months. The software vendor you selected has not delivered its product on time, your new financial policies have not been identified, your requirements keep changing, we still have not received your historical data, and ..."

"I don't give a rat's ass about your challenges, Matt. I'm paying you guys twenty-four million dollars to install my new financial system, and I expect it to be delivered on time." Guerrero turned to face Calvert. "Dan, when you convinced me to award this contract to LightCurve, you told me that you had more than 160,000 employees worldwide and that you would assemble your best team to deliver this system on time. Clearly, that has not happened. Who's responsible for this monumental failure?"

Every eye in the room focused on Calvert. As a senior partner, it was his duty to assume full responsibility for the actions of his employees. Calvert looked at Matt. "Mr. Curtis, can you tell us who is responsible for this monumental failure?"

Matt couldn't believe that son of a bitch passed the buck to him. He evaluated his options quickly. Should he place the blame on his project team, the software vendor, or Guerrero's financial analysts? "I'm responsible." He glared into Calvert's malicious eyes. "You can blame me."

Guerrero stood up and paced around the room. "Matt, you know Carponi Communications is under investigation by the Securities Exchange Commission for securities fraud. They think someone cooked the books, and they think I'm the culprit. I must have this new system in place as soon as possible to prove my innocence. Otherwise, the SEC is gonna throw me in jail. Do you want an innocent man to go to jail, Matt?"

"No," Matt answered. Although he put up a good front, Matt would have been quite pleased to see Guerrero behind bars. He hardly believed that the scumbucket was innocent.

The corporate rumor mill held that Guerrero had falsified a horde of financial statements, causing the Carponi stock price to soar over ninety dollars a share. By exercising his stock options with impeccable timing and insider information, Guerrero had accumulated millions of dollars in cash. Many Carponi employees had suspected that he had used his position to hide personal expenses that he had charged to the company, including chartered planes to Las Vegas, hotel suites in Barbados, and lavish gifts for his many female companions. When the telecommunications industry crashed after the Internet bubble burst, the Carponi stock price plummeted to $1.10 a share, and allegations of financial deception put the company on the verge of bankruptcy. Carponi stockholders lost billions of dollars while Guerrero lived the high life on the company's nickel. By installing a new financial system, Guerrero would have the opportunity to "inadvertently misplace" certain historical records that could have served as evidence of his crimes.

Calvert sat up in his chair. "Arman, I'm certain we'll find a way to get this project back on track. LightCurve won't let you down."

"Dan, if you don't deliver this system soon, I swear I'll sue you for breach of contract, and I'll find a way to drag LightCurve into the SEC investigation. If I have to take the heat for this, I'll make sure that some of the blame falls on you. Now, I'm going back to my office, and I suggest you get to work immediately. Call me when you actually have a plan to save my ass from the judicial system. I'll see myself to the elevator." Guerrero stalked out of the conference room.

Like mice running from a fire, the four managers scurried out of the conference room, leaving Matt alone to face his boss. "Dan, before you signed this contract, I told you there was no way we could meet Arman's deadline. It's impossible to do this much work in such a short amount of time. Every person on my team is working eighteen hours a day, seven days a week. They're burned out and pissed off. I've told you repeatedly that this project is in jeopardy, and I'm afraid this is going to turn into another Enron-Arthur Andersen situation."

"I don't want to hear your whining, Matt. Do what you have to do to get this project back on schedule. We're the biggest consulting firm in the world, and we're famous for our ability to deliver the tough jobs. If you fail, Arman will drag us into a long, expensive court battle, and then he'll give the job to IBM Global Business Services, just for spite. Our image will be ruined. More importantly, my reputation will be destroyed. If that happens, I'll fire you and your entire team." Calvert turned his back to Matt and took off down the hall.

"I need to put at least a dozen more people on the team, but we don't have anyone available. Can you help me find some resources, Dan?"

Calvert kept walking. "Sorry, Matt, I have a conference call that starts in ten minutes. You're on your own." He waved his hand good-bye as he disappeared around a corner.

You are such an asshole, Matt thought. He stormed back to his office and threw himself into his uncomfortable chair. "Dammit!" His MBA from Virginia Tech hadn't prepared him for this situation. Praying for good fortune, he put in a desperate call to the LightCurve human resources department, searching for warm bodies that could work on his project. No luck. Hoping for a flash of brilliance, Matt pored over his detailed work plans, trying to find a way to salvage his job and his reputation in the firm.

Matt's best friend, Mike Wozniak, also a LightCurve senior manager, poked his head in Matt's office. "I heard you had an exciting status meeting this morning."

"I'm in a buttload of trouble, Woz. My day can't get any worse." Matt leaned back in his chair and put his hands on his head.

"Actually, it can. I have some bad news for you." Mike entered the office and closed the door. A grimace made his thirty-five-year-old face look ten years older, and thick patches of prematurely gray hair on his temples didn't help the cause.

"What is it?"

"Jill Forcythe is dead."

Chapter 3

Walking through the lobby of Tysons Tower, Brooks and Tessa spotted Karen Williams standing in front of a large window, crying over the death of her little sister. Karen's striking facial features and auburn hair confirmed her genetic connection to Jill.

"Mrs. Williams, my name is Detective Brooks Barrington. I'm sorry for your loss."

"Thank you." Karen sobbed into a clump of tissues.

"I know you've already spoken with Detective McBride, but I'd like to ask you a few additional questions about Jill. Would that be all right?"

"Certainly."

They stepped across the polished-stone floor of the lobby to a reception area with two large sofas, four comfortable chairs, a decorative floor lamp, and a stone fireplace. Tessa sat beside Karen on a sofa. Facing them, Brooks maneuvered himself into a soft chair. "Mrs. Williams, do you know what Jill did last night?"

"She had dinner at my house with me and my daughters, Kayla and Jenna. The girls adore their aunt Jill. My husband, Rob, is out of town on business, so Jill came over to keep us company. After dinner, Jill went to Nordstrom at Tysons Corner to buy a pair of shoes." Karen fought back a flood of tears. "She called me when she got home and told me she bought a pair of red Prada pumps."

"What time did Jill call you?" Brooks asked.

"Around nine thirty. We talked for a few minutes about our plans to visit our parents in Richmond over the Fourth of July holiday. She told me she was tired and wanted to go to bed. Then she said, 'I love you, sis,' and hung up." As two men wheeled a body bag through the lobby, Karen burst into tears. "Oh my God. This is horrible."

After Brooks gave Karen a few minutes to compose herself, he continued with his questions. "Did Jill have any bad habits?"

"Like what?"

"Drugs, alcohol, other addictions?"

"No way! Not Jill. She never used drugs—not even in college. Her limit was one glass of wine with dinner. Her only addiction is … was … expensive shoes."

"OK. What about her health—did she have any physical problems?"

"Jill was born with a hole between the two bottom chambers of her heart. It decreased the blood flow to her lungs, so she didn't have a lot of oxygen in her blood. When she was about a year old, she had surgery to fix the problem, but it left her with a weak heart."

"Did she mention any *recent* problems with her heart?" Brooks asked. In the back of his mind, he worried about his own heart problems.

"No. Not lately."

"All right, Karen. Just a few more questions, and we'll be done. You told Detective McBride that you found Jill in her closet with the door closed."

"That's right. I can't believe she died in a closet at night. It's so weird."

Brooks leaned forward. "Why?"

"When Jill was about seven years old, she would wake up in the middle of the night, screaming—it was just piercing. She said the moonlight mixed with the darkness in her bedroom and made shadow faces that moved around her room. She thought they lived in her closet. It happened quite a lot. After a few months of these night terrors, our dad made up a ritual to help her sleep. Every night, he tucked her into bed and went through an elaborate formal procedure to close the closet door, which would keep the shadow faces away."

Karen paused to wipe her eyes and blow her nose. "One night, Jill fell asleep watching TV in the living room. Dad carried her upstairs to her room and put her in bed, but he forgot to close her closet door. Around two in the morning, she started screaming. We ran into her bedroom and found her standing in the closet, terrified out of her mind. She looked so pitiful, standing there in her Barbie pajamas, screaming hysterically. It took us an hour to calm her down. She told us she woke up and saw a man standing in her closet. He had the shadow faces all around him, and he whispered her name over and over. According to Jill, the faces swirled around the room and carried her into the closet. The man smiled at her, and then he stuck his hand into her chest and grabbed her heart. She said the pain was what made her scream. Of course, she claimed the man disappeared when we ran into the room."

Struggling to keep her composure, Karen clasped her hands together and stared at Brooks with her tear-filled eyes. "From that night on, she refused to set foot in her bedroom and, for many years, she was too scared to sleep alone. We shared my bedroom until I went to college. I don't think she saw the shadow faces or the man again. I just wrote it off as a bad dream, but it bothered her so much that Mom and Dad became worried about her mental stability. They took her to see a child psychologist, but the therapy didn't help. She swore the man in the closet and the shadow faces were real. She never slept with the closet door open. I know it sounds silly, but that one night changed Jill's life forever."

Tessa tried to bring the conversation back into the real world. "Karen, children have vivid imaginations. I remember when I was a kid in New Orleans, my little sister, Erin, had a string of bad dreams about an old cat that lived in our neighborhood, but she grew out of it. She moved on with her life, and I'm sure Jill did the same thing. I don't believe her death had anything to do with her childhood nightmare. I'm sure it's just an odd coincidence."

Brooks remembered the excruciating pain that rifled through his chest when he entered Jill's closet. Although he would not admit it to Tessa, he was pretty damn sure that this was no coincidence. "Did Jill tell anyone else about the faces or the man who attacked her?"

"I don't think she told any of her friends about them. She didn't want people to think she was a nutcase."

"How about her boyfriends?" Brooks shifted his weight in the chair.

"Jill spent most of her time building her career. She's only dated about four guys in the past ten years. None of her relationships last very long. Jill was picky about her men—and she was a high-maintenance woman."

"We should talk to them. Do you remember their names?"

"I think so. In her senior year of college, she had a steady boyfriend—a lanky guy from New Jersey named Craig Helgeson. They broke up after graduation. Then she went out with Mark Harrison for a few months. He's a trumpet player for the National Symphony at the Kennedy Center. For a couple of years, she dated Mac McQuaid, a golf pro at the Tournament Players Club at Avenel in Potomac, Maryland. Mac asked Jill to go with him on the PGA tour, but she didn't want to give up her career, so they called it quits. Her most recent relationship flamed out fast. It lasted only about three months. They broke up about a year ago. Jill wasn't ready to make a long-term commitment, and he was all hot to get married. I think he scared her away. He works for LightCurve Consulting. His name is Matt Curtis."

Chapter 4

The Fairfax Memorial Hospital Women's Center buzzed with excitement. Expectant mothers in various stages of delivery filled the fifth floor labor and delivery unit. Nervous first-time dads wandered through the halls, searching for snack machines and *Sports Illustrated* magazines to occupy their minds while they waited for fatherhood to arrive.

In birthing room 516, a sweaty woman who looked like she was going to explode grabbed Cullen Rhea's right forearm. "If you don't get this baby out of me in the next two minutes, I'm gonna rip your arm off."

"You're almost ready to push, Geraldine." Cullen pulled a rubber ball from the left-side pocket of her dark blue scrub jacket and placed it in the woman's left hand. "Squeeze this ball as hard as you can. You can do this." The pretty registered nurse with the straight black ponytail adjusted her patient's wad of pillows.

"No, I can't. I've changed my mind. I don't want to have natural childbirth. Give me drugs. A truckload of drugs. Give me an epidural. Hit me between the eyes with a sledge hammer. Please, do something to help me!" A huge contraction slammed into the woman. "Oh! My God! This hurts like hell!"

"You're too far along to have an epidural, Geraldine. The last time Dr. Monroe checked your progress, you were nine centimeters dilated. Just one more centimeter to go, and then we can rock and roll. We're coming up to the finish line. Hang on, honey."

"Why don't you get your little buns of steel in gear and go find my doctor? Tell her I can't wait anymore. And get me some more ice chips. And tell my idiot husband to stop watching *Judge Judy* and get in here to comfort me."

"I can't leave you alone right now, Geraldine. Dr. Monroe knows you're close, and she'll be here any minute." Another contraction launched Geraldine into an ear-piercing shriek of torture.

As the contraction faded away, Dr. Daria Monroe, a thirty-nine-year-old obstetrician, walked into the birthing room. Right behind her, Geraldine's husband, Stuart, a little man with panic smeared all over his face, snuck into the room, doing his best to stay out of the line of fire.

"OK, Geraldine, it's just about time for your baby to make his grand entrance," Dr. Monroe announced.

"I want drugs. I neeeeeeeeeed drugs, and this friggin' nurse won't give me any medication." She looked at Cullen. "No offense."

"None taken." Cullen flashed an understanding smile. She had heard far worse language from many other expectant mothers in the same situation.

"Come on, Dr. Monroe, help me out here. Give me an epidural."

"You'll be fine, sweetheart," Stuart said.

"Shut up, Stuart. This is all your fault. You are never gonna touch me again."

Dr. Monroe examined her patient. "You're ten centimeters dilated, Geraldine. You're too far into labor to have any drugs. It's time to push. Cullen is one of our best nurses, and she's going to help you deliver this baby."

Nurses flew around the room preparing for the arrival of Geraldine's baby. A seasoned veteran, Cullen coached the new mom with Lamaze breathing techniques. Stuart videotaped the blessed event, until the images became too graphic. Then he hyperventilated and fell into a chair. Woozy and petrified, he stumbled back to Geraldine and gripped his wife's right hand. With a ghostly white face, he listened intently as his wife threatened to shove the video camera into a very uncomfortable place if he even thought about turning the damn thing on again. For the next hour, Geraldine pushed and cussed her way to motherhood while Stuart just kept his mouth shut.

Worn out and frustrated, Geraldine slumped back into her six pillows. "I can't do this anymore," she wheezed.

"You have to, Geraldine," Cullen directed. "Come on, honey. One more big push, then you can see your new baby." Geraldine groaned with all of the strength she had left, and Cullen grunted right along with her. With one final collective moan from everyone in the room, Dr. Monroe gently pulled the baby out of its warm sanctuary into the cold, strange room.

"Happy birthday!" Dr. Monroe shouted. The baby let out a huge cry, and everyone cheered. Overcome with excitement at the birth of his son, Stuart forgot about his nausea and summoned up enough courage to cut the umbilical cord.

"Say hello to your son, Geraldine." Cullen tenderly placed the baby on the exhausted woman's chest.

"Oh, you are so beautiful." The new mom wept as she embraced her baby and kissed him lightly on his tiny red cheeks. His blue eyes struggled to adjust to the bright lights. Softly holding his round little feet, Cullen cooed at the new arrival. Tufts of thin, light-colored hair made his head look like a brand new tennis ball. Stuart counted his son's tiny fingers and toes over and over until he was absolutely certain the baby had the appropriate number of digits.

After she let the couple bond with their baby for a few minutes, Cullen plowed forward with her duties. "We need to check this little guy out to make sure he's healthy. What's his name?"

"Stuart Mayfield Barry Jr.," his father announced.

"All right, Stuart Jr., let's have a look at you." Cullen took the baby in her arms, walked across the room, and situated him on an examining table. A nursery resource nurse and a neonatologist poked and prodded the infant, performing a series of tests to determine the baby's physical condition. Declaring him to be a healthy seven-pound, six-ounce boy with an Apgar score of eight, the nursery resource nurse wrapped the baby like a burrito in a toasty blue blanket and escorted Stuart Jr. and Stuart Sr. to the nursery.

Meanwhile, Cullen turned her focus to Geraldine. With compassion and precision, she worked with Dr. Monroe to help the fatigued woman recover from childbirth. While the doctor completed a series of post-delivery procedures, Cullen made sure Geraldine settled comfortably into her bed and filled an IV bag with pain medicine. An orderly knocked on the door and announced that he was there to take Geraldine to her private room. While Cullen looked after the precious IV pole, the orderly pushed the bed down the hall to room 534. After he maneuvered the bed into its proper position, he excused himself and headed off to his next transport.

The tired woman looked up at Cullen through a pair of groggy eyes. "I'm sorry I was so mean to you. You must think I'm a real bitch."

"I think you're a strong woman, and you're going to be a great mom." Cullen placed a cool washcloth on Geraldine's forehead.

"You're so sweet. Do you have any kids?"

"Never had the good fortune. I'm hoping one day I'll get a chance to be the woman in the bed. I'd like that."

"Are you married?" Geraldine slurred her words as the pain medicine took hold.

"Nope."

"Do you have a boyfriend?"

"Yep." Cullen tucked the bedsheets tightly around her patient's weary body.

"Is he your Mr. Right?"

A bashful smile swept across Cullen's blushing face. Her dark brown eyes danced. "Maybe."

"That look tells me he's the one for you." Geraldine giggled like a teenager.

"All right, that concludes our riveting discussion of my love life. It's time for you to get some rest. I gotta go. Give me a big ol' mommy hug." Cullen wrapped her arms around Geraldine. "Take good care of that baby."

As Cullen walked out of the room and down the hall to the nurses' locker room, she compared her day to Geraldine's. That morning, Cullen had woken up, taken a shower, eaten a bowl of Cheerios with a banana, driven to work, and helped a woman have a baby—just a normal day at the office. During the past ten years as a labor and delivery nurse, she had participated in more than two thousand births. It had been a typical Wednesday in June, not particularly memorable for Cullen.

Geraldine, however, had awakened in a panic when her water broke at 4:23 AM. She rode to the hospital with her madman husband behind the wheel and screamed in misery all the way. For nine hours, Geraldine endured the greatest amount of suffering a human being could endure, and then she experienced the birth of her first child. That Wednesday was a day Geraldine would never forget.

In the locker room, Cullen changed into a clean pair of green scrubs and washed her hands. Then she headed to the break room. Opening the refrigerator, she took out a chef salad, a raspberry yogurt, and a bottle of water. While she ate her lunch, she watched the news on television. Depressing stories dominated the telecast. American forces in the Middle East continued to suffer casualties, large corporations planned to lay off hundreds of workers, and a woman named Jill Forcythe was found dead in her condo in Tysons Tower.

A burst of fresh air filled the break room as Jenny Pace, a registered nurse, bounced through the door. "Hey, Cullen, after work a few of us are going to happy hour at Grevey's. You wanna join us?" She flipped her light brown, shoulder-length hair out of her face.

"Can't. I have plans for dinner."

"With who?" Jenny plopped down at the table facing Cullen, brimming with interest and ignoring the fact that her light blue scrub jacket was stained with newborn baby goo.

"A guy I've been dating for a few months."

"What? You've been holding out on me, girlfriend. Give me the scoop. Who is this guy?" Jenny put her elbows on the table and propped her chin in her hands.

"Well, he lives in McLean, and his name is Matt Curtis."

Chapter 5

While they waited for the medical examiner to complete Jill's autopsy, Brooks and Tessa ate lunch in Tysons Corner at a small Asian restaurant called Can You Smell What the Wok is Cookin'.

Tessa grazed on her steamed vegetables and avoided the carbohydrate-laden white rice as if it were laced with arsenic. Because Brooks had not eaten for more than four hours, his stomach ached for food. He tore into a pile of sweet-and-sour pork. Between heaping bites, Brooks pored over some interesting facts about Chinese culture that were listed on the menu. "Hey, Tessa, did you know that the standard writing system in China uses more than 6,500 characters?"

"Yes, that's fascinating, Brooks."

"The characters look like little houses and trees and stick figures. I wonder what would happen if you had poor penmanship in China. What if you tried to write a note to someone like, 'I went to the store to get milk and bread,' but because of your poor handwriting, you actually wrote, 'Dear Wienerhead, your mother smells like a yak, and your butt is as big as a Buick.' You could never recover from that kind of screw-up."

"Yes, Brooks. Can we please eat and talk about the Jill Forcythe case?"

"Do you think they have a Chinese version of *Wheel of Fortune* on TV in mainland China? Good Lord, with 6,500 characters, it could take hours to solve a puzzle." He shoveled a forkful of pork into his mouth.

"I don't know, Brooks. Look, I think we need to discuss your work ethic."

"What's the matter with my work ethic?"

"You don't seem to have one. For the past twelve months, you have been consistently late for work, and you've lost your focus on the job."

"Don't lecture me, Tessa. I was solving cases when you were in high school. I've been a good cop for over twenty years, and I'm still a good cop." Brooks slammed his fork on the table.

"Then act like a good cop! I know you've had some rough things to deal with lately. But it's been a year since the accident. You have to get on with your life."

"Have you ever buried a spouse and a child at the same time?"

"No."

"Then you have no idea what I'm going through." A year ago, on a pleasant Saturday night, Brooks and his family were on their way to his daughter's ballet recital. In a matter of seconds, he found himself trapped in a car that was wrapped around a tree. Within minutes, he was forced to say good-bye to the two people he loved more than anything. "You never get over that, Tessa. You can't just 'get on with your life.' It's not that easy. And by the way, I didn't lose my leg. I know what happened to it. I didn't just wake up one morning and say, 'Oh, my goodness! I can't find my left leg.' I know where it went. The paramedics cut it off above my knee so they could pull me out of my car. I wish they had let me die with my family. Now, I have to limp around with this stupid artificial leg, and everyone treats me like I'm a freak. Dammit, I hate living like this."

"I'm sorry I upset you, Brooks." Tessa poked at her vegetables. "Just trying to help."

Brooks knew he had made his partner and close friend feel like a one hundred and twelve-pound bag of crap. He devoured an egg roll in two bites. "I'm sorry, too, Tessa. I know I've let you down. I'll try to do better." Brooks returned to his mound of pork. They finished their meal in silence.

As Brooks polished off his fourth egg roll, his cell phone beeped. He listened to the caller and then said, "Stan Bogart has some preliminary findings on Jill Forcythe. He wants to see us—right now."

Tessa left a tip on the table while Brooks paid the bill at a small checkout counter. Because he was a regular customer, Brooks had become close friends with the family who owned the restaurant. He asked the young woman behind the counter, Huan Yue, about her mother, father, two sisters, brother, and grandmother. The woman loved to hear his Southern drawl, so he cranked it up full blast for her. A line formed behind Brooks at the counter.

After a few minutes of idle chitchat, a man in line became restless. "Move it along, Jethro. I have things to do," the man blurted. He wore a light blue Oxford shirt with khakis and a navy blazer. A thinning plot of short black hair stuck straight up on top of his head with the assistance of a handful of styling gel.

Ignoring the man, Brooks kept talking. Visibly annoyed, the man launched another attack. "Hey, plowboy, shouldn't you be watching a NASCAR race or shucking some corn?" The man moved in behind Brooks and continued his assault. "Hey, Gomer, why don't you go back to Mayberry? Or maybe you're too stupid to find your way back home to Opie and Aunt Bea, you inbred redneck."

Brooks turned to face the man. "So, just because I have a Southern accent, you automatically assume that I'm just a booger-eatin', backward-ass, mouth-breathin', slack-jawed yokel with the IQ of a turnip. Well, let me invalidate the stereotype that's bouncing around in your pointy little head. I didn't grow up in a run-down shack in the Great Smoky Mountains. I was born in Chapel Hill, North Carolina, and my parents were not related. In fact, they were electrical engineers for IBM in the Research Triangle office. I've never slept with my sister or any of my cousins."

Brooks stepped closer to the man. "I have never seen a UFO or a crop circle. I have all of my original teeth. I actually wear shoes, and I own more than one pair. I have never used the phrase 'kiss my grits' in a conversation. I don't own a pickup truck. I have never worn a mullet. No one in my family has ever appeared on *The Jerry Springer Show*. I have never been a member of the KKK, and I am not a racist. My ancestors did not own slaves."

Tessa tried to subdue her partner with a firm hand on his shoulder. "That's enough, Brooks."

"It ain't nearly enough." Leaning toward the man's face, Brooks worked up a full head of steam. "No, I do not think professional wrestling is real. I have never appeared on an episode of *Cops* running through a trailer park without a shirt on. I have never eaten road kill. I believe 'Freebird' is the greatest song ever written, and if you don't agree with me, I don't give a shit. Now, if you still have a problem with me, you can just kiss my fat, hairy, pasty-white, Southern ass. Have a nice day, peckerhead." Brooks turned his back on the little weasel and walked out the front door.

When the man started to follow Brooks out the door, Tessa stepped in his path, flashed her badge, and stared him down. "It would be in your best interest to leave him alone. If you insist on harassing Detective Barrington, you'll quickly find yourself in the emergency room, and a doctor will have to surgically remove his artificial foot from your butt. I don't think you want to do that. Pay for your meal, and get the hell out of here." Reluctantly, the man returned to his place in line. Tessa chuckled to herself. That was the first time she had seen Brooks get fired up about anything in the past year.

She met Brooks on the sidewalk next to his car. "How did it feel to blow off some steam?"

"Felt great." Brooks beamed. "Get in the car. We gotta find out what happened to Jill Forcythe. Stan Bogart said her initial results were unusual."

"Unusual? In what way?"

"He wouldn't tell me over the phone, but he said he had never seen anything like it."

Chapter 6

For four hours, Matt Curtis stared at his computer and hoped an epiphany would smack him in the forehead and rescue him from the corporate hell his boss had created for him. Maybe Matt wasn't smart enough to solve his problem, or maybe he simply wasn't cut out to be a high-powered management consultant. Self-confidence issues aside, he owned a project that had slipped into a deep ditch, and he had to find a way to get it back on the road.

A thud on his office door snapped him out of his work-induced coma. He peered through his thin vertical office window to see his executive assistant, Kim, standing impatiently with a goofy grin on her tawny face.

When he opened the door, Kim burst into his office juggling two colossal pieces of birthday cake and a cup of coffee. "Time to take a break. Let's eat!"

"Sounds like a great idea," Matt said. "But you didn't have to get me coffee."

"I didn't. This is my coffee. You know my rule—you get your own coffee. I'm an EA, not a waitress. I brought you a treat because you've had a lousy day … and because I'll look pathetic if I eat two big honkin' pieces of cake by myself."

"Where did you get the cake?"

"They're having a birthday party for some chick down in the accounting department on the sixth floor. My sugar detector went off, so I crashed the party and acted like I knew her. You know I'll do almost anything for a nice hunk of cake." Kim sat in a chair next to Matt's desk.

"Have I ever told you that you're the best EA on the planet?"

"Yes. Keep going." Kim tossed her soft black hair away from her face.

"And you're extremely intelligent."

"And …"

"You're very funny."

"And …"

"You have a spectacular set of …"

"Watch yourself!" Her warm chestnut eyes danced.

"Staplers."

Exploding with laughter, Kim sat back in the chair and crossed her suntanned legs. Wearing a low-cut, scarlet and white business blouse with a matching scarlet skirt, Kim revealed enough cleavage and thigh to make Matt forget about his failing project.

"Oh, here. Let me get an extra-special coaster for you." Matt dug into his bottom desk drawer.

"A what?"

Matt pulled out a set of silver coasters with the Microsoft logo engraved in the middle. "A Microsoft sales rep gave me these coasters as a Christmas present. She was sucking up to me because we were thinking about buying a lot of software from her to use on a project for the Department of Defense. I have never used these ultra-sophisticated coasters, but I think this is the perfect time to break them out."

Kim chuckled as she set her coffee cup on the elaborate coaster. "Your mother would be so proud of you."

"My mother is dead."

Kim winced. "Oh, I'm sorry, Matt. I forgot. In all the years we've worked together, you've rarely mentioned your parents."

"I don't like to talk about my family or my childhood." Matt paused, contemplating whether he should reveal any vital information that would make him self-conscious in front of Kim. He swallowed a bite of cake and cautiously proceeded to tell his tale. "My mom died when I was born. Complications in labor. There were no doctors there to help her. My parents belonged to the Jacksonville Church of God with Signs Following. It's a primitive religion that was popular among the people who lived way back in the Blue Ridge Mountains of southwestern Virginia. The church doesn't believe in doctors or medicine made by humans. Instead, when someone gets sick, a group of devout church members pray over the person. If it's God's will, the person will be healed by the power of God. For some reason, God didn't want my mother to live. He never told me why."

Kim stared at her cake. "That must have been tough on you, growing up without a mom."

"It sucked."

"So I guess you and your dad became close."

"My dad was a mean son of a bitch. He blamed me for my mother's death. Said I took her away from him. He never forgave me for it. He treated my brother and me like farmhands. Even though we worked every day for him in the fields, he refused to let us do anything fun. No TV, no radio, no phone. We were a lightbulb away from being Amish. I hated every minute I lived with him."

"Tough way to grow up." Kim sipped her coffee. "I didn't know you had a brother."

"His name was Paul. He died when I was ten years old. He was thirteen."

"Did Paul die from an illness?"

"No." Tears welled up in Matt's eyes. "He fell down a flight of stairs." Matt sat the cake on his desk and wiped his eyes.

"I'm really sorry, Matt. I apologize for asking so many personal questions. I should just shut up and get back to my desk." Kim stood up and moved toward the door.

"No!" Matt grabbed her hand and stood to face her. "Please, stay with me. I like being with you. You're the only one around here that I can actually talk to about my personal life." He squeezed her hand and gently pulled her toward him.

Their bodies came together as Matt stared into Kim's gleaming brown eyes. Just as they were about to leap over a personal boundary that they both knew they shouldn't cross, Kim looked over at a picture of Matt's girlfriend that sat on his desk next to his phone. "So how are you and Cullen doing?" She forced a look of interest as she awkwardly backed away from her boss.

Matt picked up his cake and jammed a forkful of white icing into his mouth to hide his embarrassment. "We're doing great. Just great," he mumbled. "How is Karl feeling?"

"Good. His shoulder is almost completely healed, and he's scheduled to go back to work soon. He had a nasty injury. I worry about him, but that's what you get when you're married to a fireman. We'll celebrate our seventh wedding anniversary next month." Kim covered her blushing face with her LightCurve coffee mug.

"That's great. I'm happy for you guys." Matt smiled at Kim. It took a few uncomfortable seconds for the emotional atmosphere to return to normal.

He was thankful when Kim changed the subject. "Mike Wozniak told me that you knew the girl they found dead in her closet."

"Yes. Jill Forcythe. We dated for a while. I was infatuated with her, but she broke my heart."

"Hearts are fragile. You can't mess around with them. Even the smallest impulsive mistake can shatter a heart into pieces."

"Yes. You're absolutely right." Matt looked at Cullen's picture. Relieved that he had controlled an urge that could have severely complicated his love life, Matt tossed his crumb-covered Styrofoam plate into the trash can beside his desk. "Well, I'd better get back to work."

"Yeah, me too." Kim straightened her short skirt and walked to the door.

"Hey, Kim, do me a favor and tell Karl that I think he's a very lucky man."

Kim spun around with a huge smile. "He already knows that. But I'll tell him anyway," she chuckled. "You tell Cullen that I think you are a sweet guy. And you have a really cute butt." She opened the office door and paused. "On second thought, maybe we should keep that cute butt comment between you and me."

Chapter 7

It took thirty minutes for Brooks and Tessa to drive eight miles from the restaurant to the Fairfax County Morgue. In Northern Virginia, the mind-numbing rush hour starts at three o'clock and lasts for five hours—on a good day.

After they parked their cars, Brooks met Tessa at the front door. "I can't stand this place," he moaned. They pushed through the heavy double doors of the morgue and walked down a cold, gray hallway to the sterile examination area.

A young man wearing a pair of small, round glasses and white lab coat looked up from a microscope. His pimple-covered face brightened. "Hi, Tessa!"

"Hello, Troy. Nice to see you again."

"Did you get the flowers and note I sent you?" He adjusted his glasses and ran his right hand through his messy hair.

"Yes. They were beautiful. Thank you."

"I hope you had a great birthday. Did you do anything special? With anyone special?"

"I spent a relaxing day with my sister, Erin. We hung out in my apartment and watched my favorite movie, *When Harry Met Sally*."

Brooks smacked his forehead. "Aw, crap. I forgot your birthday again."

"Yes, you did—fourth year in a row." Tessa crossed her arms in playful disgust.

"Sorry." He ducked his head like a scolded puppy.

"Don't worry about it, Brooks." Tessa shifted her focus to the task at hand. "Troy, could you please bring Detective Barrington a large bucket?"

"Sure. I'll be right back." The medical assistant bounded off to a storage room.

"Bucket? I don't need no stinkin' bucket," Brooks complained.

"I'm just planning ahead." Tessa casually toured the room, looking for nothing in particular. Attempting to act unaffected by the creepiness of the morgue, she avoided the body on the stainless steel examination table, covered with a white sheet. She steered clear of the biohazardous waste container, with its signature red bag folded neatly over the rim, and the set of steel bowls that sat on a nearby counter. You never know what you'll see in a bowl in a morgue, she thought.

Troy returned to the room holding a large, blue plastic bucket. "You got a new haircut, Tessa. I like it short. Now you look just like Halle Berry!"

"Hey, Troy, who do I look like?" Brooks asked.

"A fat Tony Orlando." The lab assistant burst into laughter.

"You're real funny. Just give me the damn bucket, and go get Stan." Brooks snatched the pail from Troy and smacked it down on a wide desk a few feet away from the table.

Medical examiner Stan Bogart, a short, gray-haired man in his mid-fifties, entered the room with his youthful assistant following closely on his heels. The men washed their hands and put on surgical gloves. Troy handed latex-free gloves to Brooks and Tessa.

Stan took his standard position at the right side of the table. "I'm ready to get started. Brooks, do you have a bucket handy?"

"Yeah. Now, can we please get this over with?"

"Sure. Let's take a look." Grabbing the edge of the white sheet near the head of the corpse, Stan quickly pulled it away, revealing a naked female with a huge Y carved into the middle of her torso. Sliced open from both her shoulders to her abdomen, Jill's body looked like a special effect in a movie. Small patches of coagulated blood were randomly scattered around the cavernous opening.

"Jill was relatively healthy. She didn't smoke. Stomach contents consisted of spaghetti and tomato sauce with ground beef—probably consumed sometime around 6:00 PM," Stan explained.

Against his better judgment, Brooks moved forward to observe Jill's body. The smell of decaying flesh mixed with the lab chemicals created a foul stench of death. Sweat rolled down the side of Brooks's face. "Stan, can you tell me if … bbbggguuuhhh." Brooks slapped his hand over his mouth as his stomach began to erupt. He reached for the blue bucket and barfed into it.

"Happens every time. Just like clockwork, the Southern man blows grits," Stan howled. "What did he have for lunch today, Troy?"

The assistant surveyed the contents of the bucket. "Chinese food. Looks like sweet-and-sour pork. And a whole bunch of egg rolls."

Trying to settle his nerves, Brooks took three deep, cleansing breaths. "You guys have a twisted sense of humor. That's what happens when you spend ten hours a day with dead people. Good Lord, have mercy. You'd think I'd get used to this after twenty years on the job." Brooks gulped an entire glass of water and regained his composure. "Stan, did you find any problems with Jill's heart?"

"Yes, she had some serious issues concerning her heart. How did you know that?"

"When she was a kid, she had surgery to fix a hole in her heart. Her sister told us it remained weak for the rest of her life. Is that what killed her?"

"No. But look at this." Stan retrieved one of the steel bowls from the counter and gently lifted out Jill's heart for Brooks and Tessa to see. Weighing a normal nine ounces, the heart measured about five inches in length and a bit over three inches in breadth.

Brooks fought hard to keep from hurling a second time. With trepidation, he viewed the organ that was still covered with blood.

"When I cut her chest open to examine her, I discovered that the pericardium was engorged with blood."

Brooks, taking longer than usual to recover from the vomiting episode, interjected, "What about her Pierre Cardin?"

Stan, Troy, and Tessa rolled their eyes in unison. "Her pericardium," Stan explained, "The sac that completely surrounds the heart. Fortunately, the blood had coagulated enough that it didn't make too big of a mess on the poor girl when I cut it open to get to the heart. As I cleared away the bloody mess, the heart came out as well. It had been completely severed from *within* the pericardium."

"What do you mean, that her aorta burst or something?" Tessa asked.

"I mean the four vessels that transport blood to and from the heart were all severed with surgical precision, at the point of their insertion into the heart, without compromising the pericardium. When those vessels were cut, she died from internal bleeding within just a few minutes. It must have been extremely painful. That's probably why she clenched her fists."

"How do you explain this, Stan?" Brooks averted his eyes.

"I can't. It looks like her heart was detached from the inside with a sharp-edged instrument. That's impossible, especially since there were no lacerations on her chest, let alone her pericardium. I've never seen anything like it."

"Are you just messing with us?" Tessa pressed. "I know how much you love to pull practical jokes. Tell us the truth, Stan. She just died of a heart attack, right?"

"I'm not kidding around, Tessa. Her heart was attacked, but this was no ordinary organic occurrence. The incisions are too precise to be a biological malfunction. I can't begin to imagine how it happened."

Brooks peeled off his surgical gloves and gave them to Tessa to dispose of. With a disgusted frown, she handed them right back to him. Tossing his gloves in the biohazardous waste trash can, Brooks asked, "What are you going to write in your official report, Stan?"

"Cause of death—Internal exsanguination from indeterminate severing of primary cardiac vessels. Needs further investigation."

Tessa looked at the young woman's pretty face. "I wonder what went through your mind when this happened to you, Jill?"

"I think this poor girl was scared to death. Something terrifying happened in that closet, and her worst fear came true," Brooks said.

"Oh, please, you don't seriously believe Jill's childhood nightmares had anything to do with this, do you?" Tessa ripped her gloves off and threw them away.

"You heard Stan. Her heart was detached—from the inside. Doesn't that sound just a little bit strange to you?"

"So what are you saying, Brooks? The bogeyman killed Jill? You must be out of your damn mind."

"Maybe I am." Feeling the need for some fresh air, Brooks carefully edged his way around the examining table, averting his eyes from the body, and then he made a quick exit into the hallway.

A soaring fever suddenly engulfed Brooks's head and back. He grabbed his chest as a razor-sharp pain whipped through his upper body and down his left arm. An enormous burst of nausea propelled a surge of vomit out of his body and onto the hallway floor. Brooks collapsed against a wall. "Tessa, help me!" His left arm went numb. The pain in his chest spiked exponentially. Then he slumped to the floor, and everything went black.

Chapter 8

At 6:15 PM, Matt Curtis shut down his laptop and stuffed a stack of project reports into his briefcase. He poked his head outside his office door to make sure the hallway was empty. Heading toward the elevator in a near sprint, he scooted past Dan Calvert's office with his head down and his face turned away from Dan's line of sight.

"Where the hell do you think you're going?" Calvert barked.

Busted. Matt backed into Dan's doorway. "I have a ... uh ... a dinner meeting. I gotta run. See you tomorrow." Matt took off down the corridor, hoping that Calvert wouldn't follow him.

"Your project is in ruins, and you have the balls to leave the office early?" Calvert thundered down the hall to confront Matt face-to-face. "I can't believe you, Curtis. If I were you, I'd get my ass back in my office and figure out how to get my project out of the toilet. How can you do this to the firm—leaving your team at such a critical time?"

"I have complete confidence in my managers and in my team. They have their assignments, and now they need time to work. Tonight, I have a dinner commitment that I have to keep. I can't cancel."

"Who are you meeting for dinner? It had better be someone important."

"It is. This person is very important." Matt blinked his eyes. Then he blinked again. He knew he should have offered more details, but no good ones came to mind.

"Well, who is it?"

"It's a potential new client. He asked me to keep this meeting confidential."

"You should be working with your project team, not selling new work. That's my job. I'm a senior partner in this firm, and nothing should be kept confidential from me. Who is this new client?"

Matt's eyes darted around the office. "He's an executive VP with ..." A telephone rang in a nearby office. "... Dogwood Telecom. I'm meeting him at a restaurant in Dulles, beside the Dogwood headquarters. I really need to go. I can't be late. I'll give you an update tomorrow."

Matt whirled around to make a speedy exit. He didn't want to wait for an elevator because Calvert would certainly catch him and chew his face off. Passing the elevators, Matt ducked into the stairwell. As he hurried down the nine flights of stairs, he contemplated the professional suicide he had just committed.

Flinging open the stairwell door leading to the lobby, Matt ran headfirst into Calvert. "Consider this a warning, Matt. If you turn your back and walk away from me again, you'll be scrubbing urinals for a living. And if you're lying to me about this dinner meeting, I'll have your head on a stick. Are we clear?"

"Yes, sir." Matt looked down at the floor. Calvert huffed back to the bank of elevators, and Matt made his way to the parking garage. "I bust my hump every freakin' day for that bastard, and he still wants more. God forbid I actually have a personal life. I don't live for the sole purpose of serving LightCurve Consulting. Dan Calvert doesn't own me. I should tell him to shove that project up his platinum-plated ass."

Throwing his briefcase into the passenger seat of his blue BMW Z4 Roadster, Matt revved the engine, pulled out of the parking garage, and sped toward his home in McLean. Calvert would certainly hold Matt's pathetic lie against him for years to come, but he had promised to make dinner for Cullen, and he couldn't break his word. He wanted to have a nice romantic date with her, and he wasn't about to let his jackass boss screw it up.

At 6:45 PM, Matt's car came to a halt, stuck in traffic on the Dulles Toll Road. He was supposed to have dinner ready for Cullen at 7:30, so he made an executive decision to call Rocco's Italian Restaurant in McLean and place an order for delivery. If he was lucky, the food would arrive just as he got home.

Creeping along in the rush-hour crush, Matt finally felt the impact of Jill's death. When they had been together, he was deeply in love with her. Obsessed with Jill from the day they met; he had planned to spend the rest of his life with her. On their fourth date, he had asked her to marry him. Jill had been the center of his universe. Unfortunately, she didn't have the same feelings for him, so she abruptly ended the relationship, which threw Matt into a dismal depression.

One would think he'd be used to dealing with breakups since he had been dumped so many times before. Paige Whitaker, Matt's college sweetheart, had refused to accept an engagement ring from him on Christmas Eve. The next love of his life, Tahara Caron, Matt's interior designer, had cheated on him with another client. His most disastrous relationship was with Nikki Fox, a twenty-four-year-old wild child who had absolutely no intention of settling down and becoming Mrs. Matt Curtis. Now, Cullen Rhea had full custody of his affections, and Matt was certain that he had finally found the perfect woman, again. He hoped Cullen felt the same way about him.

The Rocco's delivery man was standing at the front door as Matt pulled into his driveway at 7:20. Matt tipped the driver thirty percent for getting there in a hurry, and he carried the food inside his house.

"Joe, I'm home," Matt called. His roommate and closest friend for the past twelve years didn't answer.

Matt walked into the kitchen. "Joe, it's time for dinner. Where are you?" After he laid out the food on his best dinnerware and set the table in the formal dining room, Matt searched the house.

He found his black cocker spaniel snoring in a plush indigo chair in the formal living room, the dog's favorite spot to snooze. "Joe, wake up." No movement. "Joe, come on. Get up. Cullen will be here in a couple of minutes." The dog opened his bleary eyes, yawned, and slowly rolled his body off the couch. Two stretches and three scratches later, Joe moseyed past Matt into the kitchen. His long, curly-haired ears dipped into his bowl as he drank some fresh water.

Just then, a chili-pepper red Saturn ION coupe pulled into Matt's driveway. From his living room window, Matt watched the driver get out of the car. Dressed in a simple mauve blouse and jeans, she strolled up the walkway to the front door. Watching her walk was a special event for Matt. How could a woman that beautiful fall in love with him? Matt hurried to greet her. As he opened the door to welcome his guest, Joe flew around the corner and jumped up to say hello to Cullen.

"Hi, Joe!" Cullen gave the dog a big smooch on the snout and rubbed his ears. "Let me guess, you've been drinking water. Your ears are all soggy, you silly dog." Joe licked Cullen's face, raced around her feet, and peed on the floor.

"Sorry about that. He really likes you, and he gets excited when you come to visit." Matt wiped up the mess with a paper towel. "I have to admit, I get excited when I see you, too."

"You're not gonna pee on the floor, are you?"

"If you rub my ears I might." They laughed and walked into the dining room. Cullen sat down in a middle chair at the cherry dining room table, facing a bay window that looked out into the woods behind Matt's house. Joe plopped down on the floor next to her because Cullen was a total marshmallow who would feed him scraps throughout dinner. "So, how was your day at work?" she asked.

"It sucked. I don't want to talk about it." Matt made a poor attempt to forget his professional problems and focus on his personal life. As he and Cullen dug into their meal, they discussed their favorite Mel Gibson movies and speculated on the latest editions of *Survivor* and *The Apprentice*. Cullen slipped morsels of pasta, bread, and meat to Joe on a consistent basis to keep him happy.

"I'm full, and so is Joe," she said. "Let's crash on the sofa and watch some TV."

Displaying the only domestic talent he possessed, Matt cleared the dishes and piled them in the dishwasher. Then he joined Cullen and Joe on his comfy couch in the den. He wrapped his left arm around Cullen, and she laid her head softly on his shoulder. Life was good.

After a few minutes of snuggling, Matt turned his face toward Cullen and gently kissed her cheek. Cullen tenderly touched her lips to Matt's. "You smell like lasagna," she laughed.

"Sorry." Matt pulled away in embarrassment.

"Don't be sorry. I love Rocco's lasagna. Now, shut up and kiss me." Cullen placed her hand on Matt's cheek. Then she caressed Matt's neck and gently moved her fingers through his hair.

Sensing a moment of opportunity, Matt moved his right hand along Cullen's left arm and around her shoulder. He cautiously moved his hand down the front of her body.

"Matt, quit it!" She pushed his hand away to a safe distance.

"But, I just thought—"

"Don't think. I just want to have a relaxing evening, OK?" she snapped. Rolling her eyes, she scooted away from Matt and focused her attention on a rerun of *Friends*.

"What's wrong?" Matt asked.

"I don't want you to touch me like that." Cullen's eyes started to tear up.

"But we've been dating for six months. I'm ready to be more intimate with you. I love you, and I want to be with you."

"I'm just not ready, Matt." Tears streamed down her face.

"Cullen, have I done something wrong? Can we talk about this?" Matt reached out for her, but she avoided his touch.

"I don't want to talk about it." She wiped her eyes, walked across the room to the bay window, and stared at the rising yellow moon.

"Why not?"

"Matt, I'll talk about it when I'm damn good and ready."

Perplexed and perturbed, Matt smacked the padded arm of his couch. "Fine."

"Fine!" Cullen shouted back. "I'm leaving." Cullen stomped through the house and snatched her purse off the circular wooden table in the foyer. "I'm going home. Don't call me tonight. I need to be alone. I'll call you tomorrow if I feel like it." Slamming the front door behind her, she sprinted to her car.

Matt watched her speed out of his neighborhood. "What the hell just happened?"

Chapter 9

When Brooks opened his eyes, he found himself staring into a bright, white light. *Oh, shit. I'm dead. Oops. I shouldn't say "shit" because I might be on my way to heaven, and they don't like that kind of language. I hope I'm going to heaven. What if I get to the pearly gates and Saint Peter says, "What are you doing here? This isn't your stop."*

"Brooks? Brooks, can you hear me?" a man's voice asked.

"Yes, I can hear you. Who are you, and where am I?"

"I'm Dr. Connor Kevit. You're in the emergency room at Fairfax Memorial Hospital." From behind the light, a face appeared. Wearing baggy blue scrubs and a stethoscope around his neck, the doctor reminded Brooks of Doogie Howser, MD.

"So, I'm not dead?"

"Not yet." Dr. Kevit held Brooks's left eyelid open and examined his inner eye with the help of a small flashlight.

Brooks tried to sit up, but Dr. Kevit placed his hands on Brooks's shoulders and eased him back onto a stiff pillow. Looking down and across at his bulky body, Brooks saw an IV tube sticking out of the back of his left hand. Three heart monitor pads were taped to his chest, and an oxygen tube was jammed up his nose. "What happened to me?"

"You have acute angina."

"Gee, thanks, doc, but I didn't even know I had an angina."

Dr. Kevit ignored the smart-ass comment. "You experienced myocardial ischemia—a problem with your heart that precipitated acute angina."

"Oh my God! So does that mean I have to give up egg rolls?" Brooks asked as the beeps of his heart monitor picked up speed.

"Angina is pain in the chest that happens when some part of the heart temporarily doesn't receive enough oxygen and blood. It occurs when vessels that carry blood to the heart become blocked for a short period of time. It's triggered by physical exertion or extreme emotional stress. Although it's very painful, angina doesn't permanently damage the heart muscle."

"That's great news! Thanks, doc. I'm outta here." Brooks peeled off a heart monitor pad. He cringed as he yanked out a wad of salt-and-pepper chest hair.

"Hold on, Brooks." Dr. Kevit reapplied the pad on Brooks's chest with a new strip of tape. "Angina means that you have some form of coronary heart disease. You got lucky this time, but you're a heart attack waiting to happen. Your blood pressure is 155 over 102, your cholesterol is 285, and you have a fatty liver. I'd guess you're about sixty pounds overweight, you smoke, and clearly you haven't seen the inside of a gym in more than a decade. Your body gave you a wake-up call."

"Look, you don't have to tell me I'm fat. I get winded when I lean over to tie my shoes. Tell me something I don't know."

"Heart disease is a vicious killer, and it's about to make you its next victim. Your arteries are clogged with a lot of gunk, and one day very soon, they'll be completely blocked. That's when you'll have a massive heart attack, and either you'll suffer permanent heart damage or you'll die. Brooks, you're digging your own grave with a fork. You have to take better care of yourself—starting right now."

"Yeah, yeah. I've heard it all before. I should stop smoking, stop eating food that tastes good, stop having fun, stop chasing women half my age, and stop drinking bottles of Southern Comfort for dinner. Blah, blah, blah. I know you're trying to help me, but I'm a lost cause. I should have died a year ago. At this point in my crappy life, I don't care what happens to me."

"I care," Tessa whispered. She sat in a chair in the corner of the room.

"How long have you been sitting there?" Brooks asked.

"The entire time you've been here in the emergency room." She stepped to the side of Brooks's bed.

"You should be working on Jill Forcythe's case."

"You should quit feeling sorry for yourself and listen to the doctor."

Brooks smirked at Tessa and turned to Dr. Kevit. "Can I go home now?"

"I'd like to admit you for the night so we can observe your progress. I want you to see a cardiologist, and I want you to get some sleep. Maybe you'll be well enough to go home tomorrow morning." Dr. Kevit wrote a long list of instructions on Brooks's medical chart.

"Can I get a sponge bath from a cute nurse?"

"Nope."

"Can I have a cheeseburger and fries for dinner?"

"Absolutely not."

"Can I get some really strong drugs that will help me sleep?"

"Yes."

"OK. I'm in. I haven't slept through the night in a long time. But I'm serious about that sponge bath. Maybe from a spicy Latino RN?" Brooks raised his bushy eyebrows.

"There is one nurse who might accommodate you. His name is Ramon."

"I'll take a pass."

"Suit yourself. I'll have an orderly move you up to your room in a few minutes, and I'll check on you in a couple of hours." The doctor patted Brooks on the shoulder.

"I need a private room. I don't want anyone around me tonight. It has to be a private room. Do you understand?" Brooks insisted.

"No problem. I'll take care of it," Dr. Kevit said. "I need to move on to my other patients. You should get some rest."

"All right. Hey, doc, did you meet my friend, Tessa? She's single and very desperate for male companionship."

Dr. Kevit grinned at Tessa on his way out the door. "Oh yes, we've met. I hope to see you again, Detective McBride." As he maintained eye contact with the attractive detective, he walked into the door frame. Managing a mortified wave and a stupid grin, he quickly left the room.

Tessa returned his wave, fighting through the embarrassment inflicted by her partner. "I am not desperate." She wheeled around to face Brooks. "I can get my own dates. You don't need to be my matchmaker."

"Oh yeah? How many guys have hit on you in the past six months? Not including Troy."

"None."

"Then you have officially earned the label of 'desperate.' You rarely leave your apartment when you're not working. You can't live your life holed up like a hermit, watching *Seinfeld* and running on your treadmill like a hamster."

"I'm comfortable in my apartment. I'm a homebody, and I like to spend my free time by myself. There's nothing wrong with that. Sometimes, when I'm around a lot of people I don't know, I get nervous ... anxious. I don't know why. I guess I'm just weird. Being alone works for me." She watched the monitors beside the bed so she could evade Brooks's skeptical frown.

"Tessa, after a while, being alone really sucks. Believe me. I know what I'm talking about. You've got to get out of the house and make some friends, meet new people. Look, Kevit is a nice guy, and he's a doctor. Not to mention the fact that he obviously has the hots for you. Now, get outta here and go talk to him."

"What do you know about romance? You haven't been on a date for a year."

"I have an excuse. I'm a pudgy, middle-aged guy with a fake leg and a grumpy attitude. You're a beautiful thirty-six-year-old—"

"Thirty-two."

"... thirty-two-year-old woman with the body of an aerobics instructor. All you have to do is walk down the street, and guys fall all over themselves to talk to you. You have the bait. All you gotta do is hop in the boat and go fishin' for the right guy."

"You are so full of crap, Brooks. I'm going home to grab something for dinner, change my clothes, and feed my fish. I'll come back and sit with you for a while so you don't do something stupid, like order a pizza or rip your heart monitors off just to get some attention from the nurses."

"OK. Hey, when you come back, bring me some brownies. I love brownies."

"Yeah, sure. And on my way out, I'll tell Ramon you're ready for your sponge bath."

Chapter 10

After a long day at school, a parent-teacher conference, and a marathon staff meeting, Paige Whitaker guided her green Honda Accord into the narrow one-car garage that also served as the basement of her townhouse. Although her three-bedroom home was tiny by Northern Virginia standards, it took every penny she made as a third-grade teacher to make the mortgage payments and pay the utilities on time. Thank goodness she had a set of helpful parents and a roommate with a job.

When she had bought the townhouse, her father had said, "Paige, the three most important factors in real estate are location, location, and location. Reston is a high-demand area." But for her, the three most important factors in real estate turned out to be money, money, and money.

She lugged her briefcase filled with homework assignments up the stairs to her kitchen, dropped it on the tile floor, and made a beeline for the refrigerator. A yellow sticky note stuck to the door read, "Paige, I'm having dinner with Evan tonight. I'm wearing my sexy underwear, so don't wait up for me. See you tomorrow. Nat." For the past three months, Paige's roommate, Natalie Shoemaker, had been trying to get Evan Slater, a lawyer in her office, to pay attention to her. Evidently, her miniskirts and tight sweaters had finally paid off.

Paige ate a slice of cold pepperoni pizza as she changed out of her conservative teacher garb into a comfortable pair of shorts and a Susan G. Komen "Race for the Cure" T-shirt. She wrestled her frizzy, mousy blond hair into a bushy ponytail and washed her face with Noxzema.

Syndicated reruns of *Everybody Loves Raymond* and *Will & Grace* played in the background while Paige pored over her students' assignments. With just a week left in the school year, she could tell that they were sick of homework. So was she.

At 10:45 PM, she fired up her laptop and logged on to her America Online account. She had received three e-mails from parents with questions about a homework assignment due on Friday. An e-mail from her mother detailed every activity she and Paige's father had experienced during the past two days on their trip to Virginia Beach. Finally, she opened an e-mail from her perfect sister, Valerie, which included a slew of perfect pictures of her three perfect kids and her perfect husband on their perfect vacation at Disney World.

Making her appointed rounds to her favorite Web sites, she clicked through CNN.com, USAToday.com, DrPhil.com, Washingtonpost.com, and Amazon.com. Finally, she worked up the courage to go to Match.com, an online dating service. Five weeks earlier, Paige had filled out a personal profile and had posted her picture on the site. She had yet to receive a single message from a gentleman Web surfer. Maybe her picture made her look fat, or maybe her profile was too boring. Who would want to date someone who just likes to watch TV and read? With hundreds of available thrill-seeking hotties—who get turned on by long walks on the beach, skinny-dipping, sex in public, and white-water rafting—why would anyone be interested in a dull third-grade teacher?

A cynical attitude grew into antipathy as Paige clicked through profiles of single men in their thirties who were an "ideal match" for her. A handsome insurance salesman caught her eye, but she passed because he didn't want to have children. She sent an e-mail to a hunky hiker who was sure to ignore her message. A few more men looked interesting, but Paige didn't act on her urge to contact them. Why bother?

An instant message window popped onto her computer screen. Paige was sure it was either her mom or her sister, until she looked at the message.

LazarusKaine: Hello, Paige.

She stared at the screen name. She had never heard of anyone named Lazarus Kaine. Cautiously, Paige answered his message.

MissPaigeGrade3: who r u?
LazarusKaine: My name is Lazarus Kaine.
MissPaigeGrade3: what do u want?
LazarusKaine: We need to talk.
MissPaigeGrade3: about what?
LazarusKaine: About you, of course.
MissPaigeGrade3: do i know u?
LazarusKaine: No, but I know you quite well.
MissPaigeGrade3: prove it

Paige wanted to get rid of this wingnut, but she couldn't figure out how he got her screen name. She gave it only to her close friends. Someone was probably playing a joke on her. She decided to play along for a few more minutes, and then she would blow the guy off.

LazarusKaine: You were born in Arlington, Virginia. You graduated from Virginia Tech with a bachelor's degree in early childhood education, and you teach third grade at Reston Elementary School.

MissPaigeGrade3: easy information anyone can find on the net. i'm not impressed

LazarusKaine: How about this, you have a small scar on your chin from the time your sister, Valerie, pushed you off your hobby horse when you were two years old. You cheated on a calculus test your freshman year in college and were almost kicked out of school. Your left breast is slightly larger than your right breast. You hate Siamese cats and you're afraid of heights.

MissPaigeGrade3: who put u up to this?

LazarusKaine: You have gained thirty-four pounds since you graduated from college. Your butt looks like two gigantic mounds of cottage cheese. You haven't had a date in more than three years. The last time you had sex was four years, one month, and two days ago with a guy named Todd who never called you again.

MissPaigeGrade3: how do u know all that?

LazarusKaine: I know everything.

MissPaigeGrade3: this isn't funny anymore. i don't know who the hell u are, but i'm feeling very uncomfortable about this. please leave me alone.

LazarusKaine: I understand your discomfort. I'll sign off for now. Oh, yes, one more thing, Paige. You have a small hole in your "Race for the Cure" shirt just below the capital letter "C."

Paige looked down and stuck her right index finger through a hole the size of a dime, just below the capital "C." Her fingers shook as she typed frantically.

MissPaigeGrade3: r u looking at me now? where r u?

LazarusKaine: I see everything.

MissPaigeGrade3: stop this right now or i'm gonna call the cops.

LazarusKaine: Good-bye for now, Miss Paige. I'll speak with you soon when we will discuss your relationship with Matt Curtis.

LazarusKaine signed off.

Chapter 11

Matt polished off his fifth Michelob as the credits rolled on an *ER* episode. Although he had stared at the TV for hours, Matt had no idea what he had just watched. Why did Cullen reject his advances? What was wrong with him? Did she find him physically repulsive? Did he say something stupid? Thousands of questions raced through his head, but not one answer showed itself.

Hoping a night of sleep would wipe away the residue of a miserable day, Matt went upstairs into the master bathroom to brush his teeth. The tube of Crest slipped out of his grasp three times. *God, when will this wretched day ever end?* As he lathered his molars, he thought he heard someone calling his name. It must be the beer talking to him, mocking him. He heard it again. Someone called his name, and it sounded like the voice came from his bedroom.

Matt quickly disposed of his mouthful of toothpaste and scrutinized his bedroom from behind the bathroom door. His security alarm was silent, but he decided to look around the house, just to satisfy his curiosity. He looked down the curved foyer stairs to make sure his front door was closed. As he peered through the darkness, he heard footsteps creak on the floor in the spare bedroom at the end of the hall. Matt backed into the master bedroom to get a Louisville Slugger out of his closet, then eased down the hall to investigate.

With his bat in striking position, he opened the door and looked into the unlit guest bedroom. Nothing unusual. A queen-size bed was perfectly made, a small desk sat at peace, and a floor lamp stood without disruption. Just as his pulse returned to a low thunder, Matt heard footsteps dashing down the stairs in the foyer.

"Who's there?" Matt called. He ran back down the hall to the stairs and, again, found nothing. He searched his house for another twenty minutes, looking for an intruder who obviously didn't exist.

"All right, that's it. No more alcohol after nine when I'm alone in the house." Matt poured himself a shot of Jim Beam. "Starting tomorrow."

He maintained his level of high alert as he walked upstairs to his bedroom and placed the bat under his bed as a precautionary measure.

After putting on a pair of thin, gray pajama pants and turning down his bed, Matt looked over at the corner of the room where Joe snored peacefully on his soft dog pillow. The cocker spaniel had slept through Matt's entire exploration.

"Thanks for the help, Joe. Some guard dog you turned out to be," Matt said. Joe slowly opened one eye to look at Matt, then rolled over and went back to his snoring.

Matt crawled into bed, pulled his sheet up to his face, and buried his head in his pillow. "Relax. Come on, relax," he kept telling himself. After thirty-five minutes of coaxing, Matt's heartbeat finally slowed down, and he fell into a deep sleep. The stress of the day had taken quite a toll on his body, and it craved rest.

At 2:22 AM, a battery of pops and cracks startled Matt. It sounded like someone was walking around in his attic. When he sat up in bed, the noises stopped. "This is nuts. Now I'm hearing things in my sleep."

As Matt laid his head back down on his pillow, a movement to his right caught his eye. Moonlight streamed through a tree outside the bedroom window and created a shadow on the bedroom wall in the shape of a face. The movement of the leaves in the wind caused the face to sway slowly back and forth along the wall. The face glided effortlessly until its dark eyes focused on Matt.

"That's an odd shadow. Never seen one like that." Matt turned away from the shadow and tried to go back to sleep. A few minutes went by, and Matt's curiosity got the best of him. He had to see the shadow again. He turned his head toward the wall and saw two faces staring at him.

The faces moved in shadowy synchronized waves on the wall as the wind gently rustled the leaves. Their hypnotic dance intrigued Matt and made him feel relaxed and serene. A clump of clouds passed in front of the moon, forcing the faces to dissolve into the darkness. Matt hoped they would return soon because they made him feel a quiet peacefulness that he had never felt before.

A few minutes later, the clouds moved away, and the faces resumed their rhythmic ballet. Suddenly, their eyes changed from a soothing expression to an intense glare. The faces melted into each other and then separated into four faces, all of which had the same concentrated glower focused on Matt. The faces moved swiftly around the room and multiplied exponentially. They swirled through each other, over the bed, on the ceiling, across the floor, and around Matt's head until they gathered together into a pulsating swarm at the foot of the bed. The faces melted into each other, forming an object that looked like a solid mass of light mingled with darkness. Matt couldn't take his eyes off the object as it molded itself into the shape of a human body. Slowly, the object took on the features of a tall, slender man. His face gradually shifted into position to reveal a sharp jaw line and a narrow nose. The man's short, brown hair was spiked straight up. He was dressed in a classy black suit, an azure shirt with a white tab collar and white French cuffs, and a matching azure tie. His shiny black shoes looked as if they had never been worn.

"Hello, Matt. My name is Lazarus Kaine. We need to talk," the man said in a low voice.

Matt sat frozen in his bed, staring at the creepy, well-dressed man at the foot of his bed. "This is just a dream, right?" *I will never drink alcohol again, I swear.* "I'm just gonna go back to sleep. When I wake up, you'll be gone."

"This is no dream."

Matt eased to the side of his bed and casually lowered his right hand toward his bat. Quickly, he grabbed the bat and ran toward the intruder. Using all of his strength, Matt swung at the man's head. Lazarus didn't move. The Louisville Slugger passed through Lazarus's skull with no resistance at all. Matt swung again. The bat sliced through the man's body as if it weren't there. "Are you a ghost?"

"Ghosts can't do this." Lazarus snatched the bat from Matt's trembling hand. With a home run swing like Barry Bonds, Lazarus cracked Matt's right knee with the bat, knocking him to the floor. Wincing in pain, Matt crawled to his nightstand and extended his right hand toward his phone.

Lazarus grabbed Matt's wrist. "No one can help you. Now, why don't you just calm down and sit on your bed. Let's chat for a bit."

Realizing he was no match for the dark man, Matt conceded, and Lazarus released his hold. After Matt struggled to return to his bed, he placed a pillow under his throbbing knee. "What do you want from me?"

"You brought me here."

"No, I'm pretty sure that I did not invite you into my bedroom."

"Your life has become complicated, difficult, and frustrating. You're failing at work, and you're failing in your relationship with Cullen, just as you failed with every other woman you've dated. Your world is crumbling, and you can't stop it. People are starting to discover the 'real' Matt Curtis—the worthless piece of white trash from the backwoods of Jacksonville County, Virginia. For years, you've pretended to be a hot-shot consultant with lots of money and pretty women on your arm. It's all a lie, Matt. You don't deserve the life you're living, and you're afraid you're going to lose it all. Your desperation brought me here."

Lazarus walked across the room. He stood at Matt's window and peered into the night. "Most people have your average, run-of-the-mill phobias such as the fear of spiders, snakes, and public speaking. Boring crap. On very rare occasions, a person will develop a group of fears that will take over his life and will affect the lives of others around them."

He shifted his shadowy gaze to Matt. "You, my friend, have an exceptionally strong set of psychological terrors rattling around in your well-educated head. You're struggling with a distinct fear of inadequacy, the dread of losing people close to you, and—my personal favorite—the horror of being alone. You can't handle the emotional strain. You're losing control, Matt. That's where I come in. My job is to make your worst fears come alive."

"And how are you gonna do that?" Matt wished he hadn't asked such a wise-ass question. He cringed as a rush of pain sliced through his battered knee.

"You'll see," Lazarus said. "I've already set my plan into motion. Last night, I paid a visit to Jill Forcythe. You remember Jill. Sweet girl. Nice legs. Lots of shoes. She broke your heart, so I returned the favor and broke her heart. Jill was a good start, but I have some good stuff planned for the next few nights."

"Why are you doing this?"

"Because you don't have the balls to stop me." Lazarus flashed a vile grin. "Your troubles have just begun, Matt, and they're about to get worse. I have a date tonight with one of your old girlfriends, Paige Whitaker. It's getting late, so I must be on my way. But before I go, I'll be a friend and mend that knee." Lazarus passed his right hand over Matt's injury, repairing the broken bones like a supernatural orthopedic surgeon. "You and I will talk again soon. Good night, Matt."

Lazarus closed his eyes and crossed his arms. His body disintegrated into a cloud of shadows. In a second, he was gone.

Chapter 12

After her disturbing instant messaging conversation, Paige Whitaker closed every blind in her house, checked that her doors were locked, and ate half a gallon of Ben & Jerry's Chunky Monkey ice cream. Her eyes were wide open during the *Tonight Show* and *Late Night*, but *Carson Daly* found a way to put her to sleep.

At 3:14 AM, Paige's alarm clock went off, blurting out a commercial for WKYS, "Kiss FM," a local rhythm and blues radio station. She turned off the alarm and checked the time it was set for. Green numbers glowed in the dark—7:00 AM. "That's weird. There must be something wrong with this stupid thing." As she gathered up her sheets to reconfigure her sleeping nest, Paige noticed an unusual shadow on her bedroom wall. It looked like a face, formed by darkness and moonlight. Its eyes looked angry. "Holy cannoli, I don't need this staring at me all night." Paige got up and closed her bedroom curtains to eliminate the face. She crawled back into bed, adjusted her sheets, and released a cleansing sigh in an effort to relax.

Nine minutes later, the alarm clock blared the Alicia Keys hit "Fallin'." With her eyes closed, Paige rolled over and felt around her nightstand for the stupid clock. Her right hand finally discovered the annoying device, and she worked her hand up to the top of the clock. As she reached for the off switch, she touched something cold and clammy. She felt it move and realized it was a human hand.

"Oh my God!" Paige recoiled back on her bed. It seemed like many minutes before her eyes could adjust to the darkness. Eventually, a tall, thin man came into focus, standing by her bed.

"Hello, Paige. My name is Lazarus Kaine. We need to talk."

"No! No! No! Help me! Help me! Please, somebody, help!" Paige yelled until her voice went hoarse. She was too scared to run and too frozen with fear to fight the man in the designer suit. Sheer terror trapped Paige in her own bed.

Lazarus stood motionless and stared at Paige while she shrieked. "My goodness. I haven't heard that much screaming since the Salem witch trials. I hope you're finished, because I need to speak with you."

"What do you want from me?" Paige whispered through a sob. "Take my jewelry, my money, anything you want. Just please don't hurt me."

"I don't want your knockoff jewelry or the pitiful $34.28 in your purse. I want to talk about your relationship with Matt Curtis."

"What about it?" Paige clutched her pillow in front of her like a shield.

"You and Matt were college sweethearts, young and in love, right?"

"We were close ... for a while."

"Close? You spent all of your spare time together. You took him home on school vacations to spend time with your family. You said you loved him." Lazarus moved closer to the bed.

"I was in love with the idea of being in love. We had some fun in college, but when we graduated, we grew apart."

"Don't you mean you pushed away from him?"

"I needed my space. I wanted to find out who I was as a person."

"So in your zeal to explore your new age, self-discovery bullshit, you humiliated a young man who was deeply in love with you. You refused his engagement ring—on Christmas Eve of all days. You were such a bitch to him. By the way, how did that decision work out for you? Let's see, you don't have two nickels to rub together, your thighs get bigger every day, your ass is huge, and the only men who are interested in you are two guys named Ben and Jerry."

"I told Matt I was sorry." Tears streamed down her face.

"Sorry doesn't heal the deep wounds that you inflicted on Matt." Lazarus sat down on the edge of Paige's bed and slowly leaned toward her.

"What are you doing?" Paige eased her way to the other side of the bed.

"Matt fell for you, and he got hurt. Now, it's your turn to fall." Lazarus reached for Paige.

"Get away from me!" Paige jumped off the bed. She expected her feet to hit the floor, but they didn't. The floor was gone. It had turned into an inexplicable black abyss. As she began to tumble into the mysterious hole, Paige reached up and grabbed the bedsheet. Dangling in the darkness, Paige tried to comprehend her situation. Her walnut dresser, its matching nightstand, and her iron frame bed stood securely in place, but her floor had completely disappeared. She couldn't see the bottom of the hole, and she sure as hell didn't want to fall to find it. Paige clawed her way up the sheet and nearly pulled herself back onto the bed.

Just as her right hand reached up to grab the mattress, the sheet slipped. Paige fell back down into the gaping hole, clinging to a scrap of the bedding with her left hand. "Oh, dear God! Help me!"

Lazarus stuck his head over the side of the bed and smiled at the troubled woman suspended in the ominous void. "Good-bye, Paige." He loosened the sheet and dropped her into the darkness.

After the first few seconds of her fall, Paige couldn't hear her own screams anymore. She felt her body cut through the air, but she couldn't see anything. Paige closed her eyes, expecting a devastating impact at any time. She heard a faint noise coming from below. As she drew closer to the sound, she realized it was her own voice crying out in horror. Without warning, she crashed, crushing her bones and tearing her flesh. Paige's demolished body quivered in shock as one final breath escaped her damaged lungs. Paige Whitaker came to a solemn rest—lying on her own bed.

Chapter 13

Although the mattress on his bed was thin and the alleged chicken he ate for dinner tasted like a hunk of drywall, Brooks enjoyed his stay at Fairfax Memorial Hospital.

His eyes brightened when a perky nurse popped into his room to deliver his medication for the evening. A big dose of Ambien, a popular sleep aid, earned the distinction of becoming Brooks's extra-special hospital companion. The drug kicked into gear and put him out of commission for hours.

After passing through a series of dreams starring Cindy Margolis and the Coors Light twins, Brooks woke up to the sound of someone rattling around in his hospital room. "All right! Time for another round of sleeping pills. I love this place."

Brooks turned over in his bed, expecting to see a nurse holding a cup filled with another hit of Ambien. Instead, he saw a lean man in a dark suit staring at him with wicked eyes.

"Hello, Brooks."

"Hello, Lazarus." Brooks sat up in bed. "I've been expecting you."

"Sweet of you to think of me. I'm touched. How's your leg?"

"Still gone. Thanks for asking."

"It's been a year since the accident, and you're still bitter. What a shame."

"It was no accident, and you know it. You killed my wife and daughter, you son of a bitch." Brooks started to lunge at Lazarus, but he pulled back when he realized he was still hooked up to an IV bag and a heart monitor.

"I seem to recall that you had been drinking beer with your fishing buddies on that mournful day and that your blood alcohol level was three times the legal limit. You chose to get behind the wheel of your car, and you killed your wife and daughter." Lazarus attacked with the authority of a prosecuting attorney.

"You disabled the brakes on my car."

"You couldn't maintain control of the automobile because you were smashed. For years, you lived with the fear that your drinking would cause you to lose your loving wife, Maureen, and your precious little daughter, Holly. I just helped your fear come to fruition."

"You bastard! I lost a piece of my soul when you took my family away from me." Brooks continued to fight the impulse to jump at his shadowy visitor's throat.

"Those things happen, Brooks. I've moved on. So should you." Lazarus sauntered around the room, examining the medical equipment that was tracking Brooks's condition. He leaned down to inspect the display on the heart monitor. "Trouble with the old ticker, huh? Maybe you should try the South Beach Diet. Carbohydrates can kill you."

"I don't care."

"Yes, I'm aware of that. You're not afraid of death. You have other fears clattering around that giant punkinhead of yours. For example, you haven't solved a case since the accident. Your boss, Lieutenant Malone, thinks you're an idiot, and she's looking for a reason to fire your lazy ass. What would happen to you if you were to find yourself stuck with a series of unsolved mysteries? You'd probably lose your job—right, Brooks? Because you don't know how to do anything else, you would probably end up working the night shift as a security guard at some remote office building. In your spare time, you would park your enormous beer gut in a La-Z-Boy, eat super-size bags of Cheetos for dinner, and watch *Star Trek: The Next Generation* reruns until one day, you'd find yourself asking moronic questions like, 'If Captain Jean-Luc Picard grew up in France, then why does he speak with a British accent?' Eventually, you'd get fed up with your miserable life, bite down hard on the business end of a pistol, and blow the back of your freakin' head off."

"And I suppose you're going to make all of this happen to me?" Brooks asked.

"I've already started."

"With Jill Forcythe?"

"Yes, lovely Jill. She had a bad heart, so I disconnected it." Lazarus casually strolled around the room.

"Why did you kill her?"

Lazarus spun around to face Brooks. "You're supposed to be a detective. You figure it out."

"Is Jill your only victim, or will there be more murders?"

"Oh, there will be more. In fact, I had an exhilarating encounter with another woman earlier this evening." Lazarus paced around the hospital bed.

"Who is she? What did you do to her?"

"I'm sure you'll get all the details from your partner, Miss McBride. She's the one who does all of the real work for you."

"Does Jill Forcythe have a connection to the woman you just killed?"

"Of course she does."

"What is it?" Brooks snapped.

"I'm not going to tell you, Brooks. That would spoil all of the fun." Lazarus's thin face expanded into a vicious grin.

"Why do you take such pleasure in destroying the lives of innocent people?"

"It's a gift. Since the time Neanderthals stumbled through the woods hunting for food, I've lived in the mind of every human being that has walked the planet. In the old days, humans had uncomplicated fears, like getting eaten by a lion or falling off a cliff. As humans evolved, so did their fears. When religions formed around the world, I became quite powerful because many beliefs embraced and capitalized on the concept of fear. As the years went by, fear developed into a motivating force for wars, social conflicts, religious hostilities, and terrorism. In his first inaugural address, Franklin D. Roosevelt said, 'Let me assert my firm belief that the only thing we have to fear is fear itself—nameless, unreasoning, unjustified terror which paralyzes needed efforts to convert retreat into advance.' He was talking about me, Brooks. I am fear itself."

"Thanks for the spellbinding history lesson, Lazarus. You're quite a storyteller."

"I've had lots of practice."

"So why do you call yourself Lazarus Kaine?"

"I got tired of being nameless. In the late 1950s, I whacked a guy named Lazarus Kaine, a bartender from Reno, Nevada. I thought it sounded like a cool name, so I took it. He didn't need it anymore."

"Oh, I see," Brooks said. "Here's another question. Has anyone ever told you that you look like Christopher Walken?"

"I can assume any form I choose. In case you haven't noticed, Mr. Walken is a fine-looking man. I like to describe his unique appearance as 'disturbed elegance.' He's also a wonderful dancer. The man is quite talented." Lazarus stepped toward the window. "Look, I'd love to stay and chat, but I must be on my way."

"Before you go, could you at least tell me the name of the second victim and where she is, so we can find the poor girl's body?" Brooks pressed.

"Good-bye, Brooks." Lazarus faded into the night.

Chapter 14

Matt woke up with the unsettling feeling that someone was staring at him. He opened his groggy eyes to see Joe sitting at the side of his bed, holding his leash in his mouth.

"OK, I'm coming," Matt grunted. "I had the weirdest dream last night, Joe. It seemed so real." The cocker spaniel showed no interest in Matt's story because his canine bladder was about to burst.

Matt rolled his body to the side of his bed and gently set his feet on the floor. As he shifted his weight to stand up, a jagged pain ripped through his right knee, sending Matt to the ground in a groaning heap. His knee looked like a black and blue cantaloupe. Although Lazarus had healed Matt's bones, the surrounding tissue remained quite damaged.

After painfully hobbling into the bathroom, Matt forced down two Extra Strength Tylenols and wrapped his sore knee with an Ace bandage. He then hobbled to take Joe outside, where the dog frolicked while Matt took as few short, agonizing steps as possible. A hot shower soothed Matt's aching joint, and a heavy additional dose of Advil got Matt to the point where he could drive to work.

Although he tried to focus on his failing project, he couldn't help thinking about his encounter with Lazarus. How could that shadow of a man be real? Matt's logical side told him that his experience was just a figment of his overactive imagination. But his right knee had a different opinion.

It took Matt fifteen minutes to limp from his car in the parking garage to his office across the street in the LightCurve office complex. He dropped his briefcase on his desk, unpacked his laptop computer, and shuffled down the hallway to his Thursday morning project status meeting.

"What happened to you, Hopalong?" Matt paused and turned to see Kim walking toward him.

"I fell down and hurt my knee last night."

Kim looked into Matt's red-veined eyes. "Yeah, gravity sucks when you drink too much."

"I didn't drink too much last night. Actually, I don't think I drank nearly enough. I have to get to my staff meeting. Is there anything I should know before I go in there?"

"Dan Calvert is really pissed off at you—even more than normal. He was in full rampage mode when I got here at seven. Avoid him at all costs."

"Thanks for looking out for me, Kim."

"No problem. Now get in that conference room and get to work. I'll check in on you later." She gave him a sexy wink.

"Yes, ma'am." Matt smiled as he took a minute to watch Kim walk down the hall to her cubicle. He had personally hired her seven years before, straight out of West Virginia University. She got the job because she was smart, creative, and way overqualified for an executive assistant's position. The fact that she had a cute face and a rockin' body had absolutely no influence on his decision to hire her. Really. No kidding. That was his story, and he stuck to it faithfully. Their relationship never got personal because she was happily married to her husband, Karl, a firefighter, and Matt always seemed to be in a relationship with his soul mate du jour. Matt treasured Kim's friendship, and he loved the way she filled out her business suits.

Matt could hear his project managers in the midst of a heated argument before he even opened the conference room door. "What's going on in here?" He limped into the room. Matt stopped cold upon seeing Tom Albert, the system design team leader, pounding his fist on the table and yelling at the top of his lungs.

"These system requirements are changing on a daily basis, Ben. My team can't build a functional system without clear, specific requirements," Tom ranted.

"The Carponi Communications finance guys won't cooperate with us, Tom. They refuse to give us the information we need to generate a usable set of system requirements, and they won't hand over their historical data. My team is working day and night, but we need more time to build relationships with the Carponi folks. They hate us, and they don't trust us."

"We don't have time to make friends. You guys have to push the Carponi people harder. My team members can't do their jobs properly until your lousy bunch of lugnuts get off their butts and pull their load."

"Lay off my team, Tom. They worked until one o'clock this morning, and they're busting their humps to get this project back on track."

"If you ask me, your team sucks."

"I didn't ask you, asshole." Ben lunged at Tom.

"All right! That's enough from both of you!" Matt hobbled between the two men before they came to blows. "You guys need to calm down and get back to work. You're acting like teenagers. You're poisoning the entire project."

A new voice cut through the noise. "Having some management problems, Matt?" Matt whipped his head around to see Calvert standing at the door. Matt had no idea how long he had been standing there, but he assumed Calvert heard the whole argument. "Can I talk to you for a moment, Matt? In private?"

Matt limped into the hallway, where Calvert leaned against a wall with his arms folded tightly across his navy blue suit.

"You've lost control of your project, Matt. I'm very disappointed."

"We'll be fine. Everyone is just under a lot of stress right now. We'll work our way through it." Matt straightened his red tie.

"I'm giving you three days to develop a plan to put this engagement back on track. If you can't get the job done, I'm going to replace you with another senior manager."

"I can do this." Matt held eye contact with Calvert.

"I wish I could believe you, but I fully expect you to fail. You should focus your energy on a more productive task, like working on your resume. You're going to need it very soon." Calvert moved closer to Matt, invading his personal space until Matt could smell the starch on his custom-tailored shirt. "You lied to me last night, you little son of a bitch. I know you didn't meet with a client. You had a dinner date with your hot little girlfriend. I hope she was worth it. That stunt is going to cost you your career."

"I'm sorry, Dan." Matt lowered his head. "How did you find out about that?"

"I had an intern follow you home," Calvert scowled. "I can't wait to throw your lying ass out of this firm."

Chapter 15

Brooks woke up abruptly and pulled three heart monitor pads off his chest, ripping chunks of black and gray hairs out by their roots. Then he tried to yank the IV tube out of his left hand.

A middle-aged nurse raced into the room. "What are you doing, Mr. Barrington? You have to leave your heart monitors on and your IV in until your doctor discharges you." She tried to put the monitors back into place, but Brooks refused to let her do her job.

"I have to get outta here." Brooks pulled the IV most of the way out of his hand. Blood squirted from his wound.

"Stop it! You're going to hurt yourself." With strength she had developed over the course of her twenty-seven-year nursing career, the woman clamped down on his arm, carefully removed the rest of the IV needle, and bandaged his hand to stop the bleeding.

"Where are my clothes? I'm leaving."

"Your doctor needs to examine you, Mr. Barrington. He'll be here soon. Go ahead and take a shower. Your clothes are in the closet. I'll bring you some breakfast. You can eat while you wait for your doctor to arrive."

Realizing he smelled like a hospital bed and his stomach was growling, Brooks grudgingly cooperated. As soon as the nurse left the room, Brooks reached for his telephone. The phone on the other end rang four times.

A sleepy female voice answered. "Hello. Who is this? It had better be an emergency."

"Tessa, it's me, Brooks," he whispered.

"Why the hell are you calling me so early? Aren't you in the hospital?"

"You have to come pick me up, right now."

"Why?"

"There's been another murder."

"No one has called me about another murder. I think those drugs you're on are making you imagine things, Brooks. Just take another dose of sleeping pills, and I'll pick you up at ten o'clock. Now, I'm going back to sleep. Bye, Brooks."

"No! Tessa, wait! Don't hang up. I'm telling you, another woman was murdered last night, and we have to find her." He stood up beside his bed.

"What's her name? Where is she?"

"I don't know."

"You don't know who or where she is? Then how do you know about this anonymous murder?" Tessa's voice cut through the receiver.

"I just know. Come on, Tessa. Please come and get me."

"I'll see you at ten o'clock. Goodbye, Brooks." Tessa hung up the phone. Brooks had lost two arguments before he had taken his morning pee. This was bound to be a great day.

Brooks took a hot shower, watched the local morning news, and ate a glob of yellow stuff rumored to be scrambled eggs. During his second cup of weak coffee, the nurse returned to reattach his heart monitor pads and to check his vital signs. After she wrote a few notes on his medical chart, she left without saying good-bye. A few moments later, Dr. Thomas Yager, a heart specialist, walked into Brooks's room carrying a handful of brochures.

"Good morning, Brooks. How are you feeling?" Dr. Yager scrutinized the heart monitor display.

"I feel like a hundred bucks, doc. Can I go now? I have to get to work."

Dr. Yager listened to Brooks's heart and lungs through a frosty stethoscope. After poring through a stack of medical charts and taking one final look at the heart monitor, the doctor caved in to Brooks's relentless requests. "All right, Mr. Barrington. I'm going to discharge you, but I don't want you to go back to work for three days. Stay away from stressful situations. You need to start eating correctly and exercising. I've brought you some brochures to help you get started, and I want to see you in my office next week."

The door to Brooks's hospital room squeaked open, and Tessa stuck her head inside. "Good morning, sunshine," Brooks called out. "Why are you so early?" The stern look on Tessa's face told Brooks something was very wrong.

"As I said, Mr. Barrington, I don't want you to go to work for three days." Dr. Yager made eye contact with Tessa.

"Yes sir, doc. My friend Tessa is going to take me straight home."

Dr. Yager read the strained expression on Tessa's face and the concern in Brooks's eyes. "Please take care of yourself, Mr. Barrington."

"I'll see you next week. Scout's honor." Brooks flashed the Boy Scout hand sign and grinned broadly while he waited for Dr. Yager to leave the room. After the door closed behind the doctor, Brooks asked Tessa, "What's wrong?"

"You were right. There has been another unusual death—a woman in a Reston townhouse. Come on, I'll take you home."

"I'm not going home. You're taking me to the crime scene."

"But the doctor just said—"

"I don't give a damn what the doctor said. I need to get to that crime scene right now."

Knowing she would never change his mind, Tessa helped Brooks gather his belongings. After a hospital worker wheeled Brooks to the front exit, he and Tessa walked to her silver Toyota Prius, which was parked in a patient pickup lane.

"This car is a hybrid, right?" Brooks guided his artificial leg into the passenger side of the car. "Part gasoline, part electric?"

"Yep."

"How fast can it go?"

Tessa slipped on a pair of dark sunglasses. "Let's find out." She zipped out of the parking area and floored the accelerator as she turned right onto Fellows Road. Tessa didn't slow down on the long entrance ramp past Arlington Boulevard to the Capital Beltway. She weaved through the morning rush-hour traffic with the precision of a NASCAR driver and made a left turn onto the Dulles Toll Road without using her brakes. Slowing momentarily at the toll booth, she gunned the hybrid past the 90 mph mark. Twelve minutes later, they arrived at Paige Whitaker's townhouse.

Tessa and Brooks pressed through police officers, nosy neighbors, and TV reporters to get inside. They found Stan Bogart standing in the doorway to Paige's bedroom, rubbing his temples.

"Brooks! I thought you were in the hospital. What are you doing here?" Stan swallowed three Tylenol caplets without the help of any water.

"I feel fine, but *you* look like crap. What's wrong with you, Stan?"

"Take a look at this." Stan turned so they could see Paige's mangled body lying on her bed.

"Good Lord! What happened in there?" Brooks tried to keep his simulated scrambled eggs from making a return appearance.

"Her name is Paige Whitaker. Single. Thirty-four years old," Mitchell Sparks, a crime scene investigator, explained. "Her roommate, Natalie Shoemaker, came home this morning at about six fifteen and found Paige just as you see her now."

"It looks like her body has been beaten mercilessly." Tessa entered the room and walked to the bed. Paige's broken arms and legs were contorted at unnatural angles. Her torso was smashed and three ribs stuck out of her body. Her face was viciously bruised, virtually unrecognizable.

"Actually, her injuries are consistent with a fall from a very high elevation—I'd guess twenty or twenty-five stories," Mitchell clarified.

"So, she fell from a tall building, and someone moved her body here?" Tessa's face scrunched up with confusion.

Mitchell looked to Stan for direction. "Go ahead, Mitch. Tell them the rest of the story." Stan rubbed his eyes.

The investigator cleared his throat a couple of times, licked his lips, and adjusted his Washington Nationals baseball cap. "She landed right here, in her own bed."

"What?" Tessa snapped. "Did you say she landed here? No freakin' way."

Mitchell took a deep breath and made his case. "Judging from the blood spatter patterns on the bed, the floor, the walls, and the ceiling, her body definitely landed in her bed. No question about it. It would be impossible for a person to recreate those patterns so perfectly."

Tessa threw her hands in the air. "A person can't fall twenty-five stories in a room with a ten-foot ceiling. How do you explain this, Mitch?"

"I can't."

Tessa fired off another question in Stan's direction. "What do you think about all of this?"

The long-experienced and well-practiced medical examiner stared her down. "I have no idea how this happened, Tessa."

"Have you found any connection between Paige and the woman you processed yesterday, Jill Forcythe?" Brooks asked.

A puzzled look flew across Stan's face. "No. Why do you think they're connected, Brooks?"

"Let's just call it a hunch. Tessa and I will interview the roommate. As you guys search this place, look for anything that links this woman to Ms. Forcythe."

"We'll call you when we discover some physical evidence. To commit a crime this violent, I'm sure the murderer dropped some DNA somewhere along the way," Mitchell said.

Brooks shook his head. "Knock yourself out, Mitch, but I bet you won't find any."

Chapter 16

Matt hunkered down in his small, sterile office, trying to salvage what was left of his career. Every few minutes, he would glance at the meaningless abstract corporate art hanging above his desk, wondering why his personal and professional lives were imploding.

He closed his door to shut out the rest of the world and turned his phone off to avoid pointless interruptions. His voice mail would catch the usual multitude of daily emergencies and hold them until he felt like dealing with the common disasters.

As he pored over status reports and incomplete system requirement documents, Matt sipped on his black coffee and nibbled on a blueberry muffin. He ignored the endless stream of e-mails that flooded his inbox. Suddenly, an instant message from Mike Wozniak jumped up on his computer screen, startling Matt out of his monotonous work coma.

WozOSU94: Matt. You'd better take a look at this …
http://www.washingtonpost.com/dyn/articles/A22435/local-woman.html

Sensing that the article was going to tell him bad news, Matt slowly moved the cursor over the hyperlink and clicked his mouse. He read the first two lines of the story over and over. "Fairfax County detectives are investigating the unusual death of Paige Whitaker, thirty-four years old, of Reston, Virginia. This morning, the woman's mangled body was discovered in her own bed."

Oh, God! Lazarus Kaine was real. Why did he have to kill Jill and Paige? Is there something about me that's causing this? Guilt pulled Matt's head into his hands. *I should tell the police about this. But they might take me to jail … or think I'm nuts. What should I do? Jill and Paige didn't deserve to die because of their relationships with me. I loved them both—maybe too much. I would have made long-term commitments to either of them if they had just given me a chance. That's all I wanted, a chance to love someone who would be with me forever.*

Matt had never had a devoted relationship with anyone for an extended period of time. His mother had been taken from him before he got to know her. Halsey Curtis, Matt's father, wasn't the kind of man that any person could love. The man pushed his two sons like workhorses and whipped them with a tattered belt when they strayed the least bit. Like a hard-ass slave driver, he made them bale hay in the hot summer sun and milk 140 cows every day and night without a word of thanks.

Paul, the elder son, was an A student and excelled in everything he attempted. With his rugged good looks, Paul drew attention to himself without the least bit of effort. Teenage girls laughed at his jokes, and all of the boys, especially Matt, wanted to be him.

On a sweltering Friday afternoon in July 1978, Matt and Paul finished stacking a large load of hay bales in the back of the barn. Thirteen-year-old Paul parked their rundown John Deere tractor in front of the hay bales and went inside the farmhouse to start dinner.

Because his father was picking up rolls of chicken wire and twine at the Farmer's Supply store in Jacksonville, Matt found himself unsupervised with time on his hands, a rare treat. He ran behind the barn and slid under a dogwood tree, where he had buried a shoe box filled with special treasures he had gathered during the past few months, including a stack of worn baseball cards, a broken yo-yo, twelve dollars in cash, a picture of a black Pontiac Trans Am with a golden firebird painted on the hood, a tiny box of old matches, and a pack of cigarettes he found in a bathroom at school months earlier.

For weeks, he had tried to work up the courage to light a cigarette. A few of his friends at school bragged about their smoking prowess, but Matt didn't believe them. This time, he was actually going to smoke a butt. He would be so cool. Maybe even Paul would be impressed.

Matt opened the pack, stuck a cigarette in his mouth, struck a match, and tried to light the death stick. Nothing happened. He had put the cigarette in backward and had tried to light the filter. The match hissed as it flamed out—as if it were laughing at his incompetence. Matt pulled another cigarette from the pack and attempted to fire it up. No luck. Most of the matches were damp and useless. Match after match failed to spark. Finally, his last effort exploded into a blaze. Matt nervously lit his first cigarette.

As he took a long drag on the butt, smoke infiltrated Matt's lungs like an army of nicotine-laced soldiers, attacking his system with fury. His head felt like it was going to blast off his shoulders. A rush of nausea assaulted his stomach. Matt dropped the cigarette and fell to the ground. Suddenly, a flood of what seemed like forty-eight gallons of vomit charged out of his body. He tried to stand up, but another shot of sickness sent him back to the ground. He crawled around the corner of the barn toward the farmhouse. His painful journey ended in a coughing fit on the back porch that was loud enough to bring Paul running to his side.

"What the heck is wrong with you?" Paul helped his brother to the white porch swing.

"I ... *cough* ... I tried to smoke a cigarette so you would think I was cool," Matt wheezed. "It didn't quite work out the way I had it planned. How do people smoke those things? They're awful!"

"Look, bonehead, don't ever do that again," Paul counseled his stupid ten-year-old brother. "Just sit here for a while and try to suck some fresh air into your lungs. I'll call you when dinner is ready." Paul laughed as he walked back into the house.

After a few minutes, Matt's breathing returned to normal, but he smelled an unusual odor, like something was burning. He guessed Paul had overcooked a part of their dinner and dismissed the scent. Then Matt noticed a cloud of smoke drifting into the air from behind the barn. The smell became more intense, and Matt saw flames leaping from the roof of the barn.

"Paul! The barn's on fire!" Matt screamed. "Paul! Get out here! Now!" His brother burst through the door, and the two boys ran around to the rear of the barn to see a wall of fire cascading over the top of the building.

"Grab some buckets, and run to the spring house. Get as much water as you can. Hurry!" Paul yelled. The boys made a valiant attempt to put the flames out, but the fire was way ahead of them. Without running water on the farm, they didn't even have a garden hose to use on the fire. Their father's refusal to put a telephone in the house left the boys with no way of calling for help. Defeated, exhausted, and covered with smoke, the boys watched the ramshackle barn, which had been in their family for decades, burn to ashes.

Halsey Curtis drove his pickup truck down Route 746, gunned the engine, and raced up his gravel driveway. "Get in the truck!" he barked at the boys. They jumped into the bed of the truck, and Halsey took off to the Jacksonville volunteer fire department, ten miles away. Two fire trucks responded, and three hours later, the fire was put to rest.

Later that evening, after the last of the embers went dark, Halsey called his boys into the living room. Matt felt like he was standing in front of a firing squad.

"Which one of you boys is responsible for the fire?" Halsey stared first into Paul's stoic expression and then into Matt's tear-filled eyes. Fearing the beating that would most certainly come with a confession, Matt stood motionless as tears streamed down his face. Time stopped while the boys maintained a united front.

Paul broke the silence. "It's my fault, Daddy."

Matt snapped his head around and looked at his brother in disbelief.

"Son, are you sure it's your fault?" Halsey questioned. The shock on Matt's face clearly gave away Paul's lie. "Tell me what really happened, boy. I want the truth."

Paul cleared his throat. "I was smokin' a cigarette behind the barn. I thought I had stomped it out on the ground, but I guess it caught some twigs on fire, and it spread to the barn."

"Is that the way it happened, Matthew?" Halsey shifted his piercing gaze to his younger son.

Matt didn't know what to do. Staring at the threadbare rug on the floor, he mumbled, "Yes, sir."

"All right, Paul, go out and cut me a switch. Bring it up to your room." Halsey stood up and walked upstairs to prepare for the whipping.

Matt grabbed his brother by the shoulders. "Why did you do that, Paul? Daddy's gonna beat the hell outta you. It's my fault. I started the fire, and I should have owned up to it. I'm so sorry, Paul." Matt burst into tears.

"I'm bigger and stronger that you. I can take Daddy's whippin'. It'll hurt for a while, but the pain will go away. I'll be all right." Paul placed his right hand on his kid brother's shoulder.

Paul took his time walking outside. He used a small pocketknife to cut a thin branch from an enormous maple tree that had stood in the Curtis family front yard for eighty-five years. He pulled the leaves off the branch to make it more aerodynamic, just the way Halsey liked his switches. Paul carried the branch upstairs and looked down at his brother, who was still in tears. "I'll be fine."

Too afraid to move, Matt stood at the base of the stairs. Then he listened as Halsey commanded Paul to drop his jeans to the floor. Matt could hear the switch whip through the air as Halsey slashed at the back of Paul's legs. Usually, whippings only lasted through a few strikes, but not this time. Halsey's anger shot through his right arm, and the beating became the worst one of Paul's short life.

Initially, Paul remained silent and took the whipping like a man, but when blood starting running down the backs of his legs, Paul pleaded for Halsey to stop. But the old man refused. The blows became more intense, and Paul had taken enough. The thirteen-year-old summoned the courage to clench his fist and hit his father's weathered face as hard as he could. But Halsey didn't flinch. He looked like an enraged animal as he lunged toward his son. Paul ran out of the room. Filled with fury, Halsey chased after him and took a mighty swing at Paul as he reached the top of the stairs. When the switch struck Paul in the back, the boy lost his balance and fell headfirst down the stairs. Chilling sounds filled the old country house. Matt could almost feel Paul's pain as he tumbled out of control and landed in an awkward heap on the hardwood floor at the bottom of the stairway, right in front of Matt.

Paul wasn't breathing. His body lay broken, bleeding, and lifeless on the floor. "Daddy, you killed him!" Matt screamed.

Halsey sneered down at his frantic son. "No, Matthew. You started the fire, and you didn't have the guts to own up to it. You're a coward. You are the one responsible for your brother's suffering. *You* killed him."

Chapter 17

"How long have you and Paige been roommates?" Brooks looked into the foggy eyes of Natalie Shoemaker as she sat on the couch in her Reston living room with a green fleece blanket wrapped around her legs.

"Since I moved here from Philly in 1999. Paige needed a roommate, and I needed a place to crash. She became the best friend I've ever had." Natalie fought back tears and tried to hide her massive hangover.

"Where were you last night, Natalie?" Tessa asked.

"I slept over at a guy's house. First, we went to dinner at Maggiano's in Tysons Corner, and then we took a couple of bottles of white wine back to his place," Natalie confessed.

"What's his name?"

"Evan Slater. He's a lawyer in my office." Natalie twirled her straight, dark hair out of nervous habit.

"So, if we talk to Evan, he'll verify your story?"

"Oh yeah, he was still smiling when I kissed him good-bye this morning. He won't forget last night for a long time."

"Did Paige know a woman named Jill Forcythe?" Brooks asked.

Natalie made a weak effort to straighten up and pay attention. "Lemme think …" The question seemed to bounce off the few sober brain cells in Natalie's head. "I don't know. I've never heard Paige talk about anyone with that name."

Brooks gritted his teeth. "Did Paige have any boyfriends?"

"Are you kidding? Paige? You obviously didn't know my girl, Paige. She hasn't had a steady boyfriend since college, when a guy actually asked her to marry him, and she said no! Can you believe that?"

"What was his name?"

"Matt Curtis."

The name was familiar to Brooks. "Tessa, look in your notes from yesterday."

"I'm way ahead of you." Tessa thumbed through her notepad. "Yes, here it is. Matt Curtis also dated Jill Forcythe."

"Did Paige speak with Mr. Curtis recently?"

"I doubt it. Paige would have told me about that."

Tessa shook Natalie's hand. "Thank you for your time, Miss Shoemaker. You've been very helpful."

"If you need me to answer any more questions, I'll be at Evan's house." Natalie paused to wipe her eyes. "I can't stay here anymore without Paige." A tear dripped down Natalie's right cheek.

"I understand. Take care of yourself."

Brooks headed outside to the car as fast as he could. He grabbed his phone from its holster and called an administrative assistant at the police station. "Hello, Cary. This is Brooks. I need you to do a search and locate a man who probably lives in Fairfax County. His name is Matthew Curtis. I need to know where he lives and where he works. Call me back as soon as you find him." Brooks snapped his phone shut.

Tessa had followed Brooks and now leaned against her car. "So, you want to tell me how you knew about this woman's death before it was reported?"

"Lucky guess."

"Come on, Brooks. Tell me the truth."

"You wouldn't believe me if I told you."

"Try me."

"All right. Last night in the hospital—" Brooks's cell phone cut his explanation off. "Hey, Cary. Did you find Curtis?" He stared at Tessa as his assistant reported her findings. She had found three men named Matt Curtis in Fairfax County. "OK, just give me the details on the one who is in his thirties." Brooks took a small notepad out of his coat pocket and wrote down the description. His eyes traveled along Sunrise Valley Drive toward the Reston Town Center, and he spied the tallest building in the area. He snapped his phone shut. "Tessa, let's go for a walk."

"Where are we going?"

"See that big building with the LightCurve logo on the front? That's where Matt Curtis works."

"His office is within a quarter mile of the crime scene?"

"Apparently. Let's go see what he has to say for himself."

They passed Morton's Restaurant and Starbucks on their way to the palatial lobby of the LightCurve building. Bouquets of flowers and opaque glass walls dominated the space.

Behind a large mahogany desk, an attractive, conservatively dressed receptionist with golden blond corporate hair greeted the detectives. "Hello! Welcome to LightCurve. My name is Christine. How can I help you today?"

"Hi, Christine. My name is Brooks Barrington, and this is my partner, Tessa McBride. We're Fairfax County police detectives, and we need to speak with Mr. Matthew Curtis."

"Certainly, sir. Is Mr. Curtis expecting you?"

"I doubt it." Out of habit, Brooks stole a quick look at the guest log.

"I see. Sir, I'm not sure if Mr. Curtis will be able to see you if you don't have an appointment. But I'll call his executive assistant and find out if he is available."

Brooks leaned over the desk. "Christine, Miss McBride and I are homicide detectives," he whispered. "If Mr. Curtis isn't available, he needs to get available immediately. Do you understand?"

"Perfectly," Christine whispered back. She dialed Kim Taggert's extension and relayed the urgency of the situation. Four minutes later, Kim met the detectives in the lobby and escorted them to a conference room on the ninth floor.

"Matt will be right with you. Can I get you anything while you wait? Coffee? Water? A soda?" Kim asked.

"No thanks. We're fine." Brooks watched Kim leave the room then plunked himself into a soft, black leather chair at the head of the twenty-foot conference table. "Man, these guys really work in style. I could get used to this." He looked out over the Reston skyline.

The glass conference room door opened slowly, and Matt stuck his head inside the room. "Hello, I'm Matt Curtis. Kim said you wanted to see me."

Brooks and Tessa shook Matt's hand and introduced themselves. Matt limped slowly to a chair close to the door and sat down. He carefully arranged a Toshiba laptop, Palm Pilot, Blackberry, cell phone, notepad, and Cross pen in front of him. Tessa chose a seat across the table from him. Brooks moved to the chair beside Matt.

"What can I do for you?" Matt asked. He started tapping a pen on the conference table, a nervous habit he had never been able to break, especially in tense situations.

Brooks turned his chair toward Matt. "Let's just talk for a while. Mr. Curtis, you're a management consultant. What does that really mean? What the heck do you do for a living?"

"We help companies solve complex business problems, and we implement large-scale information systems."

Brooks formed a steeple with his hands. "Oh, you find businesses that are really screwed up and charge them exorbitant fees to fix the problems that they should have been able to fix themselves."

"That's a very simplistic view of the consulting industry."

"I'm a simple man, Matt. You know, I've been around a few consultants over the past few years—people who tried to show us how to be better detectives. They didn't know a damn thing about police work. They charged us $250 an hour per consultant to tell us what we already knew. Consultants remind me of the smart kids in school who conned the slow kids out of their lunch money."

"I'm sorry you feel that way, Detective." Matt tapped his pen faster on the table.

Crossing his arms over his unrestrained stomach, Brooks leaned back in his chair. "I'm sure I'll get over it someday. Let's move on, Matt. We need to ask you some questions about a couple of old girlfriends of yours."

"Who?" Matt knew exactly where the conversation was headed.

"When was the last time you spoke with Jill Forcythe?"

"I saw her at the Da Domenico restaurant in Tysons Corner a few months ago. She was with her sister, Karen."

"What did the two of you talk about?"

"I didn't speak to her."

"Really? That's odd. We understand that at one time, you were very much in love with Jill. Why didn't you talk to her?"

Matt's pen tapped even faster. "When we broke up, she said she never wanted to speak to me again. It was a messy situation." Matt looked into the wood grain of the conference table.

"You haven't seen her since?"

"No. I heard about her death. It's tragic." Matt rapped his pen as if he were pounding out an SOS in Morse code.

"Yeah. Tragic. How about Paige Whitaker? Any recent contact with her?" Brooks shifted his weight and leaned his right elbow on the conference table.

"No. I haven't seen Paige in years."

"No kidding? That seems strange since she lived so close to you."

"What do you mean?"

Brooks pointed over the conference room table, through the huge window, toward Reston. "You can see her townhouse from here. Certainly you must have seen her at some time."

"I didn't know she lived in Reston. I haven't spoken with her since we stopped seeing each other."

"Why? What happened?"

"I asked her to marry me. She turned me down. She really hurt me."

"Enough for you to hurt her?" Brooks pushed.

"I didn't kill Jill or Paige, if that's what you're asking." Matt smacked his pen on the table like a jackhammer.

Brooks snatched the pen out of Matt's hand and moved his face within inches of Matt's. "Where were you Tuesday night?"

"At home in McLean."

"Were you with anyone who can verify that?" Brooks shot back quickly.

"My dog, Joe."

"Don't be a smart-ass. Now is not the time to screw with me. What about last night?"

"I had dinner with my girlfriend, Cullen Rhea, at my house."

"Was she there all night?"

"No, she left a little after nine o'clock."

Brooks stood up and moved slowly behind Matt. "Did you, by any chance, have a visitor late last night?"

Matt stopped breathing. Why did the detective ask that question? He couldn't tell them about Lazarus because the detectives would think he was a whack job. "No, I was alone the rest of the night."

Brooks sat on the end of the conference table. "So, you're absolutely sure you didn't speak with anyone late last night? Think carefully before you answer."

Matt's blue eyes darted from Brooks to Tessa to the conference table to his shoes to his laptop. "No, I'm sure of it. I didn't talk to anyone last night." *God, when would this interrogation ever end?*

Brooks stared into Matt's eyeballs. "Son, over the years, I have developed a pretty efficient bullshit detector, and I'm sure that you're lying to me. I believe you're associated with the deaths of these women."

"No. I didn't kill them. And I don't know who did. I swear."

"We'll see. Right now, I need to know the names of any other women you have dated seriously."

"Why?"

"They're in serious danger because they have a history with you. Tell me their names. Now, dammit!" Brooks's round face turned beet red when he yelled at Matt.

"OK, OK, I also dated Nikki Fox and Tahara Caron. Those relationships have been over for quite a while. Cullen has been my girlfriend for a few months."

Brooks's jaw muscles flexed. He placed his heavy right hand on Matt's left shoulder and squeezed with an enormous amount of pressure. "Write down their addresses and phone numbers. And you'd better pray for God to have mercy on them."

Chapter 18

Gretchen Carlsen's black Jimmy Choo pumps clicked on the white marble floor of the Neiman Marcus store at Tysons Galleria. Dressed in a gray business suit by Donna Karan, she passed the fine china display and hurried up two escalator flights to the third level of the store.

She had only an hour to shop because she was due in court to slug through a painful divorce. A senior partner with Carlsen, Costello, Deutschman, and Friedman, Gretchen was one of the top divorce lawyers in Northern Virginia. Separating a host of wealthy men from their cash, real estate, and personal property for the past fifteen years had made her aggressive, impatient, and very rich.

Stalking through the designer outfits like a lioness on the prowl, Gretchen noticed a number of wealthy women browsing through the latest fashions. Capable of dropping a thousand dollars for a small purse or a pair of shoes without thinking twice about it, such women made up a significant target market of potential clients for Gretchen's practice.

After looking at her diamond watch for the fifth time in two minutes, Gretchen stopped a store employee in the middle of the Dolce & Gabbana collection. "Excuse, I'm looking for my personal shopper, Nikki Fox. Could you help me find her?"

"Certainly, ma'am. I'll page Nikki and have her meet you right here."

"Thank you, and please don't call me ma'am. My name is Gretchen Carlsen." The employee disappeared into a forest of dresses and suits, leaving the lawyer alone, muttering to herself. "Ma'am! I am not a ma'am. That word makes me sound like I'm eighty years old. Why couldn't she have called me miss? I'm only fifty-four. With a half-gallon of Botox in my face, I should still be able to qualify as a miss."

A few feet behind Gretchen, a familiar voice cut through the department store chaos. "Hello, Ms. Carlsen!"

Gretchen turned around to see a scorching redhead who looked as if she had just stepped off the cover of *Cosmopolitan*. Wearing a white suit with a white satin blouse, the young woman had chosen to wear her Caribbean aqua contact lenses because they looked stunning with her ensemble.

Gretchen stood on her toes to hug her statuesque friend. "Hello, Nikki. I love this suit you picked out for me."

"It looks great on you, and I have some new outfits that I think you're going to like. Come on. Let's go shopping!" Nikki led Gretchen through the store to a secluded dressing room. The powerful attorney found five designer outfits waiting for her, all high fashion and extremely expensive.

After a few brief fittings, Gretchen decided on a fuchsia sheath dress and a pearl-halter dress. Modeling a champagne-colored, three-piece silk suit, Gretchen frowned. "These clothes are all so beautiful, but for some reason, I just don't feel like a real woman in anything I wear. I've become a gun for hire. Men see me only as a nut crusher."

"Ms. Carlsen, you're a beautiful, gifted, self-sufficient woman. I believe you can be very sexy. You just need to turn up the heat once in a while."

"And how would I do that?"

"Try this. One day, when you're scheduled to be in court, wear this silk suit, but don't put on any underwear."

"Oh my goodness! I don't know, Nikki. What if someone found out about it?" Gretchen covered her mouth in shock.

"That's the whole idea, Ms. Carlsen. Enjoy the excitement. Going commando can be very liberating!"

"Lawyers tend to be quite conventional with their dressing habits. I would be such a rebel."

"Yes, Ms. Carlsen. Trust me. You'll love the way it makes you feel."

"You really think that crazy idea will work?" Gretchen's eyes sparkled.

"It's working for me right now!"

Gretchen laughed out loud. "You're such a naughty girl, Nikki."

"Oh, you don't know the half of it, Ms. Carlsen." She slipped covers with the Neiman Marcus logo over the classy outfits and processed the sale by swiping Gretchen's platinum American Express card. "And if you're attracted to a certain man, get on an elevator with him. When the two of you are alone, just casually let him know that you're not wearing any panties. That will drive him beyond crazy."

"Well, there is a judge who I think is very handsome, but he's awfully traditional. What would he think about me if I did that?"

"I'll bet it would put a little extra wood in his gavel."

Gretchen chuckled and playfully smacked her provocative friend's hand. "So, are you dating anyone special these days, Nikki?"

"Some men are more special than others."

"Have you ever had a steady boyfriend, or have you always played the field?"

"There was one guy, Matt, who fell in love with me. On our third date, he told me that he wanted to spend the rest of his life with me and that he couldn't bear to live without me. He bought me flowers, jewelry, and gourmet chocolate."

"Sounds like a good catch. So, what happened?"

"After a few dates, I dumped him."

Gretchen twisted her face into a question mark. "Why? Was he weird?"

"No! Not at all. He was a sweet man … and very good-looking"

"Then why the hell did you dump him?"

"Because I was immature and stupid. I didn't want to commit to a relationship. When I broke it off, I just stopped answering his calls without any explanation. It was as if I had simply disappeared in a puff of smoke."

"He must have been devastated." Gretchen collected her purchases and her credit card.

"I'm sure he was hurt. I never apologized, and I never spoke to him again. I still feel guilty about burning him like that. I was so bad."

"And since then, have you dated a lot of men?"

"I've dated more than my share. A few good ones. Lots of bad ones." Nikki escorted her client to the escalator.

"Do you have a gentleman caller lined up for tonight?"

"I have a dinner date, and if he plays his cards right, it could get pretty steamy."

Chapter 19

"This is gonna be brutal," Brooks said. He looked at his watch. It said 4:57—three minutes since the last time he checked. Standing outside of Lieutenant Turquoise Malone's office, he felt like a derelict elementary school kid waiting to see the principal.

How was he going to explain the fact that they had found no usable physical evidence concerning the deaths of Jill Forcythe and Paige Whitaker? Telling the lieutenant about Lazarus would probably get him thrown off the case and into a straightjacket. Brooks's instincts told him that Lazarus had set his sights on Matt Curtis. For some reason, that evil creature was committed to making Matt's life—and the lives of the people associated with him—an agonizing torment. Brooks knew he had to stop Lazarus, but he had no idea how to do it.

Tessa paced in front of the lieutenant's door as she and Brooks waited for the grilling to begin. Brooks tried to pass the time by watching criminals pass through the police station on their way to questioning or to jail. "Tessa, have you noticed that almost everyone has a tattoo? Some guys have those big, ugly tattoos that climb out of their shirts and up their necks. Lots of men have tattoos on their forearms or their shoulders. And now it's common to see women with tattoos on their ankles, their shoulders, or their lower backs. I'm starting to think that you and I are the only two people on the planet who don't have tattoos."

"Sorry, you're by yourself on that one, Brooks." Tessa leaned against the wall.

Brooks whipped his head around with his bloodshot gray eyes bulging out of their sockets. "You have a tattoo?"

"Yeah, so what?"

"We've worked together every day for the past four years, and now I find out that you have a tattoo. I'm shocked. What is it? Where is it? Lemme see it."

"It's a flower. To be even more specific, it's a rose, and it's in a special place where you will never see it."

"Come on, Tessa. At least tell me where it is?" Brooks begged.

"No way, Southern man. You'll just have to use your imagination," Tessa grinned.

"How long have you had it?"

"Since I was a junior at Tulane. My roommate, Callie, and I spent my twenty-first birthday drinking ourselves down Bourbon Street. We wound up at a bar called the Tropical Isle that served these special drinks called hand grenades that could knock your ass in the dirt. After three of those and four upside-down margaritas, we came up with the brilliant idea to get tattoos. Callie and I stumbled into the nearest tattoo parlor and picked out the cutest tattoos we could find before we lost our nerve or passed out."

Brooks was enthralled. "That's a lovely story. I bet it's on your butt. It is, isn't it? Left cheek or right cheek? Lemme see it."

"Not a chance."

"You're cruel."

"You need a girlfriend."

For twenty-five minutes, Brooks and Tessa waited for their boss to finish a phone conversation that was not going well. Malone's voice boomed through her hollow office door. "I will never give up custody of the boys. You left me, you son of a bitch, so don't come crying to me about your limited time with the kids. You should have thought about that when you packed up your clothes and moved out of the house without even telling me that you were leaving. I wish I'd never met you. I hate you, Jared! You've screwed up my life. I hope you're satisfied, you bastard!" She slammed down the phone.

After the muscular black woman took a minute to transform herself from a jilted wife into a police lieutenant, she swung her door open. "Barrington and McBride, get in here, right now!"

Brooks and Tessa plodded into the spotless office as if they were walking to the gallows. Although he knew he should just keep quiet, Brooks's tongue flew into gear before he could stop it. "We don't want to disturb you, Lieutenant. You've got other things on your mind. We can do this some other time."

Malone cut her eyes at Brooks. "Disturb me? Do you know what really disturbs me? A husband who cheats on his wife and two kids with his executive assistant—that's what disturbs me, Brooks."

"Yes, ma'am. I'm sure the thought of your husband with another woman is very disturbing." Brooks regretted every word.

"My husband's executive assistant's name is Steve."

It took Brooks a few seconds to process this information. "Oh, dear. That must be very ... confusing for you and your kids." It was like he was sticking his head inside the mouth of an alligator. Pretty soon, Malone would snap his head off.

Tessa gaped at Brooks, as if to say, "Please shut up, before you get us both killed."

Adjusting a stack of documents on her desk, Lieutenant Malone tried to focus on the job at hand. She rubbed her temples and spoke through her personal anger. "Tell me about your progress on the Forcythe and Whitaker deaths."

Brooks cleared his throat. "The crime scene team has not been able to find any physical evidence that would help us identify a suspect in either case."

"So let me get this straight, Brooks. One girl has her heart disconnected from the inside, while another girl falls to death in her own bedroom, and we have no evidence to help us solve these crimes. That's pitiful." Malone glared at the detectives.

"We were able to find one person who had a relationship with both women." Brooks said. "His name is Matt Curtis. He lives in McLean and works at LightCurve Consulting in Reston."

"Does this Curtis guy have an alibi?" Malone chewed on a pen.

"Nothing we can verify. He says he was at home alone on both nights."

"So you think Curtis is responsible for these deaths?"

"Yes ... no ... sort of. It's complicated." Brooks could feel beads of sweat trickling down his face.

"What the hell does that mean?"

"You see there's a man—" In an act of self-preservation, Brooks stopped himself before he spoke openly about Lazarus.

Tessa jumped into the conversation. "Matt Curtis is our main suspect. We are still actively looking for any physical evidence or a witness who can link Mr. Curtis to one or both of the cases."

"There won't be any physical evidence," Brooks blurted. Tessa winced as she heard the statement fly out of Brooks's mouth.

"I've had enough of your bullshit, Brooks. You two need to get out to the crime scenes and find some evidence. Do you understand me?"

"The crime scene investigators have been all over both scenes. They're clean," Tessa explained.

Malone placed her hands on her desk and stretched toward the detectives. "I'm telling you to find some evidence that implicates Mr. Curtis."

Tessa looked at Brooks with a puzzled expression on her face. She moved her focus back to Malone. "Lieutenant, are you telling us to plant evidence that would incriminate Matt Curtis?"

"I don't care what you have to do. Just solve the cases, detective." Malone shuffled through the papers on her desk, ignoring the impropriety in her actions.

"I will do no such thing, Lieutenant. There is no way I will go outside the law to solve a crime."

"Are you refusing an order from your superior officer?" Malone stood up quickly.

"Yes, ma'am. I most certainly am." Tessa bolted up out of her chair.

The veins in Malone's forehead pulsed. "Tessa, do you have a problem with me because I'm a strong black woman? I can understand how you could be intimidated by me."

"That's ridiculous. *I* am a strong black woman."

"Your light brown skin and that cute button nose tell me you are not a black woman. Back home in the projects, the sisters would call you a high yellow. A mulatto."

"I'm biracial—the product of an African-American father and a white mother. I have chosen to consider myself a black woman, but I recognize and respect my white heritage."

"Mutts like you just pretend to be black when it's convenient. You're like an Oreo cookie—dark on the outside, white on the inside. You may try to pass yourself off as a black woman, but the fact is you have the heart of a prissy little white girl."

"Lieutenant, I've dealt with this issue since I was a French Quarter kid in New Orleans. In school, kids called me zebra and Oreo, just as you did. It was hard to fit in. Over the years, I've realized that I don't want to fit in with people like you—ignorant people who judge people by the color of their skin or the shape of their nose. Your racism is repulsive, but it doesn't affect me. I've been insulted by people who are even more obnoxious than you, and I've moved past the point of being hurt." Tessa moved toward the door. "I couldn't care less about your opinion of me as a person. If you don't like me, tough shit. That's not my cross to bear. I know I'm a good cop, and I'll find a way to solve these cases, legally. You just sit here in your office and obsess about your gay husband. I'm going back to work." With a confident smirk, she left the room.

Without making eye contact with his boss, Brooks stood up and got the hell out of the office. He found Tessa seething in the break room as she poured a cup of coffee. Straightening his jacket, Brooks blew out a deep breath. "That went well."

Chapter 20

After his ninth message on her voice mail, Cullen finally responded to Matt's desperate attempts to contact her. "All right. I'll have dinner with you," Cullen conceded. "I could use a nice meal before I start the graveyard shift tonight."

"Great! I'll meet you at Samuel & David's at seven o'clock," Matt said.

All afternoon, Matt fixated on the date. Would this be the end of yet another relationship? Would she use the customary "It's not you; it's me" line that he had heard so many times before? Or would she come up with a creative excuse to break up with him? What if she actually came out and said, "Matt, you're an insecure, immature dorkwad, and I can't stand the thought of being with you for another second. Don't call me ever again."

A surge of doubt swelled inside Matt's psyche. Tension held a tight grip on the back of his neck. He completely lost his focus in two afternoon meetings, and he found it impossible to answer the deluge of nasty e-mails from Arman Guerrero asking when the project would be back on schedule. By six o'clock, his nerves were toasted.

He packed up his consultant's gear and hobbled out of the office without bothering to sneak around every corner. His boss was tied up at the Thursday partners meeting. Calvert was probably going to fire him in a couple of days anyway, so it didn't matter if he left the office early.

Navigating his car through the standstill on the Dulles Toll Road took forever. Then he weaved through the stop-and-go traffic on Route 7 to Samuel & David's, an upscale restaurant located in the heart of Tysons Corner.

Dropping his keys into the valet's hand, Matt passed slowly under a maroon canopy into the reception area. He was surprised to see the stunning brunette in a pastel blue sundress waiting for him in the lobby. Considering Matt's track record with women, he had fully expected to be stood up.

Cullen greeted him with a warm hug and a soft kiss. "You're late."

"Sorry. Lots of traffic on the toll road today. Have you been waiting long?"

"Fourteen minutes and thirty-two seconds, but who's counting?" They laughed at Cullen's legendary anal-retentive nature as they entered the restaurant. "Why are you limping?" Nurses notice everything.

"I tripped and fell on the stairs at home." Matt hid his lying eyes from Cullen. "I just bruised my knee. I'm fine."

"Did you see a doctor?"

"No. It's not that bad." He cringed with every step. *What the heck would I tell a doctor? A man made of shadows cracked me in the knee with a baseball bat. Then he healed the bones and disappeared into the darkness. My knee is still a little sore. Can I have a big dose of pain medicine? A story like that would get me a free trip to the psych ward.*

Surrounded by intense business discussions and romantic first dates, Matt and Cullen sat at their table and pored over the menus. "Hey, did you hear about those two women who died?" Cullen asked as she ate a piece of bread. "I saw it on the news. They found one woman in a closet in Tysons Tower, and the other woman died in her own bedroom in Reston. Isn't that weird?"

You don't know the half of "weird," Matt thought. *Should I tell her that I dated both of those women? And that I may have been the cause of their deaths? And that I'm a suspect in two murder investigations? Hell, no.* "Yeah, I heard about them. Very strange. I need some more wine." He waved to a waiter and asked for a refill.

As they finished their salads, Cullen said, "Matt, I have to say something to you."

Oh, no, here it comes.

"I know what you're going to say, Cullen. It's fine. I understand completely. We had some great times together, and I hope you'll still be my friend, although that never actually happens in real life. I promise I'll leave you alone."

"What the hell are you talking about?" A bewildered look twisted Cullen's face.

"Well, after last night, I just figured you would want to break up with me."

"No, I don't. How did you get that idea?"

"You were really upset when I tried to touch you, and then I was certain that you hated me. So are you saying that you don't want to break up with me?" Matt reached for his glass of wine and took a big gulp.

"I love you, and I want to spend the rest of my life with you. What I wanted to tell you tonight is that I have some issues I need to work though when it comes to intimacy. I just can't do what you want to do—physically. I've been in therapy for quite a while, but it will take more time for me to deal with my problem."

"What brought this on?"

"I don't want to talk about the details."

"Maybe I can help you work through your problems. I love you, Cullen. You can tell me anything."

"No!" Sensing an impending meltdown, Cullen stood up. "I'm going to the ladies' room to pull myself together. I'll be back in a few minutes." She quickly plotted a course through the restaurant to the restroom, boldly trying to hold her composure.

Matt chewed on a piece of broccoli and tried to look like nothing was wrong. Realizing he had consumed three glasses of wine and two large Amstel Lights, Matt also made his way to the bathroom. His gait was improving, and his knee felt better. Apparently the alcohol had served as a pain reliever.

After he answered the call of nature, Matt washed his hands and looked into the mirror. Although his face had changed over the years, he could still see the self-doubting country boy that was his true identity.

As he opened the bathroom door, he bumped into a man with platinum blond hair entering the room. "Excuse me." He edged past the man and headed toward Cullen.

"Hey, Matt! How are you doing, buddy?" a voice called to him.

Matt swung around to see that the man was Simon Fletcher, a friend of his from the Tysons Sport and Health Club. A sports therapist for the club, Simon made his living by helping clients wince through muscle cramps and sore shoulders. Nearly six feet tall with a runner's body, he had the kind of flat stomach that women love and men covet.

"Hi, Simon. Good to see you." Matt stretched his neck to see if Cullen had returned to their table.

"So, what's up? I haven't seen you in the club for a few days."

"I've been buried at work. I really should get back to my girlfriend. I'll see you at the gym." Matt started to walk away.

"You know, I've never met your girlfriend. Are you trying to hide her from me? Afraid I'll use my charm and good looks to steal her away from you?" Simon playfully punched Matt in the left shoulder.

"Oh, no. Why don't you come by our table, and I'll introduce you to her?" Matt wanted to wrap up the conversation so he could get back to Cullen.

"Sounds great. I'll see you on my way out."

By the time Matt arrived at his chair, he had completely forgotten about Simon. Cullen appeared to be back in one piece. Hoping the drama was over, Matt dug into a set of jumbo lump crab cakes while Cullen pushed her roasted chicken around her plate a few times until she finally worked up the appetite to eat it. They purposely avoided all provocative subjects in their dinner conversation. Instead, they discussed Cullen's mother's schoolgirl crush on *American Idol* runner-up Clay Aiken, her father's toy train collection, and the famous in-state rivalry between their alma maters, Virginia Tech and the University of Virginia.

While a waitress cleared their plates and took their orders for decaf coffee, Matt noticed Simon approaching from behind Cullen. He acknowledged his friend with a small wave. "Cullen, I want to introduce you to a friend of mine from the athletic club."

Cullen spun around to see the Nordic man's face. "Oh, my God!" she screamed. Her body shuddered violently as she leaped from her chair. She raced through the restaurant, crashing into tables and shocking patrons.

Hobbling as fast as he could after her, Matt hurried through the restaurant, out the door, and down the sidewalk. "Cullen, stop! What's wrong? Cullen, what is going on?" Sharp bolts of lightning shot through Matt's bruised knee, but he forced himself to sprint through the pain. *Why is Cullen running away? Shit! My knee is killing me. Maybe I should see a doctor.*

Sixty yards of cement and asphalt felt like twenty miles. Cullen broke a strap on her blue Nine West pump, whacked her kneecap on the bumper of a parked car, and eventually ran out of breath. She collapsed against the front fender of a black Lexus, crying hysterically.

Matt reached her in a panic. He sat next to her on the sidewalk, and she buried her face in his chest. "Honey, what's wrong?"

"That man …" Cullen couldn't continue.

"Simon? What about him?"

Cullen looked up into Matt's blue eyes as tears streamed down her face. "He raped me," she sobbed. Without a clue on how to respond, Matt wrapped his arms around her. His instincts told him to keep his mouth shut and hold her until she was ready to talk.

Fifteen long minutes went by. Then Cullen summoned the courage to tell her horror story. "I met him at UVA. I was in my third year, and he was in med school. We had some friends in common. One Friday night after midterms, my roommate, Lisha, and I went to a restaurant called the Hardware Store to blow off some steam. Simon was there with a bunch of his buddies. After a while, he started hitting on me. He kept buying me watermelon shooters, and I kept knocking them down. By ten o'clock, I was smashed. I knew I couldn't drive, so I asked him to take me home. He practically carried me to his Camaro. I leaned the seat back and closed my eyes because I was afraid I was going to hurl all over his dashboard."

Cullen wiped her eyes. "We had been in his car for quite a while before I realized that we were outside of Charlottesville on a secluded stretch of Route 29, heading away from the city. Simon pulled off the road and started pawing at me. He ripped my blouse. I fought back as hard as I could, and I managed to get out of the car. I tried to run away, but he caught me and dragged me to the ground. He tore my skirt and underwear to shreds and … and then that son of a bitch raped me."

She ran her hands through her hair. "I was so drunk. I didn't have the strength to push him off me. When I yelled for help, he hit me in the mouth and choked me to keep me quiet. After he finished, he took my clothes and jumped into his car, leaving me on the side of the road in the middle of the night. I flagged down the first set of headlights I saw. It was a school bus carrying the Albemarle High School football team home from a game. I climbed on that bus, totally naked in front of all those teenage boys. I was mortified. The coach gave me a jacket and a pair of sweats. Thank goodness he was nice enough to take me home and to call the police."

"Cullen, I'm so sorry." Matt gently placed his hands on her cheeks.

"Now you know why I'm so weird about sex. I haven't been naked in front of another person since that night."

"I understand." Matt clutched Cullen's hands. "Was Simon prosecuted?"

"You bet your sweet ass he was! I testified against him. Evidently, I wasn't his first victim. The jury sentenced him to eight years in prison, but I heard he got out after four years. Not nearly enough, if you ask me." Cullen stood up, straightened her blue dress, and pushed her black hair away from her face. "I'm all right now, Matt. Let's go."

"I'll take you home."

"No. I'm going to work my shift. I need to go about my normal routine. That bastard is not going to screw up my life again."

Matt held her by her waist and walked her back to the restaurant. After Matt paid for their meal, they waited in silence under the canopy for the valet to bring their cars around to the front of the restaurant. Cullen's Saturn arrived first. She planted a passionate kiss on Matt's lips. "I will always love you. Never doubt me, Matt." She pressed her forehead against his.

"I love you too, baby. Be careful." As Cullen drove off toward the hospital, Matt noticed the shadows around his feet moving. An odd presence formed, just off his right shoulder.

"Looks like Simon really screwed up Cullen's head." Lazarus's voice poisoned the night air.

Matt turned his shoulders to face the sinister man, dressed in a gray, pin-striped, double-breasted suit and a deep purple tie. "And I just made it worse," Matt admitted. "I can't believe I became friends with the man who raped my girlfriend, and then I brought the two of them together. What a bizarre coincidence."

A smile slithered over Lazarus's lips. "There are no coincidences."

Chapter 21

"What's yo name, little girrrrrrl? What's yo name?" Brooks wailed the Lynyrd Skynyrd hit while his canary yellow Corvette crawled along Lee Highway in the height of rush-hour traffic. During the past few years, the daily bumper-to-bumper crunch had become a fact of life for Brooks. To confront the annoying situation, he treated himself to a heavy helping of Southern rock. With his satellite radio tuned to a classic rock channel, the Black Crowes blasted out "Remedy" as he hung a left into the Fairfax Gables Shopping Center, passed by a flower shop, and eased into a parking space behind a restaurant called Jeannette's Hot Grill.

Strolling into the place, he felt like Norm Peterson from *Cheers*. Everybody knew his name. Brooks greeted four of the terminally frisky waitresses and waved to his longtime pal, Jeannette, a raven-haired institution who possessed the eighth and ninth wonders of the world. His favorite table sat empty, as if it were reserved for him. Brooks liked to sit in the booth against the wall, straight across from the pickup station. The table provided him with a perfect view of the waitresses as they picked up their orders and a direct line of sight to the big-screen television that was locked on ESPN. In Brooks's world, it didn't get any better than that.

A killer blond bounced across the restaurant, gave Brooks a big hug, and kissed him on the cheek. "Hey, sugar! I missed you the last couple of days. Where have you been?"

A warm, comfortable feeling spread over Brooks's entire body when he heard her sweet Southern accent. "Hi, Carlene. I missed you, too. I was tied up with work. What's new?"

"Nothing much. I talked to Daddy last night. He asked how you were doing and said to tell you hello."

Brooks smiled as he thought about Carlene's father, Jimmy Baxter, his best friend since third grade. Inseparable partners in crime, Brooks and Jimmy had been closer than brothers throughout high school and college. During their sophomore year at UNC Chapel Hill, Brooks had introduced Jimmy to Elizabeth Montrose, who later became Jimmy's wife and Carlene's mother.

"Tell ol' Jimmy I'm feeling fine, and I'm keeping an eye on you—just like I promised him I would." Brooks couldn't stop staring at Carlene's incredible physical assets.

Carlene looked down at her exposed ample cleavage, jeweled butterfly belly ring, and bright blue micro shorts. "I don't think this is what Daddy had in mind," she said with a bashful grin.

"So, I'm guessing Jimmy thinks that you're still in grad school at Georgetown."

"Yes. I haven't been able to work up the guts to tell him that I dropped out last fall. It's just … everyone there is so rich and smart. I didn't fit in with those people. I'm just a simple girl from North Carolina."

"A simple girl with a 3.9 GPA in economics from North Carolina State University! You earned your way into that MBA program, Carlene. You deserve to be there. Don't let those blue-blooded snots intimidate you. You're just as smart as they are, and you're way better lookin'."

Carlene playfully whacked his wrist. "All right, that's enough outta you. I need to get back to work. You want your Thursday night usual, right?"

"You know it. Thanks, Carlene."

Brooks watched the young woman move about the restaurant without blinking his eyes, refusing to miss a single movement of her body. Ten minutes later, she returned with a heaping plate of Cajun chicken wings, a bowl of coleslaw, an extra-large order of curly fries, and a frosty mug of Samuel Adams beer. *Dr. Kevit would probably pop an aneurysm if he saw the spread in front of me. Screw him.*

"Here ya go, sugar. Do you need anything else?" she asked.

"I need you to have dinner with me, Carlene."

"Brooks, I've known you my entire life. You're like a favorite uncle to me. Going out with you would be … unconventional."

"But I'm not your uncle. Look, just try going out with me one time. That's all I ask. If it feels too strange, we'll call it a night—no harm, no foul."

"I don't know. What would my father think?" Carlene worried.

"I'll handle your father. He owes me." Brooks sipped his beer.

"Owes you? For what?"

"For lots of things that he doesn't want you to know about, including a particularly sticky situation involving a North Carolina state trooper and a bag of pot."

"Oooooh! Tell me all the details." Carlene leaned on Brooks's shoulder.

"I'll tell you everything, if you'll go out with me."

"That's bribery."

"Hey, look at me. I'm not exactly what you would call a Brad Pitt look-alike. I have to use every trick I can to get a woman like you to go out on a date with me, including bribery. Come on. Make your old friend Brooks a happy man and say yes."

Carlene picked up a curly fry and popped it into her mouth. She flashed a seductive smile. "I'll think about it." She slowly strolled away for a few steps, and then she turned around quickly to catch Brooks watching her.

"Brooks! Are you checking out my butt?"

"Yes, ma'am."

"Shame on you!" She laughed out loud. "Carry on, detective."

Brooks never lost track of the young woman as he ate his dinner. While the horny male segment of his brain focused on his gorgeous female friend, his homicide detective brain cells reviewed his plan of action. He had to find Nikki Fox, Tahara Caron, and Cullen Rhea and warn them about Lazarus—tonight. Midway through his third Samuel Adams, he decided that it was time to get going.

Carlene delivered his bill and kissed Brooks on the cheek. "I'll see you tomorrow, sugar."

"Will you give me a straight answer on our date?"

"Maybe," she purred.

Brooks handed her a stack of cash for his dinner, including a twenty-dollar tip that had "Go back to school" written on the bill next to Andrew Jackson's picture. He took a few steps toward the door and spun around quickly to catch Carlene's attention. "Hey, are you lookin' at my butt?"

"Nope," she burst into laughter.

Brooks grinned and waved good-bye. Battling the effects of three ice-cold beers, he shuffled to his car. Digging through his briefcase, he looked for a printout of the home addresses of Nikki Fox, Tahara Caron, and Cullen Rhea that had been prepared by his assistant, Cary. After he sat in his car for a few minutes to let the beer fog drain from his eyeballs, he set out in search of Tahara Caron's home in Fairfax Station.

Chapter 22

Simon Fletcher strode into the lobby of the Baron Cameron Care Center. He hurried up two flights of stairs to room 316 and knocked on the door. Without an invitation, he entered the room. The smell of ammonia smacked him in the face.

On the far side of the room, a woman sat in a wheelchair that was pointed in the direction of a television. Her left arm lay useless in her lap. The woman's legs were situated in an uncomfortable knock-kneed arrangement. But it didn't matter, she couldn't feel them anyway. The left side of her face drooped downward, misshapen into a mask that no one would ever want to wear.

"Momma, it's me, Simon." He touched her right hand. The woman didn't acknowledge him. He brushed a wisp of silver hair from her face.

"How are you feeling?" he asked as if she were actually going to respond. "I see you're watching a rerun of *Bewitched*. Remember how we used to watch that show together? Of course you don't. You don't remember a damn thing."

A male nurse tapped on the door and pushed it open, holding a tray with jars of processed food on it. "I'll take that," Simon said. "You can go ahead to your next patient. I'll handle her evening snack and put her to bed."

"Thank you, Mr. Fletcher. Your mom has had a pretty good day." He backed out of the room.

Simon opened a jar of puréed apples that looked like baby food. Grasping a small plastic spoon, he started to feed his mother. Her throat muscles convulsed when he shoveled the food into her mouth. Two-thirds of the apples wound up on her chin, her pink flowered dress, and Simon's white shirt. The doctors had said eating would get easier, but that was years ago, and she had not graduated to solid food. Nothing had become easier. And she would never get better.

When Simon was a kid in Richmond, Virginia, his mother, Roberta, worked as a vibrant OB/GYN who loved to help women bring their babies into the world. She became addicted to the late-night rush to the hospital to deliver a child for an excited mother. Drawing on an endless supply of energy, Roberta tended to her patients and her only son with empathy and kindness. She tried to be a role model for Simon because his dad was far from an example of a good father.

Leon Fletcher, a successful office products salesman, was a statue of a man with wavy light-colored hair. He was certain that every woman in his field of vision was attracted to him. Obsessed with quantity instead of quality, he screwed anything in a skirt.

One day, when Simon was eight years old, he came home from school, eager to show his father his stellar report card. Loud, unfamiliar voices came from his parents' bedroom. Simon walked up the stairs and down the hallway to investigate. The bedroom door stood wide open. He stuck his head inside the room and saw his father in bed with two women he had never seen before. Frozen with confusion, Simon stared at them from the doorway, unsure what he should do or say. One woman, a skinny girl with long dark hair, saw Simon and said, "Hello, cutie," without bothering to cover her naked body.

Leon sat up in bed and laughed. "Go downstairs and find something to do, Simon. Can't you see Daddy's busy?" His father dove back into the welcoming arms of the bony brunette and a chunky bleached blond.

Throughout the 1970s, Leon drove the free love train into every willing station he could find. From a forty-something lady with a lazy eye who worked behind the counter at the Swifty Dry Cleaners to a ditzy nineteen-year-old Denny's waitress with thick ankles and a lisp, Leon's list of conquests filled three little black books. After putting up with her husband's infidelity for twelve years, Roberta kicked his cheating ass out of the house. From then on, Simon saw his father only on major holidays and for a few days every summer. On a hot day in August 1984, a construction worker named Charles Bigby came home early and caught Leon having sex on his dining room table with his wife, Trenise. Charles fetched his Blackhawk pistol from his pickup and killed them both. Then he shot himself in the head.

As Simon's only male influence, Leon burned his image into Simon's pliable young mind. Roberta tried to convince her son that Leon was a callous man whose actions were not to be imitated. But Simon couldn't help himself. He felt as if he were genetically predisposed to take advantage of every woman he could find.

When he was thirteen, Simon discarded his virginity with a sixteen-year-old skank named Alicia Blevins. He gave her fifteen bucks, and she gave him a wild ride in the back seat of her father's Dodge Swinger. That night, Simon learned that you can't buy love, but you can rent it for thirty minutes with the right girl.

After high school, Simon went to the University of Virginia to become an OB/GYN, just like his mother. His grades were excellent, and his inherent charm made his patients comfortable. Throughout his college career, Simon had sex with a wide assortment of women, whether they wanted to or not. None of them complained, except Cullen Rhea.

She led him on. She wanted it. She asked for it. That was Simon's defense, but it didn't work. In a small courtroom in Charlottesville, Virginia, Cullen testified against Simon. Her tearful testimony convinced a jury to sentence him to eight years in prison.

Faithful and supportive, Roberta went to every court appearance with her only son, but the strain taxed her body. Her blood pressure flew out of control, and stress rampaged through her system. On the day Simon received his sentence, Roberta kissed her son and told him to be strong in prison. Four hours later, she suffered a massive stroke in her kitchen.

In Roberta's case, a blood vessel in her brain burst and spilled blood into the spaces surrounding her brain cells. The left side of her body shut down. She couldn't see or speak. Her memory was shattered beyond repair.

Brain cells die when they no longer receive oxygen and nutrients from the blood. With timely treatment, those cells can be saved, but there was no one in the house to help Roberta. By chance, her neighbor, Hattie Newbury, stopped by to check in on Roberta and found her on the kitchen floor. If it weren't for Hattie, Roberta would have died. Maybe that would have been a more satisfying outcome. The once effervescent woman was forever trapped in the body of an invalid with no way to escape.

Simon's dream of becoming a doctor ended when the judge confirmed his sentence. No woman in her right mind would go to a gynecologist who was a registered sex offender. After four years of living in a cramped jail cell and fighting off amorous inmates, Simon stepped back into the free world without a plan. Great jobs don't exist for men who are branded sexual predators, so Simon resorted to working as a sports therapist, making lousy money and living in a ratty, one-bedroom basement apartment in Herndon, Virginia. All of his extra cash went to pay for his mother's care.

After he finished feeding Roberta her evening snack, he changed her clothes and maneuvered her into bed. Simon sat beside his mother, running his fingers through her hair, just as she had done to him when he was a child.

"I have some good news for you," he whispered. "Tonight, I found the woman that ruined our lives. Remember her name? Cullen Rhea. I've made up my mind, Momma. I'm going to kill her."

Chapter 23

Driving down Ox Road in search of Tahara Caron's home, Brooks rehearsed his speech, warning the woman of the horrible acts that Lazarus was capable of committing. In his own head, he sounded like an incoherent drunk, rambling on about a malicious being that didn't really exist. Maybe this wasn't such a good idea.

Brooks drove steadily through a housing development called Hampton Chase, a community of $850,000 homes. He spied Tahara's address on the side of a mailbox and parked his car on the street in front of the woman's house. Walking around the immaculate landscaping, Brooks was still undecided about what he should say to her.

He knocked on the door and announced himself as a Fairfax County police officer. No answer, but he could hear music playing in the house. He rang the doorbell. No answer. Brooks knocked repeatedly on the door. After a few minutes dragged by, Brooks took out a business card and wrote "Ms. Caron, please call me ASAP" on the back. Just as he was sticking the card in the doorjamb, a man dressed only in a pair of light blue boxer shorts opened the door.

"What do you want?" the man grumbled. The Los Lonely Boys hit "Heaven" grooved from an upstairs bedroom.

"My name is Detective Brooks Barrington. I'm with the Fairfax County Police Department." Brooks held up his badge. "I need to speak with Tahara Caron."

"I'm her husband, Antonio Palmeiro. Why do you want to talk to my wife?" The swarthy man stood in the doorway, making no effort to invite Brooks into the house.

Measuring his words, Brooks said, "It's about a case I'm working on. I promise it will take only a few minutes." A woman appeared in the foyer behind Antonio, wearing a man's white dress shirt as a makeshift robe. She struggled with her disobedient cinnamon-colored hair to make it somewhat presentable. Shifting his attention to her, Brooks said, "Ms. Caron, may I speak with you for a few minutes?"

The woman looked at Antonio, and then at Brooks. Taking an unusually long time to respond, her eyes reflected her growing anxiety. "I'm not Ms. Caron," the woman said. "My name is Janessa Cole. I live next door."

"Oh. I see. When will Ms. Caron be available?" Brooks focused on Antonio, trying to ignore the sensitive situation he had disrupted.

"Tahara's in New York on a shopping trip with her sister, Marita. She'll be home tomorrow evening. Will there be anything else, Detective?"

"No, you two can go back to whatever you were doing. Could you please do me a favor and have Tahara call me at this number as soon as possible?" Brooks handed the man his business card. "I'd also like to try to reach her on her cell phone. Do you know her number?"

"It's 703-555-0479," Antonio said. "If that's all you need from me, detective, I would appreciate your … discretion when you speak with my wife." He shifted his eyes toward Janessa.

"Thank you for your time." Brooks nodded his head and punched the phone number into his cell phone. "Sorry to bother you, Ms. Cole."

In the safety of his Corvette, Brooks called Tahara's cell phone number. Four rings went unanswered, and then a voice mail greeting directed him to leave a message. "Hello, Ms. Caron, this is Detective Brooks Barrington with the Fairfax County Police Department. Could you please call me at 703-555-6529 as soon as you get this message? I need to speak with you immediately. Thank you."

Feeling as if he had stepped into an episode of *Desperate Housewives*, Brooks looked back at the house filled with infidelity. Never known for his moral sensibility, Brooks did not feel the need to tell Tahara about her husband's betrayal. It's not a crime for a man to sleep with his neighbor. Brooks was under no legal obligation to rat out Antonio, so Tahara would have to find out on her own. Putting his car into gear, Brooks set his attention on Cullen Rhea's townhouse in Fair Lakes.

With the help of a Northern Virginia street map, Brooks made turn after turn until he found Cullen's townhouse in the Elden Glen development. He parked in a space marked "Reserved for guests" and walked up ten steps to her front door. Once again, Brooks went through his paces with rapid knocks on the door and the doorbell. He called her home phone and left a message.

Brooks's last stop of the night was Nikki Fox's home in Tysons Corner. Within walking distance of Tysons Galleria Mall and the surrounding office buildings, Nikki's condominium complex, the Luxor Building, was a haven for young prosperous executives. Brooks used his police badge to pass through a gate at the parking garage. A beefy guard stopped him at the security desk in the lobby and asked for identification. After approving the ID, the guard called Nikki's condo and announced Brooks as a visitor. The guard waved Brooks on and told him to take the elevator up to condo number 4035.

Standing at Nikki's door, Brooks practiced his speech. Before he could raise his hand to knock, the door opened abruptly. A sizzling redhead in a lacy, hot-pink top and a pair of tight faded jeans said, "Hi, I'm Nikki Fox. Can I help you?"

Caught off guard by her good looks and assertive demeanor, Brooks fumbled for words. "I'm Brooks Barrington, and I'm a detective for Fairfax County." He displayed his badge. "May I come in?"

The redhead motioned toward a plush cobalt blue couch in her living room. Brooks suffered sensory overload from the dramatic red, blue, and purple that dominated the condo. Vivid abstract art leaped off the walls, and ornate sculptures looked as if they could move at any moment. Nikki leaned back into a feathery cream-colored chair and swung her left leg over its arm.

"I'm sorry to bother you, Ms. Fox, but I understand that, at one time, you had a relationship with Matt Curtis."

"Yes. What about it?"

"In the past two nights, two of Matt's ex-girlfriends, Jill Forcythe and Paige Whitaker, were killed by … well, let's just say they died very unusual deaths."

"What are you trying to say, Detective?"

"I believe you're in danger."

"Why? Did Matt kill them?" Nikki stared at Brooks without blinking.

"No. They were killed by a man named Lazarus Kaine. Now, I know this is going to sound very strange, but this man has unusual abilities that allow him to travel through shadows and darkness. Kaine can manipulate his surroundings. He preys on a person's worst fears. He loves to kill."

"You don't really expect me to believe that, do you?" Nikki smirked.

"I've seen his work firsthand. He's lethal, and he won't stop until he has finished tormenting everyone associated with an individual that he has singled out, which, in this case, is Matt Curtis."

"Look, Detective, I'm a big girl. I've been on my own since I was sixteen, and I'm certain I can protect myself against your shadow man. I appreciate your concern, but you don't need to worry about me." Nikki stood up, signaling an end to the conversation.

"Take my advice; sleep with the lights on." Brooks handed Nikki his business card. "Call me immediately if anything unusual happens." He walked to the door.

"Sure. I'll also place crosses all around my bed and wear a garlic necklace. Then I'll load my gun with a silver bullet and put my priest on speed dial," Nikki chuckled. "I'll be fine, Detective," Nikki said as she placed her right hand on Brooks's left shoulder.

"You're in a dangerous situation, Ms. Fox."

"Whatever you say. Thanks for the warning. Have a wonderful night." Nikki closed the door. Through the peephole, she watched Brooks limp down the hall and onto the elevator.

A smile snuck across Nikki's face. Then her body twisted into a mass of black iniquity. Mystifying shadows swirled like a tornado of malevolence. A gathering of light and darkness reformed itself into the shape of a man. "Oh, Brooks, you stupid, stupid man," he said. "You can't even tell when you're talking to your old friend Lazarus. Some detective you are!" Then he melted into the night.

Chapter 24

"I don't wanna have a C-section!" Arnez Wilkerson screamed.

Cullen hurried to the side of the woman's hospital bed. "We talked about this situation two hours ago, honey. You are a tiny woman with a big honkin' baby trapped inside of your belly. Your water broke four hours ago, but you have dilated to only three centimeters. There is no chance you're going to get to ten centimeters any time soon. We need to get that little rascal out of there, right now, and the only way we can do that is by C-section."

"Oh, I don't know about this." Arnez looked over at her petrified husband, LeBron. "This is not the way we had our delivery planned. My doctor assured us that we wouldn't have any problems. Why is this happening to us, Cullen?"

"You're experiencing protective inertia, which means your body knows that the baby is way too big to deliver naturally. It's very common. We do a lot of C-sections. It's the best solution for your situation."

"Tell me the truth, Cullen. Will a C-section create any adverse effects on the baby?" Arnez ran her trembling hands over her cornrows.

"Well, when he leaves the house, he'll have an uncontrollable urge to go out through the side window, but eventually that will go away," Cullen said with a straight face. Arnez exploded into a huge laugh, which turned into an earsplitting scream when a contraction caught her by surprise.

"I thought you gave her something for pain," LeBron said. As he kept a close watch on the monitors that were attached to his wife, his shaved head glistened with sweat.

"I did, but it must be wearing off." Cullen checked the woman's IV bag. "Arnez, when we prepare you for surgery in a few minutes, you'll get a new blast of medication. You'll be numb from the chest down. You won't feel a thing."

"Can I get that in writing?" Arnez asked through her gritted teeth.

Cullen could hear LeBron praying for his wife's suffering to end and for God to give him the strength to endure the C-section without passing out.

A knock on the door announced the arrival of Dr. Dave Adell, the anesthesiologist on duty. "Hello, Cullen. Is Mrs. Wilkerson ready for her C-section?"

"She's all yours, Dave. I'm going to check with her obstetrician to make sure he's ready to go." Cullen turned to her apprehensive patient. "Arnez, you're in good hands. Dave is a very capable anesthesiologist. You'll be fine. I'll see you when you get out of surgery."

Cullen searched the halls for Dr. Nazar DerBedrosian. After looking in five hospital rooms and three offices, she found the short, round man camped out at the reception desk. "What are you doing? Your patient is getting ready for surgery. Would you like to join us for the delivery?"

"I have been waiting for you to treat me with the respect I deserve. I believe I have earned that benefit during my twenty-three years of exemplary service to this hospital. Now, go and get me a bottle of water and prepare my scrubs," he directed.

"You can get your own water and scrubs. I'm a nurse, not your handmaiden."

Shaking his plump index finger at Cullen, Nazar said, "You will do as I say. I am in charge."

"Look, you little sawed-off buttwipe, if you don't get your finger out of my face, you're going to draw back a bloody stump. You may be a doctor, but you're not in charge of me."

"Why do you hate me so, Cullen? Because I am Armenian; that is why. Your heart is prejudiced against me." Nazar emphasized his accent.

"I couldn't care less where you're from. You annoy the hell out of me because you're a lousy doctor."

"I'm going to report you to the director of nursing for your impudence!" Nazar slammed his fist on the reception desk.

Cullen sneered into Nazar's fat face. "Fine! And I'll report you to the director of obstetrics for gross malpractice. Over the past five years, I've documented more than fifty cases where my nurses bailed your sorry ass out of trouble because you made inappropriate medical decisions. Now, I would love to stand here and verbally abuse you, but Arnez Wilkerson needs to deliver her baby. I suggest you stuff your gigantic ego into your back pocket and get to work."

"I won't forget this, Cullen." Nazar waddled down the hallway toward the operating room.

"I'm sure you won't, jerkwad," Cullen whispered. "God, I hate that squatty little dipshit."

Because Arnez had transferred into the capable care of the operating room staff, Cullen took a moment to rid her body of its Nazar toxins. Seizing a rare opportunity to sit down, she settled into a chair at the nurses' desk to chill out.

Realizing she hadn't checked her voice mail all day, she pulled out her cell phone and retrieved one new message, from a police detective named Brooks Barrington, asking her to call him. She checked her watch and figured the detective probably wouldn't appreciate a call at 1:35 AM, so she made a mental note to give him a ring after she completed her shift.

Mandy Bain, a licensed practical nurse, passed by on her way to the newborn nursery. "Hey, Cullen, a guy came by looking for you about thirty minutes ago. He left a message for you." She dug into the pocket of her mauve scrub jacket for the paper.

"Who was it?"

"He didn't tell me his name, but he was really cute."

"Did he have brown hair, blue eyes, and dimples?" Cullen figured that Matt was checking up on her.

"This guy had really blond hair—almost white. I didn't see any dimples. Here's the note." Mandy handed over the crumpled piece of paper.

Cullen's pulse accelerated. "My dear Cullen, great to see you tonight. You're still as beautiful as ever. Let's get together soon. It will be just like old times. Always thinking of you, Simon."

Chapter 25

"So, Nikki, are you going to invite me up for a drink?" Richard Attenborough asked.

Standing in the middle of the lobby of the Luxor Building, Nikki looked over at the security desk to make sure a guard was available, just in case she needed one. "I don't think that would be a good idea, Richard."

"Why not?"

"Because for the past three hours, you have bored me out of my mind. You talked about yourself the entire time we were at Morton's. Even the waitress got sick of your droning."

"I thought my stories were quite interesting." He placed his left hand on her hip, which she promptly brushed off.

"You went into explicit detail about every bullet point on your resume. It was like you were interviewing for a job. I'm sorry, Richard, but you're not getting any kind of job tonight."

Unaccustomed to rejection, Richard tightened his conventional red tie and made another run at Nikki. "I don't understand. I'm nice-looking, I'm wealthy, and I'll probably be elected as a senator within the next few years. What more do you want?"

"A personality would be nice."

Richard stared into Nikki's uncooperative glare. A distant cousin of an extremely wealthy family from Massachusetts, Richard had successfully used his familial connection to score with women throughout his adult life. His last name and a stack of family cash managed to seal the deal every time.

Not nearly as striking as his famous cousins, Richard had never reached the inner circle of the Attenborough clan. In fact, many members of the family didn't even know he existed. A privileged kid from Potomac, Maryland, he had been accepted into the University of Maryland because his father made a significant donation to the school. After six years in college, Richard barely graduated with a degree in political science. Politics seemed like the best career move for him because he could take full advantage of his Attenborough affiliation, and keeping a seat warm in a public office didn't require him to do any real work. Richard made money the old-fashioned way—his father gave it to him.

"One more chance. That's all I'm asking for. Have dinner with me tomorrow," Richard begged. "Then I'll take you shopping. You can buy anything you want. I don't care what it costs."

"Good-bye, Richard." She turned her back on him and rushed toward the elevators.

"I'll call you."

"I won't answer." The elevator doors closed. She leaned back against the wall, relieved to be away from that pompous loser. Although she had just wasted three hours, the huge piece of Morton's fabulous New York cheesecake was a fantastic reward for putting up with Richard. When she had met him at work last Wednesday, he seemed like a nice guy. Too bad being nice was just an act.

Nikki opened the door to her condo and kicked off her shoes. She changed out of her Melissa Masse kimono top and matching pants into her favorite sleepwear—an ivory Natori tank top with boy-leg briefs.

Too keyed up from her blowout with Richard to sleep, she fell on her bed, grabbed the remote control, and zipped through the channels. *Late night TV sucks.* On E! Entertainment Television, a *True Hollywood Story* about the sitcom *Growing Pains* caught her attention for a few minutes, and then she moved on to a movie called *Backdraft* that starred Kurt Russell. Thirty minutes later, Nikki caught herself drifting off to sleep, so she turned off the tube and pulled the covers over her head.

In the middle of a romantic dream involving Matt Damon, an unusual crackling noise startled Nikki. It reminded her of the sound of someone walking through the woods, but the sound came from her bedroom. She stuck her head out of the covers. A shadow moved along the wall directly across from her window and took the shape of a human face. On the floor in front of her closet, a silhouette of a man's face traveled gracefully over a clump of discarded clothes and up the wall to join the first face. *This is really weird.* A third face emerged from a large mirror that stood on her cherry chest of drawers. It hovered in the air, defying physics and reason. The third face glided over Nikki's sleigh bed, toured the room as if to survey its surroundings, and then joined the first two faces on the far wall.

Frightened and mystified, Nikki decided she should get the hell out of the room. She slipped out of bed and tore toward the door as fast as she could. The faces darted across the walls and slammed the door shut. Unable to stop herself in time, she smashed into the door, almost dislocating her left shoulder. Lying on the floor in a crumpled heap, Nikki watched the shadow faces soar through the room and swirl in an outlandish ballet of changing shapes. The faces combined in a perverse accumulation of darkness and moonlight to create the figure of a man.

Dressed in a black pin-striped suit with a white tab collar shirt and a cerulean blue tie, the man opened his black eyes and stared into her soul. "Hello, Nikki. My name is Lazarus Kaine. We need to talk."

"What are you?"

"Good question. How should I describe myself?" Lazarus paced around the room. "Let's say you're driving your car late at night, and you've had a few too many cocktails. You crank your radio up with some crappy music like the Backstreet Boys to keep you awake, but it doesn't work. After a few miles, you nod off for just a second, and then you jolt yourself awake. You roll down the windows, hoping the fresh air will invigorate your mind. This idea works for about five miles; then your brain shuts off, and your eyelids pull themselves shut. Sleep covers your body like a warm blanket of relaxation. For some unexplained reason, you open your eyes to see that you have drifted into the oncoming lane of traffic and are about to slam headfirst into an eighteen-wheeler. Adrenaline surges through your bloodstream. Your hands begin to tremble, and your body shudders with violent apprehension. You hear yourself scream, 'Oh, God, no! I don't want to die!' When you realize your life is completely out of your control, a feeling of sheer terror seizes you. That's when I take over. I exist as unadulterated fear. I decide whether you live or die."

It took a few moments for Lazarus's explanation to sink in. This apparition had to be a dream. Nikki stood up and grabbed the doorknob, but it wouldn't budge. No exit.

"What do you want from me? Take anything. Just please don't hurt me," Nikki pleaded.

"Right now, I just want to want to talk about you, the real you."

"What do you mean?"

"The pretend life of Nikki Fox is over. For years, you ran from the tubby, bucktoothed girl of your childhood. What was her name? Oh, yes. Nicole Quesenbury of Bluefield, West Virginia. Talk about a genetic mishap—five feet ten inches of butt ugly. Nobody wanted to get near her. What happened to Nicole? Well, she saved the money she made as a late night waitress at IHOP and used it to create a whole new person. Thousands of dollars worth of dental work, cheek implants, liposuction, and, of course, a brand new set of gravity-defying breasts turned the beast Nicole Quesenbury into the beautiful Nikki Fox."

"Yeah. I had some work done. What about it?"

"Don't get me wrong, Nikki. I love a great pair of fake tits just as much as the next guy. But something disturbing happened to you when you left Nicole behind. You used your constructed beauty to manipulate men for your amusement. Sex became a weapon that you used to torment unsuspecting men, just like the cute teenage boys tormented you when you were a repulsive porker in high school. The most appalling display of your reckless disregard was with a man named Matt Curtis. You remember Matt, don't you, Nikki? The guy who fell madly in love with you, and then you blew him off without even speaking to him again. You really blazed him, Nikki. Matt was devastated."

"Look, I'm sorry. I'm not perfect. If it means that much to you, I'll apologize to him. I'll make it up to Matt, somehow. Now, will you please leave me alone?" She tried to remember the techniques she'd learned in self-defense class, but none came to mind.

"You're going to make it up to him tonight, Nikki. In fact, you're about to pay for all of your sins." Lazarus stalked across the room and sat down on the edge of the bed.

"I don't understand. What are you talking about?"

"I have an assignment for you." He gently rubbed his hand along the white satin sheets.

"What kind of assignment?" Nikki wished she had kept her big mouth shut.

"Doing what you do best."

Lazarus's arms and legs melted into shadows that crawled toward the terrified woman. The shadows spread across the room, cutting off any possible escape route. They crept onto her feet and moved up her legs.

"Let's go for a little ride," Lazarus said. Then the shadows swallowed Nikki's body.

Chapter 26

"She's not coming out to see you, Joe. It's way after midnight," Matt reasoned with his best friend. "Sophie is probably asleep. You can see her in the morning. I need to go to bed."

The jet black cocker spaniel watched his beloved Sophie's doggie door, waiting patiently for her to appear. He had been infatuated with the energetic blond cocker spaniel since her owners brought her home four years ago, when she was only twelve weeks old. Sophie liked to tease Joe. With her long eyelashes and silky ears, she drove him crazy on a daily basis, and now it was even worse because she was in heat.

Tugging at Joe's leash, Matt dragged him down the sidewalk, away from his true love. After scraping his nails on the cement for twenty-five feet, Joe gave up the fight and padded alongside Matt's left leg. Every few steps, Joe looked back just to make sure he didn't miss her.

As soon as Matt opened the back door of his house, Joe scurried straight for the laundry room and assumed a perfect dog show sit in preparation for an Old Mother Hubbard doggie treat. Matt gave him three of the small treats to satisfy Joe's late-night craving.

The time on the microwave displayed 1:00. The glowing red numbers pierced the darkness of the room. "That was your last trip, Joe. Don't ask to go outside anymore tonight. Let's go to bed." His canine companion scampered up the stairs into Matt's bedroom. Digging into his cedar pillow next to Matt's bed, Joe turned around three times and flopped on his belly. By the time Matt finished brushing his teeth, Joe was snoring. The pain in Matt's knee was almost gone, but he took a dose of Advil for good measure.

Matt stepped out of his bathroom, pulled off his Virginia Tech football T-shirt, and threw it in the general direction of the clothes hamper in the corner of the room. Tonight he would sleep only in his Joe Boxers.

For the previous four hours, Matt had tried a wide assortment of diversions to get his mind off of Cullen's dreadful experience with Simon Fletcher. From Ric Edelman's book, *The Truth about Money,* to an old World Series issue of *Sports Illustrated* to a bad *Baywatch Hawaii* rerun, nothing could keep him from thinking about how that son of a bitch had hurt her. Just before 2:00 AM, the three Coronas he had slugged down after dinner kicked in, and he finally fell asleep.

At 2:22, he sensed someone watching him. He blew it off as part of a dream, but the feeling didn't go away. He opened his eyes to see a shadowy face hovering about two feet above him. A second face rose from the foot of the bed and passed over Joe, as if to make sure the "guard dog" was still asleep. The faces of fear melded into each other, generating the sound of unrestrained energy. Their conversion birthed another appearance of Lazarus, wearing a medium gray, three-button suit, a cream-colored shirt with French cuffs, and a sapphire tie.

"Hello, Matt. Having trouble sleeping?" Lazarus asked.

"I am now."

"You're worried about Cullen. I understand your concern, but she's a strong woman. I'm sure she'll get over Simon Fletcher—one way or another. She's not going to have sex with you anytime in the foreseeable future, but other than that, she'll be just fine. It must be frustrating, having a lovely girlfriend with a smokin' body that's completely off limits. That must drive you insane."

"I'll manage." Matt frowned at his sarcastic visitor.

"How? By watching *Baywatch*? Rushing out to the mailbox to get the latest edition of the Victoria's Secret catalog? Downloading Pamela Anderson screensavers? A healthy young man like you has needs, desires, and fantasies that ache to be fulfilled. What are you going to do, Matt? Wait for Cullen to come around to her sexual senses? You don't have that kind of time."

"I love Cullen."

"So what? You loved Jill Forcythe and Paige Whitaker. Look where that got you. How about Nikki Fox? Did you love her?"

Matt paused. If he told a lie, Lazarus would call him on it. He stared out the window at the streetlights that stood in front of his neighbor's house. "Yes, I loved her." But the truth did not set him free.

"Of course you did. You fell in love with Nikki the first time you saw her in Neiman Marcus. You wanted her. Oh, dear God, how you wanted her. That girl rocked your world even though you never slept with her. But then, for some unexplained reason, she didn't want to see you anymore, did she?"

"No." Matt struggled to keep his game face on. His obsession with Nikki had continued to burn white-hot for months after she dumped him. Like a pathetic Peeping Tom, he had trailed her while she was at work in the store, just to get a glimpse of her. He tried to phone her, but she refused to return his calls. Why did she brutally reject him? What was wrong with him?

"Did she ever talk to you again, Matt?"

"No. I never spoke to her after the relationship ended." Matt lowered his head.

"Well, my friend, I have a surprise for you. As you will recall, I healed the bones in your knee and made you feel better. Tonight, I'm going to make sure the rest of you feels fantastic." Lazarus passed his hands over Matt's bed, creating a surge of shadows. The accumulation of darkness pulsed and twisted to arrange itself into the contour of a human body. The shadows dissipated, revealing Nikki Fox.

"Nikki, say hello to Matt," Lazarus commanded.

"Hi, Matt," she complied.

"What's going on?" Although Matt was shocked at the circumstances, he couldn't help being excited to see the sensuous redhead on his bed.

"I am so sorry I hurt you." Nikki slid closer to Matt. She reached out and touched his cheek. Her soft, warm skin smelled like jasmine.

"Nikki needs to make amends for the way she treated you." Lazarus strolled around the bed, admiring her surgically enhanced resources. "She's going to give you the night you always wanted. And she brought along her bag of sexual tricks. She's mastered some exciting Kama Sutra positions that will drive you wild."

Running her fingers over Matt's shoulders and chest, she gently kissed him, then she caressed his stomach with both hands. Although Matt savored every second of the attention, he fought to control his libido. With an unbelievable amount of willpower and an equivalent quantity of regret, he moved her hands off his body. "Nikki, I can't do this. I'm in love with Cullen. I won't cheat on her."

Lazarus smacked his left hand on his forehead. "Dammit, Matt! What are you thinking? You have an opportunity to have a night of untamed sex with a gorgeous woman. Admit it. You want her. You need her. You gotta, gotta have her. Cullen will never find out about it. Live your life, boy!"

Nikki threw her leg over Matt's hips and straddled him like a feisty cowgirl. "Come on, baby. Let's have some fun." She peeled off her tank top, tossed it across the room, and enticed him with long, adoring kisses. Although his conscience told him to stop, his body wouldn't listen. Nikki felt too good to resist.

"Enjoy yourself, Matt. You can thank me later. I'll see myself out," Lazarus said. Then he departed into the moonlight.

Chapter 27

"Have you taken your lunch break, Cullen?" Lisha Hayford asked. She dropped her stethoscope on the nurses' work desk.

"No, not yet. I've had a busy and very weird night." Cullen finished writing her notes describing the events of Arnez Wilkerson's childbirth.

"Is everything OK? You look tired."

"It's a quarter to three and I've worked on four deliveries without a break. Of course I'm tired," Cullen said with a weak smile. She slipped Arnez's chart into a white folder and placed it in a hanging file.

"I've seen you chug through sixteen hours without breaking a sweat. You're a workhorse. Something is bothering you. Spill it, Cullen." Lisha leaned over the desk to make their conversation more private. Best friends since high school, they had always shared their most intimate problems with each other. After Cullen's rape, Lisha provided the constant support Cullen needed to finish college and move on with her life. She even helped Cullen get her first nursing job at Fairfax Memorial Hospital.

Cullen thumbed through a stack of medical charts to keep her hands busy. She bit her lower lip and fought back a reservoir of tears. "I saw Simon Fletcher tonight."

"No way! Where?" Lisha's green eyes soared out of their sockets.

"At Samuel & David's in Tysons Corner. He lives here in Northern Virginia. And—get this—he's friends with Matt."

"You have got to be freakin' kidding me." Lisha's shoulder-length, sandy blond hair flew in every direction.

"It's true. Simon works at Matt's athletic club. That's how they met. Matt didn't know anything about my history with Simon. While we were having dinner, Simon came over to our table. When I saw that bastard's face looking down at me, the whole experience flashed through my mind, as if it was about to happen again. I bolted out of the restaurant like a rampaging lunatic. Matt ran after me, and then I told him the whole story."

"You had to tell him sometime."

"Yeah, well, that wasn't the way I wanted to tell him."

"How did he take the news?"

"Matt was very sweet and understanding." Tears streamed down Cullen's face. "I love him so much, Lisha."

"I know you do. I'm glad the night ended on a positive note."

Cullen wiped her tears with a tissue. "That's the problem. It didn't. Somehow Simon tracked me down here at the hospital tonight and left me this note." She pulled the piece of paper out of her scrub jacket pocket and handed it to Lisha.

"This is creepy. He's stalking you. You've got to tell the police about Simon. Get a restraining order against him. Get a big-ass pistol. Get a pit bull. I don't care what you get, but you need to protect yourself. He's dangerous." Lisha waved the note at Cullen.

"I'm a big girl. I can take care of myself, and I'm not going to let that testosterone-impaired psycho screw up my life anymore. If he does anything else, I promise I'll call the police. Satisfied?" Cullen swiped the note out of her friend's hand.

"I still think the big-ass pistol is a good idea."

"We'll call that Plan B."

"Yeah, baby." Lisha gave Cullen a high-five.

"All right, now that our little female bonding moment is over, I'm going to lunch." Cullen hugged Lisha and left her friend chuckling at the nurses' desk.

Retrieving her lunchbox from her locker, Cullen walked down the hall to the break room. Although she had worked the graveyard shift for years, she had never gotten used to the concept of eating lunch at three in the morning.

A haphazard collection of used furniture filled the labor and delivery break room, including an old conference table surrounded by various wooden and metal chairs that didn't match. An old coffee pot chugged on a countertop. An advertisement for malpractice insurance hung on a bulletin board next to a picture of Dr. Nazar DerBedrosian with a thumbtack stuck in the middle of his forehead.

In the far corner of the room, a man sat by himself. He was drinking coffee and watching CNN on a television that sat on the counter next to the microwave. Slender with short brown hair that stuck straight up without the help of fancy mousse, the man wore a white lab coat that covered a blue button-down shirt and striped tie. A name embroidered in black thread on the coat read "Dr. L. Kaine." The man greeted her with a pleasant smile.

Cullen smiled back. "Hi. Are you new here at the hospital?" She unpacked her lunch—a chef salad, strawberry yogurt, an apple, and a bottle of water.

"Oh, no. I've been around for many years. I just stopped by to get a cup of your delicious coffee. My name is Dr. Lazarus Kaine." He stood up to shake Cullen's hand.

"I'm Cullen Rhea. I'm the charge nurse in labor and delivery. It's nice to meet you, Dr. Kaine. So, what's your specialty?"

"Head trauma."

"Wow. That's exciting stuff, but very risky. I guess a lot of your patients end up dying after you work on them."

"Yes. It happens quite often." Lazarus said. "It's interesting that we serve two very different purposes, you and I. You bring people into the world, and I take them out."

Lazarus looked at his watch, threw his Styrofoam cup into a black metal trash can, and walked toward the door. "I'd love to stick around, but it's time for me to get back to work. It was nice to meet you, Cullen. I'm sure we'll see each other again very soon." He handed her the TV remote control. "Why don't you check out channel 54? A new reality show just started. You might like it." He turned to leave the room.

"Thank you, Dr. Kaine. Pleasure to meet you. See ya later," she said. Placing the remote beside her apple, she dug into her salad. A CNN reporter blathered on with yet another mind-numbing analysis of terrorist activities in the Middle East. "Ugh. Enough already," Cullen said. Lazarus had piqued her curiosity, so she picked up the remote and punched in channel 54. A nude woman's back filled the screen. The camera slowly pulled back to reveal an attractive redhead in bed with a very lucky man.

"Oh, baby, you feel so good." The woman moaned and whipped her long red hair away from her face.

"I don't need to see this while I'm eating," Cullen grumbled. Grasping the remote, she changed the station one notch to channel 55. There was the same redhead, writhing in ecstasy. *This is odd.* She changed the channel again. Same bedroom, same couple. "What's going on with the stupid TV?" She flipped around the dial, but she couldn't get away from the sexual gymnast.

On the screen, the redhead groaned with pleasure. "I love the way you touch me. Matt, you are unbelievable."

Cullen dropped her fork and moved closer to the TV. The camera shifted to the side of the bed, revealing Matt Curtis with a look of undeniable delight on his face. He explored her body with gentle caresses. She responded with moves straight out of the Kama Sutra. "What the hell is going on? Matt, why are you doing this?" Cullen screamed at the television.

The redhead ravaged Matt. Grabbing his wrists, she held his arms over his head and nibbled on his neck. Then she turned her head and looked directly into the camera. "See, Cullen, this is what Matt really likes." She kissed him as if she were going to devour him.

"No! No! You can't do this to me!" Cullen pushed the power button, but the disturbing images refused to go away. Again and again, she tried to turn the TV off—with no success. She ripped the power cord out of the electrical socket, but the redhead continued to mock Cullen with her explicit display of unbridled sexuality. With a strength powered by absolute anger, Cullen picked the television up and slammed it on the hard tile floor, cracking the screen. But the sudden impact didn't stop that damn woman from tormenting Cullen.

"Ooooh, Matt, you make me so hot. I'm burning up, baby," the redhead growled.

Grabbing a metal folding chair, Cullen whacked the television screen with every pound of force she could muster. She pummeled the television into pieces, but Cullen could still hear that bitch making love to Matt. As she raised the chair above her head in preparation for another mighty blow, she heard a voice calling to her from the doorway.

"Cullen, what do you think you're doing?" Lisha yelled at her frantic friend.

Lowering the chair, Cullen scanned her brain for a couple of seconds to find something close to a rational excuse for her strange behavior. "I was watching *Entertainment Tonight,* and I experienced a Paris Hilton overdose. I couldn't take it anymore. I had to stop the stupidity." With her hands still shaking with bitterness, she looked down at the mangled heap of electronic parts that used to be a television. The images were gone.

Chapter 28

"Ooooh, don't stop, baby." Nikki threw her head back with passion.

Matt wanted to say something sexy back to her, but all he could come up with was, "Oh, Nikki." Not very original, but direct and effective. Although his pillow talk was weak, Matt excelled in many other, more essential, areas of performance.

Guilt gnawed at him. He had never even thought about cheating on Cullen, or anyone else for that matter. Although he knew his actions were way beyond wrong, he didn't want to stop. Nikki was so beautiful and so accomplished at lovemaking that his starving male desire overruled his shame.

Uninhibited and experimental, Nikki gave Matt permission to try things he had imagined but had never expected to come true. Every kiss, every touch, and every movement she made sent shock waves through Matt's body. He didn't know where she had learned this stuff, and he didn't care. These moves definitely weren't the kind of techniques a woman picked up from *Good Housekeeping*.

Disturbed by the noise, Joe stood up on his pillow, stretched, huffed in distain, and padded downstairs to find a quiet spot to sleep. Nikki and Matt didn't notice that Joe had left the room because their tantric sex session required their full attention.

As Matt moved his fingers over her naked back, Nikki suddenly felt like she had a fever. She broke into a sensual sweat. "I feel dizzy." She ran her hands through her hair.

"Do you want to take a break? Get some water?"

"No, let's keep going. I can't get enough of you." Nikki fell into Matt's arms and kissed him. He could feel her temperature rising. She trembled, but it wasn't from sexual arousal. As Nikki sat up on Matt's waist, her hands started shaking. Pain swept across her face. Her lips quivered.

"Nikki, what's wrong?"

"I don't know." Blood trickled from her nose. An intense heat radiated from Nikki's body. "My hands feel like they're going to explode," she said. Her fingers vibrated violently as she held them in front of her face. Then her fingers burst into flames. Nikki cried out in agony.

Scrambling from underneath her, Matt tried to cover Nikki with the bedsheets to extinguish the fire. No effect. He rushed to the bathroom to get wet towels. It seemed to take hours for the water to saturate the towels, even though he had cranked the tub faucet to full blast. Nikki's screams got louder by the second. When he returned to the room, Nikki's arms were ablaze. He wrapped the towels around her and tried to snuff out the flames. But the fire refused to die.

Nikki's eyes looked odd, almost viscous. "Matt, I can't see anything!" They began to liquefy and ooze out of their sockets. "Oh, God! Please help me!" Her eyes melted and poured down her cheeks, steaming with heat. Beauty faded, swallowed up with terror. The severe temperature caused her face to soften, as if it were about to slip off of her skull. Like a Roman candle, Nikki's luxurious red hair caught fire and burned to the roots.

Her blood boiled, ripping holes near major arteries to free itself from the intense combustion. Tissue fused to bone. Skin disintegrated into the underlying muscles. Her internal organs turned to burnt clumps of indeterminate organic material.

The smell of fiery flesh made Matt sick to his stomach. Helpless and terrified, he threw more wet towels over Nikki's blazing carcass, but it was too late. Within five minutes, Nikki's body was burned beyond recognition. To keep the fire from spreading, Matt used an old bathrobe to smother the stray flames that hissed across his bed. Gray smoke rose from the charred remainder, creating a cloud of death over the room.

Matt collapsed on the floor, crying at the horror that lay on his bed. "I know you did this, Lazarus!" he yelled at the shadow of death. "Show yourself, you son of a bitch! Crawl out of the darkness, and see what you've done to her!" But the night remained still.

"Forgive me, Nikki. This is my fault." Matt stared at the pieces of scorched cadaver strewn across his bed. "I'm so sorry."

Recognizing the end of the carnage and sensing his best friend's sadness, Joe entered the bedroom and sat next to him. Matt hugged his dog and said a prayer for Nikki.

I've got to call 911. But what am I going to tell them? Hello, a woman just burned to death in my bed? The smell of the smoldering residue became too much for Matt to handle, so he pulled his boxers on and headed downstairs to make his unusual phone call.

Matt could barely breathe as he picked up the receiver. He dialed 9 ... 1, then the upstairs smoke alarm screeched an ear-piercing blast. He ran upstairs through the cloud of smoke that had formed in his two-story foyer. After he shut off the alarm, he heard a crackling sound coming from his bedroom.

Smoke billowed out of the bedroom and stung Matt's eyes as he investigated the strange noise. He edged into the room, terrified at what he might see. With blurred vision, he saw Nikki's remains pulsate. Pieces of muscle and bone crumbled. The blood that had covered his bed and the floor evaporated and disappeared into the cloud of smoke. The lingering collection of humanity that used to be Nikki Fox shuddered and disintegrated into dust. A flurry of smoke whirled through the room, amassing the ash and dirt into a small, but powerful windstorm. In a sudden flash of blinding light, the storm disappeared.

    Matt's sheets and pillows returned to their initial state, showing no signs of the fire that he had seen burn them to a crisp. Not even a hint of smoke hung in the air. He examined his bed, but he couldn't find the smallest trace of Nikki's existence. It was as if she had never been there.

Chapter 29

At 3:45 AM, Tessa McBride's eyes snapped open. She bolted upright in her bed, her heart racing like the engine of a Formula One speedster. *What is wrong with me?*

Sweat discharged from virtually every pore. Her lungs felt like someone sucked the air out of them with an enormous bellows. Although she gasped for oxygen, she couldn't inhale fast enough.

Hot flushes took turns with chills, which sent stinging sensations through Tessa's entire body. Nausea invaded her system, sending her running to the toilet to suffer through a maddening installment of the dry heaves. Was she about to die? *I'll just sit down here on the floor for a minute. If I faint, at least I won't have far to fall.* She leaned her head against the cold porcelain bowl.

When she finally worked up the nerve to stand, dizziness threw her around the room, causing her to stumble on her way back to bed. "I've got to stop this, but I don't know how. I think I'm going crazy," she said in a quivering whisper.

Her legs started to shiver and shudder. Grabbing her calves, she commanded them to settle down, but they wouldn't listen. Her quadriceps flexed with nervous energy as if she were an Olympic sprinter preparing to run for a gold medal. "This is ridiculous! Why am I acting like a panic-stricken loon?"

Feeling the impulse to move around, Tessa paced throughout her apartment, trying to find something to take her mind off of her high level of anxiety. She turned on the television, but all she could find was an infomercial about a suntanning miracle that could be administered with a simple cloth, a VH1 *Behind the Music* episode about Aerosmith, and a movie on the SciFi Channel about a mutant fish with a bad attitude. "This isn't gonna work." She switched the television off with a wavering thumb. Reading didn't help either. Even *People* magazine couldn't calm her down. Finally, around 5:00 AM, her nervousness subsided. Tessa drifted to sleep in her comfortable leather recliner.

A few minutes after 7:00 AM, Tessa's cell phone blasted the theme from *Mission Impossible*. She crawled out of her recliner and edged slowly toward her glass coffee table. The caller ID told her that "Turquoise Malone" was on the other end of the line. *This can't be good.* "Hello, boss, what's up?"

"We have another murder," Malone said without a hint of emotion.

Tessa closed her eyes and shook her head. The last two murder investigations had worn her out. Now a third death would make her life even more complicated. "What are the details?"

Malone explained the specifics about a woman, Nikki Fox, who had burned to death in her home. "Sounds like it could be an accident. Do we really need to investigate something like this?" Tessa tried to sound rational, but her main goal was to keep her Friday unencumbered with yet another homicide.

"It was no accident. Get in touch with Barrington, and get over to the crime scene as soon as possible."

Tessa's right hand trembled as she held the phone to her ear. *Dammit*! Her stomach felt queasy, and her pulse quickened. She didn't want to leave her apartment today. Now she would have to confront people, ask questions, and function in public as an officer of the law. Just the thought of human contact made her edgy.

"Lieutenant, I'm not feeling very well. Maybe Brooks should handle this one by himself." She battled the urge to hang up the phone and crawl back into her safe recliner.

"I don't trust Barrington to work a case alone. What the hell's wrong with you?"

"I ... um ..." Tessa couldn't tell her boss that she was afraid to step out of her apartment—afraid that she would have an anxiety attack and embarrass herself in front of a crowd of people. "I'm having some stomach problems."

"All cops have stomach problems. Take a big shot of Maalox, and get your rear in gear, detective."

"Yes, ma'am. I'm on my way." She turned her cell phone off and plopped back into her recliner. The chair wrapped its loving arms around Tessa, refusing to let her go. She laid her head back on the soft black leather and practiced a breathing exercise she had learned in a yoga class. It didn't help. She couldn't bring herself to leave the devoted comfort of her only good piece of furniture.

Tessa looked down at her improvised pajamas, an Underdog T-shirt and a pair of worn gray sweatpants. The last thing she wanted to do was take a shower, slather on her makeup, and put on grown-up clothes. A sharp stick in the eye would be preferable to facing the misery of Northern Virginia traffic, and talking to people seemed out of the question. For God's sake, she just wanted to be by herself in her secure apartment where no one would judge her for acting like a fearful nutcase.

It took Tessa twenty-five minutes to pry her butt out of her recliner. She trudged into the shower and got ready for work under duress. *What is the matter with me?* This behavior was not normal for an educated, supposedly confident woman. Should she see someone? A therapist? A priest? A bartender? Who could help her shake this feeling of angst?

Question after unanswered question filled her head with self-doubt as she drove to Brooks's home. Her shaky hands almost caused her to run onto the sidewalk a couple of times along the way. "Get a grip, Tessa," she reprimanded herself. "I have got to get over this." But she had no idea how to solve her severe mental problem. Dreadful thoughts flashed through her mind. *Would I have the guts to kill myself? How bad could it be?*

Chapter 30

Sipping hot coffee, Brooks sat in a lounge chair on his back deck and read the Friday morning edition of the *Washington Post* to Mildred, his plump basset hound. "The Washington Nationals won their eighth straight game last night. They beat the Mets—nine to seven in ten innings. They can hit, but their pitching staff can't get anybody out." With an uninterested huff, Mildred rolled over on her left side.

He turned the page. "The Washington Redskins signed their first-round draft pick—Cornelius DeShazio, a linebacker out of the University of Miami—to a five-year deal including a fifteen-million-dollar signing bonus. Lord, have mercy! That's too much cash for a guy who has never played a down in the NFL, don't you think, Mildred?" The hound yawned.

The sun peeked over the line of oak trees that separated his house from his neighbor's pool. Next to his gas grill, a neighborhood squirrel that Brooks had named Rocky nibbled on a nut and kept a close eye on Mildred, just in case she decided he was worth chasing.

"Angelina Jolie has a new movie coming out. Whoa, baby! She is something else, Mildred. I'm gonna have to see it. I don't care what the movie's about. As long as Angelina is in a skimpy outfit, I'll be happy," he said as if Mildred actually cared.

While the basset powered through her morning nap, Brooks thumbed through articles on terrorist atrocities, politics, and the economy. The doorbell brought their leisurely morning to an abrupt halt.

Taking her position as chief of security seriously, Mildred scampered through the kitchen and into the foyer, ears and jowls flapping with every step. She lumbered to the front door to check out the uninvited visitor. Two quick barks and a loud "boouuuuuuu" announced her imposing seventy-two pound presence to the potential intruder.

Brooks opened the door to see Tessa standing on the front step with her arms crossed. She was wearing dark slacks, a white button-down shirt, and a navy blazer. "Good morning, Tessa. Do you want some coffee?" The woman didn't say a word as she walked into the house. Her eyes broke the bad news.

"Let me guess. Another woman is dead?"

"Yes. Nikki Fox."

"Gottdammit! I warned her ..."

"You what?"

Brooks fussed with his newspaper to avoid Tessa's glare. "I went to her home last night to tell her that she was in danger."

"I can't believe you did that." Tessa shook her head. "Let's not tell Lieutenant Malone about your little visit to the crime scene on the night of our latest murder."

"No. She wouldn't be very happy with me."

"She'd tear your freakin' head off. God, I hate that woman." Tessa jammed her hands on her hips.

"Yeah, that's no secret."

"Come on, change out of your adorable jammies, and let's get going."

Brooks looked down at his tattered blue pajama bottoms and the syrup-stained Carolina Panthers jersey that was stretched over his paunch. "Hey, cut me some slack. I'll be ready in ten minutes." He lifted himself up the stairs to his bedroom while Tessa scratched Mildred's furry belly.

Exactly ten minutes later, Brooks hobbled downstairs, wearing a gray suit with a lot of miles on it and a red tie with green stripes. "How do I look?"

"Like you're on your way to investigate a woman's death."

Rubbing Mildred's floppy ears, Brooks kissed her on the snout. "Daddy has to go to work. I'll see you soon. Be a good girl while I'm gone." He waved to her as he closed the front door.

"Isn't that sweet, a boy and his dog?"

"Shut up and get in the car." Brooks heaved his artificial leg into the passenger seat of Tessa's Prius. They rode in silence as Tessa weaved through the two-lane roads of Brooks's Chantilly, Virginia, housing development, Sutton Oaks. Gunning the engine, Tessa took a circular on-ramp onto Route 66 a bit too fast and headed toward Tysons Corner.

As she drove, Tessa's hands strangled the steering wheel, trying to hide the tremors that vibrated through her body. Unfortunately, she couldn't conceal her quivering lower lip.

"What's the matter with you?" Brooks asked.

"Nothing." Tessa bit her lower lip.

"Are you sure? You seem kinda agitated."

"Three murders in three days would agitate anybody. I'm just a little stressed out. Now, get the hell off my back, Brooks."

"All right, pardon me for being a concerned friend. Don't get your panties in a wad so early in the morning. Let's talk about the case. Tell me what you know about Nikki Fox."

"A neighbor noticed a terrible smell coming from her condo early this morning."

"What kind of smell?"

"Burnt flesh."

"Shit." Brooks rubbed his forehead. "This is gonna be bad. Fire is brutal. Relentless. Unforgiving." He watched the white lines on the road fly by the car window.

"The neighbor called 9-1-1. The rescue squad forced the door open and found Nikki in her bed, burned to a crisp." Tessa steered around weekend construction on the 495 Capital Beltway.

"I don't wanna see her," Brooks complained.

"You have to. It's your job."

"Sometimes this job really gets to me. It's so depressing to see the pain and suffering that one human being can inflict on another. We assume that we're more intelligent and more evolved than other creatures. But then you arrive at a crime scene to see that some pissed-off drunk shot his wife in the head five times just because she forgot to put mustard on his turkey sandwich, and you realize that humans are just wild animals with opposable thumbs."

"You don't have to be a detective, Brooks. You can change careers."

"And do what? Work as a private investigator? Sit in my car for ten hours a day and take pictures of cheating spouses? No thanks. I'll just put in my time on the force and retire when I'm fifty-five with full benefits."

"Yeah? And then what will you do? Buy a Krispy Kreme franchise?"

"Nope. I'm gonna move to Daytona, sell cheap T-shirts on the beach, and watch the thongs pass by. Girls will get a free shirt if they flash their boobs at me. Every day will be a new episode of *Brooks Gone Wild*."

"You really think that's gonna happen?"

"Probably not." Brooks grinned. "But the Krispy Kreme franchise is an excellent idea."

As Tessa pulled into the parking garage of the Luxor Building, they saw an army of police vehicles. They pressed through the security checkpoint in the lobby and met Stan Bogart at the door of Nikki's condo.

"Good morning, guys. This is a rough one. You'll need these." Stan handed Brooks and Tessa thick surgical masks and gloves.

Just hours before, Brooks had sat with Nikki in the living room that was now teaming with officers and crime scene investigators. Although they covered their faces with masks, the smell of cooked flesh inundated the air to the point that it was almost impossible to breathe.

Battling the powerful scent, Brooks and Tessa peered into Nikki's bedroom to see a charred human form on the bed. "Oh, dear God in heaven." Brooks ran for the bathroom.

"Can't you guys do something about that smell?" Tessa complained from behind her mask.

Burrowing into his steel-sided briefcase, Stan pulled out a small bottle of peppermint oil and three cotton balls. He doused the clumps of cotton with the potent oil and waved them around the room. The peppermint scent disguised the horrid stench enough to make the air bearable. Under duress, Brooks re-entered the room and stood by Tessa.

She squeezed her hands together as if to pray for the strength she needed to complete the task at hand without turning into a blathering idiot. "OK, Stan. Tell me what you know."

Adjusting his mask, Stan walked over to the body. "We assume that this is Nikki Fox. However, we can't be absolutely sure until we process the dental records. The subject experienced intense heat, originating in the internal organs and working its way to the outer segments of the body. When I say intense heat, I mean an extreme temperature that would be generated by a crematorium. Most of the muscle and skin have been turned to ash. The bones are quite brittle, and the blood was completely destroyed by the fire."

Mitchell Sparks, the crime scene investigator, jumped into the conversation. "The subject was not burned here because the bedsheets have not been damaged. There's no sign of fire anywhere in the condo."

"Are you saying she was virtually cremated somewhere else and transported here?" Tessa asked.

"That's the way it appears, but I don't see how the body could have been moved intact in this state. It's basically been reduced to dust," Mitchell responded. He stared at the corpse with a puzzled expression on his face. "And we have no idea why there is a pair of women's underwear on the body."

Stan swallowed hard. A pair of ivory-colored boy-leg briefs hugged the lower portion of the remains. "The underwear has not been damaged. It had to have been placed on the body after it finished burning, but that seems impossible given the extent of the damage. The legs would have fallen to pieces when someone tried to slip the underwear over them. Maybe we'll get lucky and find some of the killer's DNA when we examine the underwear at the lab."

"Who would do something like this?" Tessa marveled.

"Someone who enjoys the art of killing," Brooks said. "He loves to show off his creativity." In his mind, he pictured Lazarus's lean face, laughing at him, taunting him. He knew that Lazarus placed the underwear on the body, but he didn't dare say anything about it.

"So why don't you go find the killer and arrest him, Detective?" Lieutenant Malone's voice boomed from behind them.

Caught off guard, Tessa spun around. "Oh, Lieutenant, what are you doing here?"

"I'm doing my job, Detective McBride. Is that all right with you? I wasn't aware that I needed your permission to visit a crime scene. Do you have a problem with me being here?"

"No, ma'am."

"Is there any connection between this death and the two cases you are supposedly working on?" Malone placed a mask over her face and took a quick look at the body.

"Yes. Nikki Fox dated Matt Curtis, as did Jill Forcythe and Paige Whitaker," Tessa said.

Malone glanced at Brooks, and then she moved her arctic gaze back to Tessa. "Bring Curtis in for questioning. And I want to be there when you talk to him."

Chapter 31

A hammering headache woke Matt from a restless night's sleep. Every step made it worse, as he plodded downstairs and opened the back door so Joe could answer the call of nature. Matt rummaged through his cabinets to find two Extra-Strength Tylenol caplets, hoping they would ease his pain.

Scratching on the door, Joe signaled that he was ready to come back in. As soon as Matt let him in, he headed for his empty food bowl and did his best impression of a starving dog. Matt poured a mound of dry dog food and filled a matching bowl with fresh water.

Picking up his cordless phone, he dialed a number and paced around his kitchen as he waited for an answer. Then a pleasant female voice said, "Good morning and thank you for calling LightCurve Consulting. This is Kim Taggert."

"Hi, Kim. I'm not coming in this morning," he groaned.

"I see," she chuckled. "Let me guess what happened. You had a hot date last night, and things kinda got out of hand."

"Yeah. You could say that." Matt rubbed his eyes. "I'm going to work at home for a while. I'll be in after lunch."

"OK. I'll call you if I need you. Get some rest, drink lots of fluids, and don't forget to sign in to your instant messenger account so it looks like you're actually working." After many years of experience as Matt's assistant, she had learned that the phrase, "I'm going to work at home for a while," was executive shorthand for, "I feel like a big steaming pile of horseshit, and I'm going to hang out on the couch in front of the TV until I feel better."

Matt smiled. "Thank you, Kim. See ya later." He hung up the phone, opened his refrigerator, and evaluated his options. Although he wasn't hungry, he knew he had to eat. Scrambled eggs and bacon seemed like a good choice because that was the only hot breakfast he knew how to make. He shoveled three heaping scoops of Dunkin' Donuts coffee into his black Krupps coffeemaker and ordered it to percolate in a hurry.

After he packed a plate with six scrambled eggs and four pieces of microwaved bacon, he carried his breakfast into the living room and turned on the Cartoon Network's Boomerang channel. As a deprived farm kid living in a house ruled by his dictatorial father, Matt never experienced the joy of vegetating in front of a block of morning cartoons. Now that he had his own house and his own rules, he could finally watch episodes of *Johnny Quest*,

Space Ghost, Secret Squirrel, and *The Jetsons* that he had missed the first time around.

A knock at his front door interrupted Matt in the middle of his stirring rendition of *The Flintstones* theme song. He turned the channel to ESPN's *SportsCenter* to hide his secret cartoon addiction.

Looking through the small rectangular windows that surrounded his front door, Matt saw Cullen standing on the doorstep. He swung the door open. "I am so glad to see you." He reached out to hug her.

"Don't touch me."

Matt snapped his arms back out of harm's way. "OK, whatever you say. Come on in. I just made some coffee. You want some?"

"No." Cullen sliced Matt into pieces with her eyes. She marched into the kitchen, sat down at a small round table in the breakfast nook, and crossed her legs and arms.

Matt fetched his LightCurve coffee mug from the living room and sat at the table next to Cullen. "How was your shift at work?"

"Fine."

"That's good. I was really worried about you last night." Matt's feeble attempt at compassion went unacknowledged. Unable to think of anything else to say, Matt just drank his coffee while he stared at Cullen over the ridge of his mug.

"Who's the redhead?" Cullen asked without blinking.

Matt choked on his coffee. "What redhead?"

"The one you were in bed with last night. You remember her, don't you? Pretty face, long legs, cute little butt, big implants. Not the kind of woman a man could forget." Cullen tightened her arms, nearly cutting off the circulation to her hands.

Matt's eyes darted around the room, looking for an escape route. *How did she find out about Nikki? Should I tell the truth, or should I lie? The truth will get me into deep trouble. Lying will probably get me into deeper trouble. Oh shit! What am I going to do?* "Cullen, let me explain. See, I wasn't actually with anyone last night."

"Oh, really? Then how do you explain the fact that I saw you in bed with her, and you looked like you were having the time of your life."

"How did you see us?"

Cullen smacked her hand on the table. "That's not important. Who is she?"

Matt tried to get his breathing back to normal before he hyperventilated. "Her name is Nikki Fox. She's an old girlfriend."

"With a name like Nikki Fox, she must be a stripper ... or a hooker."

"No. She's a personal shopper for Neiman Marcus at Tysons Galleria."

"What the hell were you thinking, Matt?" The muscles in her jaws flexed.

"Look, it wasn't my fault."

"Wasn't your fault? What happened? Did you just slip, fall down, and have sex with a slutty redhead? Don't insult my intelligence, Matt. On the night I finally tell you about my rape, you sleep with another woman. How could you do this to me?" A wall of tears streamed down her face.

"Honey, you have to believe me. I didn't do this on purpose and whatever you saw wasn't real. The truth is, last night a man named Lazarus—" The doorbell cut Matt's explanation off before he got to the important part. "I'll be right back. Please give me a chance to tell you the whole story." The doorbell rang again.

Matt rushed through the foyer and saw Brooks Barrington and Tessa McBride waiting outside. He greeted them with an impatient glare. "I'm sorry, Detectives, but I'm very busy. Now is not a good time for me to talk to you."

"Mr. Curtis, if I were you, I'd make time to speak with us. We have some questions concerning your involvement with Nikki Fox," Tessa said.

"What about Nikki?"

"She's dead," Tessa answered with a stone face.

Matt felt numb as he moved aside to let the detectives walk inside. He led them to the plush white couch in his formal living room, and then he sat down on a matching chair positioned directly across the room.

Cullen appeared in the doorway. "Excuse me. Did you say that Nikki Fox is dead?"

Tessa and Brooks stood up to introduce themselves. "I'm Detective Brooks Barrington, and this is my partner, Detective Tessa McBride. You must be Cullen Rhea." He shook Cullen's clammy right hand.

"Yes. I got your message on my voice mail. Sorry I didn't return your call. I've been preoccupied." Cullen shot a piercing glance at Matt. "Why are you here?"

"Ms. Rhea, we believe Nikki Fox was murdered last night," Tessa responded.

"Murdered? Then why are you talking to Matt?" Cullen's voice wavered.

Tessa paused for a few seconds to prepare her explanation. "On the previous two nights, two women were killed, Jill Forcythe and Paige Whitaker. Last night, Ms. Fox met a very unfortunate death." She looked at Matt and then shifted to face Cullen. "Ms. Rhea, you should know that Mr. Curtis dated all three of those women."

Cullen's face turned pale. Sensing an imminent eruption of emotion, Brooks jumped into the conversation. "That's why I called you last night.

Can we talk privately?" He gently placed his hand on her shoulder and tried to lead her into the kitchen.

"No! No! No! This cannot be happening!" Cullen bolted for the front door, sprinted to her car, and tore off down the street.

Matt chased after her, but Tessa caught his arm before he made it to the front door.

"Let me go! I have to catch her. I have to explain all of this to her. Get the hell out of my way!" Matt bellowed.

"I'm sorry, Mr. Curtis, but we can't let you go anywhere. You're involved in a police investigation, and you need to answer our questions."

Ripping his arm from Tessa's grasp, Matt started toward the door. Tessa placed her hand on the 9 mm pistol strapped to her waist and stood in front of him, daring Matt to run. Realizing that Tessa was serious, Matt backed off and sulked back to the living room.

Tessa resumed her interrogation. "Where were you last night?"

"I had dinner with Cullen at Samuel & David's. I came home around ten o'clock."

"Did you go back out?"

"No. I was at home the rest of the night." Matt fidgeted with his hands.

"Were you alone?"

"Yes. I was alone. All night. By myself." He couldn't tell them about his experience with Nikki because they would certainly cart him off to a padded room.

Tessa looked up from her notebook. "Are you sure about that, Mr. Curtis?"

"Yes, ma'am." Matt's fidgeting became more pronounced.

"When was the last time you saw Nikki Fox?"

"Uh … it's been awhile. I can't remember the exact date. We broke up a long time ago."

"And you're certain that you haven't seen her since?"

"No, ma'am. May I ask how Nikki died?"

"She burned to death in a fire," Tessa said. Matt didn't think fast enough to fake a look of surprise. "Do you mind if we look around your house?" she asked.

Matt knew that if he refused to give them permission to search the premises, they would simply obtain a search warrant. In a matter of hours, they would return to wreck his house. In his mind, he replayed the vision of Nikki's smoldering body disappearing into a cloud of smoke and dust, leaving nothing behind except a horrific memory. *Let them look around*, the logical part of his brain rationalized. *They won't find any evidence.* "Help yourself, Detective. I have nothing to hide."

"I'll take the upstairs." Tessa pulled a pair of latex-free gloves out of her coat pocket.

Brooks nodded his head, walked into the kitchen, and ran his fingers along the smooth black granite countertops. Then he assessed the expensive-looking furniture that filled Matt's house. "Did you decorate your home by yourself, Matt?"

"Oh, no. A friend of mine is an interior decorator. She picked out everything for me."

"Was that an old girlfriend, perhaps?"

"Yes, as a matter of fact, she was."

"Tahara Caron?" Brooks wandered into Matt's home office.

"Yes. Good guess."

"I'm a detective. I don't guess."

Tessa's voice burst out of Matt's bedroom. "Brooks? Mr. Curtis? Could you come up here please?"

Matt led the way as Brooks hauled his prosthetic leg up the stairs. When they entered the room, they saw Tessa standing in the right-hand corner of the room next to the closet, holding a piece of clothing.

"What is that?" Brooks asked.

Tessa held up an ivory tank top. "Mr. Curtis, can you explain why you have a woman's shirt in your bedroom?"

Matt processed a series of possible explanations as he remembered Nikki stripping off the shirt, but he couldn't come up with an excuse that was anywhere near believable. "I have no idea how that got here." He felt as if the word "guilty" was tattooed on his forehead.

Tessa walked over to Matt. "This matches the underwear we found on Nikki Fox's body. Mr. Curtis, you need to come with us to the police station. We have more questions for you, and I suggest that you start telling the truth."

"Am I under arrest?" Matt asked.

Tessa paused for a few distressing seconds. "Not yet."

Chapter 32

"Antonio, I'm home," Tahara Caron called. She struggled to pull three overstuffed suitcases through the doorway of her Fairfax Station home. "Honey, can you please come help me with my bags?" No answer.

Her husband's Volvo sat in the driveway, so she assumed he was home. After she waited for a few more minutes, Tahara figured he was at a neighbor's house and hauled the matching set of Briggs & Riley luggage up an angled flight of stairs. As she reached the landing, she gasped for air. Her lungs felt as if they were about to collapse. Fishing an asthma inhaler out of her purse, she squeezed three huge puffs of relief into her lungs.

A four-foot-eleven-inch stick of dynamite, Tahara was born on a poverty-stricken street in metro Manila. She worked throughout her childhood to help support her family. As a young child, she made a pittance by operating a fruit and vegetable stand with her older sister, Marita, in the downtown farmer's market. Her mother, Dasha Zalamia, a native Filipino from the violent island of Mindanao, sat at a sewing machine six days a week in a dirty textile factory and cleaned houses on the seventh day for extra money. Tahara's father, Michel Caron, a French immigrant, served as a lineman for the Manila Electric Company until he was killed on May 20, 1976, Tahara's third birthday. As he was trying to get home to his family, Typhoon Olga trapped him in his Ford Galaxy. He drowned under a crush of floodwater.

Growing up, Tahara fought to survive in the most disaster-prone country on the planet. Typhoons, earthquakes, volcanic eruptions, floods, garbage landslides, and military action against Muslim insurgents were just some of the problems she had to live through. Ferdinand Marcos ruled as a virtual dictator until 1986. Communist and Muslim guerrillas constantly attacked the regime. Many nights, Tahara woke up to the sound of gunfire just outside her window. Marita held her and told her that everything would be all right, but both girls knew the truth. They wished they were somewhere else, anywhere else. By the time she was seventeen, Tahara had endured all of the natural and human disasters she could stand. With the help of their mother, Tahara and Marita fled to the United States without a clue what they would do when they got to the Los Angeles International Airport.

Floundering around Southern California for three months left the young women broke and disillusioned about the American dream. Realizing they needed more than their high school educations to qualify for jobs that didn't involve paper hats and fries, the sisters took the SAT and applied to various colleges in the area. Menial housekeeping jobs at a downtown Marriott kept them alive while they attended school. Marita received a degree in accounting from UCLA's Anderson School of Management. Tahara graduated with honors in interior design from the Fashion Institute of Design and Merchandising, an ironic success for a girl who had slept on an ant-infested cot for the first seventeen years of her life.

Upon graduation, Tahara accepted an entry-level designer's position with Buckingham and Associates, an upscale interior design boutique in McLean. Three thousand miles later, she moved into a two-bedroom, high-rise apartment in Tysons Corner and began a new life as a young professional, barely resembling the little Filipino girl in ratty sneakers and a secondhand dress who sold mangos in Manila.

Female clients loved Tahara because of her exuberant personality and her innate ability to come up with creative ideas. Her boss, Michelle Buckingham, grew to rely on Tahara and trusted her with the most persnickety clients. With an uncanny ease, Tahara captivated her male customers with her exotic dark eyes and rich black hair.

Tahara loved her job and usually worked sixty to seventy hours a week. Given her limited leisure time, she dated clients so she could have a semblance of a social life. Some relationships lasted longer than others, and many of them hinged on the magnitude of the interior design project associated with the respective male client. A few of the men fell in love with her, but when they ran out of cash, she ran out of affection. Love was an expensive upgrade. To Tahara, men were like twenty-five-percent-off sales at Macy's—just wait a few of days and another one would come along.

A couple of years prior, a wealthy Cuban immigration lawyer named Antonio Palmeiro gave Tahara a blank check to decorate his home. Four months later, she moved into Antonio's house. On a three-day weekend trip to Las Vegas, Antonio proposed to her, under an indoor waterfall at Kokomo's Restaurant in the Mirage Hotel. After they finished their tropical fruit desserts, they went to the Rockin' Las Vegas Wedding Chapel and signed up for the deluxe package. The French-Filipino woman and the Cuban giggled through the entire ceremony and were pronounced husband and wife by a bad Elvis impersonator—a shining example of love American style. Much to Tahara's surprise, when she kissed her new husband at the end of their wacky wedding ceremony, she realized that she was deeply in love with Antonio.

Tahara unpacked her suitcases and threw a clump of dirty laundry into the washer. After she finished with her clothes, she began to pick up random pieces of Antonio's wardrobe that were scattered around the bedroom. "How could one man make such a mess in just three days?"

She carried an armload of briefs, socks, and jeans to a clothes hamper in the master bathroom. Then she assembled a pile of button-down shirts, suit pants, and suit jackets for a trip to the dry cleaners. When she lifted a white dress shirt from the foot of the bed, a curious fragrance caught her attention. Holding the shirt up to her nose, she took a deep whiff of a feminine scent: a blend of iris, vanilla, and rose—Shalimar perfume. Tahara's heart screamed in her chest. A raging pulse pounded in her ears. She didn't wear Shalimar.

Chapter 33

"Would you like something to drink? A Coke? Some water?" Tessa offered.

"No thanks. Can we just get this over with? I need to get to work." Matt squirmed on the hard wooden chair. He sat at a large oak conference table, directly across from Brooks.

"Our speed depends on you, Mr. Curtis." Tessa removed her navy blazer and hung it on the back of her chair. She strolled around the table and sat on the edge, close to Matt. "Truth is faster than fiction."

Matt had seen enough episodes of *Law & Order* to recognize that he was dangerously close to a jail cell. He knew that someone was probably watching him from behind the mirror on the far wall, waiting for him to say something stupid or incriminating, or both.

Crossing her arms, Tessa launched into her interview. "Mr. Curtis, can you explain your involvement with Nikki Fox last night?"

Before he responded, Matt paused to contemplate his situation. "I should wait for my lawyer to get here before I answer any questions."

Brooks leaned over the table. "Look here, Hoss, we're not going to try to trick you into confessing or run that moronic good cop–bad cop game they play on TV. We just want the real story. Three women are dead, and they all dated you. Don't you think that's a bit unusual?" Matt nodded his head. "Then tell us what happened last night. We know Nikki was in your bedroom, and I'm pretty sure she wasn't reading you a bedtime story. Come on, son, help us out here."

Matt sucked in a deep breath. "I want to see my lawyer."

Taking a different route, Brooks searched for the truth. "Did something odd, something unexplainable, happen to Nikki last night?"

"What do you mean?" Matt adjusted his position on the rigid chair because the lower portion of his back started to hurt.

"Did anything unnatural occur while you were with Nikki?"

Pictures of the redhead's horrid death spun through Matt's head, like a terrifying film he couldn't stop. He remembered how her eyes looked as they began to melt, how her skin felt as if it were cooking from the inside, how her charred flesh smelled as her body smoldered on his bed. Beads of sweat formed on Matt's forehead and ran down the side of his face. He clasped his hands and braced his feet against the legs of the chair. *Should I tell the truth?*

Why did Detective Barrington ask such an off-the-wall question? Would they actually believe my far-fetched story about Lazarus Kaine? Not a chance. "I want to talk to my attorney."

Tessa walked around the table to Brooks "Can I speak with you outside?" Leading him into the hallway, she closed the door hard behind her. "What kind of questions are you asking him, Brooks?"

"I'm trying to get him to open up to us. You have to admit that Nikki experienced a very unusual death. I believe something extraordinary happened in that guy's bedroom, and he's the only one who can tell us about it."

"Well, I don't think—" Tessa stopped talking when she saw Lieutenant Malone appear around the corner. Malone held a stack of papers in her left hand and a crime scene kit in her right.

"I have the results from the lab. They found male DNA—hair and fluid—on Nikki Fox's underwear. It doesn't match anyone we have on file." She handed the kit to Tessa. "Get a DNA sample from Curtis."

"He's asked to speak with his lawyer. I'm sure we'll need a warrant to obtain a sample."

"Convince him to give it to you voluntarily. Tell him it's in his best interest. Do it before his lawyer gets here."

"I'm sorry. I don't feel comfortable doing that, lieutenant."

"I don't care how you feel, McBride. Do it!" Malone snapped. She turned to Brooks. "Stop asking ridiculous questions, Barrington. You sound like an idiot." She whipped her ponytailed dreadlocks around and marched down the hall.

When the detectives returned to the interrogation room, Tessa placed the crime kit in the middle of the table. "Mr. Curtis, I need to collect a DNA sample from you."

"Why?" Matt asked.

"It's a standard procedure in a murder investigation."

"I didn't murder anyone."

"Then you don't have anything to lose by giving us a sample."

Matt considered the pros and cons of the situation. "I'd better ask my lawyer about it. Let's hold off for right now."

With her back to the observation mirror, Tessa could feel Malone's eyes firing laser beams into the back of her head. She slipped a pair of surgical gloves out of the crime kit. "Mr. Curtis, the more you cooperate, the easier this will be for you. You never know, your DNA may send you home a free man."

While Matt was still preparing his response in his mind, the door opened to reveal a man in a big hurry. "I'm Spencer Ericsson, attorney for Matthew Curtis. The questions end right now." A bow tie-and-suspenders kind of lawyer, Ericsson's personality conquered the room. "Detectives, please excuse me while I speak privately with my client." Reluctantly, Tessa and Brooks left the room.

Malone met them in the hallway. "Dammit, McBride!" she bellowed. "Now we're forced to get a warrant to collect his DNA."

"We don't have enough evidence to justify a warrant. We don't know the time of death or where the hell she died. We're getting way ahead of ourselves." Tessa glared at her boss.

"I can be very persuasive, Detective. Keep him here while I go to the CA's office. Do not let Curtis leave that room!" She stormed away to find the commonwealth's attorney.

For ninety minutes, Tessa paced in the hallway while she and Brooks waited for Malone to arrive. Ericsson met with Matt in the interrogation room, discussing his relationships with Jill, Paige, and Nikki. Matt defended his innocence, but he didn't have the guts to tell his lawyer about Lazarus. Matt figured there was no sense muddling Spencer's mind with a strange story that he couldn't prove.

Malone delivered the warrant to Tessa. "I went through hell to get this. Don't screw it up, McBride."

Tessa entered the interrogation room, threw the warrant in front of Ericsson, and pulled the exam gloves onto her hands. "All right, Mr. Curtis. This won't hurt a bit." She took a long cotton swab out of the crime kit and approached Matt.

Bursting with fear and apprehension, Matt looked at his lawyer. "Do I really have to do this, Spencer?"

The attorney perused the legal document. "Yes, I'm afraid you do, Matt."

With a tender swab of the right side of Matt's mouth, Tessa completed her task, dropped the swab into a thin evidence case, and handed it to Malone.

"I'll take this down to the lab," Malone said. "You two stay right here with Mr. Curtis. I'll be back in a few minutes."

Respecting the attorney-client relationship, Brooks and Tessa again waited in the hallway. They watched through a window in the door as Matt and Spencer mapped out their plan of action.

Forty-five minutes later, Malone returned. She pushed her way past Brooks and Tessa and burst into the interrogation room. "Matthew Curtis, you're under arrest for the murder of Nikki Fox."

"Wait a minute." Ericsson stood up. "It takes at least nine hours to process a DNA sample. You can't take him into custody without any evidence."

"Don't tell me how to do my job, counselor. I will provide you with the DNA evidence at the appropriate time as we move through the legal process.

In other words, you'll see the results when I'm damn good and ready to show them to you." Malone turned toward the door. "Barrington," she called. "Take Mr. Curtis to the processing area."

Brooks avoided eye contact with Malone as he moved across the room. He pulled Matt's hands behind him and placed a pair of handcuffs on his wrists. As he shuffled his prisoner into the hallway, Brooks whispered, "Matt, tell me what really happened to Nikki. I know you didn't kill her, and I can't stand to see an innocent man go to jail, but you need to help me."

Matt turned his body to face Brooks. *Should I tell him about Lazarus? I'm already under arrest. What have I got to lose?* "You have to believe me—"

Stepping between the men, Ericsson cut Matt off. "Don't say another word, Matt." The lawyer escorted his client to the processing area in silence while he kept a watchful eye on Brooks. He monitored every action as the detective handed Matt off to a processing officer and left the area.

Matt looked pitiful as the officer led him away. "Thanks for your help, Spencer. I didn't kill anyone."

"I know, Matt. I'll get you out of here as soon as I can. And I'll talk to Cullen. She should be aware of what's going on." Although Spencer was worried about his client, he was also concerned about how his half-sister was going to take the news that her boyfriend was under arrest for the murder of a former girlfriend.

Chapter 34

After Spencer explained Matt's situation to Cullen in a long phone call, she sat on her couch and stared at nothing while she let the disappointment sink into her body. *This isn't getting me anywhere. I should go to bed and rest. I have to work tonight. Yeah, right. Like I could actually fall sleep through this mess. I'll drive myself nuts if I stay here by myself. I'm going to the mall.* She grabbed her keys and hoped some shopping would distract her for a while.

"Here's your Brownie Batter Blizzard, ma'am. Have a great day!" An ultra-perky teenage girl with a head full of bouncin' and behavin' hair handed Cullen a heaping cup of comfort. Cullen stabbed her spoon into the ice cream and scooped the soothing dessert into her mouth like a drug addict celebrating a score. Although her personal life was spinning out of control, chocolate would always love her.

Cullen parked herself on an empty bench on the second level of Fairfield Mall in front of Lord & Taylor. While she decimated her frozen delight, Cullen watched moms push strollers and herd defiant toddlers through the mall. Would she ever get the chance to be a mother? Considering the events of the day, it didn't seem likely to happen any time in the near future. She wanted to have a child, but her boyfriend's involvement in a murder case and her strong aversion to sex were gigantic obstacles.

Major questions galloped through Cullen's mind. Why did Matt cheat on her? He swore he loved her, and Cullen believed him. Did her resistance to intimacy drive him to Nikki Fox? What about his connections to the three murders? Did he really kill those women? Should she stand by him and help him through this ordeal, or should she let him endure the pain alone? A part of her felt sorry for him. Another part wanted to gouge his eyes out with a fork—that would teach him a lesson. But what if he was innocent? He tried to explain his actions, but the detectives interrupted his account of the events. How could she ever forgive herself for abandoning him at a time when he needed her most? She still loved Matt and prayed to God there was a logical justification for this insanity. While he was tied up with the detectives, there was nothing she could do for him. At this point, Matt's strongest advocate was his lawyer, and Cullen knew Matt was in good hands

After she slurped the last drops of melted ice cream out of the paper bowl, Cullen debated whether to get another Dairy Queen Blizzard or to shop for shoes. Both sounded like viable options, but the shoes got the call. She pitched her trash into a nearby receptacle and headed into Lord & Taylor to look for a pair of red pumps that would take her mind off of the morning's disaster. Twenty-two pairs of shoes auditioned for Cullen. Each pair failed miserably.

An irritated shoe clerk named Justin scrounged around the stockroom and found a lonely pair of size six Anne Klein pumps. Fully expecting to be sent back to the stockroom, he delivered his last resort to Cullen. She slipped on the screaming red pumps with four-inch heels and sexy ankle straps. Originally priced at $249, the shoes were marked down seventy-five percent.

Cullen pranced around the store, amazed that the pumps looked spectacular, even with her old jeans. "Wrap these bad boys up for me, Justin," Cullen beamed. The rush of buying shoes at a huge discount was the closest thing to sex Cullen could experience. Justin processed Cullen's Visa payment and slid the shoe box into a white shopping bag. Cullen bopped out of the store, swinging her purchase and singing out loud to Muzak's version of Bruce Springsteen's "Pink Cadillac."

Strolling through the mall, she passed Cingular Wireless, Stride Rite, and Sephora. The gravity of a Victoria's Secret sale drew her into the store. An enormous picture of supermodel Tyra Banks in a Body by Victoria bra welcomed customers. Cullen couldn't resist picking up a stash of her favorite lotions, Pear Glacé and Vanilla Lace.

As she wandered through the store, an attractive saleswoman approached her. "We have a fantastic collection of thongs on sale today. Would you like to see them?"

"No thanks. I'm not a butt floss kind of girl," Cullen laughed. "Can you ring up these lotions for me?"

"I'd be happy to. These are my favorite scents. My husband, Charles, likes Pear Glacé the best. It always gets his engine started, if you know what I mean," she said with a chuckle. "I'm sure your special man will love it, too."

"Oh, yes, I'm sure he will." Cullen managed a weak smile. For convenience, she placed her lotions into her Lord & Taylor bag and walked toward the exit. An eight-foot poster of Heidi Klum wearing a skimpy black bra-and-panty set thanked her for shopping at the store. Admiring Heidi's perfect stomach, she began to regret the Blizzard she had wolfed down.

Meandering through the lower level of the mall, she breezed by Williams-Sonoma, Bath & Body Works, and Foot Locker. Macy's anchored the east end of the mall. In search of thick, plush bath towels, Cullen rode the escalator to the second floor of the department store. As she walked through the electronics department, she caught a glimpse of herself on a video monitor positioned to capture images of customers as they walked by. She took a quick peak at her hips on the screen and scolded herself again for the Blizzard. Moving out of the screen shot, she glanced at another video monitor that was attached to a different camera. A familiar face filled the television screen. The face belonged to Simon Fletcher.

Cullen spun around to spot Simon. He had to be behind her somewhere, but she couldn't find him. Her pulse quickened. How long had he been following her? What did he want with her? She rushed around the corner of a sixty-inch plasma screen television and ran smack into Simon Fletcher's arms.

"Well, funny running into you, gorgeous. Long time, no see. Did you get the note I left for you at work? I followed you to Matt's house this morning. Then you left in such a hurry. Did he do something to upset you, my dear?" Simon tightened his grip on Cullen's biceps.

"Let go of me," she growled.

"Oh, come on, Cullen. I've been thinking about you a lot over the years. Missing you, wanting you, hating you, making love to you over and over in my mind."

"Get your hands off of me, or I swear to God I'll scream my head off for security." Cullen tried to pull away from his grasp without success.

"Do you actually think a department store security guard will get here in the next five minutes? Don't be silly. We'll be long gone before anyone shows up."

"I'm not going anywhere with you," Cullen yelled. She slammed the heel of her Nike sneaker in the middle of Simon's right foot, causing him to loosen his hold long enough for her to tear herself free. She ran out of the store into the mall as fast as she could, past Waldenbooks and Eddie Bauer. Simon's footsteps pounded behind her, getting closer with every pace. As she ran by Mastercraft Interiors, she felt a strong tug on her Lord & Taylor bag. Simon yanked the bag to the ground and pulled Cullen down with it. He seized the bottom of the bag, while Cullen clutched the thin handles that strained to hold on.

"Let go of my bag, dammit!" she screamed.

"Not until you take a little ride with me, baby."

"I said let go of my bag, asswipe. These are my new shoes, and I got them on sale!" Cullen ripped the bag out of Simon's grasp. She scrambled to her feet and took off through a crowd of people toward the Jean Carlo department store.

"Hey, are you OK?" a generously proportioned man called. But Cullen didn't have time to stop and explain her situation.

Seizing a rare opportunity to see some action, the man blocked Simon's path. "What's your hurry, pal?" The large fellow stuck his hands on his hips to create a wall of fatty flesh.

"This is none of your business, porky. Get outta my way." Simon placed his hands on the man's belly and tried to push him aside.

"Keep runnin,' honey," the man yelled out to Cullen. "I'll keep this jerk occupied for a while."

Without looking back, Cullen ran into the store and wound through racks of dresses, coats, and blouses. Hiding behind a display filled with handbags, she periodically peered out to see if Simon had followed her. Minutes felt like hours.

A voice from behind startled her out of her crouched position. "May I help you, miss? Are you interested in one of our handbags?" a gray-haired saleswoman asked.

Cullen stood up and surveyed the accessory department for Simon. "No, um, I'm fine. Thank you," she said. Four 360-degree turns revealed no sign of her pursuer. She snuck behind a stack of decorative scarves to plan her escape route and keep watch for any sign of Simon.

A voice from two aisles behind her sent Cullen's senses into overdrive. "Excuse me, ma'am. I am looking for my girlfriend. She's about five foot five, straight black hair, perfect teeth, wearing a Dave Matthews T-shirt." Simon's composed voice disgusted Cullen.

"Yes, I've seen her. Lovely girl. She was looking at handbags just a few minutes ago," the saleswoman said, clueless that she had just assisted a rapist.

Simon passed within three feet of Cullen. She held her breath as she squatted close to the floor, praying he would overlook her. Aggravated by his lack of success, Simon stalked away from the accessory department. For twenty minutes, Cullen waited for him to give up the chase. By the time she worked up the nerve to stand up, her knees were throbbing.

Deciding it was time to make a break, Cullen dashed through the store toward the exit. She darted through the doorway into the parking lot, hoping she could get to her Saturn before Simon caught her again. Ripping her car door open, she jumped in the driver's seat, revved the engine, and screeched out of her parking space.

It took four miles of stoplights for Cullen to calm down. Her breathing didn't return to normal until she pulled into her assigned parking space at her townhouse in Elden Glen. But Cullen didn't notice that a beige Ford Focus had followed her out of the mall parking lot. Simon now knew where she lived.

Chapter 35

"Tessa, you need to eat," Brooks reprimanded. "If you don't watch out, you're gonna get too skinny. You need to put a little junk in your trunk. Guys like that. There's nothing less attractive than a flat butt."

"I'm tired. I don't want to eat right now. And I like my trunk just the way it is. We've had a long day. I just want to go home."

Brooks escorted his reluctant partner into the Bulldogger, the closest thing Northern Virginia had to a roadhouse. Famous for its rowdy reputation, the restaurant encouraged overindulgence in drinking and dining. Wide-screen televisions lined the walls, tuned to ESPN and Country Music Television. Decorated with an assorted collection of Dolly Parton's wigs, Alan Jackson's cowboy hats, and gigantic stuffed animal heads, the establishment looked as if it could easily serve as a wealthy redneck's vacation home.

A feisty hostess wearing a pair of form-fitting black pants and a red Bulldogger shirt that was strategically knotted to reveal her tiny midriff greeted the detectives with a grin. "Good evening! My name is Crickett. How many for dinner tonight?"

"Well, hello there, Crickett," Brooks gushed. "Table for two."

The young woman grabbed two menus. "Walk this way."

They followed her through the restaurant as the Big and Rich country hit "Save a Horse, Ride a Cowboy" ripped through the speaker system. Brooks watched Crickett's tight little rear end sway to the driving beat. "If I walked that way, I'd break a hip."

Laughing at Brooks, the woman gestured to an empty booth. "This is your table. Your waitress will be right with you." She strolled back to the front of the restaurant, fully aware that Brooks was savoring every step.

"You're pathetic," Tessa said.

"What are you talking about?"

"Flirting with a woman half your age. You should be ashamed of yourself, Brooks."

"I'm not ashamed at all. I'm attracted to women who are half my age, and I'll flirt with whoever I want to. I make my own choices. You can't tell me what to do. You're not the boss of me."

"You sound like a ten-year-old."

"I do not." Brooks stuck his tongue out at Tessa. "At least I try to meet new people. You act like every man on the Earth has leprosy."

A middle-aged woman, also wearing a Bulldogger shirt, khakis, and a white apron tied around her waist, walked up to the table. "Good evenin.' My name is Mavis, and I'll be your waitress tonight."

Brooks smiled. "Hello, Mavis. Tell me, do I detect a South Carolina accent?"

"Yes, you do. I lived in Charleston all my life—fifty-seven years. My husband, Lawrence, died six months ago. I was so lonely in that big ol' empty house that I decided to move up here to Virginia to be close to my grandbabies." Her face reflected the years she spent sunning herself on the beach near her home. For some reason, she found it necessary to pluck her eyebrows and paint them back on with an eyebrow pencil. Although Brooks had seen this practice before, especially as a kid, he never understood why a woman would do that. He also noticed that Mavis dyed her hair Elvis black and styled it the same way that Loretta Lynn did in the early 1970s. "I like your hairdo, Mavis. It reminds me of home."

"Oh, why thank you! You know what they say ... the higher the hair, the closer to God," she chuckled. "What can I get for y'all to drink tonight?"

"I'll have a Samuel Adams, and bring one for my friend, Tessa. She really needs a beer." Mavis scribbled the request on a tattered notepad.

"I'd like to go ahead and place my order," Tessa announced. "I'm in a hurry."

"Sure thing, honey. What can I get ya?" Mavis obliged.

"I'll just have a small side salad with low-fat ranch dressing. And a glass of water." Tessa's feet patted the floor with impatience.

Frowning at her measly request, Brooks turned to Mavis. "We'll start off with a big plate of chili nachos. Then, I'll have a double cheeseburger with steak fries."

As Mavis headed toward the kitchen, Tessa slumped down in her seat. "I'm so glad we found enough evidence to put Matt Curtis in jail. We might not be able to hang the first two murders on him, but at least he'll be punished for killing Nikki Fox. Thank God we put an end to those murders."

Brooks couldn't look her in the eyes. *Matt Curtis is an innocent man*, he thought. *Lazarus Kaine killed those women*. But Brooks would spend his leisure time in a padded cell, making origami birds, playing solitaire, and watching *The People's Court* if he told anyone about the man made of shadows. Not to mention the fact that his analytical partner would never believe him. A major question gnawed at his mind. Had Lazarus finished his job, or did he plan to kill more people? "Yeah, I hope the killing is over."

"Of course it's over. We caught the bad guy. Let's claim victory and put the past couple of days behind us. It's happy hour on a Friday afternoon. Time to forget work," Tessa said. "Now, where's that beer?"

Emerging from the kitchen with their drinks and nachos on a large tray, Mavis toddled to their table. "Here ya go. I put a little extra cheddar cheese on top, just for you." She placed her hand gently on Brooks's shoulder.

After Mavis left, Tessa's green eyes twinkled. "I think Mavis has the hots for you."

"Oh, I probably remind her of her son."

"Or her dead husband!" Tessa howled.

"Drink your beer, smart-ass."

As Tessa downed the first half of her beer, Brooks noticed that her right hand shook while she held the bottle. "Are you OK?"

"What do you mean?" She quickly jammed her hands in her lap.

"You're shaking, and it's not the first time I've seen that happen. What's going on with you?"

"Nothing. Nothing is wrong with me." She shifted her eyes away from Brooks's inquiring expression.

"Then why are you acting like you're nervous about something?"

"I don't know. Dammit!" She smacked her elbows on the table and rubbed her temples. "I wish I knew why I'm acting so weird. I'm tense and anxious, but I have no idea why I feel this way. I don't think I'm depressed or stressed out, but sometimes I have these panic attacks that I can't stop. Some days it takes hours for me to calm down enough to go to work. Public places like this make me crazy. I don't want to talk to anyone. I feel like I'm about to lose my mind, and I can't explain it. I don't know what to do." Tears streamed over her high cheekbones.

"Have you talked to anyone about this? Like a therapist or a counselor?"

"Oh God, no! They'd probably tell me I'm crazy."

"No they won't. You need to see a professional." Brooks took a pen and a small notepad out of his shirt pocket. He wrote down a name and a phone number and then handed it to Tessa.

"What's this?"

"A referral. This is my therapist, Dr. James Radford. Call him. He can help you."

"You have a therapist?"

"I have a number of personal demons that need a lot of attention. After my wife and daughter died, I wanted to put a bullet through my head. I thought about it every day for months. Every now and then, the impulse still crosses my mind. Dr. Radford keeps me from pulling the trigger."

Chapter 36

"I feel like an animal." Matt Curtis trudged in handcuffs through the Fairfax County Jail complex in front of a husky guard.

"You killed a woman. As far as I'm concerned, you are an animal. Keep walking," the guard ordered. Officer Tom Clayton kept his left hand planted on Matt's shoulder and his other hand on his pistol as he escorted Matt down a flight of stairs.

Within a matter of hours, Matt was transformed from an educated, law-abiding taxpayer into an alleged criminal. The fingerprinting ceremony seemed surreal, as if it were happening to someone else. Without saying a word, a police officer grabbed Matt's fingers and pressed them a bit too firmly onto a fingerprint card and then swiped a cloth over Matt's fingers in a token attempt to remove the ink. During the event, the officer never made eye contact with Matt, refusing to acknowledge his worth as a human being.

The strip search turned out to be as bad as Matt had imagined. Nothing could ever be as dehumanizing as standing naked in front of two policemen while another officer examined every inch of his body. Matt didn't know what they were looking for, and he damn sure wasn't about to ask.

After the ordeal, the men confiscated Matt's wallet and keys. They also took away his belt and shoelaces to keep him from attacking the other prisoners or himself. Now he had to stagger to a holding cell in a pair of sagging pants and wobbly Reeboks, like a real "gangsta."

"I didn't kill those women."

"Of course you didn't. I'm sure you're just caught up in some misunderstanding, and you're actually innocent." Clayton's words were saturated with cynicism.

"Yes! You're absolutely right!" Matt tried to spin around to face the officer.

"Shut up, turn your eyes forward, and keep walking. Everyone in this hellhole says they're innocent, but they're all guilty as sin. The evidence says you're a killer, and now you have to face the consequences. A misunderstanding won't get your ass thrown in jail, but murder will, Mr. Curtis. Your DNA was found on a dead woman. Not only are you guilty; you're stupid."

"How do you know so much about my case?"

"A murder story gets around fast in this place."

Officer Clayton stopped Matt at the door of a holding cell. The policeman unlocked his handcuffs and cautiously opened the door. Three crusty men assessed their new roommate. "Hello, gentlemen. This is Mr. Curtis, and he'll be staying with you for a while." The officer shoved Matt into the room and slammed the heavy metal door behind him.

A large man sitting on an old cot in the far corner of the room winked. "Thank you, officer. We'll take good care of him."

"I'm sure you will, Mr. Trail," Clayton said with a chuckle. Then he backed away with an incredulous smile on his face.

Leaning against a grimy cement wall, Matt tried to hide the fact that he was scared out of his freakin' mind. Like farmers appraising a new steer, his cellmates judged him by his appearance. Two of the men, both dirty and disheveled, declared Matt to be a nonthreat and resumed their conversation on the legal ramifications of drug trafficking.

The third cellmate stood up, a monster of a man who had to be at least six foot seven. Three hundred and seventy-five pounds of masculinity marched across the holding cell to welcome Matt to the community. Wearing a torn shirt memorializing the death of Tupac Shakur, the man cast an enormous shadow over Matt. His scraggly beard had bread crumbs and crusty blobs of peanut butter trapped in it—leftovers from various meals he had inhaled over the past few days. Dental hygiene didn't seem to be a priority for him; however, his gold front tooth somehow had found a way to retain its shine. His six-inch high Afro couldn't quite cover a large scar that lay across his forehead.

"What's your first name, Mr. Curtis?" the giant asked.

"Matthew. But you can call me Matt."

"I'll call you anything I want to call you, Matthew," the man rumbled. "Those two losers over there in the corner are Skillet and Ray Ray. They're junkies. Just stay away from them, and they won't hurt you."

"OK. Thanks for the advice, Mr. Trail." Matt's voice cracked.

"You don't look like you belong here, Matthew. What did you do? Insider trading? Embezzlement? Shoplifting?"

"Murder."

The giant burst into laughter so loud that it shook the bars of the cell. "Murder? You? I don't believe it. A white boy like you couldn't kill nobody."

"Well, you're the only person around here with that opinion."

Trail lumbered to his cot and waved for Matt to join him. Visions of bad prison movies made him sweat. *Oh, dear God*! He had been in jail for only ten minutes, and he was already well on his way to becoming somebody's girlfriend. Matt sat on the end of the cot as far away from the colossal man as possible.

The giant scooted closer to Matt. "Where are my manners? I should formally introduce myself." Sticking out his hand, which was as big as a catcher's mitt, the man said, "My name is Bunny Trail."

A gigglesnort blew out of Matt's nose before he could stop it. "Did you say your name is Bunny ... Trail?" He fought back a huge laugh that would lead to certain death—or worse.

"Yep. Bunny Trail is my given name. My daddy thought that having an unusual name would make me tough. When people made fun of me, I had to defend myself. His theory must have worked, because I turned out to be a mean son of a bitch. He's dead now."

"I'm sorry. How did he die?"

"I was eating a bowl of Trix cereal for breakfast this morning. He started making a whole bunch of Bunny jokes, so I busted his head with a shovel."

Matt nodded his head and chose his reply carefully. "He had it coming."

Bunny threw his meaty right arm around Matt's shoulders. "I like you, Matthew. You're gonna be my little buddy. We'll be just like the Skipper and Gilligan."

Matt forced a crooked smile, silently hoping that the Skipper would leave Gilligan alone in the middle of the night.

Chapter 37

"Hello, Ms. Caron. This is Detective Brooks Barrington with the Fairfax County Police Department. Could you please call me at 703-555-6529 as soon as you get this message? I need to speak with you immediately. Thank you."

Tahara saved the voice mail message and snapped her cell phone shut. "Wonder what he wants? I'll call him first thing Monday morning." Right now, she was focused on the Shalimar perfume she detected on her husband's shirt. Her imagination came up with a multitude of explanations for the feminine scent. All of them made her angry.

After picking at a sparse plate of tortellini that technically qualified as her dinner, Tahara decided to take a shower in a futile effort to wash the Shalimar and its implications away. As she took off her clothes, she evaluated her shape in a full-length mirror on her master bathroom wall. Yeah, she was short. Couldn't do anything about that. Pilates and running every day kept her legs in pretty good shape. Although her backside had a sprinkling of cellulite in a few places, it could still be considered a cute butt. Her stomach was fairly flat, but it wasn't a defined six-pack. For what seemed like the forty-gazillionth time, she weighed the pros and cons of surgically increasing her A cups into C cups. Lots of her friends had implants, but a big set of headlights would probably make petite Tahara look like a *Playboy* cartoon. Ugh! Why was she doing this to herself? Self-depreciation never made anyone feel better about anything. But the right pair of breasts could make her look great in a bikini. Arrrrgh! *Stop it, stop it, stop it. You're making yourself nuts.*

Many men still seemed to be attracted to her, so she raised the emotional flag of victory over her physical imperfections and got the heck away from the stupid mirror.

She looked up through the three skylight windows that watched over the master bathroom. It was about 11:00 PM, and she could see the moon peeking through the skylights. Tahara turned off all of the bathroom lights, cranked the hot water up to full power, and stepped into the shower. She loved to stand in the moonlight and let the warm water pound the worry out of her body.

As she conditioned her hair, Tahara heard a distant voice call her name. *Maybe Antonio has finally come home. Should I confront him about the*

Shalimar? How would he react? Would he admit to an affair, or would he deny any sort of infidelity? Oh, God, would he leave me for another woman?

The voice called her name again, but it didn't sound like Antonio. She had never heard the peculiar male voice before. Certainly the doors were locked and the security system enabled, right? Maybe it was someone leaving a message on the answering machine. As she rinsed a thick lather of rose exfoliating body scrub off her shoulders, she heard the voice again. This time it sounded much closer, as if it came from her bedroom.

Grabbing a towel from a nearby rack, she quickly dried off and slipped into a heavy purple velvet bathrobe. She turned on the bathroom lights and eased the door open, unsure of whom she would see. Moonlight danced with darkness to form three shadowy faces moving gracefully over her bed. The faces churned around the room, tore across the walls, and came to rest in a wingback chair in the corner of the room. In an abrupt wave of change, the shadow faces altered their appearance and composition to form a man dressed in a solid black, double-breasted suit with a white French-cuffed shirt and a burgundy tie.

"Hello, Tahara. My name is Lazarus Kaine. We need to talk," the man said in a low menacing tone.

Tahara clutched her robe together at the neck. Paralyzed by fear, she didn't know what to do or say, so she just stood perfectly still.

"Oh, there's no need to be modest, my dear. I've already seen you naked. I especially liked the way your shoulders glistened in your moonlit shower. Very sexy."

"Get out of my house!" Tahara ran back into the bathroom and slammed the door behind her. She leaned against the door, gasping for breath. Her asthma inhaler was on her nightstand on the other side of the door. She would have to survive without it.

Without warning, every lightbulb in the bathroom burst, leaving Tahara alone in the dark. Did she have a flashlight in the bathroom? No. Phone? No. Did she have anything that could be used as a weapon? Not really. A cold curling iron wouldn't do much damage.

As she stood with her back against the doorway, two shadows on the opposite wall started to move. The shapes shifted into hulks that looked like animals—large indistinguishable beasts. Within seconds, the shadows transformed into two brawny rottweilers growling with fury. Two hundred and fifty pounds of pissed-off canine snarled at Tahara. Their disgusting hot breath filled the room. Poised for battle, the dogs crouched just inches away from Tahara. As if they were given a strict command to attack, the dogs lurched at her, biting at her legs and jumping at her face. Afraid for her life, she opened the door, squeezed into the bedroom, and struggled to pin the dogs inside the bathroom. As soon as the door latched shut, the dogs went silent.

"Welcome back, Tahara. I missed you," Lazarus said.

Wheezing and bleeding from a deep bite on her left calf, Tahara darted for her bedroom door. She almost made it, but two shadow faces slammed the door shut just as she reached the door frame. "Please don't hurt me. Take my money, my jewelry—take it all. Just tell me what you want, and I'll give it to you. But please, don't hurt me."

"I want to talk about your relationship with Matt Curtis."

"Who?"

Chapter 38

"Hi, Cullen. How was your day?" A wide-eyed medical student gaped at her.

In her head, Cullen answered the question. *Well, let's see. My boyfriend cheated on me, and then he was arrested for murder. Later, I was chased through Fairfield Mall by a lunatic who wants to kill me. That's how my day went, you soft-skulled little hobbit.* Out loud, she answered, "It was just fine, Marcus. Why don't you go find a delivery to observe? Maybe you'll learn something." The youthful doctor-in-training smiled at her and trundled off to find an active birthing room.

Standing at a large circular desk, Cullen prepared a medical chart for a patient who was on her way to the hospital. Down the hall, Cullen could see Lisha giggling as she held the hand of a dark-haired man dressed in a pair of scrubs.

"Cullen, I want you to meet Dr. Jonathan Handley," Lisha surged. "Jon is on call, but he made time in his busy schedule tonight to come and see me. Isn't he sweet?"

"It's nice to meet you, Jon." She looked at Lisha as if to request an explanation.

"We've been seeing each other for a couple of weeks." Lisha hugged the man's arm.

"Oh, really?" Cullen turned her attention to the new suitor. "So, Jon, what do you do here at our fine hospital?"

From twenty feet away, an annoying nasal accent brought their conversation to a screeching halt. "Cullen, why didn't you give Mrs. Goldstein the morphine I prescribed for her pain?" Dr. Nazar DerBedrosian barreled toward Cullen like a charging bull. "You deliberately ignored my orders. This is unacceptable behavior. How do you explain your actions?"

Towering over the squatty man, Cullen leaned down into his face. "Mrs. Goldstein is allergic to morphine. You would have known that if you had read her chart. Because you were unavailable, outside sucking on a cigarette like a moron, I found your partner, Dr. Lindross, and he prescribed Entonox for her. Now Mrs. Goldstein feels much better, no thanks to you." Cullen turned away from the dumpy doctor and tried to resume her conversation with Lisha and her new beau. "I'm sorry, Jon. What did you say you did for a living?"

"I'm a rectal surgeon. I work with assholes all day." He chuckled at the cliché quoted by proctologists around the world.

Cullen cut her eyes at Dr. DerBedrosian. "Yeah, so do I."

Nazar huffed, wheeled his extended gut around, and traipsed off in a full-fledged Armenian snit.

"It was a pleasure to meet you." Cullen shook Jon's hand. She stole a quick look at her watch. "I gotta run. Lisha, you and I will talk later."

As Cullen walked along the corridor, she heard a door open behind her. A person fell in step behind her, keeping close to her quick pace. She glanced into the nursery as she turned a corner, ignoring the footsteps that continued to follow her. A young male orderly pushing a new mom in a wheelchair suddenly spun out of a semiprivate room and cut in front of Cullen, causing her to stop short. The person following her bumped into her back, nearly knocking her down.

"Oops, I'm sorry," Cullen apologized.

"No problem. It was good for me," a man's voice answered.

Cullen whipped her dark ponytail around to see Simon's face sporting a wicked grin. He grabbed for her arm, caught the sleeve of her purple scrub jacket, and tried to pull her toward him. Ripping her sleeve from his grasp, she yelled to the orderly, "Call security! This man is trying to attack me!" Then she took off with Simon chasing closely behind.

"I'm going to kill you, bitch."

Cullen flew past the nurses' desk in a dead run. "Lisha! Call security! Simon Fletcher is after me."

As Lisha picked up the phone, she saw Simon sprinting down the hall. She ducked down so he wouldn't see her. Then she crawled around to the edge of the nurses' desk. When she heard his footsteps approach, she stuck her foot out and tripped him, causing him to fall headfirst into the side rails of a stretcher that was parked against the wall. "Shit!" Blood poured out of a two-inch gash on the left side of his forehead. He wiped the river of blood out of his eye with his left hand and continued his chase.

Cullen dashed to the elevator bay and pushed the down button. Too scared to wait for the next elevator, she bolted through an exit door and hurried into the staircase. She tripped two times, but she somehow maintained her balance as she rushed down five flights of stairs. Cullen thumped into the staircase door and darted through the lobby toward the automatic doors at the exit. A jolt of physical energy knocked her into a chair in the reception area. Simon wrapped his arms around Cullen's legs like an NFL linebacker finishing a tackle. He rolled on top of her, pinning her to the ground.

"Let me go! Help! Someone help me!" She punched Simon in the face with every pound of force she could muster. An elderly couple that had just entered the lobby stood with shock on their faces as they watched Cullen fight with Simon. Shrieking in panic, a woman in a wheelchair veered herself out of harm's way.

A quick knee to Simon's groin disabled him long enough for Cullen to get to her feet, but he caught her from behind before she could get out the door. "Shut up and come with me." Simon smacked his bloody left hand over her mouth. He carried the struggling woman for a few feet but then lost his grip on Cullen's waist. She stumbled and fell to the floor, taking Simon down with her.

Without looking back, Cullen got up, lurched through the automatic doors, and sprinted across the street to the parking garage. Avoiding the enclosed spaces of the stairs and elevators, she ran between parked cars, puffed her way up a ramp, and turned a corner to finally reach her Saturn. She stuffed her right hand into her coat pocket. "Crap." Her car keys were stashed in her purse in her locker on the fifth floor of the hospital.

Hiding behind her car, Cullen heard security guards swarm through the parking garage. Their voices overlapped each other in a series of requests and commands as they searched the hospital property.

When a couple of voices came close to her, she crept from behind her car, snuck through the parking garage, and edged up to two security guards who were walking toward the exit.

Cullen approached a man who seemed to be in charge. "Where is he? Where is Simon Fletcher?"

"Who are you?" the guard grumbled.

"I'm Cullen Rhea, the woman that he just chased through the hospital. He wants to kill me. You did catch him, didn't you?"

The guard noticed the blood splattered across Cullen's purple scrub jacket. "I'm sorry, Ms. Rhea. He ran into the woods on the other side of the street. We lost him."

Chapter 39

"Matt Curtis was a client who fell in love with you and thought that you felt the same way about him," Lazarus explained to Tahara.

She stared at the intruder. *Who is this guy? How does he know anything about me?* She hesitated before she spoke to the unwelcome stranger. "Does he live in McLean? Impala black granite countertops in the kitchen? Crossville porcelain tile in the kitchen and bathrooms? Cream-colored window treatments?"

"That's the one."

Tahara arranged her robe to cover her thighs as she sat on the floor, as far away from the eccentric trespasser as she could get. "Yeah. I remember him. That was a bad situation."

Lazarus crossed his legs as he sat in the wingback chair. "Tell me about it." He sounded like a psychiatrist conducting a therapy session.

She took her time to respond. Although she was still scared, she decided to offer some information to appease the man. "Matt bought a house that had no style at all—a four-thousand-square-foot snoozer. It had dreary beige carpet in the living room and builder's linoleum on the kitchen and bathroom floors. The formal living room was decorated with hideous flowered wallpaper with colors that don't exist on this planet. Oh my God! It was awful. We had to rip out everything."

"You spent quite a bit of time with Matt while working on the house, and eventually you became intimate."

"Yes. We dated for a while, and he fell in love with me. It happens."

"But you didn't fall in love with him?"

"He was nice enough, and I liked being with him. But when the project came to an end, our relationship got kind of, you know, boring."

"By boring, you mean, Matt stopped spending money."

"Yes."

"So, what happened?"

"I sold a huge home makeover project to Antonio. The man had cash falling out of his pockets. He let me buy the most expensive furniture, window treatments, slate floors, and artwork I could find. It was a very exciting time."

"And you had an affair with Antonio while you were supposedly dating Matt exclusively?"

"Well, I suppose you could call it an affair, but as far as I was concerned, Matt and I were finished. Antonio had the Latin lover thing going for him. I just couldn't resist."

"And I guess you were also attracted to his money?"

"Of course! I'm not an idiot." Tahara threw her hands up at Lazarus.

"How did Matt react when he found out about your affair?"

"He sounded pretty upset on the phone."

"Did you ever see him again, in person, to provide the poor man with some closure?"

"No. I was too busy with Antonio's project." Keeping her eyes locked on the willowy man, she edged over to her nightstand, grabbed her asthma inhaler, and squeezed three large puffs of respiratory assistance into her lungs. Then she sat on the edge of her bed, hoping she would soon find a way out of the room.

Lazarus pushed himself out of the chair and walked toward Tahara. "Do you know where Antonio is right now?" Lazarus stood at the foot of her bed.

"No, I don't."

"Would it surprise you to hear that he's next door—with Janessa Cole?"

"Janessa is our friend. We spend a lot of time with her."

"I'm sure you do. Janessa is an attractive woman, don't you think? Long legs. Curvy. Quite the opposite of you. And did you ever notice that she wears Shalimar perfume?"

A bitter chill froze every nerve ending in Tahara's body. "Janessa is my friend. I would trust her with my life."

"But would you trust her with your husband?"

Tahara recalled the many occasions when Janessa playfully massaged Antonio's shoulders and gave him hugs that lasted a bit too long. And she had lost count of the times she caught him staring at Janessa's body. "Why should I believe you? How do you know where my husband is? And who the hell are you, anyway?"

Lazarus walked over to an antique oak rolltop desk that Tahara had purchased as a gift for Antonio to celebrate their first anniversary. The mysterious visitor waved his hand in front of a locked drawer on the lower right-hand side of the desk. With smooth precision, the locking mechanism shifted into the open position. He slid the drawer out with slow anticipation as if it contained a valuable treasure.

"Let's just say that I am the bearer of bad news." He reached into the drawer and retrieved a leather journal. Without opening the book, he handed it to Tahara. "You can be the judge of Antonio's actions. Go ahead. Read it."

Tahara's hands shuddered as she opened the journal titled, "Personal Diary of Antonio Palmeiro." Tears fell on the pages and smeared the ink as she read explicit descriptions of Antonio's three most recent relationships.

His first affair was with Maria Fernández García, a partner in his law firm. Antonio wrote about numerous "business trips" that he and Maria would orchestrate. They would spend three or four days together in a Ritz-Carlton hotel in Atlanta, rarely venturing out of their favorite room on the concierge level.

The second affair involved a woman named Yeni de Villavicencio. He met her on the Internet in the Amigar, a popular Hispanic chat room. As if they were destined to find each other, Antonio and the woman discovered that they had grown up in the same area of Cienfuegos, a historic city, located on the southern coast of the central region of Cuba. Both of them escaped Castro's regime as teenagers and found refuge with family members in Miami. With so much in common, the Cubans quickly fell into an intimate relationship, often meeting for afternoon dates at Yeni's apartment.

Details about his current affair with Janessa Cole filled the final third of the memoir. He explained how he had become addicted to the rush of maintaining a romantic relationship with someone who was so close to his wife. The story read like a Harlequin romance. It contained tales of secret sexual encounters and exciting adventures when they were almost caught in the act by Janessa's husband, Braden, an Air Force Colonel who worked at the Pentagon. Many nights, when Tahara worked long hours with her clients, Antonio and Janessa would eat take-out food from a local Chinese restaurant and then retire to his elegantly decorated master bedroom for hours of passion. In the diary, Antonio explored his feelings of fondness for Janessa, how he loved to kiss her softly on the back of her neck, and how she drove him insane with her exquisite dancer's legs. But the most striking aspect of his written confession wasn't the physical component of their relationship; it was the emotional connection Antonio shared with Janessa, a bond that he had never felt with Tahara.

The tiny Filipino woman broke down into a sobbing bundle of despair. "Why did Antonio feel the need to have these affairs? What's wrong with me? I love him, and he's supposed to love me." She bawled into a pillow.

"Infidelity is most painful when it makes a complete circle. You cheated on Matt. Antonio cheated on you. This cycle of betrayal started and ended with you, Tahara."

The ache of Antonio's disloyalty mingled with the guilt she now felt about her own unfaithfulness to Matt. Tahara huddled on the bed, a blameworthy remnant of the confident woman she used to be.

"Would you like me to put an end to your misery, Tahara?" Lazarus moved closer to her.

"Yes! Please, make it stop!" she wailed.

"As you wish."

Relaxing for the first time since she discovered Lazarus in her bedroom, Tahara stopped trembling. Then her hands began to explore her body, but she wasn't in control of them. They didn't even feel like her own fingers touching her skin. She couldn't feel her arms, as if she were paralyzed, but they moved independently with a purpose. Without permission, her hands opened her robe and tenderly stroked her stomach and chest, working their way up to her shoulders and neck. When they reached the sides of her throat, Tahara's hands paused, as if they were waiting for their next set of instructions.

"Good-bye, Tahara," Lazarus whispered. With the power of an industrial-strength vice, Tahara's hands squeezed her throat. She tried to scream, but her hands crushed her windpipe. Her lungs throbbed as she gasped for air. The lack of oxygen made Tahara's body quake with violent convulsions. The skin on her face turned shades of blue, purple, and then pale gray. After a few moments, her legs stopped flinching and her torso came to rest. With their mission now complete, Tahara's hands released their death grip.

Lazarus admired his handiwork, enjoying the view of Tahara's motionless corpse on the bed. "I love my job." The personification of fear vanished into the night.

Chapter 40

The cement felt cold against the back of Matt's shoulders. Leaning against the wall, he sat on one end of the decaying cot where Bunny had told him to sit. On the other end of the cot, the giant man snored like a chainsaw. Across the room, Skillet and Ray Ray slept next to each other for warmth and protection from Bunny.

A new arrival, DeShawn, lay passed out in front of a filthy toilet where he had deposited the undigested portions of a forty-ounce bottle of Schlitz Malt Liquor, a bag of Utz Cheese Curls, and two Chalupa Supremes from Taco Bell. Thrown in jail for driving under the influence of alcohol, DeShawn also should have been sentenced for talking under the influence of stupidity because of his penchant for making fun of Bunny. After DeShawn's third moronic comment about the large man's first name, Bunny buried his massive right fist in DeShawn's gut, which caused him to toss his chalupas. Luckily for DeShawn, he passed out before Bunny had time to kill him.

Matt spent the night keeping his mouth shut and staying out of Bunny's way. He just wanted to make it to morning without getting his brains beaten in or becoming the object of another man's affection. After being locked behind a set of green metal bars for seven hours, Mother Nature kicked in. Matt had to poop. The last thing he wanted to do was make a lot of noise and wake up the four degenerates around him. And he sure as hell didn't want to get caught with his pants around his ankles. So, he decided to hold it.

After a few arduous minutes, the poop pains went away. *OK. I'm fine. I just need to relax.* Then Matt's lower abdomen felt as if someone were stabbing him with a hunting knife. Cold sweat ran down the sides of his face. Oh no. This was gonna be bad. Should he go in his pants like a toddler? Or should he take his chances and use the toilet? Time was quickly running out. He had to make the call.

Easing off the cot, Matt tiptoed around Bunny's gigantic black Converse All-Stars. He carefully avoided DeShawn's arms, which laid in front of the toilet, bowing to the porcelain throne. Lowering his pants just enough to accomplish his mission, he sat down on the cracked seat. *Please don't make any noise*, he pleaded to his colon. An errant burst of gas exploded into the bowl like a shotgun blast. *That's it. I'm a dead man. Killed in jail over a fart.* He closed his eyes and waited for the pounding to begin, but nothing happened. Bunny kept snoring. Skillet and Ray Ray remained motionless.

Matt hurried to finish his task. But now another critical question presented itself. Should he flush? The noise would certainly wake his roommates, but the smell was already way past rank, and it would get much worse as time went by.

There was only one thing he could do. He pulled up his pants and snuck back to his assigned position on the cot. Yes, it would be difficult to deal with the smell for a while, but he would have to gut it out. If someone, namely Bunny, woke up and complained about the odor, Matt would place the blame on DeShawn. Hey, the guy was plastered out of his mind, and there was no way he would be able to remember whether or not he had gone to the bathroom. Of course, there was a strong probability that Bunny would beat the hell out of DeShawn, but that was a consequence Matt was willing to accept.

Closing his eyes, Matt pretended to sleep. A few minutes later, a set of footsteps caught his attention as they clicked toward the metal bars that fenced in his freedom. The clock at the end of the corridor read 2:22 AM. As the footsteps approached, the grim fluorescent light from the walkway mixed with the darkness and formed a small group of shadow faces that oozed and swayed, announcing another arrival of Lazarus.

"Hello, Matt." The man stood at the door of Matt's cell wearing a navy, three-button pin-striped suit, a light blue twill dress shirt, and a dark blue striped tie.

"Shhhh! Shut up. You're gonna get me killed," Matt whispered. He moved from the cot to the metal bars that separated him from Lazarus.

"Oh, don't worry about your roomies, Matt. A nuclear explosion couldn't wake them up." Phasing from flesh to a blurry cloud of drifting darkness, he passed through the bars into the cell. Then he returned to his thin human form. "So, are you enjoying your stay in this fine, taxpayer-supported facility? Having the time of your life, I bet." He wrinkled his nose. "What is that awful stench? It smells like shit in here."

"Five guys in a small room. One toilet. You do the math." Matt tried to suppress his gag reflex. "I hope you're happy now, Lazarus. I'm taking the blame for your murders. Is this what you want? To see me suffer in prison?"

"Yes. It's quite amusing. I've especially enjoyed watching your budding relationship with Bunny. I'm sure the two of you will be very happy together."

"We'll send you a wedding invitation. Now, get out of here and leave me alone." Matt turned away from Lazarus.

"I'm not even close to being through with you, Matt. There is still much work for me to do."

Matt spun around. "Haven't you done enough?"

Lazarus leaned back against the metal bars. "Let's summarize. So far, I have killed four of your former girlfriends—"

"Four? I thought it was three—Jill, Paige, and Nikki."

"Yes, four. Tonight I conducted a very interesting therapy session with Tahara Caron. My insightful observations about her proclivity for infidelity left her breathless."

"Why are you doing all of this, Lazarus?"

"It's really quite simple. You see, the most effective way to torture someone is to mutilate, disfigure, and kill people whom the subject feels affection toward. Because all members of your immediate family have been dead for quite a while, the next logical group to assault would be the women whom you have loved. It's a strategy that has been used for hundreds of years by dictators, tyrants, and terrorists. Organized crime families have turned this tactic into an art form. Did you ever watch *The Sopranos*? Those guys perfected the method. And that Tony Soprano cracked me up."

"You've had your fun with me. It's time for this to end." Matt peered into Lazarus's lifeless black eyes.

"I beg to differ, Matt. You're going to be prosecuted for the vicious murder of Nikki Fox. Your fear of failure will be fully realized when you're sentenced to twenty-five years in prison without parole. Your fear of the loss of loved ones will come to fruition within the next twenty-four hours when I complete my last homicide. Then you'll experience the worst fear imaginable—you'll be alone."

"I won't let you kill Cullen, you son of a bitch." Matt grabbed for Lazarus's neck but his hands passed through the man made of shadows.

"I'm not going to kill Cullen." Lazarus didn't acknowledge the physical advance. "Someone else is already planning that blessed event."

"Who is it? Tell me, dammit!" Matt's body tensed.

"You're a smart man. You figure it out."

Matt's brain hummed like an IBM mainframe. Who would want to hurt Cullen? Who could possibly have something against her? Only one person came to mind. "Simon Fletcher."

"Good answer, Matt." Lazarus gave him an acerbic congratulatory nod. "Too bad there's nothing you can do to stop him. Remember, you're in jail."

"I'll find a way. But if you're not planning to kill Cullen, who are you going after? You've killed all of my other girlfriends. There's no one left."

Lazarus broke into a sly grin. "Oh, yes there is. Guess who?" Then he converted back into his shadowy state of existence and disappeared.

Chapter 41

How am I going to get back to my car? Simon crouched under a group of thick bushes as he hid in the woods across the street from the hospital. For thirty minutes, he maintained his concealed position while a slew of guards passed within a few feet of him. Unable to locate him, they admitted defeat and moped back across the street to report their failure.

Calculating his next move, Simon watched the security force flock around the entrance to the hospital from which he had narrowly escaped. Three men fortified the gated entrance to the parking garage where Simon had lost sight of his prey.

For a second time, she had slipped out of his grasp. Mother would be so disappointed. Simon had given his word to her that he would kill the woman who had turned his precious mother into an invalid and had sent him to prison. But all he had to show for his efforts, so far, was a nasty two-inch gash on his forehead and a yellow button-down shirt spotted with his own blood. He swore he wouldn't let his mother down the next time he got his hands on that bitch.

It was time to get out of the woods. By now, he assumed the security guards had called the real cops, who would probably bring out their K-9 corps to sniff around. Keeping a close watch on the activities across the street, Simon crept between the trees. The darkness of 4:00 AM on a cloudy morning made it difficult for him to plot a course out of the thick underbrush. Feeling his way through three hundred yards of briars, bushes, and brambles, he reached the intersection of Fellows Road and Arlington Boulevard. He waited for two cars to pass before he sprinted across the road.

A twenty-four-hour drug store stood at the opposite end of the intersection, which seemed like a good place for him to get cleaned up. As he rushed through the empty parking lot, Simon turned his head around in every direction, wary of an errant police officer. Covering his face with his left hand to hide his identity from the video camera that watched over the front door, he passed through the automatic doors and picked up a small green shopping basket with a plastic handle. Avoiding two young men who were stocking shelves with cans of shaving cream and sticks of deodorant, he hurried to the back of the store and found a small bathroom located next to the pharmacy.

"Shit! That hurts." He dabbed the wound on his forehead with a wet paper towel. The bleeding had stopped, but splotches of blood had dried on his face and neck. He looked as if he had been in a car accident. It took six brown paper towels to make his face look presentable.

Footsteps tapped outside the bathroom door. Jumping into the single stall, he closed the steel latch and held his breath as the footsteps continued into the room. His heartbeat pounded in his ears as the footsteps clicked to the single urinal. A sigh of relief filled the room as the man completed his business. Simon closed his eyes as he waited for the man to wash his hands, which seemed to take an eternity. The automatic hand dryer clicked on for a few seconds, and then the footsteps left the room.

Hurrying out of the stall, Simon took off his shirt and ran cold water over the blood stains. His internal clock told him to get going before someone else walked in on him. He slipped his partially wet shirt back on and strolled back into the store. In a middle aisle, he saw a display of Washington Redskins merchandise. He selected a cap and a Joe Theismann throwback jersey with the number seven on it. *I hate the Redskins, but these will have to do.*

He took a quick trip down the medical aisle to pick up a tube of Neosporin. Realizing his stomach was empty, he collected a package of cheese crackers, a box of fruit bars, and two Cokes. Figuring that he could be on the run for a while, he grabbed a black backpack that he could use to carry his necessities.

I need to find something that I can use as a weapon. He walked casually through the store. After a few minutes of deliberation in the household aisle, he found a silver utility knife with a retractable carbon blade. Less than five inches long and lightweight, the knife could slice through a hunk of flesh with minimal effort.

Keeping his head low, and away from the security cameras, Simon approached the checkout area. Only one register was open and was manned by a short brown fellow with "Sanjay" written on his name tag. Simon dumped his items on the counter and added eight large Milky Way bars from the impulse section. He pretended to scratch his forehead to cover his face and his head injury.

"How are you doing tonight, sir?" Sanjay asked with a heavy Indian accent.

"Just fine, thank you."

"You must be a big fan of the Washington Redskins, as am I. Last year, I went to a game at FedExField. My brother, Vijay, got us two tickets from a scalper. It cost a great deal of money, but it was so exciting. They lost to the Philadelphia Eagles, but I did not even care. Vijay kept hogging the binoculars and looking at the cheerleaders. Have you seen those cheerleaders in their skimpy outfits? Oh my goodness, when I saw them, I almost forgot about the game. Women do not dress like that in Mumbai. Maybe this year, the Redskins will go all the way to the Super Bowl. I cannot wait for the football season to begin!" The clerk flashed a yellow-toothed grin.

Nodding to be polite, Simon answered, "Yeah, me too. Look, I'm sort of in a hurry here."

"Oh, yes, it is very late or very early, depending on your perspective." Sanjay calculated Simon's total dollar amount. "That will be $71.09."

Simon dug into his wallet. "Damn. I only have $68." He didn't want to use a credit card because the police would certainly be monitoring his transactions.

Stuffing the merchandise into two plastic bags, Sanjay winked at Simon. "Don't worry about it," he said in a whisper. "Redskins fans have to help one another."

Picking up the bags, Simon patted him on the shoulder. "You da man, Sanjay." He pulled the cap low over his forehead to cover the gash.

"Oh yes, yes. I am the man. Have a nice day. Go Redskins!" Sanjay waved to his new friend, whom he would never see again.

As the automated door closed behind him, Simon snuck around the corner into an alley separating the drug store from a gas station. Hoping he was out of the view of any security cameras, he stripped off his blood-stained shirt and pulled the jersey over his head. He stashed his shirt under a stack of newspapers in a trash can and rubbed a glob of Neosporin on his injury. After quickly shoving his purchases into his new backpack, he opened one of the Milky Ways and took a big bite of chocolate, caramel, and nougat. Feeling like a new man, Simon ambled down the sidewalk, chewing his snack and proudly displaying his football-themed disguise.

Now, I've got to get to my car so I can get the hell away from the hospital. But how? I can't just walk past a bunch of guards, and I don't have any money for a cab. Just then, a Fairfax Memorial Hospital shuttle bus drove by with "Employee Satellite Parking" written on the side in large blue letters. He jogged after the bus. It turned left on Hollow Lane Corporate Drive, and then it drove through a spacious parking area sparsely populated with cars. Trying to stride with a relaxed gait, Simon entered the lot and found a sign marked "Hospital Shuttle Pickup Area."

Fifteen minutes passed as Simon sat alone on a hard wooden bench, waiting for another shuttle to arrive. Finally, a green bus chugged up to the stop and opened its doors.

"Where's your employee badge?" the driver grunted.

"Oh, man, I must have left it at home on my dresser. I just got called in for an emergency surgery. Can you cut me a break this time and take me directly to the ER? I'll be in big trouble if I don't get there soon."

"Sure. What do I care? I get my nine-fifty an hour no matter how many people I haul or where I stop." The man threw the bus into gear.

When the shuttle pulled up to the emergency room doors, Simon thanked the man for the ride and leaped off the bus. Just to make sure the driver believed his story, he ran into the building. He pulled his hat low over his face as he passed by a security guard who was monitoring the entrance. Winding through a long hallway, he found an unguarded exit, headed back outside, and walked around the side of the building. With a nonchalant pace, he walked by the construction site of a new four-level parking garage, and then he passed in front of the hospital's Child Care Center. No security guards were in sight.

He found his Ford Focus safely stashed in the parking lot of The McLeary House, a hotel for families with children who are patients at the hospital. *The cops will be looking for my car.* Simon unlocked his vehicle, threw his backpack into the back seat, reached into the glove compartment, and pulled out a Phillips head screwdriver. In a matter of a few minutes, Simon removed the license plates from his vehicle. As he looked around the parking lot, a Chevy Blazer caught his attention. Periodically turning his eyes toward the hotel, Simon removed the Blazer's license plates and replaced them with his own. In a hurry, he screwed his new acquisitions onto his Focus. His new Virginia license plates read "ILVJSUS."

As he tightened the final screw on the rear plate, he heard a voice from behind him. "Excuse me, sir. I'm with hospital security. Can I ask you what you're doing?"

Damn. This is probably going to get ugly. "I'm just tightening the license plates on my car," Simon muttered without turning around.

"At five in the morning? Sir, you need to show me some identification."

"I'm sorry officer but ..." Simon stood up, wheeled around, and jammed the Phillips head deep into the guard's neck. "You're screwed." Simon watched the man's eyes roll back into his head. Blood gushed from the hole in the side of his thick neck. Simon removed the screwdriver from the guard's jugular vein and then repeatedly impaled the man's chest. When the guard dropped to his knees, Simon grabbed his shirt collar to keep him from falling over and spilling blood all over the parking lot. With his right hand, Simon wiped the tool on the guard's shirt before sticking the screwdriver in his back pocket.

Retrieving his car keys from the front pocket of his jeans, he popped the trunk of the Focus. "Dude, you should have cut back on the Little Debbie snack cakes." Simon heaved the man's bulky body into the tiny compartment. The guard moaned in pain when Simon smacked his head against the side of the trunk. A swift strike to the forehead with a black tire iron knocked the man unconscious.

"Let's see what you have for me," Simon said. After he removed the guard's pepper spray from its holster, he fished around and found a wallet in the man's back pocket. It held two Visa cards, a MasterCard, and $156 in cash. "Not bad." A driver's license identified him as Albert J. Mossman. "Thanks, Al. Gotta run." He slammed the trunk shut.

Sitting behind the wheel of his piece-of-shit car, Simon took a deep breath, preparing for the next twenty-four hours that would define the rest his life. He would do whatever it took to kill Cullen Rhea. If he succeeded, he could head off to Canada and assume a new identity. If he failed and got caught, he would force the police to kill him. Either way, he was not going back to prison—and someone was going to die.

Chapter 42

Stomach acid leapt through Brooks's esophagus and splashed into his throat. Storming his digestive tract, it burned through the tube that made its path. Brooks sat up in bed and tried to cough the poison out of his upper body, but it held firm and blazed his vocal cords.

Hopping into the bathroom without his prosthetic leg, Brooks gulped down three cups of water that had no effect on the potent acid. He poured a liberal dose of Maalox and belted it down like a shot of tequila. As he looked in the mirror, he felt ashamed of the dark bags that hung beneath his eyes and the hairy mounds of fat that lopped over the waistband of his light blue boxers. The forties suck.

"Come on. Hurry up and start working, stupid medicine." Rubbing his chest, he hoped he was experiencing acid reflux and not another heart attack. That was the last thing he needed.

"I knew I shouldn't have eaten those three Hershey bars at eleven o'clock." Why did he do that to himself almost every night? He knew that a late night chocolate binge always triggers a painful acid attack, but he couldn't stop himself. Idiot.

He struggled to get his wide girth back to the bed. Lack of self-control seemed to be at the root of every bad thing that had happened to Brooks. Looking down at his stump, he thought about how his addiction to alcohol had cost him his leg and, more importantly, his family, in an automobile accident that he should have been able to avoid. He could still hear his wife, Maureen, moaning in misery before she died. Holly, his sweet daughter, never made a sound. The poor child didn't get a chance to scream.

"I miss you so much." A solitary tear trickled down his face. "I'm so sorry for what I did to you." Brooks stared at a picture of his wife and daughter that sat on his dresser. Every day for the past year, he felt the agony of his loss, and his guilt refused to go away. He closed his eyes and wept for them.

"You can cry all you want, but that won't bring your family back."

Brooks opened his tear-filled eyes to see Lazarus sitting with his angular legs crossed. "Get your narrow ass out of my rocking chair."

"Calm down, big guy. I'm just here for a visit."

"What do you want, now? Lemme guess. You want to brag about how you killed Nikki Fox and got Matt Curtis arrested for the murder, right?"

"Very good, Brooks. You know me pretty well."

"Well then, pat yourself on the back and get outta my house. You've killed three women and caused an innocent man to go to jail. Why don't you go find someone else to bother?"

"I can't move on until I've finished my current assignment. Matt's pronounced set of fears won't be fully realized until I've exhausted my to-do list. And—you might want to make a note of this—I've killed four women. Tonight, I had a wonderful session with Tahara Caron."

"You can't murder people for sport."

"Actually, I can."

"You are some piece of work." Brooks shook his head. "I don't understand. What's so special about Matt Curtis? Why do you have to punish him?"

"Matt let his fears get away from him. He's terrified to be alone and, with my help, he'll discover that his worries are well-founded. For my big finish, I have a special homicide planned. I can't wait to see it."

"I know you're going after Cullen Rhea for your final murder."

"Oh, you're way off, Columbo. You're not as smart as you think you are."

Brooks frowned. *If he's not targeting Cullen, then who is he planning to kill? We haven't identified any other woman who had a relationship with Matt. Maybe I have lost my edge as a detective.*

"You know, Brooks, the most interesting aspect about this operation is how my uncommon form of homicide is affecting you." Lazarus snuck a coy grin. He stood up and walked to the side of Brooks's bed.

"What do you mean?"

"You're like a lumbering elephant, Brooks. It takes quite a few shots to put you down. Taking away Maureen and Holly was just the first leg of our journey—the leg that you lost. On the second segment of our voyage of personal destruction, I'm gradually eliminating the respect of everyone around you by committing murders you can't solve. Tessa neatly pinned Nikki Fox's death on Matt, but you have no evidence to solve the cases involving Jill Forcythe, Paige Whitaker, or Tahara Caron. And Lieutenant Malone has lost what little patience and value she had for you."

He's right. The boss thinks I'm a fool. She calls me Detective Foghorn Leghorn behind my back. I'm sure she'd love to get rid of me.

"You're deathly afraid that if you fail as a detective, your colleagues will view you as a dumb ol' redneck who couldn't cut it in the big city. When all of those murder cases remain unsolved, people will ostracize you. Eventually, no one will give a damn about the good ol' boy from North Carolina. In the end, you'll be forced to move back to Raleigh—a defeated cripple. Only a bloody suicide will bring you welcome relief."

"That's ridiculous." In the deep recesses of his psyche, Brooks recognized that Lazarus knew his true feelings.

"Every day, you find it more difficult to justify your existence as a detective to the Fairfax County Police Department. Your organization is filled with officers who think you're nothing but a loose Confederate cannon that doesn't belong. Isn't that right, Brooks?"

"Yes." He shifted his large frame to his left side to ease the pressure on his partial leg. Lying to Lazarus was pointless, and the truth was not easy to accept. Ever since he moved to Northern Virginia, he felt like an outsider. "I have to fight the redneck stereotype on a constant basis, and I despise the fact that people judge me unfairly just because I have a heavy Southern accent. I'm not a jug-eared moron. Southern is not a synonym for stupid. I'm still an asset to the department."

"You can bust your hump trying to prove your merit," Lazarus laughed. "But we both know that you're destined to fail." The lanky man stepped across the room to an oak nightstand and opened the middle drawer.

"What are you doing?" Brooks asked.

"Invading your secret space." Reaching into the drawer, Lazarus pulled out a handgun—a limited-production 9 mm revolver called a Charter Arms Pit Bull. "You bought this pistol at a gun show eleven months ago with one purpose in mind. But up until now, you haven't been man enough to finish the job." He extended his arm and held the gun in the palm of his hand. "Tonight's the night."

Brooks stared at the revolver. What would the future hold for him? More wrinkles and gray hair. A bigger beer gut. Back pain. Arthritis. Severe heart problems. And it wasn't like his leg was going to grow back. He took the pistol from Lazarus. "What will happen to me when I die? You have to tell me. Does heaven really exist? Will I ever see my wife and daughter again?" His eyes begged for answers.

"Pull the trigger and find out."

Thrusting the cold gun barrel against his right temple, Brooks pulled the hammer back and placed his trembling index finger on the trigger. Closing his eyes, he swallowed hard and held his breath.

"Come on. Do it, Brooks. Be a man. End the misery. Put that bullet through your brain, and you'll never have to suffer through another day of your pointless life."

Gritting his teeth, Brooks felt every muscle in his body contract. Sweat drenched his clothing. Then, with an earsplitting yell, he turned the gun toward Lazarus and fired the revolver at the shadow man's chest. Six bullets passed through Lazarus's lean body without resistance, lodging in the wall across the room.

"What a wretched disappointment. You can't even kill yourself," Lazarus sneered. "You're a waste of my time and effort."

"Sorry." Brooks broke into a mocking smile as he noticed that his brief display of courage seemed to throw Lazarus off his game.

The agitated figure squinted his black eyes. "I'm sick of your screw-ups, fat boy. Next time, *I'll* pull the trigger." He vaporized into a blur of murky shadows.

Chapter 43

"Just send me $29.95, plus $4.00 for shipping, and you'll receive this lovely vial of anointing oil, which I will personally pray over." A television evangelist with a bad haircut held the vial next to his face so the camera could zoom in for a close-up. "The power of God will flow through my hands when I bless this oil. And I will do this just for you—my beloved children of God. Simply place a drop of this astounding oil on your hands and touch anyone, including yourself, and you will bring about a miracle in the name of Jesus Christ. Cash, Visa, MasterCard, American Express, and Discover are accepted. No personal checks, please."

"I can't believe I'm actually watching this." Tessa amazed at her lack of a real life. "Saturday morning television is awful." She changed the channel to a *Cosby Show* rerun.

For the past three hours, she had sat in her recliner with a Snoopy blanket over her legs, trying to calm her nerves by flipping through the channels. No luck. Maybe Brooks was right. Maybe she should see his doctor and find out if she really was losing her mind or if something else was wrong with her. She held the doctor's telephone number tightly in her right hand. Couldn't call him now. He would certainly write her off as an unbalanced lunatic with no sense of time. But how would she ever make it through another day?

As she watched the show, Bill Cosby reminded her of her father, Edgerrin McBride—The Edge. Like Cosby, her father was a funny man who loved children, especially his two darling daughters. A New Orleans native, he played saxophone in the jazz bars of the French Quarter from his fourteenth birthday until he died at the age of fifty-three, a victim of prostate cancer. He hated Tessa's choice to become a police officer, which was a far too dangerous profession for his lovely little girl. "Stop messing around with criminals. Meet a good man. Settle down. Give me a whole mess of grandchildren," The Edge would often lecture. How disappointed he would be if he saw her now, sequestered inside her apartment, afraid to interact with another human being for no good reason.

A few minutes after seven, a knock on her door startled Tessa out of her TV coma. She didn't answer, hoping the person would get frustrated and go away. Three more hard knocks on the door told her the visitor wasn't about to give up. "Who could possibly need to talk to me?" She sulked to the door. Through the peephole, she saw a bulbous nose pressed against the other side of the peephole. "What do you want, Brooks?" She opened the door for her partner.

"Sorry to wake you on a Saturday morning."

"I've been awake for hours. What's up?"

"We have another dead woman. Tahara Caron." Brooks stepped into Tessa's small apartment.

"No one called me about another homicide. How did you find out about it?"

Brooks took a few seconds to answer. "I have nothing official. It's just a hunch. I need you to go with me to Tahara's home."

Tessa sat down on her cream-colored sofa. "Brooks, you know that Matt Curtis was locked up in jail last night. There's no way he could have killed Tahara Caron."

"Humor me, Tessa. I'll wait while you change your clothes. Unless, of course, you want to investigate this case wearing your Garfield pajamas."

"I'm not going anywhere."

"Why?"

"I can't leave right now. It's that anxious feeling I told you about at the restaurant. It won't go away. I need to stay home today. Please understand."

Brooks walked over to his friend and took her hand. "I know you're going through a rough time. I'll handle this one by myself. But swear to me that you'll call Dr. Radford first thing Monday morning."

She managed a weak smile. "I promise I'll call him." She gave Brooks a tight hug. "Thank you for being my friend," she whispered in his ear.

"You try to relax and get some rest. I'll call you later." He moved toward the door. Then he stopped with a confused look on his face. "Tessa, we discovered four of Matt Curtis's old girlfriends—Jill Forcythe, Paige Whitaker, Nikki Fox, and Tahara Caron, plus his current girlfriend, Cullen Rhea. Did we identify any other women he was involved with?"

Grabbing her notebook from her coffee table, she flipped through her observations. "No. I don't have any other names written down. Why?"

"I believe that there is one more woman in danger, but I don't know who it is."

Tessa looked at Brooks as if he had three heads and a hump on his back. "What are you talking about? You say Tahara Caron is dead, but it hasn't been reported, and now you think there's another woman in the mix. We caught the bad guy, Brooks. It's over."

"It won't be over until tonight."

"How the hell do you know that?"

Brooks took a deep breath and looked into Tessa's eyes. He couldn't believe he was about to say this. "An evil supernatural being systematically murdered the four women who had close relationships with Matt Curtis. Just a few hours ago, he told me that he planned to kill one more woman tonight, but it was not Cullen Rhea."

Tessa sat perfectly still with a blank look on her face. Then she burst into hysterical laughter. "Have you been drinking tequila sunrises for breakfast again? Man, I don't know how you came up with that one, but that's the funniest thing you've said in a long time. A supernatural being? Does he live in a haunted castle? Does he speak with a heavy Transylvanian accent and turn into a bat?"

"I'm not kidding."

"Stop it!" she cackled. "You're killing me, Brooks. Whew. I feel better already."

"You don't believe me? Then how do you explain these weird deaths?" A hurt expression took over his face.

"If this supernatural creature is what you've been dropping hints about over the last few days, you need see your therapist immediately. I'm sure there's a logical explanation to everything that's happened over the past few days. We just have to figure out what it is. Now, quit goofing around." Tessa stood up and shuffled Brooks out of her apartment. "Get outta here and let me rest." She leaned back against the door, shaking her head in bemusement.

Chapter 44

"What's that smell?" Bunny rubbed his leathery hands over his face to wake himself up.

Panic slashed through Matt's chest. *Oh, please blame DeShawn, please blame DeShawn.* Holding his position on the end of the cot, afraid to move or make a sound, Matt watched the hulking man walk over to the toilet.

"Who dropped a load and forgot to flush?" Bunny pushed the handle down to rid the room of the putrid pile. Snatching DeShawn up by his silky red shirt, Bunny gave him a brain-rattling shake. "Did you do this?" he asked the thin man who was still quite drunk.

"I don't remember," he moaned. "Hey, man, get yo damn hands off me. I paid twelve dollars for this shirt. Give a brother a break." DeShawn swung his arms in a sorry effort to break free from the big man's grip.

Drawing back his massive right fist, Bunny prepared to ram it into DeShawn's face. The skinny alcoholic closed his eyes and winced in advance for the pain that was about to shatter his nasal cavity.

"Put him down." On the other side of the metal bars, Sergeant Lance Florez placed his right hand on his sidearm, daring Bunny to do something he would regret.

The giant slowly lowered DeShawn back to the ground and patted him hard on the shoulder. "If you smell this place up again, I'm gonna tear your head clean off."

Bunny plodded over to the cell door. "What can we do for you this morning, officer?"

"I'm here for Matthew Curtis." Florez looked over at Matt, who leaped from his cot. "You're out on bail. Let's go." He released a metal lock and kept a close watch on Bunny and the other criminals.

When he reached the cell door, Bunny wrapped his burly right arm around Matt's neck. "Take care of yourself, little buddy. And stay out of trouble."

"You too, Bunny." He grinned at his supersized friend.

Locking the door behind Matt, Sergeant Florez escorted him down the hall. "So, let me get this straight. Mr. Trail lets you call him Bunny?"

"Yeah. Bunny and I are tight."

As the men entered a large office area, Matt saw his attorney waiting in front of a cluttered reception desk. Wearing a white oxford shirt with khakis and a navy blazer, the thirty-seven-year-old lawyer looked as if he had just stepped off the University of Virginia campus. "How did you get me out?" Matt pumped Spencer's hand in thanks.

"With twenty thousand bucks in bail money. And you're lucky that I play racquetball with the judge who happened to draw this case."

"I don't know how to thank you, Spence."

"A cashier's check for twenty thousand would be a good start." Spencer accompanied Matt to the property cage to pick up his personal effects.

"I'm innocent, Spence. I swear I am."

"I know you are, Matt. Let's get you home. Cullen's waiting for you. She needs to see you. She had a tough night." They walked into the parking lot and climbed into Spencer's black Lexus SUV.

On the way to Matt's house, Spencer told him about Simon's assault on Cullen at the hospital. "If I find Simon, I'll kill him." Matt slammed his fist on the dashboard.

"I didn't hear that," Spencer said. "And don't say that around anyone else. You're in enough trouble as it is. Let the police do their job."

When they pulled into Matt's driveway, the front door flew open, and Cullen ran out to the car. Before the Lexus stopped moving, Matt jumped out and wrapped his arms around her. "Are you all right?" He held her face in his hands.

"I'm OK. Really scared, but I'll get over it. Was the jail horrible?"

"Yes. Thank God, Spence got me out. I made a new friend. His name is Bunny."

"Bunny? I don't think I want to hear any of the details." Cullen pulled Matt toward the house. "Let's get some coffee." She turned to Spencer, who was still sitting behind the wheel of his SUV. "Thanks for everything, Spence!"

"No problem. That's what brothers and lawyers are for. I've got to run. Carol and the kids are waiting for me at home. The Fairfax County police are supposed to send over a uniform to stay with you until they catch Simon. He should be here soon. Call me if you have any problems." Spencer backed out of the driveway.

Cullen and Matt waved good-bye as they walked into the house, holding each other around the waist. "Cullen, I need to explain why things have been so weird during the past few days."

"Yes, you do. I'll get the coffee and meet you in the living room."

Just then, Joe rounded a corner and slid across the slick hardwood floor. Matt picked up his best friend, hugged him tightly, and planted a big smooch on his snout. "I missed you so much," he whispered in the dog's floppy ear. Joe licked his face.

As if he were holding a baby, Matt carried Joe into the living room and sat on the sofa with the curly-haired dog on his lap. Cullen brought a steaming mug of coffee to him. "All right, what the hell's been going on with you?" She sat down in a comfortable chair across the room, prepared to act as judge and jury.

One small sip of coffee turned into half a cup while Matt prepared his story. He started from the beginning and explained how Lazarus had methodically killed his old girlfriends in order to ruin his life. Cullen didn't say a word, giving no indication to Matt that she had met the illustrious Mr. Kaine in the hospital. Listening with intent interest, she let him blurt out a detailed description of his Nikki Fox experience, fully admitting that he had made an inexcusable mistake and asking for her forgiveness.

When Matt completed his exposition, Cullen stood up and stepped into the kitchen. She poured herself a second cup of coffee, returned to the living room, and stood directly in front of Matt. "Do you really expect me to believe your ridiculous story?"

"It's the truth. I swear."

"Sounds like an episode from *The Twilight Zone*."

"Look, I know this is hard to wrap your head around, but I am not making it up. Please believe me, Cullen."

"Why should I?" She paced around the room to increase the squirm factor.

"Because I love you."

"Don't try to get out of trouble by using the 'L' word."

"Sorry." *Maybe if I make her laugh, she'll come around.* "Look at Joe." He propped the dog up to face Cullen with his soulful brown eyes. "He believes me."

"Joe sleeps twenty hours a day, licks his butt, and eats cat poop. He's not what you would call a great character witness." A hint of a smile broke across her lips. "All right, Matt. I'll accept your tall tale as truth, for now." She pointed a daunting index finger at him. "But if you ever touch another woman, so help me, I'll crush your—"

"OK, I get it. I'm all out of second chances." Moving Joe off his lap, Matt stood up and hugged Cullen. "Thank you, baby." He held her in his arms as he relaxed for the first time in three days.

A knock at the door broke them out of their long embrace. Joe dashed to the front door, as if it were someone to see him. Looking out the side window, Matt saw a muscular police officer with a crew cut standing on his welcome mat. "Good morning, officer." Through his recent jail time, he had learned the importance of making friends with guys in uniform.

Presenting his badge for inspection, the officer said, "I'm Police Officer Adrian Foley of the Fairfax County Police Department. I need to speak with Ms. Cullen Rhea."

"Oh, yes, certainly. Come on in." Matt ushered the officer through his home.

With an unwavering formality, Foley shook Cullen's hand. "Hello, ma'am. My name is Police Officer Adrian Foley. I'll be responsible for your safety for the next twenty-four hours. I'll do everything I can to make sure Fletcher doesn't hurt you. You can just go about your normal business. I promise I'll stay out of your way."

"Well, right now I'd really like to go home and get some rest. I have to be back at work tonight at 10:45."

Matt stepped in front of Cullen, just inches from her face. "Why don't you stay here until they catch Simon? You'll be safer with me and a policeman to protect you." He couldn't let Cullen out of his sight while the rapist was still at large.

"I want to sleep in my own bed, Matt. I'm exhausted. And I need to go to work to get my life back to somewhere near normal. I'm not going to change my routine for that freakin' Simon Fletcher. Besides, I have Officer Foley to watch out for me." She picked her purse up off the kitchen table and turned to the officer. "I'm ready to go."

She walked with Foley to the front door and waited for him to get into his police car. Throwing her arms around Matt, she kissed him on the lips. "I will always love you, Matt," she whispered. He put his forehead against hers, wishing she would stay. As she walked to her car, Cullen waved good-bye.

"Please be careful," Matt called to her.

"I have my own personal policeman. What could possibly happen?"

Chapter 45

"This is Detective Barrington of the Fairfax County Police Department. Is anyone home?" Brooks knocked on the front door of Tahara Caron's home. He rang the doorbell for the third time. No answer.

Just as he prepared to force the door open, Brooks heard footsteps in the grass around the corner of the house. Antonio Palmeiro appeared from behind a large holly bush, looking as if he had been awake all night. "What are you doing here?" he asked.

"I just wanted to make sure Tahara was all right."

"She's fine."

"I'm glad to hear it. Can I speak with her?"

"She's probably still asleep." Antonio tucked his shirttail into his black pleated pants.

"You're not sure?" Brooks noticed what looked like lipstick smudged on the shoulder of Antonio's wrinkled blue shirt.

"I got up early this morning to go into my office to do some work."

Right. The only thing this guy was doing was his neighbor's wife. "I'd like to talk to Tahara. Could you please open the door?"

Giving in to the persistent detective's request, Antonio obliged and unlocked the front door. "Tahara, there is someone here to see you," he called from the foyer. Silence. "Tahara, are you awake?" Antonio looked at Brooks. "I'll go get her."

"No. You stay here. I'll check on Tahara." Hurrying up the stairs as fast as his prosthetic leg and heavy frame would allow, Brooks rushed into the room to see the woman lying on her bed, staring at the ceiling with a dead gaze. Lazarus had claimed another prize.

Disobeying the detective's order, Antonio entered the bedroom. When he saw Tahara's blank stare, he let out a loud yell. "Oh, no! What's wrong with her? Tahara, wake up! Help her! Do CPR! You have to save her!" Antonio screamed.

Brooks felt the jugular vein in her neck. "It's too late. She's gone."

The fiery Cuban clenched his fists and drove them into his temples as he fell to his knees, crying over the death of his wife.

Brooks stepped around the grieving man to get a close look at Tahara. With a gentle touch, he felt her rigid left arm. At least this murder wasn't messy, which was a welcome relief for his sensitive stomach. After so many years of looking at dead bodies, he could tell that she had entered rigor mortis, the state a body reaches when the oxygen supply to the muscles ceases but the cells continue to respire. Lactic acid builds up in the blood cells, which causes the muscles to harden. In most situations, the body becomes stiff after about three hours.

Brooks took note of the odd positioning of Tahara's arms. Her elbows were even with her shoulders and her hands lay on her pillow, close to her ears. Bruises on her neck formed the shapes of two small hand prints. Brooks closed his eyes. *Dear God, Lazarus made this woman choke herself to death.*

After Brooks called 9-1-1 and his office to report Tahara's death, he sat down with Antonio at a square oak kitchen table. "Where were you last night?"

"I was working in my office."

"Bullshit. Tell me the truth." Brooks leaned over the table. "You were nailing your neighbor's wife, weren't you?"

The Cuban lowered his head. "All right, yes. I spent the night next door with Janessa Cole. Her husband is out of town. I told Tahara I was working late and planned to sleep on the couch in my office. I feel awful about this."

"You should," Brooks said. "And I guess you forgot to tell your wife that I came by and needed to talk to her."

Guilt weighed on Antonio's shoulders. "Yes, I forgot." Antonio stood up and looked through a bay window that overlooked his backyard. "I should have been here to protect her."

"There's nothing you could have done."

"How could you possibly know that?"

"Policeman's intuition." Brooks got up and limped through the kitchen toward the front door. "I don't have any more questions for you, Mr. Palmeiro. The crime scene team should be here soon. I need you to wait outside with me."

As Antonio took a seat on his front doorstep and wallowed in guilt, Brooks stood in the Saturday sunshine. *In just a few hours, Lazarus will kill again. But who will his victim be?* A ball of stress formed in his chest. Brooks walked to his car and retrieved a pack of Marlboros from a cup holder. He should quit smoking—but not today.

Two cigarettes later, the Fairfax County crime scene team arrived. Brooks gave a quick description of the situation to the team and to Stan. As the team mobilized into action, Lieutenant Malone pulled up in her green Nissan Pathfinder. *Great. This is just freakin' great.* Slamming her car door, she set her sights on Brooks.

"You and McBride put Matt Curtis in jail yesterday, which was supposed to put an end to these homicides. Now another girlfriend is dead. How do you explain this, Barrington?"

"Matt Curtis didn't kill anyone, Lieutenant." Brooks glared at her like a cowboy ready for a gunfight.

"Then who did?"

Brooks deliberated about how he should answer the question. He couldn't tell her about Lazarus because she would probably fire him on the spot, and he couldn't say there were no other suspects, because she would think he was a poor excuse for a detective. "The crime team is gathering evidence now. I'll give you a full report when I have a definitive answer."

"Let me translate your truckload of crap into English. You don't have a clue who killed these four women."

"I didn't say that," Brooks said without flinching.

"Then what are you saying?"

"I'm saying that you need to get the hell outta my face and let me work." *Oh shit, I just committed professional suicide.*

Malone glowered into Brooks's eyes as if she were trying to scorch his retinas. "You have twenty-four hours to bring me something that remotely resembles a piece of evidence. If you come up empty, I'm taking you and McBride off these cases and replacing you with detectives who can make an arrest. Are we clear, Brooks?"

"Yes, ma'am." Behind his back, Brooks flipped her the bird.

"By the way, where is McBride?"

"Tessa's not feeling well today, but she'll be back at work Monday. You can count on her."

"I wish I had the same level of confidence in McBride that you seem to have."

"I wish you did too, Lieutenant. Tessa's earned it." Brooks turned his back on his boss and walked toward his Corvette.

"Where are you going now, Detective? Shouldn't you be inside looking for evidence with the crime scene guys?"

"Nope. I have an interview to conduct at another location. I'll talk to you later," Brooks said without looking back. Then he waved his right hand good-bye to his superior officer and possibly to his career.

Chapter 46

"You like combo?" the middle-aged Hispanic woman asked. She wore a plastic name tag that displayed the name "Adalia" and a Skeeter's Burger Palace cap that was way too small for her head.

"No. I want a Skeeter's Special Heavy Duty Burger, an apple turnover, and a large Coke." Simon pulled his Redskins hat low over his eyes.

"You like combo?" the woman asked again with a vacant gawk.

"No. I said I want a Skeeter's Special Heavy Duty Burger, an apple turnover, and a large Coke, you moron. What is your problem? This is not a complicated order."

The woman blinked twice. "Uno combo." She searched for a picture on the cash register.

Simon placed his hands on the counter. "Look, if you're going to work here in the United States, you should learn to speak English. Is that too much to ask? Is that an unreasonable request? If I worked in a fast food restaurant in Mexico, wouldn't you expect me to speak Spanish?"

Hoping to avoid a scene, a Hispanic man wearing a manager's badge that said "Julio" stepped in front of Adalia and punched Simon's order into the system. "That will be $5.26," he said with a mandatory smile.

Simon handed over the money and tapped his fingers on the counter as he waited for his lunch. With an oblivious grin on her face, Adalia passed him his food. "Thank you coming Skeeter's Burger Palace."

Without acknowledging her, Simon carried his order to a secluded booth in the back of the restaurant. Opening the environmentally safe container in a rush, Simon dove into his sandwich. It had been sixteen hours since his last meal. In the middle of his first bite, Simon noticed something strange about his burger. Removing the top bun, he saw that the meat was missing. "Unbelievable." He huffed back to the cash registers.

"I want to see the manager. Where the hell is the manager?" He threw the sandwich down on the counter.

Julio appeared from the drive-through window cubby. "Yes, sir. Can I help you?"

"Look at this burger. It's supposed to have two big ol' beef patties, secret sauce, lettuce, onions, pickles, and cheese on a tasty bun. How can you possibly forget the two big ol' beef patties? They're the first ingredients listed in your theme song. What kind of idiots do you have working here?"

"I'm very sorry, sir. I'll get you another burger." Julio barked out the order in Spanish. As he returned to the counter with the replacement, Simon looked behind the man and saw two Hispanic women laughing hysterically.

"Ha, ha, very funny. Bite me." *I wish I had a gun. I'd blow those grins right off their faces. I should tell them I work for the U.S. Immigration Service. That would shut them up in a hurry.* Realizing his need to maintain a low profile, Simon snatched his new burger off the counter, returned to his seat, and inhaled his lunch. After one final glare at the mischievous cooks, he left the restaurant and headed to Fairfield Mall to kill some time before his late night date with Cullen.

He debated whether he should dispose of Albert Mossman's body or let him rot in the trunk of his car. *Knowing my luck, I'll get caught dumping the body. I'd better leave him where he is for now. I just hope the smell doesn't get too bad.*

After parking his car near the Macy's entrance, Simon sauntered through the parking lot watching soccer moms fill their gigantic SUVs with their coveted catches of the day. He wondered if they were happy with their predictable suburban lives, or if they secretly ached for some real excitement—the kind of uninhibited exhilaration that Simon could give them.

Walking through the mall, he saw a group of TV sets stacked in front of an electronics store. A local news anchorwoman was reporting a breaking story. "Fairfax County police are looking for a man who assaulted a woman last night at Fairfax Memorial Hospital. His name is Simon Fletcher." Simon's mug shot flashed on the screen. "If you see this man, call 9-1-1 immediately."

Oh, shit. I need a better disguise. He surveyed a listing of stores on the mall's directory and decided on the Goofyfoot Boardshop on the upper level.

Keeping his head low as he shopped for a new persona, Simon collected a pair of green and red Nikes, a pair of black wraparound Ray-Ban sunglasses, a red skateboard with a blue dragon painted on the top, a pair of green plaid shorts, a black and white checkerboard bandana tied to look like a do-rag, and a white *South Park* T-shirt that said, "Cartman for President." Dumping his items at the register, Simon hid his face from the checkout girl.

"Hi! My name is Janie. Did you find everything you were looking for today?" She bubbled with eighteen-year-old eagerness. Simon just nodded.

"Your total is $226.45. Will that be cash or credit?" The girl scratched at her nose stud and flipped her blue-tipped hair out of her eyes.

"Credit." Simon casually laid Albert Mossman's Visa on the counter. Waiting for the transaction to clear, he fiddled with his Redskins hat to shield his identity from the security camera. With a slight smirk, he scribbled a messy fake signature on the receipt. *I wonder if Albert has been reported missing yet? Probably not. He's only been gone a few hours.*

"Thank you, Mr. Mossman. Have a great day," Janie beamed.

"You can call me Al." Grabbing his bag of goodies, Simon strolled out of the store. He hung a quick left into a department store and ducked into the bathroom. Locking himself in the handicapped stall, Simon shed his Redskins merchandise and assumed his new skateboard character. Opening the stall door, he couldn't help laugh at the ridiculous reflection he saw in the mirror. After disposing of his old identity in the bottom of a large metal trash can, Simon ambled out of the restroom a new dude, ready for fun and adventure.

Back in the parking lot, he decided it was time to ditch his car—along with the smelly dead guy stuffed in his trunk. Remembering an ad he saw a few days ago on television, Simon drove to Kirk Paxton Chevrolet, a couple of miles down Route 50.

As soon as he parked the Focus in the visitor's section in front of the car dealership, a salesman pounced on him. "Hello! My name is Earl Winger. What can I do for you on this lovely Saturday afternoon?" The man pumped Simon's hand with a powerful clench.

"Hi, Earl. I saw one of your commercials on TV, and I'd like to take advantage of your take-it-home test drive offer. Can I take a Chevy Malibu home with me today?" Simon feigned excitement.

"Certainly! I'd be happy to show you what we have in stock. What's your name?"

"Albert Mossman, but you can call me Al." *I'm getting a lot of mileage out of old Albert.*

"All right, Al. Come with me." The salesman led Simon to a herd of cars parked along the side of the dealership. "Would you like to go for a test drive before we do the paperwork? We can take one for a spin around the block if you'd like."

Standing in front of a shiny Malibu, Simon tapped the hood of the car. "I've already made up my mind. Let's go with this one, Earl. Blue is my favorite color. Wrap her up for me."

The men walked through a pair of glass doors into the dealership and sat down at Earl's tiny cluttered desk. "Let me explain how the take-it-home test drive works. I'll need a valid driver's license and proof of insurance. You must be at least twenty-one years old, and you must leave your current vehicle here at the dealership. You must stay within one hundred miles of the dealership. Usually we limit the test to twenty-four hours, but since we're not open on Sunday, you'll need to return the car by nine o'clock Monday morning. Do you understand all of these requirements?"

"Absolutely, Earl. Whatever you say." Simon gave the salesman a self-assured nod. He pulled Albert's wallet out of his back pocket and handed over Albert's driver's license and Allstate insurance card. With his black and white checkered do-rag wrapped low on his forehead and his Ray-Bans hiding his blue eyes, Simon easily passed for Albert. Besides, since Earl smelled a sale, he looked at the driver's license only long enough to verify that his potential buyer was over the age of twenty-one.

After he signed the necessary documentation with another forged Albert Mossman signature, Simon stood up. "I really gotta run, Earl. I'm on a tight schedule. Can I get the keys to the Malibu?"

The salesman tossed a set of keys to Simon. "Do you need to get anything out of your car before you leave?"

"A couple of things. Then I'll be on my way. I'll leave my keys in the ignition. Oh yeah, the rear of the car might smell a little funky. I think something is wrong with my exhaust system. Just ignore it."

"I'll see you Monday when you bring the Malibu back." Earl shook Simon's hand with a hint of Willy Loman's desperation in his eyes.

"Great. Then we can throw some numbers around. Sharpen your pencil, and we'll work out a deal for that sweet ride." Simon sauntered out the front door of the dealership. *Have a nice life, Earl. You'll never see my skinny ass again.*

In less than a minute, he collected his skateboard and his backpack filled with basic necessities he purchased at the drugstore. He walked around to the rear of his car and thumped the trunk lid. *So long, Albert.* Then he hopped into his brand new Malibu and drove toward Cullen's house.

Chapter 47

"Hello. This is Matt Curtis."

"Where the hell are you?" Dan Calvert's gravelly voice thundered out of the tiny cell phone speaker.

"I'm at home."

"Well, I'm in the office, and I just checked in on your project team. They worked for eighteen hours yesterday, and they've been here since seven o'clock this morning. They also told me that you didn't come in to the office at all yesterday, and they haven't heard from you today. Is that true, Matt?"

"Yes, that's true. Yesterday I was detained. And today, I have some personal matters to take care of," Matt said. *There is no way Calvert will buy that lame excuse.* "I trust my managers and the team. Before I left the office on Thursday, we came up with a number of good ideas on how we can reuse some software we developed for a similar project. That should save us a lot of time and get us back on schedule."

"So when will you be here today?"

"I'm not coming in. As I said, I have some pressing personal business that I have to tend to." Matt paced around his kitchen table.

"A good senior manager puts in his hours with his team," Calvert preached.

"A good senior manager lets his team focus on their work without hovering over their shoulder every minute of every day. They'll be successful, and I'll make sure they're rewarded for their hard work and long hours." The speed of Matt's pacing increased.

"The firm comes first, Matt."

"No. My life comes first. The firm is a distant second. It's just a job." It was getting difficult for him breathe.

"Then you won't be upset when I fire you."

"I've been an excellent employee for years, and I have the progress reviews with your signatures on them to prove it. I'm one of the best senior managers in the firm. You need me more than I need you. You can't fire me, Dan." Matt's heart hammered.

"The hell I can't!"

"If you fire me, I'll sue the firm for wrongful termination, and I'll drag your gold-plated butt into court just to see you sweat."

"You wouldn't dare do that to the firm, you little son of a bitch."

"Try me." *Hey, I sound a little like Clint Eastwood. This is really cool. I'll probably lose my job, but at least I defended myself.*

Silence on the other end of the phone indicated that Calvert was way past pissed off. He sucked in a deep breath and cleared his throat. "Be in my office at nine o'clock Monday morning."

That's it. I'm fired. He's telling me when and where I'll get my public execution. I fought a good fight, but now it's over, and Dan's gonna lay my guts out in front of the entire office.

"I want to see your work plan—every detail. Show me how you're going to get your project out of the mud. And your plan had better work."

Shocked at the fact that he still had a small semblance of a career, Matt stopped pacing. "Fine. See you Monday morning." He hung up his cell phone before he said something stupid to ruin the moment. A deluge of confidence like he had never experienced flooded Matt's ego. Fighting Calvert had made him feel bulletproof.

He hurried into his home office and began to create a presentation that would prove to Calvert that he wasn't just mouthing off. He knew his ideas were creative, and he would force Calvert to admit that he had the project under control.

In less than an hour, Matt created twelve PowerPoint slides that were sure to impress Calvert, even on his most apprehensive day. He printed them out and stuck them in his briefcase. He was now locked and loaded for his battle with his boss.

Just as Matt shut his computer down, a knock at the door sent Joe into a barking fit. Looking through his office window, Matt saw Brooks on his front stoop.

Holding Joe by his bright blue collar, Matt opened the door. "The last time I talked to you, I wound up in jail. If you have any more questions, you'll have to talk to my lawyer. Good-bye, Detective." He started to close the door in Brooks's face.

"I know you're innocent, Matt." Brooks placed his hand out to hold the door open.

"So you let me spend the night in jail for the fun of it? Thanks a lot. Please don't do me any more favors."

"I'm here to talk about Lazarus Kaine."

Frozen by Brooks's words, Matt didn't know what to say. He just stood at the door searching for a response that made sense. "How do you know about him?"

"Let's just say that Lazarus and I have some history together. Can I come in?"

Flustered, Matt opened the door and walked with Brooks toward the living room. "Tell me everything you know about Lazarus."

Brooks sat on one end of the couch and stretched his prosthetic leg under the coffee table. Taking a seat in a chair across the room, Matt faced the detective, anxious to hear about his tormentor.

Leaving out no details, Brooks described the horrific car crash that killed his wife and daughter. He held Lazarus responsible for the incident, but he took his own share of the blame for driving drunk.

Equally as truthful, Matt illustrated his experiences with the wicked creature and explained how his fears had led to the deaths of four former girlfriends. "Lazarus said that he planned to kill one more woman tonight."

"Who?"

"He wouldn't tell me. I don't know who it could be. I haven't had a serious, intimate relationship with any other woman. And Lazarus explicitly told me that it would not be Cullen."

"Yes, he told me the same thing. Cullen has her own problems with this other guy. What's his name?"

"Simon Fletcher. He raped Cullen when they were in college. Her testimony put him in jail, and now he wants retribution."

"Does she have a uniform with her now?"

Matt nodded his head. "But I'm still worried about her."

"You should be. Whack jobs like this Fletcher don't care what they have to do or who they have to kill to achieve a violent thought that invades their warped brains."

"Gee, thanks. That makes me feel so much better." Matt frowned.

"Sorry to be blunt, but you should be prepared for the worse."

"I understand." Matt stood up because he needed to pace. "So how do we stop Lazarus from killing his last victim?"

"I wish I knew." Brooks looked at his watch. He grabbed the arm of the couch and pushed himself to a standing position. "I'm sorry, but I have to get going. I'm due at the medical examiner's office. We have to process Tahara Caron."

Matt winced at the thought of his former girlfriend's lifeless body. "How did she die?"

"Lazarus made her strangle herself."

The blood drained from Matt's face. "How awful."

Brooks handed him a business card. "Listen to me. I want you to rack your brain and come up with the name of this last woman that Lazarus has his eye on. When you do, call me on my cell phone." He limped toward the front door. "And don't do anything courageous like going after Simon Fletcher. Let the police officers do their thing," Brooks placed his right hand on Matt's shoulder. "This ordeal will be over tonight. You gotta have faith that everything will turn out all right."

"Faith has never worked very well for me."

Chapter 48

"Karl, are you absolutely sure your shoulder feels OK?" Kim Taggert leaned on the door frame of their master bedroom.

"Yes, I'm sure. I feel fine." He packed a pair of white socks into a blue nylon overnight bag.

"You know you don't have to go back to work if you're not completely ready."

Wrapping his arms around her, he kissed her forehead. "I'm ready. I can't sit in this house for one more day. If I have to watch one more minute of reality TV or those freaks on the daytime talk shows, I'm going to lose my mind. Trust me. It's time for me to get back to the station."

"But what if your shoulder isn't healed yet? What if you get hurt again? What if—"

He playfully placed his hand over Kim's mouth. "No more what ifs. I'm going back to work, and that's final."

Kim pushed his hand away. "Fine. Go ahead. Suit yourself, ya big lunkhead."

"Who are you calling a lunkhead?" Karl started tickling Kim's ribs through her dark blue and gold West Virginia University T-shirt.

"You're the only lunkhead in this house." She tickled back. They fell onto their king-size bed and proceeded to pick and poke at each other until they couldn't laugh anymore. Kim threw her arms around Karl's neck and kissed him on the lips. "Please do me a favor. Don't act like a wild man tonight just to prove to the guys that you're back to full strength. There are other firemen who have the skills to save people, you know. You don't have to go all superhero on your first day back."

"No guarantees, babe. I have to do what the situation calls for."

"Geez, you are so stubborn." She whacked him on the upper part of his right bicep.

Karl winced in pain. "Ow, my shoulder! I think it's messed up again. Call a doctor. Call 9-1-1. Get an ambulance." He rolled on the bed in agony.

"Wrong shoulder, doofus." She chuckled at her husband. "Finish packing your bag. I'll go fix you a turkey sandwich and some snacks for the station."

Walking down the stairs of their three-bedroom home, she couldn't help but think back to the night twelve weeks ago when she received a call from

Karl's boss. It was the call she had dreaded for the past seven years—the call telling her that he had been hurt in a rescue.

Karl's station responded to an automobile accident on a curvy two-lane road in a remote section of Clifton. Rain-soaked pavement and a high rate of speed caused a man to lose control of his silver Infinity Q45 sedan. The car had hydroplaned and veered into a ditch. It had then rolled into a maple tree, which pinned the driver underneath.

When Karl arrived on the scene, his instincts told him that the man had probably sustained serious damage to his back and neck. The driver needed to get to a hospital immediately to treat his life-threatening injuries.

Leading his team by example, Karl searched for ways to extricate the man from his car. Using the Jaws of Life and an improvised pulley system, the firemen shifted the vehicle just enough to enable them to slide the man out of his car to safety. As the paramedics positioned the man on a backboard and prepared him for transport, Karl heard a loud crack behind him. Before he could turn around, a large portion of the shattered maple tree snapped off its trunk and crashed on top of Karl, which crushed the bones in his left shoulder. He lost consciousness.

In the emergency room, Kim could tell that he had been critically injured, but she was smart enough not to ask too many questions that would uncover too many frightening details. No one told Kim that Karl almost died in the ambulance on the way to the hospital because of severe blood loss. Some facts are better left unmentioned.

Three operations to rebuild his shoulder, weeks of arduous physical therapy, and Kim's loving care rehabilitated Karl. He wasn't back to his old self, but he was well enough to return to his job. She was glad to have him in one piece, and Kim hated the fact that he could get hurt again within a matter of dangerous seconds.

Karl walked into the kitchen wearing his Fairfax County Fire Department uniform. He bent over and petted their yellow lab, Chief, as the dog munched on a big bowl of dry food. "See ya tomorrow. Be a good boy, and don't eat the furniture while Mom's at work." The dog raised his head as if to say good-bye while he continued to crunch his dinner.

"I guess I'd better get going. My shift starts at seven." He threw his duffle bag over his right shoulder.

After taking one final inventory of his appearance, Kim reached up and kissed her husband. "I'm a sucker for a hunky fireman." She handed him his lunch bucket, hugged him tightly, and then pinched his butt. "All right, get outta here before I start crying again."

"Don't worry. Nothing is gonna happen to me."

"Yeah, that's what you said last time you left for work, and you ended up in intensive care."

"That was a freak accident. I promise I'll keep a close watch for falling trees this time." Karl squeezed her butt. "Keep those sweet buns warm for me. I'll see you in twenty-four hours. Love you, babe."

"Love you, too." She wrestled with her emotions as she closed the door behind him and locked the dead bolt. In an act of reassurance, Chief walked over to Kim and leaned his heavy body against her right leg, which is the universally recognized Labrador retriever symbol for "You're my best friend in the whole world. Pet me."

"Looks like it's just you and me tonight, pal." She scratched the dog behind his ears.

Although she wasn't hungry, she figured she should eat something that would qualify as dinner. Standing in the doorway of her walk-in pantry, she selected one of her all-time favorite entrées—Frosted Flakes. Hey, there was no law saying you couldn't eat cereal for dinner.

After pouring a heaping bowl of her sugary feast, she carried her evening meal into the living room and placed it on a workstation desk that sat in the corner. She cranked up her Dell desktop computer and dined with Tony the Tiger while she surfed the Web, making her daily visits to Oprah.com and a local Labrador retriever rescue site. Then she double-clicked the Microsoft Outlook icon to check her e-mail.

Three new messages popped into her inbox. The first e-mail was from her father and included a list of stupid jokes about ducks, blonds, and flatulent pigs. The second note contained an ad for Bandolino, an online shoe store.

Although she didn't recognize the cryptic address on the third message, the subject line piqued her interest. "RE: Matt Curtis." How odd. Why would someone send an e-mail to her home account about her boss?

With her curiosity turned up to full blast, she opened the e-mail. "Hello, Kim. My name is Lazarus Kaine. We need to talk."

Chapter 49

Simon Fletcher huddled in the Malibu. "Nine o'clock. Time to set things into motion." He had scouted out the park, woods, and playgrounds that surrounded Cullen's townhouse complex. For three hours, he hid in his car around the corner, preparing for the next fifteen minutes that would make or break his mission.

Like a casual visitor, he drove into the townhouse parking lot and guided his car into the perfect position—just two parking spaces away from Cullen's Saturn. Next to her car, a police cruiser filled a visitor's spot. Taking an unassuming attitude, he collected his new skateboard and backpack, got out of the car, and walked down the sidewalk to a bike path that led into a stand of trees. Crouching at the edge of the woods, he held up the car's keyless remote and pressed a red button that set off the car alarm. Every light on the car flashed, and the horn blasted out an obnoxious, repetitive honk.

Watching Cullen's home, he waited for his plan to take effect. Then, just as he had expected, the front door opened. A police officer stepped out of her house with his hand on his pistol, ready to remove it from its holster. Stalking down the sidewalk, the officer surveyed the immediate area as he approached the vehicle. When the cop reached the driver's side of the car, Simon pushed the red button again to stop the alarm.

"Showtime." Simon pushed off on his skateboard, rolling directly toward the officer. Gliding down the sidewalk, doing his best to look like a stereotypical skater, Simon gave the cop a slacker head nod. "What up, lawman?" He skidded to a stop just in front of the officer.

Officer Foley sized up the slender boarder in the *South Park* T-shirt and the checkerboard do-rag. "Do you know who owns this car?"

"Naw. No idea," Simon said. "Gotta jet." He stepped on his board, wheeled down the sidewalk for about twenty feet, and then scratched the back of his board on the sidewalk to stop. He picked up his board. "Oh hey, sheriff, can I ask you a question?"

Already on his way back to his post in Cullen's home, Foley turned to face the skater. "I'm not a sheriff. I'm a police officer. What's your question? And make it quick."

"I saw on TV that you guys are looking for that Fletcher guy, right?"

"Yes. What's your point?"

"Check this out, I saw a dude that looked a lot like him hanging around the common area, back behind that row of townhouses." Simon pointed to a clearing behind Cullen's home.

Foley unsnapped the strap of his holster. "When did you see this man?"

"Just a few minutes ago." Simon plastered a clueless look on his face. His do-rag was pulled low over his eyes to hide his true identity from the streetlights.

"Could you take me to where you saw him?" Foley asked.

"Sure. Anything to help out John Law."

"Thank you for your help. What's your name?"

"You can call me Al." Pretending to be Albert Mossman had turned into an amusing hobby.

"Lead the way, Al." Foley gestured for the skater to go ahead of him.

"With pleasure, officer ..."

"Foley."

"Officer Foley. Cool. What's your first name?" He tucked his skateboard under his left arm and moseyed down the sidewalk.

"Adrian. Officer Adrian Foley." The officer walked with the skater toward the bike path that led to the common area.

"Yo, Adrian." Simon mumbled a bad impression of Sylvester Stallone's legendary character, Rocky Balboa. Then he burst into an obnoxious slacker laugh.

"Believe it or not, I've heard that line a few thousand times. It's never funny. Can we just concentrate on finding the man you say looks like Simon Fletcher?"

"You got it, Adrian. I saw him in a clearing on the other side of these woods." He led Foley along the bike path that cut into a broad patch of trees and bushes. "Man, I'm wicked hungry. How about you? Wanna Milky Way or some cheese crackers?"

Frustrated with his moronic guide, Foley grabbed Simon's arm. "No! Would you please be quiet? If Fletcher is out here, I don't want to tip him off."

"OK, but I need to eat somethin' or I'll get a bitchin' headache." Simon unzipped his backpack. He let the officer walk a bit ahead of him while he burrowed into the pack. Keeping a close watch on the officer, Simon pulled out Albert Mossman's pepper spray and hid it in his right hand. "Yo, Adrian, look at this."

When the policeman turned around, Simon shot the pepper spray directly into his eyes. Foley dropped to the ground, held his hands over his face, and moaned in pain. Simon threw off his pack and grabbed the back end of his skateboard with both hands. "Later, dude." He smashed the front edge of his skateboard deep into Foley's forehead. With a sinful sense of achievement, Simon methodically crushed the officer's skull with a dozen powerful strikes.

When Foley's body stopped twitching, Simon relieved the officer of his 9 mm Glock pistol and stuck it into the waistband of his pants. As he quickly took the officer's handcuffs and shoved them into the left front pocket of his pants, he looked around for any witnesses. Then he removed the handcuff key from a key ring holder that was attached to the officer's belt and stuck it in his right front pants pocket.

"Stupid muscle head. You weigh a ton." He dragged the man's body under a thick honeysuckle bush. With a wry smile on his face, Simon stuck the front of his skateboard in the ground about a foot from Foley's traumatized head. Covered with blood and gray matter, the board served as a crude tombstone for the man who was just trying to do his job.

Simon threw his backpack over his shoulder and jogged back to Cullen's house. So far, so good.

Chapter 50

"I hate this. I hate this. I hate this." Kim pounded out her last mile on the treadmill as it whirred in her basement recreation room. Sweat soaked through her West Virginia University T-shirt and black running shorts, a sign that her five-mile run was almost over.

The Barenaked Ladies' CD *Everything to Everyone* rocked through her headphones while Chief slept like a furry yellow rock on the off-white Berber carpet next to the treadmill.

She reduced her speed setting and flattened the incline to cool her muscles down. Gradually slowing to a walk and then to a full stop, she wiped her face with a purple towel and hopped off the machine.

"Chief, go up to the kitchen." No movement. "Here we go, Chief." She snapped her fingers. Still no movement. Bending down, she patted the lab on his belly and scratched his head.

Chief opened one eye as if to say, "Keep going. I'll tell you when to stop."

"If you come to the kitchen with me, I'll give you a treat," she whispered into his soft left ear. The dog immediately jolted from his sleeping position and raced up the stairs to a kitchen closet that contained a box of dog treats. He wagged his tail as fast as he could and licked his chops. "Works every time." She handed him a peanut butter-flavored treat that he gingerly took from her hand.

After chugging the last half of a bottle of water, she packed her lunch for the following day and stuck it in the refrigerator. "Time to take a shower and go to bed." As she walked through the kitchen into the foyer, Chief followed her through the house, but he stopped at the front door and sat down.

"What are you doing? It's bedtime."

The big dog sat perfectly still with a look on his face that meant, "I gotta pee."

"You just went outside a couple of hours ago. It's late. I'm not taking you out again." Chief didn't budge. Knowing how stubborn the lab could be, she hooked the dog's red leash to his matching red collar. "All right, make it snappy. I don't like standing around in the dark."

Out in the small front yard, Chief sniffed and snuffed in the grass, but he just couldn't find the perfect place to whiz. While he searched for the ultimate spot, Kim noticed three teenage boys walking up the sidewalk toward her. "Hurry up, Chief." But the dog didn't pay any attention to her.

As the teens got closer, she could hear them talking. "Hey, look at them legs. Ooooh, I'd like to get me summa that. Hot and juicy." The boys quickly closed the gap between them and Kim.

"Inside, Chief. Now!" She pulled at his red leash.

One of the boys ran up the sidewalk and cut off her path to the front door. "Where you goin' so fast, baby?" the African-American teenager asked. Standing in her way with his arms crossed, he wore a Baltimore Ravens cap with the bill pulled to the side of his shaved head, a Detroit Pistons jersey with Ben Wallace's number three on it, a gigantic pair of Tommy Hilfiger jeans that rode far below his waist, and a pair of brown work boots.

The other two boys took positions on either side of her, creating a triangle with Kim and Chief in the middle. "We just lookin' for a good time, sweet thang," said one of the boys, a white kid who was trying way too hard to act like his black homey. Wearing a 50 Cent T-shirt, an Oakland Raiders knit cap, and a thick gold chain with three enormous dollar signs hanging from it, the boy had no clue how ridiculous his Vanilla Ice guise looked and sounded.

"Please, just let me go in my house." Kim wrapped Chief's leash around her hand. "Look, guys, I don't want any trouble."

"Trouble?" the third kid laughed. "We don't want no trouble. We jus' want you to give us some good lovin,'" the kid said with a Spanglish accent. He bumped knuckles with the white boy. Holding a Biggie-size container of Wendy's fries and wearing a green shirt with a red bandanna covering his head, the teen moved closer to Kim. Showing his teeth, Chief growled at the boy who approached her, but his angry demeanor subsided when the boy offered him a salty fry.

The triangle around Kim began to collapse. Assuming he was the leader of the pack, Kim stared at the black kid, trying to conceal the fear that charged through her body. As he stepped closer to her, Chief sensed the boy's violent intentions and jumped at him, barking like an attack dog and biting at his thick clothes. The other two boys backed away from Chief, afraid that the powerful lab would take a chunk out of them.

Feeling an opening in the triangle, Kim turned around and raced down the sidewalk with Chief galloping alongside her. "Help me! Help!" She yelled as loud as she could, hoping her neighbors would save her. But no one came to her defense.

The teenagers chased her as if she were their prey. Running down the sidewalk and into the road, she could hear them laughing behind her, fueled by the excitement of the hunt. Although the five-mile run on the treadmill weakened her legs, repeated shots of adrenaline kept her a few yards in front of the aggressive boys.

Winding between parked cars and common area trees, Kim ran about three-quarters of a mile through two neighborhoods with Chief panting loudly next to her left leg. It occurred to her that she could run up to a front door and scream for help, but the boys were so close behind her that they would easily catch her before anyone had time to answer. She didn't even want to think about what they would do to her if they got their hands on her. The only viable option was to keep running for her life.

The Hispanic kid drew within a few feet of Kim and leaped at her. He grabbed her ankle, which sent her into a hard tumble onto the asphalt. The teenager also lost his footing and landed face first on the pavement, ripping a large patch of skin from his right cheek.

Too scared to check for blood, Kim scrambled to her feet and pulled Chief's leash to make a hard right turn. The other two boys stopped just long enough to see if their Hispanic buddy was alive and then continued the chase, leaving their bleeding friend behind.

Running and crying in desperation, she dashed around the corner of a house that stood on the corner of two cross streets. The house was owned by her friends, Ted and Arlene Nicholson. Knowing the home had a pool in the backyard with an equipment shed, she ran past the kidney-shaped pool and straight for the shed. *Please be unlocked*, she begged as she arrived at the wooden door of the small building. Fumbling with the latch, her hands shook with terror. *God, please help me get this thing open*. Finally, the rusty latch released, and Kim pulled Chief into the tiny shed, which was filled with swimming pool chemicals, brushes, leaf nets, and spare parts for the Jacuzzi. Crouching next to her dog, Kim held his snout shut to keep him from making noise.

She heard the white kid say, "Where'd she go?" Footsteps padded on the concrete around the pool.

"I dunno, but watch out for that big-ass dog," the black kid said.

Chief let out a soft high-pitched whine. Hiding in a toolshed with two hands around his muzzle was not his idea of a good time. "Shhhh, be quiet," Kim whispered.

"This is useless, man. I don't see her anywhere. She's gone. Let's get outta here before somebody calls the cops on us," the white kid rationalized.

"Yeah. Bitch ain't worth the hassle."

As she heard footsteps take the boys away from the pool area, Kim let out a breath she hadn't realized she'd been holding. She continued to clutch Chief's snout, just in case. After she gave the teenagers a few minutes to find something else to do or someone else to bother, she stuck her head out the door and looked around for any sign of the teenage gangsta posse. Sneaking around the deep end of the pool, Kim and Chief passed in front of a motion detector, which triggered a blinding flood of white light.

Hustling Chief toward the house, she knocked on the patio door. "Ted? Arlene? Is anybody home? It's me, Kim Taggert. I need your help." Afraid that the boys would return, she pounded on the door with both fists. No one answered.

Chapter 51

I need to leave for work. Where the heck did Officer Foley go? Cullen looked out of her front window. *What could he be doing all this time? Did he get lost? Don't be silly. Did he find Simon? Did Simon hurt him? Oh, that's ridiculous. Foley's a cop. He's trained to defend himself. Maybe I should go look for him. No, I shouldn't leave the house. But what if he needs help? Yeah, right. Like I could help a policeman. Crap. I need to leave right now or I'll be late. I'll leave him a note.*

She fetched a pencil and a yellow sticky notepad from her kitchen counter. In a hurry, she wrote, "Officer Foley, I have to go to work. Please meet me at the hospital. Hope you're OK. Cullen." Then she stuck the note on a mirror in her foyer.

Slipping on her purple scrub jacket over her hospital-issued misty green scrubs, she picked up her lunchbox, threw her purse over her shoulder, and dropped her cell phone into her jacket pocket. Cautiously, she opened her front door and looked around for Foley. His car had not been moved. *Something is not right.*

With her head on a swivel, she rushed to her car and unlocked it with her keyless entry remote. As she pulled the handle up to open the car door, a sinuous arm wrapped around her left shoulder and thin fingers covered her mouth and nose, cutting off her airway. The round barrel of a pistol jammed between her shoulder blades.

"Don't say a word, or I'll shoot you right here," Simon whispered in her right ear. Cullen nodded compliance as she struggled to breathe. "Listen to me very carefully and do exactly what I say. Open the door, and then hold out your left hand."

Her lungs burned for air as she pulled the door open. As she extended her left arm, Simon snatched Foley's handcuffs from his left pants pocket and snapped a restraint on her left wrist. Still holding the pistol to her back, he clicked the other restraint around the Saturn's black steering wheel.

"Now, put the driver's seat up so I can get into the back seat. If you scream, I'll put a bullet in your skull." She desperately wanted to yell, but she was certain that Simon would be true to his word.

Crawling into the back seat, Simon kept the pistol pointed at Cullen's head. "I hate two-door coupes. No legroom." He folded his body into the car. "Get in. We're going for a ride."

Sliding into the driver's seat, she started the car. *How am I going to get out of this? I should hit my OnStar button, but then he'll probably kill me.* Nearing a state of absolute panic, Cullen's arms shook with fear. *Stop it. I can't let him see that I'm afraid. That's exactly what he wants. I'm not going to give him the pleasure of turning me into a blundering fool.*

Simon pushed the barrel of the gun hard against the back of Cullen's head. "You drive where I tell you to go. No deviations. No detours. No signals to other drivers. Don't make me kill you before I'm ready. I want to enjoy every moment of your death." He hunched in the cramped back seat. "Take the Reston Parkway all the way through Reston to Route 7."

"Where are we going?" Cullen pulled out of the Elden Glen parking lot.

"You'll find out soon enough. Shut your mouth and drive."

Cullen drove for a few miles in silence, but after a while, she just couldn't keep quiet any longer. "Why are you doing this, Simon?" She looked at him in the rearview mirror.

"You demolished my life and turned my mother into a vegetable. I'd say that's a couple of pretty good reasons." He shoved the barrel of the pistol against Cullen's right temple and clicked the safety off.

"I just told the truth in court."

"Well, this time, your precious truth won't help you. In fact, in exchange for your honesty on the stand, you're going to get maimed and murdered."

"You started all of this by raping me, Simon." Tears streamed from her eyes as she drove past the Reston Town Centre.

"Yes, and I'm going to finish it. Violence leads to more violence. It's almost poetic, don't you think?"

"I think you're a lunatic. No matter what you do to me, Simon, the police will eventually catch you and throw your demented ass back in jail."

"I'm not going back to jail. By the time the police find the remnants of what used to be your body, I'll be lying on a secluded beach, knocking down tequila shots with a couple of hookers—living the life I should have had years ago."

"Why don't you just forget about me and leave now?" Cullen drove through Reston, looking for a way to signal to someone that she was in trouble.

"Because, I want you to suffer. I want to see the pain travel across your face. I want to feel your screams as they come rushing out of your mouth. I want to hear your skin tear and your bones break as I rip you to shreds. I want to split you open and watch your self-righteous soul drift out your body."

"And what will that do for you?" Cullen probed, fully aware that she sounded like Dr. Phil talking to a nutcase.

"Your excruciating death will give me a sense of great fulfillment. Satisfaction in a job well done. Contentment. Pure, unadulterated joy. Sexual gratification. Would you like me to continue?"

"I get the picture."

"Good. Now take a left on Route 7, then a right on Georgetown Pike. And no more questions. You're giving me a headache."

Cullen made the turns and drove through the rolling hills of the Great Falls area, an elite community filled with wealthy owners of million-dollar estates. While she drove, she kept telling herself to be strong. *Do whatever you have to do to stay alive.*

The ringing of her cell phone cut through an awkward silence. As she instinctively reached for her scrub jacket pocket with her right hand, Simon clutched her wrist. "You don't think I'm stupid enough to let you answer that, do you?" He took the phone from her pocket, turned it off, and dropped it in his backpack.

After they passed the entrance to Great Falls Park, a national park famous for its scenic waterfalls and hiking trails, Cullen could hear Simon's breathing become noticeably faster. "Turn right on Old Dominion Drive." He huffed like a bull preparing for a charge. A mile and a half down the winding two-lane road, Simon fidgeted in his seat. "Pull off the road here, and stop the car."

Cullen guided her Saturn off the pavement next to a narrow bridge and shifted the car into park. She slipped the keys into her pocket and waited impatiently for her captor's next command.

"Lean forward, and let me out of the car." He pushed the seat hard against Cullen's back, squeezing her against the steering wheel. Taking his backpack with his right hand while pointing the gun at Cullen with his left, Simon forced his way out of the back seat. After he stretched his cramped legs, he clicked the safety on the pistol and stuck it into the waistband of his pants. Leaning into the car, he whispered in Cullen's ear, "Your time has come."

Taking the handcuff key from his right front pants pocket, Simon unlocked the handcuff restraint from the steering wheel and clicked it around his right wrist. "Let's go for a walk."

As they edged their way over an embankment, Cullen moved her free hand to the Fairfax Memorial Hospital employee badge hanging around her neck on a silver chain. Making sure Simon was looking the other way, she slipped the chain over her head and dropped the badge on the ground.

Chapter 52

"If a relaxing moment turns into the right moment, will you be ready? Click here for cheap prices on Viagra, Levitra, and Cialis." Bold blue letters made the e-mail message pop off the screen.

"How did these people get my e-mail address? I don't have any problems in that area. At least, I don't think I do. No! Of course I don't. This is stupid." Matt poked the delete key.

Throughout the evening, he had attempted to use television and the Internet as diversions to keep from worrying about Cullen and Simon. But they didn't work. Surfing the Internet for an hour and a half seemed like a good idea at first, but visiting ESPN.com and Wallstreetjournal.com didn't do anything to calm his nerves. He even tried reading through every article concerning Virginia Tech athletics on Hokiesports.com, but he couldn't stop thinking about Cullen.

Five minutes into the 11:00 PM edition of *SportsCenter*, the phone rang. Matt's stomach instantly turned into a tight knot.

"Matt, this is Lisha Hayford. Is Cullen there?"

"She's working tonight."

"I'm at work. She's not here. Cullen is twenty minutes late. That girl's never been twenty minutes late for anything in her life. I'm worried about her. I just called her at home and on her cell phone, but she's not answering. Something is wrong, I can feel it. Oh God, what if Simon got to her."

"I'm sure she's OK. Lisha, there's no reason to panic." *What a load of crap—she has every reason to panic.* "I'll call you as soon as I find her. I promise."

"I'm really scared, Matt." Lisha's voice wavered. "Call the police. Call the FBI. I don't care who you call. Just get somebody to help you find her."

"Nothing is going to happen to her. I'll talk to you soon." He hung up the phone and searched for Brooks Barrington's business card.

The trembling of his hands made him misdial the number twice before he heard the phone ring on the other end. "Barrington," a groggy voice answered.

"Detective, this is Matt Curtis. Cullen is missing."

"What do you mean she's missing?" Brooks's voice was swallowed by the thunder of a rowdy crowd of drunks.

"She didn't show up for work, and she's not answering her cell phone."

"All right, I'll go check out her house. I'm just a few minutes away from there."

"Where are you?"

"None of your gottdamn business," Brooks snapped. "I'll let you know when I locate her."

"No. I'll meet you at her house."

"Stay put, Matt."

"See you in fifteen minutes." Matt hung up on Brooks. Snatching his keys, Blackberry, and wallet from his desk, he pulled on a pair of white Nikes and ran out to his car.

He sped through his neighborhood and squealed his tires along the on-ramp to Interstate 495. The blue BMW hummed at more than ninety miles per hour as Matt took the Route 50 exit way too fast heading toward Fairfax. Nearly losing control of his car, Matt almost clipped a Chevy Suburban. He ran three stoplights as he raced to Cullen's townhouse.

Revolving blue lights from a police car circled the parking lot in front of Cullen's home. Brooks's yellow Corvette sat next to the police cruiser with a flashing blue light stuck on the hood. Two uniformed officers stood at the Corvette, taking their orders from Brooks.

As Matt walked up, one of the officers broke rank and headed around Cullen's townhouse in a dead run. Brooks saw Matt approaching in his peripheral vision. "Do you have a key to Cullen's house?"

Matt dug into his pocket, pulled out a keychain with the words "Nurses Rock" on it, and handed it to a stout female officer. She opened the front door and searched Cullen's house while Brooks and Matt waited outside.

"Do you see Cullen's car anywhere?" Brooks asked.

Matt surveyed the parking lot, evaluating every vehicle. "No. It's not here." His pulse quickened. *Simon has her*, he thought, but he didn't want to say it out loud.

The officer returned from her search of the house. "No one in there."

A scratchy communication burst out of the speaker attached to her shoulder. "Officer down. Request assistance. We've located Foley. Severe injuries evident."

"Copy that. I'm on my way." The policewoman sprinted toward the woods.

Matt shot a look of dread at Brooks. "Where the hell is Cullen?"

"Probably with her car. Does she have any type of vehicle recovery device like a LoJack?"

"No. She just has a basic Saturn ION coupe."

"Saturn is a GM vehicle. Does Cullen have OnStar in her car?"

"Yes, she activated it when she bought the car a few months ago."

"Good. OnStar has a global positioning system. Let's see if it works." Brooks flipped his cell phone open. He dialed the number for the police dispatcher. "Hi, Linda. This is Brooks Barrington. Can you patch me through to the OnStar stolen vehicle location department?" A few seconds went by while the call went through. A woman's voice finally flowed out of the cell phone. "Thank you for calling OnStar. My name is Helena. How may I help you?"

"This is Detective Brooks Barrington of the Fairfax County Virginia Police Department. I need you to locate a stolen car for me."

"Certainly, sir. What is the name of the owner of the vehicle in question?"

"Cullen Rhea. The last name is spelled r-h-e-a. Her address is 13529 Westwood Circle, Fairfax, Virginia. The vehicle is a Saturn ION coupe."

"Please hold while I access our global positioning system to locate the vehicle."

Matt stared at Brooks, afraid to breathe. Seconds felt like hours.

"Detective, the Saturn is located on Old Dominion Drive in Great Falls, Virginia," Helena said. "It is approximately two miles from the intersection of Old Dominion and Georgetown Pike."

"Thank you for your help, Helena."

"Good luck, Detective."

Snapping his phone shut, Brooks hurried to the driver's side of his Corvette. "Go home, Matt. I'll call you when I find her."

"I'm going with you, and I should drive."

"Why?" Insult was plastered all over Brooks's face.

"Because you smell like hot wings and beer. How many drinks have you had tonight?"

"A few, but I'm fine. I can drive."

"Driving drunk is exactly what Lazarus would want you to do. Don't let him trap you again the way he did with your wife and daughter. If you get us both killed, he wins."

Torn between reason and ego, Brooks gripped his car keys. Then he stuck his keys in his pocket. "You're right. You drive. But you'd better haul ass, boy."

Brooks maneuvered his prosthetic leg into Matt's BMW and pulled the seat belt over the barbecue sauce splatters on his belly. Matt spun out of the parking lot and drove down Route 50, disregarding every traffic regulation that stood in his way.

As he turned onto the Reston Parkway, Matt noticed a Subaru Forrester driving in front of him with a West Virginia University sticker on the rear window. "Oh my God! It's Kim."

"What in the hell are you talking about?" Brooks asked.

"Lazarus's last target. It's my executive assistant, Kim Taggert."

"How do you know that?"

"Kim and I have always been very close."

"You boinked your secretary? That's pretty cliché, don't you think?"

"She's an executive assistant. And, no, we never became intimate because she's been happily married for years. I've always been attracted to her, and I'm pretty sure that she's attracted to me. We flirt a lot, but that's as far as it ever goes. Maybe if things had been different—"

"Then you would have boinked your secretary. Sorry, executive assistant."

"Yes, but I didn't. Let's be clear about that. Kim is very important to me. I care about her. We can't let that son of a bitch kill her." He turned to face Brooks. "But how do we protect Kim and look for Cullen at the same time?

"We phone a friend." Brooks fished his phone out of his denim shirt pocket and punched in a familiar number.

"Hello?" a woman's voice answered.

"Tessa, I need your help."

"Brooks? It's late. What's going on?"

"I believe another woman could be in danger. It's Kim Taggert, Matt Curtis's executive assistant. I need you to check on her and keep her safe tonight."

"Um, I don't know if I can, Brooks. I've had a pretty rough night fighting off panic attacks. Why can't you check on her?"

"Because Cullen Rhea has been abducted. I'm on my way to Great Falls to search for her. Tessa, I know this is going to be difficult for you, but this woman could be fighting for her life tonight. We can't leave her alone to fend for herself. Tessa, I need you to help this woman. She doesn't deserve to die."

"OK, OK. I'll try. Where does she live?"

"I have no idea." Brooks looked at Matt for information.

"Her address is in my Blackberry. He pulled the electronic device out of his shirt pocket and handed it to his passenger. "I never leave home without it."

Brooks tapped the screen with the thin stylus a few times. "She lives at 4628 Barlow Road. Hurry. And, Tessa, be very careful."

Chapter 53

"Come on, you guys. Open up. I'm not messing around." Kim smacked Ted and Arlene's patio door.

Cupping her hands to the window in the door, she squinted to see into the family room. A blue and white striped couch sat on the far wall and faced a stone fireplace. Decked out with Penn State football memorabilia, the room celebrated Ted's illustrious career as a fourth-string fullback for coach Joe Paterno's Nittany Lions. In his senior year, Ted had actually played a few minutes and had caught a pass for a touchdown in the fourth quarter of a blowout against Purdue.

"Where are they?" Then she remembered that Ted and Arlene were on their second honeymoon—a seven-night eastern Caribbean cruise. *That's just perfect. I'm standing on their patio so scared that I'm about to pee in my pants, and they're stuffing their faces with jumbo shrimp at the late night buffet with Gopher and Captain Stubing on The Love Boat.*

"Let's see if we can find somebody on this block who can give us a ride home," she said to her canine partner. Hoping the teenagers were not waiting for her in the bushes, she walked around the house and hurried down the sidewalk.

I don't know anyone else in this neighborhood besides Ted and Arlene. Guess I'll have to ask a stranger for help. Someone must still be awake. Darkened houses lined both sides of the street. Every extraneous noise she heard made her more jumpy.

At the corner of Kennesaw Street, lights on the main level of a colonial home gave Kim a glimmer of optimism. She and Chief stepped along a stone pathway that led to the front door. *Come on. Come on.* She walked up to the door and rapped the heavy door knocker. No answer.

From behind an emerald-green curtain in a side window, a pair of elderly female Asian eyes peered at the late night visitors. When Kim made eye contact, they hid behind the curtain.

She banged on the door. "Hello? Can you help me?" Still no answer. Then the lights went off. "I saw you in the window. I know you're home. Please answer the door."

Minutes went by while Kim continued to knock and ring the doorbell. With a final exasperated whack on the door, she gave up. "Fine. Be that way."

Leading Chief back to the sidewalk, she concocted a strategy. "All right. Here's the deal. We gotta get home. If those boys show up again, you need to turn into an attack dog and go Cujo on them. Understand?"

The yellow lab snuffed and stretched his long legs out in front of his body as if he were preparing to run.

"I'll take that as a yes." She patted his solid back.

Ready to run at any second, she and Chief hurried down the sidewalk through the neighborhood. After a couple of blocks, she began to relax a bit and loosened her grasp on Chief's leash. She had run through two housing developments to get away from the aggressive teenage boys, and now the trek home seemed like it would take forever.

Crossing through the intersection of Haven Oak Road and Barlow Road, she noticed a sudden change in the way the moonlight created shadows in the trees that lined the sidewalk. The shadows were moving and changing with the sway of the trees in the summer wind. Fascinated with the unusual sight, she watched the shadows shift into the forms of four eerie faces. Then Kim realized that the shadowy faces were coming toward her.

Sensing that something was wrong, Chief began to whine and bark. Kim tightened her grip on his leash as the faces flew through the trees, over the pavement, and around parked cars. Scared and bewildered, Kim took off running as fast as she could down the sidewalk, pulling Chief along with her. She wasn't sure if the shadow faces were real or if they were just a figment of her overactive imagination. But either way, they frightened the hell out of her.

As she rounded a corner, she looked back to see if the faces were following her. Unaware that Chief had drifted over into her running path, Kim stepped on Chief's leash and got tangled up with his legs. An out of control ball of woman and dog rolled on the cement and smashed into a pair of male legs.

Stunned and embarrassed in a crumpled heap on the ground, Kim looked up to see a man staring down at her. Wearing a dark blue pin-striped suit with a light blue dress shirt and a yellow paisley tie, the man looked as if he were on his way to a corporate board meeting. Short spiked hair stood up on his head, and his eyes looked like two chunks of coal.

The man reached his right hand down to Kim in an offer to help her to her feet. "I am so sorry about that. I was running and tripped over my dog. Are you OK?"

"Hello, Kim. My name is Lazarus Kaine. We need to talk."

That's what that weird e-mail said. "Do I know you?" She racked her brain as she tried to recognize the sharply dressed man.

"Not yet. But recently I have had a number of interactions with your boss, Matt Curtis."

"I haven't seen you in the office. What company do you work for?"

"I work alone."

Disapproving of the slender man's ominous looks, Chief initiated a low, rumbling growl and lurched toward Lazarus. Hoping to intimidate the man, the yellow lab showed his upper incisors and threatened to attack.

Unaffected by the dog's aggressiveness, Lazarus leaned over and petted the dog's head. "My, what big teeth you have, Chief."

"How do you know his name?" Kim asked, unsettled by the man's actions and his unexpected familiarity with her life.

"It's written on his dog tag." Lazarus rubbed Chief's ears, making friends with the big dog.

"Oh, yeah." Kim felt as if she had "moron" tattooed on her forehead. "Looks like Chief found a new buddy. He's usually pretty ornery with new people. You must be a dog person."

"Yes, I love dogs." A devious smile slid across his face. "They're delicious."

Unable to tell if the man was just kidding or super creepy, Kim let out an uncomfortable chuckle. "Well, we'd better be on our way. Nice to meet you, Mr. Kaine. Let's go, Chief." Tugging at the dog's red leash, she walked past Lazarus, but his cold hand grabbed her right shoulder.

Moving his body directly behind Kim's, Lazarus pulled her close. "Karl doesn't know about your relationship with Matt Curtis, does he?" His icy breath crawled across the back of her neck, giving her a gargantuan case of the willies.

"What are you talking about? Matt's my boss." She wheeled around

"He's more than a boss to you, isn't he, Kim?"

"Matt's my friend." She locked eyes with Lazarus's manic stare.

"We both know he's far more than a friend."

"What do you mean? What are you talking about?" She slowly backed away from the disturbing man.

"You're attracted to him. Ever since you interviewed with him seven years ago, you've wanted to jump Matt's bones. But for some silly reason, you let your marriage to Karl stand in your way."

"That's absolutely ridiculous." Kim crossed her arms in defiance.

"Oh, is it? Then why do you flirt with him so much? You laugh at his lousy jokes. Your hands linger when you touch him. You wear sexy short skirts because you know he'll sneak looks. You like to feel his eyes embrace your body as he watches you walk down the corridor. You often stand very close to him because he likes it—and so do you. You frequently wish that you had the nerve to drop the faithful wife persona for just a moment and act on your impulse to show Matt how you feel about him. You want to get naughty with him. There's no denying it."

How does this guy know so much about me? It's like he has been listening to the dialogue that runs through my head. "All right, I'll admit that I am attracted to Matt. Yes, I flirt with him, but I swear I have not slept with him. I've thought about it, a lot, but I haven't gone through with it. I love my husband, and I would never do anything to hurt him or put our marriage in jeopardy."

"But you constantly send Matt mixed signals. You tempt him and playfully seduce him, which activates his launch sequence. Then, at the last second, you abort the mission and leave him stranded with a full tank of rocket fuel and nowhere to go. Do you have any idea how frustrating that must be for him?"

Kim stared at the sidewalk. "It probably drives him crazy."

"Well, tonight, I'm going to help you fully understand the meaning of the word "frustration." You'll find out what it's like to be in a futile situation that you can't control. Maybe then you'll be able to empathize with Matt Curtis." Lazarus stepped toward Kim.

She backed away from the man, who analyzed her like a peculiar psychotherapist. "I don't need your help, Mr. Kaine. Look, I need to get going. You have yourself a wonderful night. See ya later." She turned toward her home and pulled Chief's leash, intent on quickly getting away from the weird guy in the designer suit.

Lunging after Kim, Lazarus seized her right forearm, nearly yanking her off her feet. He pulled her face just inches from his. "You're not going anywhere."

Chapter 54

"Keep up with me, dammit," Simon snapped at Cullen.

"You're walking too fast. Slow down."

"God, you are such a pain." He tugged at the handcuffs that shackled them together.

She had no intention of making the journey easy. Every step of the way, she annoyed the ever-lovin' crap out of him by stepping on his heels, tripping over weeds, and grousing about everything that came into her mind. During their expedition along the narrow path, Cullen had emptied her scrub jacket pockets, dropping a ballpoint pen, a tin of Altoids, and her stethoscope with the hope that someone would find her improvised popcorn trail before Simon had time to complete his task.

They stumbled past a small sign labeled, "Difficult Run Trail." The hiking path followed the Difficult Run Stream, a tributary of the Potomac River that functioned as the southern border of Great Falls Park. Rambling over mostly flat terrain, the trail offered a number of slightly elevated clearings that provided moonlit views of picturesque waterfalls and diminutive white-water rapids. In a different circumstance, the most charming clearing could have served as a secluded location for a romantic evening with a bottle of wine overlooking the falls; however, Simon had a very different set of plans that included excruciating pain and a dramatic murder.

Sensing that she was approaching her final destination, Cullen let her entire body go limp. She collapsed on the ground as if she was paralyzed.

Aggravation burned in his chest as Simon grappled with 110 pounds of defiance. "What are you doing? Get up and walk."

"No." Cullen transformed her body into an uncooperative collection of bones and muscle. She dug the heels of her Reeboks into the dirt and jerked on the handcuffs with both arms, scraping the skin off of Simon's right wrist.

"That's it. I've had enough outta you." He aimed the pistol at Cullen's head.

Cullen closed her eyes and started praying. *Our Father, who art in heaven, hallowed be thy* ... Click. *Thy kingdom come, thy will be* ... Click. Click. *What is that clicking noise? I should be dead by now.* She opened her right eye just enough to see Simon remove the ammunition clip from the pistol.

"I don't believe this." Simon examined the clip and shook his head.

"It's empty? You tried to kill me with an empty gun?" Cullen laughed. "Wow, you really suck at this." She howled in delight and relief because she was still alive.

"Shut up. Just shut up." He smacked the clip back into place. "What kind of dumb-ass cop forgets to load his gun?" He heaved the useless weapon into the dark woods. Pulling at the handcuffs, he tried to haul Cullen to her feet, but she wouldn't budge, refusing to oblige her hapless would-be killer.

"If you take the handcuffs off, I'll walk."

"I'm not that stupid, Cullen. I know you'll try to run away. We don't have far to go."

"Suit yourself." Wrenching her body in a flurry of dramatic convulsions, she flopped on the ground like a fish on a line.

After fighting with her for about ten feet, Simon stopped. "All right, I'll take the cuffs off. But if you run, I swear to Jesus, Mary, and Joseph, I'll slit your throat." Simon reached into his pants pocket, retrieved the handcuff key, and released her from the handcuffs.

"Thank you." She rubbed her scraped wrist. "That feels much better." She stood up. "Hey, you're bleeding. It looks pretty bad."

Struggling with Cullen had caused Simon's handcuff to dig deep into his forearm, tearing his skin into a wide wound. Shifting his focus away from his annoying captive, he fumbled with the tiny key to unlock his side of the metal restraint.

Seizing an opportunity to escape, Cullen took off running as fast as she could. Realizing he had been played for a fool, Simon chased after her like a crazed killer in a horror movie sequel.

Random humps in the hiking trail worked like nature's speed bumps, slowing Cullen down. She could hear Simon thundering behind her, drawing closer with every stride as his feet pounded the ground. *Keep going. Got to stay alive.*

Assuming Simon was familiar with the trail, she decided to lunge into the obscurity of the forest. Stumbling through the brush, she scraped her ankles on huge rocks that lay hidden in the night. Sharp briars tore at her hospital scrubs. Virginia creeper vines reached up from the ground and grabbed at her feet as she thrashed through the summer foliage. Huge oak trees swung their thick branches at her head as if they were protecting their homeland from an unwelcome intruder.

Exhausted from the chase, she stopped for a second under a large maple tree to catch her breath. Afraid of what she might hear, she stood still and listened for signs of Simon's pursuit. To her great surprise, the only audible sounds came from the leaves rustling in the soft evening breeze. But the serene tranquility of the great outdoors couldn't calm her down. She could feel Simon lurking in the shadows. Hunting her. Hating her.

Studying her surroundings, Cullen didn't have a clue how far off the trail she had wandered. As if being chased through the woods by a homicidal maniac wasn't bad enough; now she was lost.

Chapter 55

"Let go of me, you crazy son of a bitch."

"What's the matter, Kim?" Lazarus sneered. "Feeling a bit irritated? It's about to get a lot worse."

Eager to protect his best friend, Chief lunged at Lazarus, landing his heavy paws on the man's left side and snapping at his arm. Without losing his hold on Kim, Lazarus waved his hand in front of the big dog's face like a magician performing a trick. As if he had mainlined a muscle relaxant, Chief's fury dissipated. A gray mist clouded his eyes, and his legs collapsed, sending him sagging to the sidewalk—a clump of comatose canine.

"Chief! Chief, get up!" Kim yelled. "What did you do to him?"

"Your dog is fine. He's just going to take a little nap while I finish with you." Lazarus wrapped his arms around Kim and manhandled her out into the street.

Kicking and screaming, she brawled with a strength she didn't realize she possessed, but it wasn't enough to break her free. He dragged her into the middle of the intersection of Haven Oak and Barlow roads.

"Now you're going to find out what it feels like to be trapped in a situation where you have no control of the outcome, the same way Matt feels when he's with you. Ever since he met you, he has desperately wanted to act on his impulses, but you wouldn't let him. On a daily basis, you tease him, seduce him, and then you push him away. You encourage his desire, then you lock him inside an emotional jail cell, a disturbed man, unable to express his feelings. Tonight, you'll be consumed by your sins of infatuation. You'll experience the frustration and pain you've inflicted on Matt for so many years."

"I'm willing to take responsibility for my actions, and I promise I'll apologize to Matt. Just please let me go."

"It's too late for a last-ditch effort to save your soul with a pathetic confession. It's time for you to suffer." The street under Kim's feet began to soften. Asphalt oozed over her sneakers, gradually pulling her down into a cold pit of crushed gravel and tar. The road sucked her into its grasp as if it were alive. It drew her into the pavement, clutched her calves, and devoured her thighs. She thrashed and battled to extricate her legs, but the road refused to let her go.

"Get me out of here! Help me! Somebody help me! I don't want to die this way."

"You ain't seen nothin' yet, sweet cheeks. Good-bye, Kim." Leaving her with a final, cunning chuckle, his body burst into hundreds of small shadow faces that crawled into the night. Within moments, the faces were gone.

Descending slowly into the road, Kim thought about the old Tarzan movies she watched as a kid in which people found themselves trapped in quicksand. Because this was a similar situation, she remembered the sage advice the people always received from their jungle guides—just hold your body completely still, and you'll stop sinking. She didn't know if the advice was a viable solution for this dilemma, but it was the only answer she could come up with on the fly. With nothing to lose, she slowed her breathing and held her arms and legs motionless. For a few terrible seconds, she continued to drop into the asphalt. But as the pavement covered her black running shorts and encircled her waist, she stopped sinking. Then the blacktop reverted back to its original hardened state. The road held Kim hostage in the middle of the intersection.

With the top half of her body sticking up out of the road like a bizarre Kim-in-the-box, she thanked God for her stay of execution. "Now I just have to wait on somebody to drive by and call for help. The fire department will dig me out of this hole. I'll be fine, except for the crap I'll have to take for the rest of my life from Karl and his buddies for getting myself into this predicament. This is really embarrassing, but at least I'm alive."

At the far end of Haven Oak Road, the engine of a black Ford Excursion fired into action, and a bright pair of headlights sliced through the darkness, shining directly into Kim's eyes. "All right! This is good. This person will see me and call 9-1-1. I'll be outta here in no time."

The enormous sport utility vehicle pulled out of its parking space and drove toward Kim. She yelled and waved her arms in the air as the Excursion approached. Then she noticed that the SUV was accelerating, as if the driver were pushing the gas pedal to the floorboard. The powerful vehicle's automatic transmission cranked into overdrive and hurtled itself at her.

"Slow down! I can't move! I need help!" She flailed her arms.

The Excursion picked up speed as it continued on its collision course with the upper half of Kim's body. Its license plate was aimed squarely at her head. The headlights became larger and brighter, almost blinding Kim with their intensity. "Oh God, no, no, no!" The SUV tore over the pavement with homicidal intent.

As Kim came to terms with her certain death, she heard another vehicle approaching from her left on Barlow Road. A set of sedan headlights advanced toward her. The two vehicles raced on perpendicular paths, destined to intersect at Kim's trapped torso. She clenched her fists and prepared for the brutal impact.

The silver Toyota Prius lurched as its driver stomped on the gas, only twenty yards away from her. The Excursion's engine screamed on its way to the inevitable crash. Fifteen yards away. Ten yards away. Kim covered her head with her arms, afraid to look at the autos that were about to mutilate her.

As the Excursion came within striking distance, the Prius smashed into the right front fender of the mammoth SUV. Veering ever so slightly off course, the Excursion slid to the side of Kim's body. Its bulky black bumper missed her head by less than a foot. Almost rolling over, the Excursion roared out of control and plowed into the back of a red Chevrolet Monte Carlo that was parked on the side of the road. The sedan's tires squealed as it spun around in the road and came to rest, wedged between a street light and a stop sign.

The sedan groaned and sputtered as its engine died, which signaled the end of its suicide mission. Opening the crumpled driver's side door, a woman climbed out from underneath a deployed airbag. Dressed in a pair of Puma running shoes, jeans, a cream-colored blouse, and a brown bomber jacket, the woman had a smear of blood on the left side of her forehead. Favoring her left leg and holding her left arm close to her side, she limped to Kim. "Are you hurt?" She winced.

"I need a beer, two shots of tequila, and a Valium to settle my nerves, but other than that, I think I'm fine." Kim wiped tears of relief from her eyes. "Thank you for helping me."

"I'm glad you're all right."

From out of nowhere, a huge ball of fur-covered excitement slammed into Kim and slobbered all over her face. "Chief! Thank God you're safe." Kim gave the massive canine a tight hug.

Kim looked up at Tessa with a humiliated expression on her face. "You're not going to believe what happened."

"After the past few days, I'd believe almost anything." Tessa held her left elbow to keep it stable. "I'd better check on the other driver."

She limped over to the crushed hunk of black metal that used to be a Ford Excursion. Bracing herself for what she was about to see, she took a deep breath and pried the passenger's door open. No one was behind the wheel.

Chapter 56

"That's Cullen's car." Matt swerved off Old Dominion Drive. He parked behind his girlfriend's Saturn, jumped out of his BMW, and sprinted for her vehicle.

"Get your head down, Matt." *This guy's gonna get us both killed.* Brooks eased his way around to the right side of the Saturn. Unsnapping the latch holding his .357 Sig pistol, he pulled the gun out of its holster. Brooks peered inside Cullen's car to see a blue sweater and a stack of fashion magazines in the back seat. A purse and a lunchbox sat on the passenger's seat.

"Where is she?" Matt squinted into the shadows of the surrounding woods.

"Hard to tell. I can't see a damn thing out here. Do you have a flashlight in your car?"

"Yeah, I'll get it."

As Matt mined his small cluttered trunk for a flashlight, Brooks let his instincts guide him. After Matt delivered the flashlight, Brooks scrutinized the ground on the driver's side of the Saturn. "Scuff marks in the dirt indicate a struggle, and then they headed north." He pointed in the direction of an embankment. With some trepidation, Brooks slipped his pistol back into its holster.

Flipping his cell phone open, he speed-dialed the police dispatcher. "Hi, Linda. This is Brooks Barrington. Please send assistance to Old Dominion Drive in Great Falls at the Difficult Run Bridge. I am in pursuit of suspect Simon Fletcher. Give me every officer you have available. Also, roll an ambulance, just in case." He snapped the phone shut. "Let's go."

They walked toward the embankment, staring at gravel and weeds. After a few steps, the flashlight beam passed over a small shiny object. Brooks groaned as he bent over his protruding paunch to inspect the item. "Cullen's employee badge. He must have taken her on the hiking trail."

"There's a trail around here? How did you know that?"

"I used to hike in this area with my family. There's a stream not very far along, and a clearing where my daughter, Holly, loved to sit and watch the water splash over the rocks." Brooks tramped into a patch of tall grass.

"I'm sure you must miss her."

"You have no idea." They walked in uncomfortable silence as Brooks led Matt to a weathered hiking trail.

"Which way do we go? Left or right?" Matt asked.

"Let's see if Cullen was smart enough to help us." Brooks shined the flashlight up and down the path to see if she had dropped another article for them to find.

"I don't see anything," Matt said.

"Let's go to the right."

"Why?"

"I'm certain they went to the right."

"What makes you so sure?"

"Stop asking annoying questions, Matt," Brooks snapped. "Just trust me. I'm a professional. I know what I'm doing."

They trudged for about fifty yards along the uneven path while they strained to see the ground. Then Matt caught a glimpse of something that reflected light. He dug into the grass on the side of the trail and picked up Cullen's stethoscope. "You were right. This is the way, Brooks. How did you know they went in this direction?"

"Training, experience, and a great deal of intelligence."

"In other words, it was a lucky guess."

"Yep."

As they worked their way along the trail, Brooks found a ballpoint pen and a tin of Altoids, which were both dropped in strategic locations to help potential rescuers make the proper turns on their expedition. A symphony of insects filled the night air with an opus of repetitive clicks, chirps, and hums that vibrated the forest with sounds of chaos. Squirrels scurried through the underbrush, rummaging for bits of food and running from predators.

A quarter of a mile into their search, Brooks felt an uncomfortable pressure in his chest as if someone were squeezing his heart with a huge pair of pliers. Shards of agony spread to his shoulders, neck, and arms. A feeling of lightheadedness made him dizzy to the point where he almost fainted. Sweat poured from his head and stained his denim shirt. Nausea swept over him like a hot, putrid breeze. Breath escaped from his lungs but refused to come back. He dropped to the ground on his good knee, gasped for air, and clutched his chest.

"Brooks, are you all right?"

"What kind of silly-ass question is that? Do I look like I'm all right?" He felt as if his eyeballs were going to fly out of his head. The fourteen chicken wings, tub of coleslaw, and six beers in his stomach ached to get out of their unstable gastrointestinal prison, but Brooks's stubborn will kept them in their place.

"You should go back to the car. The ambulance will get there soon. I'll find Cullen by myself."

"The hell you will. I came this far, and I'm not giving up just because I have a little heart problem. You can't do this by yourself, Matt. You've never been face to face with a brutal killer like Simon."

"Have you?"

"Of course I have, but it's been a few years." Brooks fought to get to his feet. "Cullen doesn't have much time. We need to get to her before Simon decides to kill her." He sucked in as much air as his lungs could hold, hoping the fresh dose of oxygen would clear his head.

With a combination of selfless bravery and adrenaline-induced stupidity, Brooks resumed his chase to find Cullen and Simon. Maybe it was his genuine concern for Cullen's well-being—or maybe it was his selfish need to prove to himself that he still had the ability prevent a violent crime—that motivated Brooks to push his broken-down body along the wooded trail. Either way, he had to continue the hunt.

As the pain in his chest subsided, Brooks regained his normal breathing pattern, and his pulse slowed down to a low roar. *This is a good sign. I'm going to be OK ... until my heart explodes.*

Chapter 57

"Oh, my God!" Cullen's right shoulder bumped into something warm and hairy that clung to the side of an old maple tree. She stared into the yellow-tinged eyes of something that was the size of a cat with gray fur, a pointed pink nose, and black ears. The startled animal hissed and growled, showing a mouthful of sharp teeth.

Backing away from the small beast, she tripped over a root that stuck up from the loose dirt. She crashed into a prickly bush and thumped hard on the ground. Looking up in the moonlight, she could see that the animal was a surprised opossum that had just been minding its own business.

"Sorry about that." She brushed the leaves and grass off her aching backside. So frightened that it was unable to flee, the opossum fell into an involuntary shock-like state and hung motionless, hugging the sturdy tree. "It's OK, little fella. I'm not going to hurt you. Have a pleasant evening." Cullen smiled at the terrified marsupial. "I'm standing in the woods in the middle of the night, holding a conversation with an opossum. Now it's official. I have lost my freakin' mind."

Cullen gazed at the moon as if it had some magic ability to show her the way out of the forest. Instead, the moon slipped behind a group of clouds and avoided any interaction with her.

Walking to her left for no logical reason, she figured that eventually she would find the trail, the stream, or Simon. Then she heard footsteps beating through the underbrush behind her. *Oh shit! I gave away my location when I screamed at that opossum.* She tore around bushes, between trees, through massive spiderwebs, over dead branches, and into the darkest section of the forest.

As if running through a darkened gauntlet, Cullen covered her head with her arms and took the punishment inflicted by fat branches and long tree limbs. Sharp leaves sliced at her face, and stringy vines snatched at her ankles. The moon peeked from behind its cloud cover to watch her as she struggled to find freedom. Then it quickly disappeared, leaving her alone in the dark.

She didn't see a pointed rock that rose from the ground like a geological road block. Her right foot caught the top of the rock, which sent her tumbling head first into an open space. Falling and rolling, she smacked her left elbow hard on the ground and finally came to rest in the middle of the hiking trail that had been so elusive. Beaten, battered, and bruised, Cullen moaned as she stood up. Unable to get her bearings, she placed blind faith in her intuition and headed to her left down the trail, hoping like hell that she was walking toward her car.

Moving faster with every step, she felt more confident that she would find her way out of the forest. At random intervals, she stopped and listened for Simon, but all she could hear was the steady drone of the nocturnal world that surrounded her.

Passing a stand of holly bushes that looked sort of familiar, she broke into a run. She encouraged her throbbing legs to keep going even though they had taken an awful pounding from the forest.

Feeling a strong second wind, she could hear the Difficult Run Stream drifting in the night. *I think I'm getting closer.* Figuring that a little assistance from above couldn't hurt, she prayed. *Hey, God. It's me, Cullen. You know I don't ask you for much, but I could use a little help down here. Look, if I get out of this alive, I promise I'll go to church every Sunday, and I'll try my best to be nice to the people that bug the heck outta me. I'll be more affectionate to Matt. I'll call my mom more often. I promise to stop saying bad words, unless I'm really mad. And I promise to eat less chocolate.* She paused. *No. I need to take that one back. But I will donate a lot of clothes to a battered women's shelter, and I'll volunteer at the animal rescue foundation. Please, God, help me get outta here.*

A cluster of puffy clouds parted, allowing the moon to shine on the path. Shadows created by tall trees shifted back and forth along the trail like surreptitious escorts leading Cullen to her fate. The wind picked up, which caused the shadows to move aggressively through the trees and over the land. Like Dorothy dashing through the Haunted Forest, she just wanted to go home.

Sprinting as fast as she could, Cullen took a hairpin curve too fast. Her left foot skidded on a patch of loose rocks, sending her stumbling into the trunk of a small dogwood tree. "Dammit! Oops. Sorry, God. That one just slipped out." Anxious to get to safety, she scrambled to her feet. *This is nuts. I'm running through the woods like a crazy woman.*

Fifteen yards down the trail, Cullen heard something rustling in the bushes in front of her. She stopped, unable to decide whether she should ignore it or run in the other direction. Maybe it was Simon preparing to attack her. Maybe it was a bear hunting for some tender white meat. Then a plump brown rabbit bounced out of the underbrush. A woman on the edge, Cullen almost jumped out of her scrubs. The bunny stopped and looked at her, trying to determine if she was a predator or just a pretty young woman with an overactive imagination. It twitched its nose a couple of times, adjusted its rabbit ears, and leisurely hopped away.

Laughing at herself for being scared of a fuzzy bunny, Cullen resumed her pace. Then a powerful hand grabbed her injured left elbow from behind. When she tried to turn around, a lean arm wrapped around her right side, yanking her back against a man's chest. Fear blew through her body with the power of a jet engine. A pair of lips behind her right ear whispered, "Hello, Cullen."

Chapter 58

"Do you see her? I can't see her. Where is she? Do you think she's all right?"

"For the love of God, would you please shut up?" Brooks whacked Matt on the shoulder with his left hand. "We don't want to let Simon know that we're out here. Just keep your eyes open and your mouth closed." Matt frowned and grudgingly complied with Brooks's orders.

As they walked along the path, Brooks fell behind. A stream of sweat ran down the side of his face. "Matt, hold up a minute."

"What's the matter? Are you sick again?"

"No. I gotta pee like a racehorse."

"We don't have time for that, Brooks."

"When a middle-aged bladder is full, you have to take care of it. This will only take a minute." Brooks turned toward a poplar tree and prepared to answer the call of nature.

Matt paced while Brooks purged the six bottles of Samuel Adams from his body. In midstream, a woman's scream sliced through the darkness. "No! Let go of me!"

"Come on!" Matt raced down the path.

"Gottdammit." Brooks strained to cut off his rivulet of relief. He yanked at his relaxed-fit Wrangler jeans and stumbled along the trail, trying to zip his fly and run at the same time. "Turn the flashlight off," Brooks whispered.

They stalked through the darkness until they saw two figures thrashing on the trail ahead of them. The male form had both arms wrapped around the smaller female, dragging her as she fought to get away.

"Simon's probably trying to get her to the clearing that's just up ahead," Brooks guessed.

"We have to stop him." Matt bolted toward Simon and Cullen.

"Hold on there, cowboy." Brooks caught Matt by the right wrist before he made any progress. "We can't just run up on him. Simon probably has a weapon, and if he gets excited, he'll kill her."

"Then take out your pistol and shoot him."

"It's not that easy."

"Why not?" Matt glared into Brooks's concerned face.

"There's not a clear line to him. Cullen could get hurt."

They continued down the trail, remaining out of view and a significant distance behind Simon and Cullen. "You're afraid to shoot, aren't you?" Matt pressed. "Like an idiot, you had to knock down a bellyful of beer tonight, and now you're too drunk to fire your pistol. Nice work, Detective."

"What I do when I'm off duty is none of your damn business. And for your information, my drinking has nothing to do with this situation. I'm not a very good shot—even when I'm sober."

"What do you mean? Certainly cops must pass some sort of weapons test, right?"

"Yes. But shooting at a paper target on a closed range is a lot easier than shooting at a real person moving through the woods at night. I'm afraid I'll hit Cullen. I can't take the risk."

"All right. I'll shoot him. Give me the gun."

"No way." Brooks clasped his holstered pistol.

"Hand it over, Brooks." Matt held out his right hand.

"Have you ever fired a gun?"

"Back home on our farm, I used to shoot squirrels, deer, and groundhogs. Look, I'm sure I can do this, Brooks. I have to do it for Cullen."

"Think through the consequences. If you fired a shot and injured her, you'd never forgive yourself. If you shoot Simon, you'll probably go back to jail. There is no upside in doing something foolish."

"Then what can we do? That son of a bitch is about to kill her, and we're not doing anything to stop him. I'm not going to stand here and watch."

Brooks moved his large frame in front of Matt. "Listen to me. We'll follow them until they stop walking. Then, at the appropriate time, when he moves a few feet away from Cullen, we'll surprise Simon from two sides. We'll immobilize him while he's disoriented."

"Do you actually think that pitiful plan will work? Where did you get it? *The Idiot's Guide to Catching Bad Guys? Police Work for Dummies? Magnum, P.I.?*"

"It's the best scheme I can come up with at the moment." Brooks turned his back on Matt and resumed his pursuit. Through the forest, they watched Simon jostle Cullen toward a predetermined location.

"This sucks." Out of habit, Matt looked at his wristwatch. The tiny hands pointed to 2:07 AM. A soft summer breeze increased its intensity. Tall trees waved their branches and leaves, creating a collection of swaying shadows in the moonlight. As Matt hiked through the darkness, the shadows formed faces that lined the trail—greeting him, leering at him, taunting him. Like a group of separate entities acting as a single unit, the shadow faces churned, evolved, and combined to form an accumulation of mysterious energy.

A smile spread across Matt's face. A flash of brilliance danced in his weary eyes. "Hey, Brooks," he whispered. "I've got a better idea."

Chapter 59

"Ow, that hurts! Let go of my hair." Cullen lashed out at Simon as he tugged on her ponytail.

"Quit whining and keep walking. We're almost there."

"Where?"

"The last place you'll ever see. It's actually quite beautiful—and serene. You'll love it. The soothing crash of the waterfall is so peaceful that it could lull you to sleep," Simon said softly. "It's perfect location for a gruesome death."

Exhausted and sore, Cullen tried to wrench her way out of Simon's grasp, but the long night of running through the forest had taken its toll on her body. Bashed and bruised, she could barely move her aching legs. Simon pushed her around a sharp curve in the trail and shoved her through a patch of tall grass. She staggered into a clearing on the bank of the Difficult Run Stream. In front of her, she saw a striking view of a small waterfall. Glistening in the moonlight, the waterfall looked like it belonged on a postcard as the clear water splashed into a wide section of the stream.

Pushing Cullen down on the ground and slamming her back against a huge rock, Simon held the utility knife blade against her throat. "No more running away. I'm tired of chasing you. Do you understand" His chapped lips almost touched Cullen's left cheek.

"Yeah, I get it, Simon." She nodded her head ever so slightly, avoiding contact with the knife.

Backing away from her, he retracted the carbon blade, slipped the utility knife into his right pocket, and crouched down just a few feet away from the water. Without losing eye contact with his victim, he rummaged deep into his backpack and found a Milky Way candy bar. Like an excited eight-year-old boy, he ripped open the package containing the sweet chocolate treat. "I've loved these since I was a kid. My mom used to buy them for me when I got good grades on my report card." Taking immense pleasure in the common delicacy, he chewed slowly and savored the sugar rush. "Are you hungry, Cullen?" He taunted her with his mouthful of the creamy delight.

"Yes, I'm starving." She coveted the chocolate.

"Tough shit." Simon laughed and stuffed the last half of the candy bar into his mouth. Smacking his lips like a cow chewing a clump of grass, he devoured the huge chunk of chocolate and smiled at her, revealing bits of brown that stuck to his front teeth.

Easing to the edge of the stream without losing site of Cullen, he dipped his right hand into the water and took a sip of the cool natural liquid. "Are you thirsty?"

"Of course I am."

Simon stood up, walked over to Cullen, and helped her crawl to the edge of the water. He gently held her sides as she leaned close to the water. Just as she reached her right hand into the stream, Simon grabbed the back of her head and shoved her face into the rushing water, using his entire body to get the maximum amount of leverage required to keep her skull in position.

Battling with what was left of her strength, Cullen thrashed to loosen Simon's hold. *I can't breathe. Oh God, I'm drowning.* She swung her arms and kicked her feet while water poured into her lungs. Grabbing a handful of her hair and yanking her head out of the water, Simon pulled her to safety. She collapsed on the ground, coughing, gagging, and sucking in a welcome chestful of air.

"Would you like another drink?" A wicked grin was painted on his smug mug. He hovered over her, filled with amusement as he watched her suffer.

Cullen hocked a load of spit into his self-satisfied expression. "No, thanks. I'm good for now." She wiped her mouth with the sleeve of her purple scrub jacket. "You are such an ass."

Staring down at his attractive hostage, Simon used his shirttail to dry his face. "Enough fooling around. Let's get to the good stuff." He lifted her to her feet and drew her body close. Then he kissed her forehead. "Take your clothes off."

Cullen responded with a low moan. She slowly opened her mouth and bit Simon's bottom lip as hard as she could—as if she were tearing into a tough piece of meat.

"You bitch!" Simon tasted blood that oozed from his lip. Swinging his left fist wildly, he caught Cullen on the right side of her head, sending her crumbling to the ground.

Although she was physically drained, her instincts told her to run. Cullen scrambled to her feet and darted toward the woods. With her fatigued muscles failing her, she hoped enough adrenaline would pump into her system to carry her into the darkness of the woods. She made it to an area covered with wildflowers and weeds, but just before she reached a group of thick bushes, a powerful jolt from behind knocked her to the ground.

As she strained to stand up, a pair of hands grabbed her shoulders and forcefully threw her on her back. Simon jumped on top of her, retrieved the handcuffs from his pocket, and snapped the steel clamps on her wrists.

"I told you not to run." As he stood up, he snatched the collar of Cullen's scrub jacket. Dragging her back to the clearing, he licked his swollen bottom lip, trying unsuccessfully to stop the bleeding. "I can't believe you bit me."

"You should have shared the chocolate." As Cullen's back bumped along the rocky soil, she kicked her feet and tried to twist her body. Simon lugged his uncooperative victim to a patch of soft grass just a few feet from the water's edge.

Pissed off at his inability to seal the deal, he took out the utility knife, extended the blade, and held it in front of her face. "Take your pants off."

"Simon, please don't do this."

"I said take your pants off." He moved the knife closer to her face. "I want you to get naked for me."

"You won't enjoy it. I'm in the middle of my period."

"I don't care." Simon grasped the waistband of her hospital scrubs with his left hand and pulled them down to her ankles.

Unwilling to resign herself to her impending rape, Cullen lifted her knee and aimed at Simon's groin. She missed.

Laughing at his victim's weak attempt at self-defense, Simon began pulling her white underwear off. A cell phone rang in the distance.

Chapter 60

"Aw, shit." Brooks rushed to pull his cell phone from his shirt pocket before it rang again. Juggling it in his sweaty hands, he flipped the tiny phone open and looked at the caller ID. "Tessa, I can't talk. I'm busy."

"Brooks, what's wrong? Where are you?" The woman's voice burst through the speaker. Turning down the volume, Brooks cupped his hands over his mouth to deaden the sound.

"Simon Fletcher has Cullen Rhea hostage in Great Falls Park. I can see them."

"For God's sake, don't fire your weapon. You're a terrible shot."

"Thanks for the vote of confidence. Look, I gotta go."

"I understand. I just wanted to tell you that Kim Taggert is safe. She was trapped in a bizarre situation, but now she's fine. She's with me." Sounds of many people talking at the same time created a chaotic wall of background noise behind Tessa's voice.

"Where are you?"

"I'm at the emergency room at Fairfax Memorial Hospital. I had a little accident in my car."

"What happened? Are you OK?" Brooks caught himself talking too loudly.

"I have a few cuts and bruises, but it's no big deal. I'll explain it all when I see you. Go get Fletcher. Call me when you can."

Brooks softly clapped his phone shut. "That was my partner. Kim Taggert is out of danger."

"Thank God." Matt's look of relief faded quickly. "But Simon heard your cell phone. He knows someone is out here." Through the trees, Matt could see Simon holding a knife to Cullen's neck, studying the wooded area to find the owner of the phone.

Glancing at his wristwatch, Matt's pulse quickened when he saw the time—2:22 AM. Three shadow faces flew through the trees and dove at Matt. Just a few feet in front of him, the faces became a mass of twisting black force that drew strength from the pale moonlight and the gloom that filled the night. The gathering of kinetic power shifted and surged through a bizarre embryonic phase. Then it began to advance into the form of a human. Slowly, details of the figure came into focus. The man wore a charcoal gray three-piece suit, a solid white dress shirt with French cuffs, and a magenta tie with a matching pocket handkerchief. "Good evening, boys."

"What are you doing here, Lazarus?" Brooks snapped.

"I came to watch Simon dismember Cullen. Oh, how I do love a good old-fashioned slaughter. It should be quite a show. You guys have the best seats in the woods, so I thought I'd join you."

"We're not gonna let that happen," Brooks said.

"The two of you think you're going to keep Simon from killing her? A fat, drunk, crippled cop and Mr. I'm-terrified-of-my-own-shadow? That's ridiculous." Lazarus laughed out loud.

"Anything is possible. Even you can be stopped. We know that you failed to kill Kim Taggert."

Lazarus abruptly stifled his laughter. "Yes, your little friend Tessa got in my way. She ruined a perfectly good murder. On rare occasions, fate intervenes, and dumb luck spoils the most ingenious homicide. It's an annoying part of the job. I'll get over it, eventually." Lazarus straightened his tie and smoothed his expensive lapels. "By the way, Brooks, how are you feeling? A little dizzy? Nauseated? Feeling some extra weight on your chest? Worried about the fact that you're just a sausage biscuit away from a coronary catastrophe?"

"I'll be fine." Brooks winced as his lungs tightened. The fingers on his left hand went numb and his breathing became shallow. A rocket of pain flew through his left shoulder. With his vision blurred in both eyes, he barely saw Lazarus turn to face Matt.

"And how are you this fine evening, Matthew?" The thin man moved toward Matt. The shadows around him undulated with a rhythmic sway.

"Hello, Lazarus. I'm glad to see you."

Lazarus raised his narrow eyebrows. "Oh, really? That's unusual. No one is ever glad to see me. I'm touched." He placed his right hand over his chest where a heart should have been.

"We need to talk."

"About what?"

"Your persistent efforts to screw up my life in every way imaginable. I've had enough of your bullshit, and it stops tonight."

"Let's get something straight. You brought this upon yourself. You lost control of your fears, and I merely helped them come to fruition. By giving in to your insecurities and your irrational doubts, you created a series of deadly situations for the women in your life. You are responsible for everything that has happened over the past few days. The fault falls on you." Lazarus poked his bony right index finger into Matt's collarbone.

Matt clenched his fists. "You're right. I take full responsibility for each horrible incident. Four women are dead because of me, and I'll have to live with that guilt. But most of all, I regret that I let you dominate my life. That's over."

A slight smile eased across Lazarus's slim face. "My goodness. It appears that you've developed a spine, Matt. I'm surprised. I didn't think you had the stones to accept the blame and stand up to me. You've almost earned my respect. But you still have a serious problem to deal with." Lazarus turned his body and gazed through the forest at Simon and Cullen. "That lunatic is about to scatter pieces of your girlfriend all over the ground."

"No, he's not. I'm going to stop him." Matt stepped forward so he could stare into Lazarus's black eyes. "And you're going to help me."

Chapter 61

"Don't make a sound." Simon pressed the knife blade against Cullen's neck. Positioning her body in front of his, he used her as a shield against any form of artillery that could be meant for him.

Directly in front of them, the bushes rustled. A human form appeared from behind a bundle of bulky branches. Cullen felt the urge to scream for help, but the knife at her throat kept her quiet.

A bright burst of light flooded the woods, briefly blinding Simon, but he held his victim in a rigid clench. "Turn that damn light off, or I'll slit her throat!" he yelled.

The beam went dark and a shaded figure moved through the bushes into the clearing. "Let her go, Simon," a stern male voice commanded from out of the night.

"Stop right there, whoever you are." Simon constricted his prey like a hungry boa.

The man moved cautiously into the moonlight. "Matt! Oh, thank God you're here." Simon clamped his left hand over Cullen's mouth to shut her up. Even though she could barely breathe, the sight of Matt made her feel optimistic. *Now I just have to figure out how to get away from this psycho.*

"I'm asking you as a friend, Simon. Please, let her go." Somehow Matt maintained a rational tone.

"How romantic. Trying to free your girlfriend and save the day. Well, I'm sorry, Matt, that only happens in the movies. I'm gonna carve this bitch up like a Butterball turkey, and you're going to watch me do it."

"I won't let you hurt her." Matt moved forward with deliberate purpose.

"You're willing to fight me for your girlfriend's life? That's a very courageous but stupid choice, Matt. I'll kill you just for the fun of it."

"No. I don't want to fight you." Matt continued to approach Simon. "I want to introduce you to a friend of mine."

At that instant, the wind shifted from a leisurely southern breeze to a northern gust. Shadows that lurked in the woods began to move and mutate. Darkness encompassed the forest as an indecipherable black shape formed beside Matt. Out of the trees, hundreds of shadow faces soared through the air, swirling through the night and uniting with the murky mass to make it even stronger. The figure shifted its mighty weight and heaved with power as it metamorphosed into the outline of a human.

Starting near the ground, the accumulation of shadows grew into a pair of black eelskin shoes, a black wool three-button pin-striped suit, an azure dress shirt with a white collar, and a satin azure tie. A severe face developed under a headful of short spiked hair. Finally, a pair of coal black eyes came into focus and peered at the troubled man holding the utility knife. "Hello, Simon. My name is Lazarus Kaine. We need to talk."

Simon raised his right eyebrow. "Nice entrance. What are you supposed to be? A bad imitation of David Copperfield?"

"I will admit that I do enjoy displaying my flair for the dramatic. I consider it to be a significant segment of my personality. It's a characteristic that I prefer to embrace." He made a quick assessment of Simon's slacker wardrobe. "And what are you supposed to be? A Tony Hawk wannabe? You're too old to be a dude."

"This is just a disguise, and it worked beautifully, by the way."

"On Officer Foley. You crushed his skull with a skateboard," Lazarus said without a hint of emotion. "He endured a most agonizing death."

"I watched him die. It was invigorating." Simon's chest swelled with a sense of careless pride. He took a few moments to size up the sharply dressed man with the sinister eyes. "So, let me guess. You've come here to try to convince me to let Cullen go and surrender myself peaceably."

"Oh, no, quite the contrary. Actually, I'm a murder aficionado. You could even call me a homicide junkie. I always say, 'There's nothing like a good mauling.' Tonight, I'm here as an interested spectator. I understand that you plan to butcher this lovely young woman, and I'd like to take a look at your technique."

Simon held a perplexed gape on the thin man. "Are you serious?"

"Yes. Come on. You're wasting my time. Let's see what you can do. Rip her to shreds. Tear her lungs out of her chest. Cut her stomach open, and spread her intestines all over the place. What are you waiting for? Let's see some blood." Lazarus frowned at Simon and snapped his fingers in an impatient hustle.

What first appeared to be a gallant rescue had turned grotesque, and Cullen felt fully justified in pushing her panic button. "Matt, what's going on? Stop this!" Terror stormed out of her eyes. The more she struggled, the tighter Simon held her. Kicking her feet, she fought hard to make him loosen his grip, but it didn't work.

Visibly confused and terribly worried, Matt screamed at Lazarus. "What do you think you're doing?"

"Shut it, Matt." Like a schoolteacher waiting on a dumbfounded student to answer a simple question, Lazarus let a long, silent pause eat away at Simon's confidence. After thirty unbearable seconds, Lazarus threw up his hands. "Well, Simon, are ya gonna kill her, or are ya just gonna stand there like a schmuck?"

"I can do it." He placed the sharp blade of the utility knife on the left side of Cullen's neck and gave her a soft kiss on the cheek. "Brace yourself, baby. This is really gonna hurt."

Chapter 62

Matt swallowed hard. *What have I done?*

"Quit stalling!" Lazarus yelled. "Slice her throat."

Taking a deep breath, Simon gripped the handle of the knife. Gritting his teeth, he swiftly drew the blade across Cullen's neck.

"No!" Matt bolted toward Simon, but Lazarus caught his right arm and stopped him.

Screaming in horror, Cullen instinctively rushed her hands to her throat. She looked down at her fingers, expecting them to be covered with crimson, but they weren't. Not a spot of blood stained her hands.

Realizing his initial pass had missed the mark, Simon slashed at Cullen's neck for a second time. But again, the knife blade passed over her neck without piercing the skin. "Dammit!" He hacked at her face. No luck. The utility knife had no effect on Cullen. Simon tried to bury the knife in her stomach and stab her in the lower abdomen, but the blade inflicted no harm. After two more futile swipes at her throat, Simon bitterly accepted the fact that he had failed. He released his hold on the woman who wouldn't die and ran toward a stand of laurel bushes. Then a large figure emerged from the underbrush and blocked his escape route.

"Fairfax County police. You're under arrest." Brooks pointed his pistol at Simon.

Bursting into tears, Cullen pulled her scrub pants up, ran into Matt's warm embrace, and buried her face in his chest. "I was so scared." She slumped in his arms. "I thought I was dead." He wrapped her in loving comfort.

"I don't understand." Simon examined the knife that appeared to be in fine working order. He passed his left index finger lightly across the blade, splitting the skin and drawing blood. "What just happened?"

"It's quite simple," Lazarus explained. "You suck at revenge. You're a loser. A worthless piece of pig vomit. Your mother would be so disappointed in you. What a shame. She had such high hopes for her only child, and now look at what has become of you. You can't even kill the woman who ruined your life. You're pathetic."

Dropping his knife to the dirt, Simon lowered his face in disgrace. "Just shoot me."

"No." Lazarus moved close to Simon's face.

"Why not?"

"Because you're not afraid to die."

"I'm *not* going back to jail," Simon said. "That place is a hellhole."

"I have no intention of sending you back to prison."

"Then what are you going to do to me?"

"You have a petrifying fear of becoming a vegetable—just like your mother. You can't bear the thought of being trapped inside your own body, unable to communicate or function like a normal human being. Locked inside an organic cell, your body would deteriorate while your mind would operate as it does now. How maddening that would be—watching the world pass you by as you sit in a wheelchair; drooling and defecating all over yourself; and living a hollow, wretched existence. Well, Simon, that's what you have to look forward to because I'm going to make your worst fear come true."

Lazarus seized Simon's shoulders and backed him against the broad trunk of an oak tree. The slender man placed his palms on Simon's forehead. His long fingers draped across Simon's head like a set of bony tentacles. "Brace yourself, Simon. This is really gonna hurt." Then Lazarus pushed his hands through Simon's skull and into his brain. Shrieking with terror, Simon convulsed and quivered as his central nervous system reacted violently to the shock of an unwelcome intruder.

With the skill and precision of an experienced neurosurgeon, Lazarus strategically ruptured a series of vital arteries that carried blood to the parts of Simon's brain that controlled movement and speech. With an atrocious shudder, the left side of Simon's body flew into a savage frenzy. Simon's left arm drew up against his chest with his hand locked into a deformed fist. The left side of his face appeared to pull away from his skull. Simon then lost control of his right side, with his arm and leg flinching randomly. He lost all vision in his left eye and most of the sight in his right eye. Slumping to the ground in a pile of misery, Simon let out a long groan as he became aware of the torment he would have to tolerate for the rest of his life.

Content with his work, Lazarus turned his back on Simon and joined Matt, Cullen, and Brooks in the clearing. He adjusted his suit jacket and ran his hands through his spiked hair. "Are you all right, my dear?" he asked Cullen.

Still enveloped in Matt's arms, she said, "Yes, I'm fine. Thank you for your help. You saved my life." Tears again streamed down her face as she released another wave of pent-up stress. "But I gotta tell ya. That knife thing really freaked me out."

"It was my pleasure." A grin crawled across his face. "You know, I don't usually help anyone, but in your case, I made an exception. And I'm delighted that you liked the knife trick. It's one of my favorites and great fun at parties."

Lazarus shifted to face Matt. "I never thought it would happen, but you found the courage to take charge of your fear and use it to your advantage. During my extended period of existence, very few people have been able to persuade me to serve as a collaborator in a dangerous situation. Your decision to take an enormous risk saved Cullen. You made a bold choice; for that, you've earned my respect."

"Does that mean you're finally going to leave me alone?" Matt looked hopefully at the tormentor who had become his colleague.

"For now. But what happens in the future depends on you." Lazarus winked his black eye. He touched Cullen gently on the arm as a silent goodbye. Then he turned to see Brooks attending to the lump of humanity that lay helpless on the ground.

"Well, Detective, I see you captured the man who allegedly killed those four women. It's too bad that he suffered a series of massive strokes and won't be able to defend himself in court. I assume he'll be relegated to a long-term care facility while you'll take the credit for closing a sequence of high-profile homicide cases," Lazarus said with his tongue planted firmly in his cheek.

Brooks grunted, heaving his tired body into a standing position. "Just doing my job, Lazarus. I get paid the mediocre bucks to catch the bad guys. Sometimes it's extremely dangerous, but that doesn't bother me. I live my life for the chase. Fighting for justice. Protecting and serving the citizens of this great—"

"That's enough outta you, Brooks." Lazarus chuckled at the sarcastic detective. Looking down at his silver wristwatch, the thin man sighed, "Sorry, folks, but I need to run. Duty calls. No rest for the wicked."

"Hold on a minute, Lazarus. I need to know something. Does this signify the end of our bizarre relationship?" Brooks asked.

Lazarus raised his right hand to Brooks's face and playfully patted the detective's chubby cheek. "See ya around, Brooks. And eat a salad every now and then." Then the shadow of death departed into the night.

Chapter 63

"Where are we going?" Matt fidgeted in the passenger's seat of Cullen's Saturn.

"I told you. It's a surprise. Keep your blindfold on. It looks fabulous on you." Cullen giggled as she made a sharp right turn.

"I can't see a darn thing through this black silk scarf. You wrapped it around my head so tight that it feels like a tourniquet. I think you cut off the circulation to my brain."

"Deal with it," she said. "We'll be there soon."

Matt reclined his seat all the way back, placed his hands behind his head, and enjoyed the mystery ride. Life was good again.

For the past week, he and Cullen had plunged headfirst into normalcy, trying their best to stop thinking about the most harrowing days of their lives. Seizing the reins of his floundering project, Matt had worked closely with his management team to implement a viable plan to get their faltering project back on schedule. After taking a couple of days off to heal and decompress, Cullen had returned to work, helping expectant and exasperated women push their ways to motherhood. During the week, the couple had shared two rushed lunches and had purposely avoided any discussion of Lazarus Kaine or Simon Fletcher.

"Are we there yet?" Matt sounded like an impatient six-year-old boy.

"Almost. Keep your blindfold on for another five minutes." Cullen made a long, descending right turn that seemed a lot like an exit ramp.

After a couple of extended pauses that must have been traffic lights, Matt felt the car hang a left and slowly ease to a stop. Cullen got out of the car, and a few seconds later, Matt's door opened.

"Good evening, sir," a young man's voice said. A hand reached into the car and gently clutched Matt's right arm to help him exit the automobile. Matt heard the driver's door close, and then the Saturn drove away. "Boy, I hope that was a valet." He suddenly felt like a complete dork because he was standing on a sidewalk with a blindfold covering his eyes.

"Walk with me." Cullen slipped her left arm around his waist and guided him to an unknown destination.

Twelve uncertain steps later, Cullen pulled his blindfold off. It took a few seconds for Matt's eyes to adjust to the twilight. Then he realized he was standing in front of a building with a glass exterior. Above a set of glass doors, a group of thick block letters marked the building as 1750 Tysons Boulevard. Through the glass doors, on a reception podium, he saw a familiar logo—a white circle with a palm tree in the middle.

Matt turned to his lovely escort. "You brought me to the Palm Restaurant. I love this place!" He kissed Cullen on the lips and held the door open for her.

Located next door to the glamorous Ritz-Carlton Hotel in the heart of Tysons Corner, the restaurant capitalized on its reputation as a high-end steakhouse and its proximity to the wealthy inhabitants of Fairfax County. The perfect place for power lunches with important clients or romantic dates, the Palm was the definition of traditional elegance.

Walking behind Cullen, Matt couldn't help staring at the way her body looked in her little black dress. The sleek curve of her back, the perfect shape of her calves, and the way her shiny black hair fell over her soft shoulders combined to form an image of a woman who was way out of Matt's league.

"Good evening and welcome to the Palm. My name is Sebastian," said a thirty-something maître d' with a genuine smile.

"Hello, Sebastian. We have a reservation. The name is Cullen Rhea."

"This way, ma'am." The man gestured for the couple to follow him. Winding through the 180-seat dining room, he led them to an isolated table for two that was draped with a spotless white linen tablecloth—a signature of the Palm. Caricatures of famous patrons including Larry King, Sam Donaldson, and Virginia Senator John Warner looked down on Cullen and Matt as they scanned their menus. The walls gave homage to Northern Virginia's Internet pioneers by displaying drawings of the Dulles corridor's cybergeek zillionaires.

Cullen and Matt dug into the sweet raisin bread, black pumpernickel, and crusty French bread that constitute standard fare at the restaurant. They devoured their mixed green salads as they talked through a week's worth of work-related trivia. Cullen's salmon fillet arrived broiled to perfection—crispy outside, melt-in-your-mouth tender inside. Matt's cowboy rib eye steak was cooked to order—medium rare, nicely charred, well-marbled with fat, and bursting with flavor. They spoke sparingly as they ate their exquisite meals and took in the classic ambiance.

Finishing the final hunk of his steak, Matt started to say, "About last week—"

"Matt, do we really have to talk about what happened?" Cullen asked through her last bite of salmon.

"I just want to apologize for everything that I put you through."

Cullen reached across the small table and took Matt's left hand. "Last week, I finally got the chance to exorcise the demons that plagued me for years. All of the inane fears, inhibitions, and doubts I had about myself fell away as I fought back against Simon. For the first time since that horrible night in college, I have my confidence back. And I feel great." Then she leaned over the table and whispered, "But most important, right now, I need you to do something for me."

Matt's eyes widened with suspense. "Sure. I'll do anything for you. What is it?"

"Help me flag down the waiter who has the dessert tray. I need a chocolate fix."

Laughing like two kids, they looked around the restaurant and finally spotted the dessert tray guy making his rounds on the far side of the room. They waved him over with a sense of urgency. Arriving at the table, the young Italian waiter launched into his spiel. "Good evening. My name is Anthony. Tonight our desserts include New York cheesecake, raspberry sorbet—"

"Stop right there. I'll make this easy for you." Cullen surveyed the tray. "I'll have a piece of your double chocolate fudge cake."

"Same for me," Matt said with a decadent grin.

Moments later, Anthony delivered their treats and some fresh coffee. Matt ate slowly and sipped his warm decaf as Cullen consumed her delicacy with self-indulgent pleasure. Finishing her final nibble, Cullen reached for her small black purse and stood up. "Here's the plan." She opened her purse and pulled out a small, plastic card. "I want you to wait here for thirty minutes. Have some more wine or coffee or whatever. Just promise me you'll stay here for thirty minutes. Then, I want you to walk next door to the Ritz-Carlton. Go up to room 4029, and use this card key to open the door." She dropped the card on the table next to his coffee cup.

"Why? What's going on?" Matt asked, bewildered and wildly intrigued.

"You'll see." Then she turned and left the room.

A puzzled look remained on Matt's face as he examined each caricature on the surrounding walls and tried to make the time pass. He finished his decaf and his wine, then he looked at his wristwatch. Twenty-five minutes to go. On his way back to the kitchen, Anthony stopped by the table and laid a thin leather portfolio in front of Matt. "I can take that when you're ready, sir."

Hmmm. So Cullen blindfolds me, takes me to an expensive restaurant, and sticks me with the bill. Pretty sneaky. Then he remembered how beautiful she looked in that slinky black dress, and he handed the waiter his gold MasterCard.

A trip to the bathroom and another cup of coffee filled the next twenty-two agonizing minutes. *That's close enough. I can't wait any longer.* He thanked the maître d' as he left the restaurant and walked through the opulent lobby of the Ritz-Carlton. He nervously tapped his fingers on the wall of the elevator as it took him to his destination. Two turns down the wide hallway put him in front of room 4029. He slid the card key into the lock, turned the handle, and opened the door. Lit by a single candle that sat in the middle of a dresser, the hotel suite looked like a chic boudoir. A hint of vanilla scented the air. As Matt stepped inside the room, he saw Cullen standing by the king-size bed, wearing her new red pumps—and nothing else.

Chapter 64

"That was a great movie." Tessa stretched her arms above her head. Sitting in a theater seat for the past two hours had made her muscles a bit stiff.

"What were your favorite parts?" Dr. Connor Kevit draped his right arm around Tessa's shoulders and walked her through the expansive lobby of the Fairfax Corner Cinema.

"I liked the scenes set in New Orleans. They reminded me of home. The way it used to be—before Hurricane Katrina. And I have to admit that I really like Orlando Bloom. He's a great actor. And he's cute."

"Oh, so you have a thing for skinny white guys."

"Yeah, I do." Tessa flashed a coy glance.

"I see. You know, I just happen to be a skinny white guy."

"Yes, I'm aware of that. But, of course, I am a trained detective." Tessa wrapped her left arm around Connor's hips. "Do you have a thing for athletic, biracial women who chase murderers for a living?"

Connor looked at Tessa's lovely face and raised his eyebrows. "Yeah, as a matter of fact, I do. But they're really hard to find."

They burst into laughter as they ambled through the lobby toward the exit, then a familiar voice caught Tessa's ear. She turned around, looked in the direction of the snack bar, and saw an old friend standing in line for popcorn. "Hey, Brooks!"

The hefty man spun around with a goofy grin on his face. "Tessa! I didn't expect to see you here tonight."

"I'm sure you didn't." Tessa smiled politely at a dazzling young blond who stood close to Brooks. Dressed in black heels, a black leather miniskirt, and a curve-hugging black and white striped shirt that revealed her silky left shoulder, the woman had the kind of body that could cause traffic accidents.

Brooks cleared his throat. "Tessa, I'd like you to meet Carlene Baxter. Carlene is a ... um ... she's—"

"I'm an MBA student at Georgetown University." The sexy woman shook Tessa's hand. "It's a pleasure to meet you. Brooks has told me so much about you."

"Yes, I'll bet he has." Tessa noticed that Brooks and Carlene were holding hands. "Have you two known each other very long?"

"I've known Brooks all my life. But tonight is our first official date," Carlene said in her honey-sweet Southern accent. "We're going to see the new Angelina Jolie movie."

"I'm not surprised. Brooks is obsessed with Angelina Jolie." Tessa laughed at her mortified partner. "Do you know that he's seen *Lara Croft: Tomb Raider* thirty-eight times? He has the entire script memorized."

"That's more information than we need at this point in the evening." Brooks turned to Tessa's companion. "You look really familiar. Have we met before?"

"Yes. I'm Dr. Connor Kevit. I took care of you in the emergency room last week when you had your bout with angina. How are you feeling?"

Brooks glanced over at his sizzling companion. "Believe me, I've never felt better." Shifting the attention away from himself, he said, "Tessa, you're not wearing your knee brace tonight."

"My doctor says it's healing, so he gave me permission to lose the brace." She gave her date a squeeze.

"That's great news. And you seem very relaxed. I guess the Zoloft has kicked in." A big shit-eatin' grin exploded across Brooks's face.

Tessa nodded. *Touché. He just had to get me back for that Lara Croft crack.*

"You're taking Zoloft?" Connor asked with a concerned expression.

"I'm taking it to relieve some stress. Does that bother you?" *Great. Now he's gonna think I'm bonkers. Thanks a lot, Brooks. I finally meet a nice guy, and you have to go and screw everything up.*

"No, it doesn't bother me at all. I've been taking Zoloft for the past six months. It helps me deal with the chaos in the emergency room."

Relief covered Tessa like a warm blanket. *Whew! I'd better get outta here before Brooks says something else that could get me in trouble.* "We should let you guys get your popcorn. Carlene, it was very nice meeting you. Brooks, I'll see you Monday morning."

Tessa grabbed Connor's hand and led him to the exit. Walking down the sidewalk toward the parking lot, the doctor said, "Tessa, would you be up for a moonlit stroll? There's a nice park with a lake not far from here."

"Sounds great." *Oh, yeah, baby. This guy's scoring major points.*

After a ten-minute ride in Connor's Daytona blue Nissan Z sports car, they pulled the two-seater into a small parking lot next to Morning Dove Park. As they leisurely wandered along a cobblestone path that circled a small lake, Connor told funny stories about his father, Bill, a sales executive with IBM and his mother, Elise, a high school math teacher. Tessa told stories from her childhood in the French Quarter.

They snuggled on a wooden park bench and talked into the night. Moonbeams bounced off miniature waves on the water, and lightning bugs flashed through the air. What a perfect night to start a new relationship.

Suddenly the wind shifted, dropping the temperature by ten degrees. Dressed in a thin red dress, Tessa's exposed arms broke out in goose bumps, making her shiver.

"Maybe we should go," Connor suggested.

"No. I'm fine." *This is the most romantic moment I've had in years. I'm not going anywhere. Nothing could move my butt off this park bench.*

"I have a jacket in the car. Do you want me to go get it?" Connor offered.

"Yes! That's a wonderful idea." *Smart man. He's a keeper.*

"I'll be right back. Are you sure you'll be OK by yourself?"

"I'm a cop. I have a gun in my purse. I'll be fine."

Just as Connor's hustling footsteps disappeared into the darkness, a lone figure approached on the cobblestone pathway to Tessa's left. Gradually entering the moonlight, a lean man dressed in a black three-button suit, a crisp white shirt, and a jade-green tie walked to the opposite end of the park bench, sat down, and crossed his legs. The man didn't say a word. He seemed content to stare into the night.

Feeling the need to break the awkward silence, Tessa put forward a self-conscious, "Hi."

"Hello, Tessa. My name is Lazarus Kaine. We need to talk."

About the Author

Born and raised in the Blue Ridge Mountains of Southwestern Virginia, Joel Eden spent his early years as a television, radio, and stage performer. He graduated from Virginia Tech in 1984 with a bachelor's degree in Marketing. After spending what seemed like a lifetime buried in corporate America as a middle manager, Joel created Lazarus Kaine.

Fascinated with the intricacies and mysteries that lurk deep inside the human mind, Joel loves to explore the odd thoughts and feelings we all have from time to time—especially the ones we won't admit to publically.

Joel Eden lives in Northern Virginia, with his wife, Kaye, and two sons, Andrew and Michael. He loves watching college football, coaching youth sports, spending time with his family, and spoiling his golden retriever, Louise. You can send an email to Joel at joeleden@lasariacreative.com. For more information about Joel, go to www.lasariacreative.com.

Coming soon from Joel Eden ...

Gévaudan

In the secluded mountains of Jacksonville County, Virginia, a covered bridge stretches over the Bellamont River. No one has crossed the bridge in twenty years. Some people believe that vicious beasts with retractable claws and razor-sharp fangs live on the other side. Would you have the courage to cross the bridge?

Lasaria Creative

www.lasariacreative.com

Made in the USA
Lexington, KY
27 March 2010